"Not only does Willig deliver captivating characters and a lively plot—she effortlessly channels Austen's deliciously sharp sense of wit into her own sparkling prose." —*Chicago Tribune*

"Willig is writing the best Regency-era fiction today." —*Booklist*

"Willig's writing is witty and smart, and her addictive series sparkles with lively dialogue, intelligent characters, and great plotting, which is why readers keep coming back for more. Willig represents the Regency romantic mystery at its best." —*RT Book Reviews*

"This tenth bloom to be added to Willig's popular series is just as fresh and satisfying as any of the other flowers in the best literary bouquet ever created! Fans can rejoice in finding the outstanding features they've come to count on: intriguing historical details, double-crossing deceptions, complex characters, and plenty of romance." —*Library Journal* (starred review)

"Eloise, of course, is amazing, but it's truly the plot . . . that shines . . . wonderful!" —Romance Junkies

"Humor, love, espionage—yet again there is absolutely *nothing* that this incredible author leaves out. . . . [These stories] just keep getting better and better every time!" —Once Upon a Romance

continued . . .

"Willig's sparkling series continues to elevate the Regency romance genre." —*Kirkus Reviews*

"Jane Austen for the modern girl . . . sheer fun!"
—*New York Times* bestselling author Christina Dodd

"An engaging historical romance, delightfully funny and sweet. . . . Romance's rosy glow tints even the spy adventure that unfolds . . . fine historical fiction." —*The Newark Star-Ledger*

"Another sultry spy tale. . . . The author's conflation of historical fact, quirky observations, and nicely rendered romances results in an elegant and grandly entertaining book." —*Publishers Weekly*

"There are few authors capable of matching Lauren Willig's ability to merge historical accuracy, heart-pounding romance, and biting wit."
—*BookPage*

"History textbook meets *Bridget Jones*." —*Marie Claire*

"A fun and zany time warp full of history, digestible violence, and plenty of romance." —*New York Daily News*

The Lure of the Moonflower

A PINK CARNATION NOVEL

LAUREN WILLIG

 NEW AMERICAN LIBRARY

NAL

NEW AMERICAN LIBRARY
Published by New American Library,
an imprint of Penguin Random House LLC
375 Hudson Street, New York, New York 10014

This book is an original publication of New American Library.

First Printing, August 2015

Copyright © Lauren Willig, 2015
Readers Guide copyright © Penguin Random House, 2015
Excerpt from *The Secret History of the Pink Carnation* copyright © Lauren Willig, 2005
Penguin Random House supports copyright. Copyright fuels creativity, encourages diverse
voices, promotes free speech, and creates a vibrant culture. Thank you for buying an authorized
edition of this book and for complying with copyright laws by not reproducing, scanning, or
distributing any part of it in any form without permission. You are supporting writers and
allowing Penguin Random House to continue to publish books for every reader.

New American Library and the New American Library colophon are registered trademarks of
Penguin Random House LLC.

For more information about Penguin Random House, visit penguinrandomhouse.com.

LIBRARY OF CONGRESS CATALOGING-IN-PUBLICATION DATA:
Willig, Lauren.
The lure of the Moonflower: a Pink Carnation novel/Lauren Willig.
p. cm.—(Pink Carnation; 12)
ISBN 978-0-451-47302-8 (softcover)
1. Women spies—Fiction. 2. Nobility—Portugal—Fiction.
3. Napoleonic Wars, 1800–1815—Fiction. I. Title.
PS3623.I575L87 2015
813'.6—dc23   2015012935

Printed in the United States of America
10 9 8 7 6 5 4 3 2 1

Set in Granjon LT Std Roman
Designed by Cassandra Garruzzo

PUBLISHER'S NOTE
This is a work of fiction. Names, characters, places, and incidents either are the product of the
author's imagination or are used fictitiously, and any resemblance to actual persons, living or
dead, business establishments, events, or locales is entirely coincidental.

Penguin
Random
House

To my agents, Joe Veltre and Alexandra Machinist; to my editors, Laurie Chittenden, Kara Cesare, Erika Imranyi and Danielle Perez; to my publishers, Brian Tart and Kara Welsh; and to everyone on the team in production, publicity and marketing at Dutton and NAL for seeing the Pink Carnation series through from its inception in 2003 to its final chapter in 2015.

So many thanks to you all!

The Lure
of the
Moonflower

Prologue

Sussex, 2005

Reader, I married him.

Or, rather, I was in the process of marrying him, which is a much more complicated affair. Jane Eyre didn't have to plan a wedding involving three transcontinental bridesmaids, two dysfunctional families, and one slightly battered stately home.

Of course, she did have to deal with that wife in the attic, so there you go.

There might occasionally be bats in Colin's belfry, but there were no wives in his attic. I'd checked.

"Hey! Ellie!" My little sister drifted into the drawing room, where I was busily and profanely engaged in tying bows on the chairs that had been set up for the reception. Silk ribbon, I was learning, might be attractive, but it was also more slippery than a French spy in a Crisco factory. "Delivery for you! Is that supposed to look that way?"

"It's a postmodern take on the classic bow," I said, with as much dignity as I could muster. "Think . . . Foucault's bow."

Jillian cocked a hip. "Or you could just call it lopsided."

"O, ye of little faith." I abandoned my attempts at Martha Stewartry. The guests wouldn't care if there were bows or not. They just wanted us to be happy. And an open bar. "You said there was a delivery? Please tell me it's the port-a-loos."

"There's a perfectly good bathroom down the hall. If you want to, you know, wash off that thing." Jillian gestured at the tectonic layers of mud that were beginning to crack on my face.

No, I hadn't fallen in the garden. I had fallen prey to my oldest friend, Pammy, and her Big Box of Beauty Aids. Which appeared to involve highly priced purple-tinted garden mud.

"Not for me. For the reception," I said patiently. Well, sort of patiently. My mud mask was beginning to itch.

I was pretty sure it wasn't supposed to itch.

"Not unless it's one for midgets," said Jillian.

"Cutlery? A tent?" I followed Jillian down the hall, ticking off items, and rather wishing we'd thought to invest in item number one: a wedding planner.

'Twas the afternoon before my wedding, and all through

Selwick Hall nothing was where it was supposed to be, not one thing at all. We had chosen to be married in Colin's not-so-stately home, on the theory that if you pour enough champagne, no one will notice the cracks in the plaster or the faded bits in the upholstery. We were having the ceremony in the drawing room and the reception on the grounds, which had sounded romantic in theory.

Like many things that sounded romantic in theory, it was proving more difficult in fact. Right now I was awaiting the delivery of a tent, several cartloads of china, folding chairs, half a dozen port-a-loos, and Colin's best man, who had inexplicably failed to arrive, although his explanation through the crackling cell phone connection had hinted at obstacles including pile-ups on the A23, an overturned lorry just out of London, and the sheeted dead rising and gibbering in the streets.

Translation: he'd overslept and was just now leaving.

My future mother-in-law, on the other hand, had arrived safe and sound, which just went to show that there were times when the universe didn't have its priorities straight.

With twenty-four hours left to go, I was beginning to wonder whether I shouldn't have taken my mother's advice and just had the wedding in New York.

But it was Selwick Hall that had kind of, sort of brought us together. Or at least given us the opportunity to find each other, depending on how you preferred to look at it.

I hadn't come to England for love. I'd crossed the pond in search of a spy. And if that makes me sound like an extra from a James Bond movie, it couldn't be further from the truth. The spy I was looking for was long since out of commission. My hunting grounds weren't grotty clubs or the glass-walled lair of a villain with a taste for seventies-style furnishings, but the archives of the British Library and the Public Records Office in Kew; my weapons, a few heavily underlined secondary sources and ARCHON, which might sound like the sort of acronym chosen by a criminal cartel, but was really the electronic search engine for manuscript sources in the UK. Plug in a name and—voilà!—it would locate that person's papers. Letters, diaries, random ramblings, you name it.

There was one slight problem: To find the papers, you needed a name. Spies tend not to use their real names. Unless they're Bond, James Bond. I'd always wondered why, with such a public profile, no one had succeeded in bumping him off between missions.

The Pink Carnation hadn't made the same mistake. The spy who gave the French Ministry of Police headaches, who had caused Bonaparte to gnash his molars into early extraction, didn't go by his real name. He was everywhere and nowhere, a pastel shadow in the night. Oh, people had speculated about the Carnation's identity. Some argued that he wasn't even English, but a Frenchman, cunningly pretending to be an Englishman playing a Frenchman. And if that isn't enough to make you want to reach for a gin and tonic, I don't know what is.

But I had one lead. Sort of. When you're desperate, "sort

of" starts looking pretty good. According to Carnation lore, the Carnation had his start in the League of the Purple Gentian, a spy unmasked fairly early in the game as one Lord Richard Selwick, younger son of the Marquess of Uppington.

So I'd done what any desperate grad student would do: I'd written to all the remaining descendants of Lord Richard Selwick, asking, pretty please, if anyone might happen to have any family papers lurking about in the attic or under a bed or tucked away among the lining of their sock drawers.

Did I mention that Colin just happened to be a descendant of that long-ago Lord Richard?

I found documents. I found love. I found the identity of the Pink Carnation. I didn't quite find my doctorate, but that was another story. It was all ribbons and roses and happily-ever-afters, or at least it would be as long as the caterers catered, my mother didn't kill my future mother-in-law before the ceremony, and all the bits and pieces made their way into place by roughly ten a.m. tomorrow.

I say ten a.m. because we were doing this the traditional way, morning suits and all. Everyone would be blotto by noon and hungover by sunset, but that seemed a small price to pay for the sight of Colin in a morning suit.

And yes, I may have watched *Four Weddings and a Funeral* one too many times.

"Delivery?" I reminded Jillian.

"It's a box," said Jillian informatively. "I signed for it for you."

"Did it clink?" I asked plaintively. Booze. Booze would be good. Wedding guests would forgive lopsided bows and a missing best man as long as there was enough booze.

"See for yourself." The deliverymen, in the way of deliverymen, had dropped the box smack in the middle of the hall, where it was currently impersonating a large speed bump.

Just what our wedding was missing: a do-it-yourself obstacle course.

Although, come to think of it . . .

I abandoned that tempting thought. Survival of the fittest is a principle best not applied to wedding guests. The person most likely to wipe out on the box was me, after a few gin and tonics too many at our rehearsal dinner.

I was not looking forward to the rehearsal dinner, that intimate occasion where one's nearest and dearest can shower blessings on the impending nuptials. The big problem was that Colin's nearest . . . Let's just say they weren't always dearest. There was enough bad blood there to give a vampire indigestion.

It was tough enough for Colin that his mother had run off with a younger man, a man only a decade older than Colin. Worse that she had done so while his father was dying, slowly and painfully, of cancer. But the real kicker? The younger man was Colin's own cousin.

It got even more fun when you factored in Colin's sister joining with his mother and stepfather in a coup against Colin the previous year, when they'd used the combined voting power of their shares in Selwick Hall to saddle Colin with a film company on the grounds of the Hall.

Never mind that Colin was the one who actually, you know, lived there.

For the most part, it had all been smoothed over. Colin and his sister were speaking again—just. And Colin and his stepfather had reached a tentative peace. As for Colin and his mother . . . that relationship made no more sense to me than it ever had.

The one saving grace in the mix—other than my groom himself, of course—was Colin's aunt, Arabella Selwick-Alderly. I wasn't sure whether it was her natural air of quiet dignity or the fact that she knew where all the bodies were buried, but either way, she was very effective at exerting a calming influence over feuding Selwicks.

I looked down at the box in the middle of the hall. It wasn't a box so much as a trunk, the old-fashioned kind with a domed lid and brass bands designed to hold it together through squall, shipwreck, and clumsy customs officials. It looked as though it had been sent direct from Sir Arthur Wellesley, from his headquarters in Lisbon.

"Maybe it's a wedding present?" said Jillian dubiously.

I looked from Jillian to the trunk, a smile breaking across my face. "That's exactly what it is."

Mrs. Selwick-Alderly had already given us a wedding present, and a rather nice one: a Georgian tea set, made of the sort of silver that bent the wrist when you tried to lift it. But there was no one else this could be from.

Unless the Duke of Wellington really had sent his campaign trunk from beyond the grave.

Ignoring the flaking mud on my face, I knelt down before the trunk. The box looked like it had been through several wars. The boards were warped with age and the elements; the brass tacks were crooked in parts and missing in others. But it had held together. Rather like the Selwick family.

It was also quite firmly locked. Again like the Selwick family.

I sat back on my haunches. "Was there a note? A key?"

Jillian held up her hands, palms up. "Don't look at me. I'm just the messenger."

"Eloise?" I could hear the slap of my mother's Ferragamo pumps in the passage from the kitchen to the hall. Enter Mother, stage right, looking harried. "There's a circus tent going up in your backyard."

Poor Mom. She would have been much happier with a wedding at the Cosmopolitan Club, where all the arrangements simply happened, and no one had to figure out the placement of tents. My family has never gone in for camping. Or, for that matter, circuses.

I tried to sound reassuring. "That's the marquee, Mom. It's where we're having the reception."

My mother looked unconvinced. "Are you sure they didn't rip off Ringling Brothers?"

"I don't think they have Ringling Brothers here."

My mother cast a dark glance over her shoulder. "Not anymore, they don't."

"Send in the clowns . . . ," sang Jillian, not quite sotto voce. "Don't bother. They're here."

I glowered at my sister over the domed lid of the Creepy Old Trunk. "Funny. Don't you have a senior essay to write or something?"

"Not until next month." Jillian smiled beatifically at me. "Until then, I'm all yours."

"Lucky me," I said dourly. Which, of course, really translated to *I love you*. It was, as Jillian would say, the way we rolled. We snarked because we loved. "Have I mentioned that I'm really glad you're here?"

"I know," said Jillian serenely. She gave me a one-armed hug that somehow managed to be equal parts comfort and condescension, as only a college senior knows how. "Nervous?"

"I can't imagine why." Drawing up a Selwick seating chart was like navigating a field full of land mines. And we all know how well that usually goes. Before the evening was over, someone was going to blow.

I just hoped it wouldn't be me.

"Oy," said someone from the doorway. His voice was rather muffled by the large, rectangular object on a dolly in front of him. "Where'd you want this?"

"Not in the house," I said quickly. "If you just take the path around the back to the garden, and make a right past the tent . . ."

"I'll show him," said my mother, with her best martyr look. "You can go . . ." She gestured wordlessly at my face.

"Make yourself look a little less like Barney?" Jillian suggested.

"You used to love Barney," said my mother reprovingly, and shooed the port-a-loo guys out the door.

"I was three," said Jillian, to nobody in particular.

"Yup. I'm saving that for *your* wedding."

"Hmm," said Jillian, with a look of deep speculation that did not bode well for tomorrow's maid-of-honor speech. "Where's Colin?"

"Relative wrangling." I'll say this for the Selwicks: they'd all come out of the woodwork for our wedding, flying in from the far corners of the Earth, or stumbling in from the pub down the road, depending. There was a large Canadian delegation, as well as a bunch fresh off the plane from the UAE; there were Posies and Pollys and Sallys and enough hyphenated last names to make writing out place cards an exercise in wrist strain. The Posies and Pollys and Sallys were all very well. The main concern was that Colin not be left alone with his mother or stepfather for more than five minutes. I couldn't even check in with him, since he'd left his cell phone with me, in case the tent people or the caterers called. "Oh, Lord. Would you—"

"On it," said Jillian, and whisked out the door in search of her future brother-in-law. Pity the Selwick who got in her way.

There were all sorts of useful things I could be doing: tying bows on favors, chipping off my mud mask, promoting world peace, but instead I knelt beside the trunk.

The note was there, half stuck beneath the trunk, the creamy stationery grimed. I wrestled the envelope out from under the edge.

Eloise, it said, in letters that had never seen a ballpoint pen. The handwriting was as elegant as ever, but, I noticed with a pang, less certain than I had seen it before. Mrs. Selwick-Alderly had seemed ageless when I first met her, but she wasn't ageless, any more than the rest of us, and the last two years had taken their toll.

With hands that weren't entirely steady, I slid the note from the envelope.

> *My dear Eloise,*
>
> *As you have no doubt guessed, this trunk was once the property of Miss Jane Wooliston. It traveled with her from Shropshire to Paris, from Paris to Venice, and from Venice to Lisbon.*

Miss Jane Wooliston. I lowered the note, looking at the trunk with something like awe. I had spent the past three years tracing the steps of the spy known as the Pink Carnation, following her from Shropshire to France, from France to Ireland, from Ireland to England. But in all of that, I had never encountered anything that had belonged directly to her.

This was her trunk. She had used it in her travels, packed it with her disguises. It might, I thought with rising excitement, hold secret compartments, letters, clothing, clues to the Carnation's personality.

And more than that. I had hit a wall in my research back in the fall. I could trace the Carnation to Sussex in 1805—but no further. In the spring of 1805, she had dissolved her league and gone deep undercover. So deep that none of the avenues I had explored had yielded any trace.

I had my guesses, of course. There were activities in Venice in the summer of 1807 that smacked of the Carnation's style, especially as the episode also involved the French spy known as the Gardener, the Carnation's colleague and nemesis. But I didn't speak any Italian. I could have hired someone to go to the relevant archives for me, but . . .

By then, grad school and I had already parted ways.

Like all breakups, it gave me a pang to think of it. I knew intellectually that I'd made the right choice in jettisoning my academic career, but it was still hard not to feel nostalgic sometimes. I missed it. I didn't want to go back—and I certainly didn't want to be grading student papers—but I missed it all the same.

It was Colin who had suggested that I take my notes and turn them into something else entirely, spinning the Pink Carnation's story from truth to fiction. So I'd dropped my footnotes into the garbage and spent a fevered seven months banging out the first episode in the Pink Carnation's career, closing my eyes in the midst of a Cambridge winter and trying to imagine myself back in France in the spring in 1803, when a young Jane Wooliston and her cousin, Amy Balcourt, had arrived in France.

Oh, yes, and trying to plan my wedding.

Between wedding and writing, finding out what had happened to the Carnation after that break in 1805 had drifted into the background.

Until now.

I returned to Mrs. Selwick-Alderly's note, but, maddeningly, she danced away from the main point.

> *The trunk was abandoned in Portugal in late 1807, at which point it disappeared from view for the better part of two centuries. Why it was abandoned and how it came into my possession are both tales for another day.*

I could practically hear Mrs. Selwick-Alderly's voice as I read, and see that spark of mischief in her eyes. As with all good fairy godmothers, one always had the sense that there was one last trick she was holding in reserve.

As long as she didn't turn us all into mice, I was good with that.

> *It seems only fitting that the trunk end its journeys at Selwick Hall. I give it into your care, trusting*

that you shall do your utmost to preserve the
trunk and the treasures it contains.

I remain, affectionately,
Arabella Selwick-Alderly

There was nothing at all about a key. For that matter, I
realized, swiping at the cracking mud on my face, although
there was the usual brass plate on the front, there was no key-
hole. It was as blank as a building without windows.

The trunk was like the Pink Carnation herself, a puzzle.

Like other trunks of its type, brass tacks marched in long
lines down the sides and across the lid. Ordinarily they might
have been used to spell out a monogram, but here there was
none, just the workmanlike lines of tacks.

Two of which appeared to protrude slightly more than the
others.

It would, I thought, be very like the Carnation to hide
the solution in plain sight, something so simple that one
wouldn't expect it to be right. I reached out to press the
tacks. . . .

And my jeans began vibrating.

No, no curse had been placed on the trunk. After my first
nervous jump, I realized that it was Colin's phone buzzing in
my pocket. I wriggled it out of the pocket of my jeans, hoping
fervently that it wasn't the caterers with yet another last-minute
polenta-related emergency. If it was, I might just have to go

Napoleonic on someone's nether regions. In translation: I would be politely dismayed in a rather chilly tone.

What can I say? I study the early nineteenth century, not the Middle Ages. Or rather, I had studied the early nineteenth century.

The display on the front said, RESTRICTED. Not the caterers, then.

"Hello?" I said quickly.

The voice on the other end said something staticky and incomprehensible.

"Hello?" I said again, the mud cracking around my mouth as I raised my voice. "Hello?"

Through the buzz, I heard only, "—Selwick."

"This is his fiancée," I said. "May I take a message?"

Wherever this guy was calling from, it sounded like he was underwater in a Harry Houdini cage. "Tell him . . . bring the box."

"Is this Nick?" No connection was that bad by accident. And Colin's best man was the prank-pulling kind. I knew only about half of what had gone on when they were at Oxford, and that half was more than enough. "Because if it is—"

A raspy voice interrupted me, sounding like a combination of a chronic cold and nails on sandpaper. "Tonight. Two o'clock. At the old abbey."

Donwell Abbey, presumably. The ruins lay in the backyard of the current manor house, next door to Colin's estate. If a twenty-minute drive over a bumpy road or an even longer walk along the more direct footpath counted as next door.

Yep, this was right up Nick's alley. He'd just love to dress himself up as the Phantom Monk of Donwell Abbey, complete with hooded robe and phosphorescent paint, and drag Colin out at two in the morning on the night before his wedding. The real question was whether he could refrain from snickering long enough to remember to shout, "Boo!"

"Not funny." I rolled my eyes. "If you're at the services wasting time making prank calls—"

"It's not Nick!" The voice on the other end forgot to rasp for a moment. It sounded vaguely familiar, but it definitely wasn't Nick. Dropping back into film-noir mode, the voice went on. "Tell Selwick to follow instructions—or else. . . ."

"Or else?" I should have let it go to voice mail. But underneath my annoyance I could feel a little prickle of unease. There was something seriously disturbed about that voice. "Look, I'm going to—"

"Eloise?" It was a different voice, crackly with static and tension. A voice I knew. "Eloise—"

"Mrs. Selwick-Alderly?" She'd told me to call her Aunt Arabella, as Colin did, but in the tension of the moment, I forgot. "What on—"

But she was gone. "Tell him. Bring the box."

And the line went dead.

Chapter One

Lisbon, 1807

The mood in Rossio Square was nasty.

The agent known as the Moonflower blended into the crowd, just one anonymous man among many, just another sullen face beneath the brim of a hat pulled down low against the December rain. The crowd grumbled and shifted as the Portuguese royal standard made its slow descent from the pinnacle of São Jorge Castle, but the six thousand French soldiers massed in the square put an effective stop to louder expressions of discontent. In the windows of the tall houses that framed the square, the Moonflower could see curtains twitch, as hostile eyes looked down on the display put on by the conqueror.

The French claimed to come as liberators, but the liberated didn't seem any too happy about it.

As the royal standard disappeared from view and the tricolor rose triumphant above the square, the Moonflower heard a woman sob, and a man mutter something rather uncomplimentary about his new French overlords.

The Moonflower might have stayed to listen—listening, after all, was his job—but he had another task today.

He was here to meet his new contact.

That was all he had been told: Proceed to Rossio Square and await further instructions. He would know his contact by the code phrase "The eagle nests only once."

Who in the hell came up with these lines?

Once, just once, he would appreciate a phrase that didn't involve dogs barking at midnight or doves flying by day.

The message had given no hint as to the new agent's identity; it never did. Names were dangerous in their line of work.

The Moonflower had gone by many names in his twenty-seven years.

Jaisal, his mother had called him, when she had called him anything at all. The French had called him Moonflower, just one of their many flower-named spies, a web of agents stretching from Madras to Calcutta, from London to Lyons. He'd counted himself lucky; he might as easily have been the Hydrangea. Moonflower, at least, had a certain ring to it. In Lisbon he was Alarico, a wastrel who tossed dice by the waterfront; in the Portuguese provinces he went by Rodrigo—Rodrigo the seller of baubles and trader of horses.

His father's people knew him as Jack. Jack Reid, black sheep, turncoat, and renegade.

Jack turned up the collar of his jacket, surveying the scene, keeping an eye out for likely faces.

Might it be the dangerous-looking bravo with the knife he was using to pick his teeth?

No. He looked too much like a spy to be a spy. In Jack's line of work, anonymity was key. Smoldering machismo and resentment tended to attract unwanted attention.

There was a great deal of smoldering in the crowd. Since the French had marched into Lisbon, two weeks ago, with a ragtag force that could scarcely have conquered a missionary society, they had proceeded to make themselves unpleasant, requisitioning houses, looting stores, demanding free drinks.

The people of Lisbon simmered and stewed. This lowering of the standard, this public exhibition of dominance, was all that was needed to place torch to tinder. Jack wouldn't be surprised if there were riots before the day was out.

Riots, yes. Rebellion, no. For rebellion one needed not just a cause, but a leader, and that was exactly what they didn't have right now. The Portuguese court had hopped on board the remaining ships of their fleet and scurried off to the Americas, well out of the way of danger, leaving their people to suffer the indignities of invasion.

Not that it was any of his business. Jack didn't get into the rights and wrongs of it all, not these days. Not anymore. He was a hired gun, and it just so happened that the Brits paid, if not better than the French, at least more reliably.

There was a cluster of French officers in the square, standing behind General Junot. They did go in for flashy uniforms, these imperial officers. Flashy uniforms and even flashier women. The richly dressed women hanging off the arms of the officers were earning dark stares from the members of the crowd, stares and mutterings.

Some were local girls, making up to the conqueror. Others were undoubtedly French imports, like the woman who stood to the far left of the huddled group, her dark hair a mass of bunched curls beneath the brim of a bonnet from which pale purple feathers molted with carefree abandon. Her clothes were all that was currently à la mode in Paris, her pelisse elaborately frogged, the fingers of her gloves crammed with rings.

A well-paid courtesan, at the top of her trade.

But there was something about her that caught Jack's eye. It wasn't the flashing rings. He'd seen far grander jewels in his time. No. It was the aura of stillness about her. She stood with an easy elegance of carriage at odds with all her frills and fripperies, and it seemed that the nervous energy of the crowd eddied and ebbed around her without touching her in the slightest.

Her features had the classical elegance that was all the rage. High cheekbones. Porcelain pale skin, tinted delicately pink at the cheeks. Jack had been around enough to know that it wouldn't take long for the ravages of her trade to begin to show. Those clear eyes would become shadowed; that pale skin would be replaced with white lead and other cosmetics in a desperate simulacrum of youth, a frantic attempt to catch and hold the affections of first one man and then another, until there was nothing left but the bottle—or the river.

Better, thought Jack grimly, to be a washerwoman or a fishwife, a tavern keeper or a maid. Those occupations might be hell on the hands, but the other was hell on the heart.

Not that it was any of his lookout.

The courtesan's eyes met Jack's across the crowd. Met and held. Ridiculous, of course. There was a square full of people between them, and he was just another rough rustic in a shapeless brown jacket.

But he could have sworn, for that moment, she was looking fully at him. Looking and sizing him up.

For what? He was hardly a likely protector for a French courtesan.

Go away, princess, Jack thought. *There's nothing here for you.*

The French might hold Portugal, but not for long. Rumors were spinning through the crowd. The British navy was sending ships. . . . There were British spies throughout Lisbon. . . . The royal family were returning to raise their army. . . . There were troops massing on the Northern frontier. . . . Rumor upon rumor, but who knew what might have a breath of truth?

It would all go into Jack's report. Provided he ever found

his bloody contact, who appeared to be late. The review was almost over, and still, no one had approached him.

That did not bode well.

The soldiers began to filter out of the square, marching beneath the baroque splendor of the Arco da Bandeira, the cheerful yellow of the facade in stark contrast to the bleak weather and even bleaker mood of the populace.

"Pig!" a woman hissed, and tossed a stone.

"Portugal forever!" rose another voice from the crowd.

The officers milled uneasily, looking to their leader. Junot turned, speaking urgently to the man at his side, one of the members of the Portuguese Regency Council, the nominal government that had replaced the Queen and Regent.

A bottle shattered against the tiles, among the feet of the departing soldiers, spraying glass.

"Death to the French!" shouted one bold soul, and then another took it up, and another.

Projectiles were hailing down from every direction, stones and bottles and whole cobbles pried from the street. Abuse rattled down with the stones. The French troops ducked and milled, looking anxiously to their leader, who appeared to be in the middle of a fight with the regency council, none of whom could agree with one another, much less anyone else.

And then, the sound that could turn a riot into a massacre: the crack of an old-fashioned musket, shot right into the ranks of French soldiers.

It was, Jack judged, not a healthy time to stay in the square.

Any moment now, the French were going to start firing back, and Jack didn't want to be in the middle of it. If his contact hadn't appeared by now, he wasn't coming. One thing Jack had learned after years in the game: saving one's own skin came first.

He slipped off through the heaving, shouting crowd. The various approaches to the square were already crammed with people: people surging forward, people fleeing, people fainting, people shouting, mothers grabbing their children out of the way, fishwives scrabbling at the cobbles, old men running for ancient weapons, French émigrés and sympathizers running for their lives as the crowd hurled abuse and missiles at the collaborators. Rioters were fighting hand-to-hand with French soldiers; Junot's face was red with anger as he shouted, trying to be heard above the square. A runner was making for the French barracks, undoubtedly to call up reinforcements.

Jack ducked sideways, down the Rua Áurea.

A hand grabbed at his arm. Jack automatically dodged out of the way. This wasn't his fight. And then a musical voice said, "Wait!"

It was the courtesan—the courtesan he had noticed across the square, her curls flying, her bonnet askew.

"Please," she said, and she spoke in French, a cultured, aristocratic French that caught the attention of the mob around them, made them stop and stare and growl low in their throats. "I need an escort back to my lodgings."

He'd say she did. Her voice was already attracting un-wanted attention.

But Jack didn't do rescues of maidens, fair or fallen. Don't get involved—that was the only way to survive. Even when they had a figure like a statue of Aphrodite and lips painted a luscious pink.

"Sorry, princess," he drawled, his own French heavily ac-cented, but serviceable. "I'm no one's lackey." He nodded to-wards the embattled French soldiers. "There's your escort."

"They can't even escort themselves." Her pose was appro-priately beseeching, the epitome of ladylike desperation, but there was, even now, in the midst of all the tumult, that strange calm about her. It was the eyes, Jack realized. Cool. Assessing. She lifted those eyes to his in a calculated gesture of supplica-tion, her gloved hands against the breast of his rough coat. "Please. You know that the eagle nests only once."

All around them, the hectic exodus continued. In the dis-tance Jack could hear the ominous clatter of horses' hooves against the cobbles, signaling the arrival of the cavalry.

But Jack stood where he was, frozen in the middle of the street, locked in tableau with a French courtesan. And a very pretty tableau it was. Pretty, and completely for show.

Beneath the heavy tracing of kohl that lined her eyes and darkened her lashes, her gray eyes were shrewd, and more than a little bit amused.

She raised her brows, waiting for him, giving him the

chance to speak first. It was a damnable tactic, and one Jack used himself with some frequency.

He didn't much appreciate being on the other end of it.

"The eagle," said Jack, his gaze traveling from the plunging depths of her décolletage to her painted face, "sometimes nests in uncommon strange places."

The woman didn't squirm or color. She said calmly, "The more remote the nest, the more secure the eggs."

"Puta!" taunted one of the crowd, jostling towards them.

The woman raised her voice, putting on a convincing display of arrogance tinged with fear. "I will pay for your escort. My colonel will reward you well for seeing me safely home."

"I'll see her—" shouted one man, and made a graphic hand gesture.

Loudly, in Portuguese, Jack said, "When coin is lying in the gutter, it would be foolishness not to take it, eh?" Under his breath, in French, he added, "Squeal."

Without waiting for a response, he scooped her up, over his shoulder. A ragged cheer rose up from their viewers, combined with some rather graphic suggestions. Jack waved his free hand, and then hastily had to clap it back over her bottom as she squirmed and bucked and squealed, putting on, he had to admit, an excellent show. That is, if she didn't unbalance them both.

"Easy there, princess," called Jack, with a wink for the

crowd, and, with a hard hand on her bottom, hoisted her more securely over his shoulder.

Something banged into his collarbone, making him wince.

Not all flounces, then. He'd eat his hat if that wasn't a pistol tucked into her stays.

Who—or what—in the devil was she?

"Where to?" he asked beneath his breath, staggering just a little. The woman was slim, but she was nearly as tall as he was, and burdened with a superfluity of flounces and ruffles. The street was slick beneath his feet with mud and offal.

"Down Rua Áurea and turn left on the Rua Assunção," she said, as briskly as though she were giving directions to her coachman. And then she began whacking him on the back with her parasol, screaming for help.

"Right," Jack said under his breath, and took off. Bloody hell, did she need to hit so hard? "You might be a little less convincing," he muttered.

"And ruin the deception?" Amused. The woman sounded amused.

They were past the mob now, out of the way of the men who had witnessed their little scene. Jack set her down with a thunk, right in a patch of something unmentionable. It did not do wonders for the lilac satin on her slippers.

"Sorry, princess. I'm not your sedan chair. You can walk the rest of the way."

He half expected her to argue, but she cast a look up and down the street and nodded. "Follow me."

She knew how to stay in character; Jack had to give her that. She minced along, constantly readjusting her bonnet, fidgeting with the buttons of her pelisse. Jack followed, in the slouch he'd developed in his role as Alarico the drunk, keeping an eye out for pursuers, and trying to figure out what to make of the woman trip-trapping ahead of him, making moues of distaste as she picked her way through the sodden street, her flashing rings practically an invitation to a knife at her throat.

But there was an alertness to her that suggested her attacker wouldn't fare well.

Jack remembered the hard feel of the pistol beneath her stays. That, he realized, explained the fiddling with buttons. And the hat? Jack regarded the woman in front of him with new interest. He'd be willing to wager that there was a stiletto attached to that bunch of feathers on her hat.

As for those rings, those foolish flashing rings . . . Most would-be assailants would be so dazzled by the gleam of gems on her hands that they wouldn't notice that those hands were holding a knife until it was too late.

Grudgingly, Jack had to admit that whoever the woman was, she knew what she was doing.

Which made her both very intriguing and very, very dangerous.

The house to which she led him was a private residence. Jack followed her through a gate, across a courtyard, and up a flight of stairs to a narrow iron door. His fingers briefly touched the point of the knife he kept in a sheath at his wrist.

The woman might have known the code phrase, but that didn't mean this wasn't an ambush. No secret organization was inviolable, no code unbreakable. The woman's French was impeccable, her clothes Paris-made.

Which could mean anything or nothing.

How far did her masquerade go? Jack wondered. Was there a colonel who had her in keeping? It had been done before. Sleeping with the enemy was the surest way of securing information. A man might share with a mistress what he wouldn't with a friend.

Jack's imagination painted a picture of the rooms they were about to enter: lush carpets on the floor, a gilded mirror above a dressing table laden with mysterious creams and powders, a hip bath in one corner, silk draperies falling around a wide bed. The perfect nest for a French colonel's woman.

Jack didn't consider himself prudish or squeamish; a job was a job, and they all got it done as best they could. So why the instinctive feeling of distaste that this woman, this particular woman, might sell her body for information?

From a reticule that looked too small to contain anything of use, the woman took a heavy key and fitted it into the door.

It opened onto a spartan room, the walls whitewashed, the only furniture a table, a chair, and a divan that looked as though it doubled as a bed. There was no dressing table, no gilded mirror, no bed draped with curtains.

"Surely," said Jack mockingly, "the colonel could afford better."

The woman closed the door behind them with a snap. "There is no colonel."

Now that they were inside, her movements were brisk and businesslike, with no hint of coquetry. She tossed the key on the table and crossed the room, testing the shutters on the window.

"No?" Jack lounged back against the doorframe, his hands thrust in his pockets. "You surprise me."

"I doubt that." The woman plucked the bonnet off her head, taking the dark curls with it.

Beneath it, her own hair was a pale brown, brushed to a sheen and braided tightly around and around. Without the coquettish curls, her face had the purity of a profile on a coin, the sort of face to which men ascribed abstract sentiments: Liberty, Honor, Beauty. All she needed was some Grecian draperies and a flag.

She dropped the bonnet on the table. "You have a reputation for keeping a cool head. Or have we been mistaken in you . . . Mr. Reid?"

Jack straightened slowly. "I am afraid you have the advantage of me."

No names. That was the rule. Never names. Only aliases.

One by one, the lady plucked the rings off her fingers, setting them each in a bowl on the table. "Your full name is Ian

Reid, but no has ever called you that. Your family calls you Jack. You were born in Madras to Colonel William Reid, a Scottish-American officer in the East India Company's army and his—"

"Concubine?" drawled Jack.

"—companion," the woman corrected primly, "a Rajput lady of high birth."

His mother might have been a bazaar girl for all it mattered to the English community in Madras. Her high birth had meant only that she had felt her fall all the more, reduced from a princess among her own people to a cavalry officer's kept woman.

Jack didn't like to talk about his mother. He liked it even less when other people talked about his mother.

Years of taking hard knocks kept Jack's face wooden. The only reaction was his very stillness, a stillness he knew betrayed him as much as any response. "Does this fascinating exposition have a point?"

The cool, controlled voice went inexorably on. "You served for some years in the army of the Maratha chieftain Scindia, before Scindia's French allies recruited you, and renamed you the Moonflower." The last ring clattered into the bowl. The woman stretched her bare fingers, like a pianist preparing to play, before glancing over at Jack. "You fell out with the French three years ago. People tend not to like it when you work for someone else while pretending to work for them. They like it even less when you abscond with a raja's horde of jewels."

Jack shrugged. "All's fair, they say."

The woman raised a pale brow. "In love or in war?"

From his limited experience, Jack didn't see much difference between the two. Except that those one loved might hurt one the most. "They're one and the same, princess." His eyes lingered on her décolletage with deliberate insolence. "I had thought you would know."

The woman brushed that aside, continuing with her dossier. "As a result of your little escapade with the jewels, you relocated to Portugal, where you have been positioned ever since."

Jack tilted his hat lazily over his eyes. "You are well-informed," he drawled. "Brava."

The woman's lips turned up in a Sphinx-like smile. "It *is* what I do."

She sounded so pleased with herself that Jack decided that turn and turnabout was only fair play. He'd see how she liked it with the shoe on the other foot.

"We've ascertained that you know all about me." Jack straightened to his full height, favoring her with a wolfish smile. "Now let's talk about you."

"I don't—" she began imperiously, but Jack held up a hand.

Pushing back from the wall, he prowled in a slow circle around her. "You speak French beautifully, but it's not your native tongue. You wear your French clothes well, but they're a costume, not a personal choice. Left to yourself, you don't go in for furbelows."

His eyes went to her neck, where she wore a gold locket on a silk ribbon. The rest of her jewelry was showy, and undoubtedly made of paste. The locket was simple, and it was real.

Jack nodded at her neck. "Except, perhaps, one. That locket."

The woman's hand closed over the bauble, a small but telling gesture. "Very nice, Mr. Reid. You are quite perceptive."

Jack smiled lazily. "That's what they pay me for, princess. Now, do I go on—or are you going to tell me who you are?"

He half expected her to demur. Any other woman would have. Any other woman would have teased and played.

Instead, this woman, with her elaborate rings and plain locket, looked him in the eye and said simply, "You may know me as the Carnation. The Pink Carnation."

Jack stared at her for a moment, and then he broke out in a laugh. "Pull the other one, sweetheart."

Chapter Two

*L*aughter wasn't quite the reaction that Jane Wooliston had expected.

Napoleon Bonaparte was said to break crockery at the mere mention of the name of the Pink Carnation. Hardened soldiers quailed; courtiers checked beneath their pillows for notes with the telltale pink flower; even Fouché, Napoleon's Minister of Police, was rumored to look over his shoulder and walk a little faster when there was a hint of floral scent in the air.

Some of it, Jane knew, was a reflection of her own skill, of knowing when to strike and when to retreat and, most of all, how to remain in the game. There was something to be said for longevity. Other spies, the Scarlet Pimpernel and the Purple Gentian, had been unmasked, their leagues unraveled.

Still others, Petunias and Orchids and a regular blight of Begonias, had hardly made it across the channel to France before being unceremoniously nabbed and dropped into the darker regions of the Temple prison.

But the Pink Carnation remained at liberty. And, by remaining so, acquired a reputation that owed a little to the truth and far more to the power of imagination. Any French reversal, from Napoleon's failure to launch his fleet to the burning of his breakfast croissants, was laid at her door. The Imperial Guard heard her in every shutter that creaked in the night; they looked for her under the bed. Without intending to, Jane had become something greater than herself. She had become a myth, larger than life, cloaked in mystery.

There were times when she caught sight of herself in the mirror, of her own familiar face, just a face when it came down to it, eyes and nose and lips and skin pale from the protection of bonnets and hoods, and wondered at the absurdity of it all.

There were other times, however, when it was rather convenient to be a myth. Particularly when dealing with insubordinate agents. From everything she had read in his file, insubordination was Jack Reid's middle name.

Or if it wasn't, it should be.

Whatever Jack Reid did, one could be sure it was what he wasn't meant to be doing. Sent as an apprentice to a printer, he ran away and hired himself out as a mercenary. Offered a permanent position in a prince's retinue, he accepted a job spying for the French. When the French promoted him to a position of trust, he began feeding information to the English. Jack Reid had a talent for defying expectation, and, not so incidentally, orders.

He also happened to be very good at what he did. Everyone agreed on that. He had a knack for languages, an instinct for operating unseen. And Jane was in uncertain territory, in a country where she knew only as much of the language as could be crammed into five days of study, about to embark on a mission that would take her deep into a countryside well removed from her usual networks of agents and informers.

Like it or not, she needed Jack Reid. More than that, she needed his cooperation. She needed him to follow her lead without argument, without question. In their line of work, a moment's hesitation could mean the difference between life and death.

It had been a calculated risk, revealing her nom de guerre. The more prudent course would have been to identify herself as the Moonflower's contact, nothing more. But while a man might quibble at the orders of a fellow agent, especially if said fellow agent were both female and young, no one said no to the Pink Carnation.

Almost no one.

Jane didn't waste her time arguing. That would only make her look weak. So she did what she did best: she waited. She waited until Jack Reid's laughter subsided from a guffaw into a rich chuckle. She waited until his grin faded into a frown, until his amusement turned to uncertainty.

And then she arched one brow.

"If you have done amusing yourself, Mr. Reid," said Jane, in a voice designed to evoke every governess and schoolmaster who had ever taken a ruler to his palm, "there is work to be done."

There was nothing like dignity to make a man squirm.

Mr. Reid wasn't so easily broken, however. His eyes moved over her with deliberate insolence, from her smoothly coiled hair to the absurd flounces at her hem. "The Pink Carnation has been in operation for five years, at least. You're—what? Twenty-four? Twenty-five?"

She would be twenty-six in February, although there were times when she felt at least twice that.

Not that Jack Reid should throw stones. He wouldn't be twenty-six until July, for all that he affected the world-weary air of a corsair who had raided the world twice over and found nothing in it to interest him.

It was the stubble, Jane decided. If that was stubble and not just artistically applied dirt on his chin. She'd used that trick a time or two herself, when circumstances required her to pose as a man.

"Age has nothing to do with it," Jane said quellingly. "Alexander the Great conquered Greece at the age of twenty."

Mr. Reid was unimpressed. "Alexander the Great lived in different times."

Jane knew what he really meant. "And he didn't wear a skirt."

"Actually, he did. And a rather shorter one." Jane resisted the urge to tug at her skirt as Mr. Reid conducted a lengthy perusal of the garment in question. "He also had cavalry."

"You, Mr. Reid, are my cavalry. Such as you are. You are on loan, Mr. Reid. To the League of the Pink Carnation."

"The Pink Carnation in person." The Moonflower had switched from French to English, his diction clipped, well educated, with just a hint of a lilt. His French was good, but his English was better, laced with a cutting sarcasm. "From reports, I would have thought you would be seven feet tall and carrying a saber between your teeth."

"I'm sorry to disappoint," said Jane, "but I left my saber in my other reticule. Now, if we could turn to the matter at hand . . ."

"Ah, yes. My secondment." He drew out the word, making it a mockery. "I assume you have orders for me?"

"Wasn't the eagle's nest enough for you? Or do you need documents drawn up by a lawyer and signed in triplicate?" Jane smiled condescendingly at the Moonflower. "It would be an amateur's error to carry anything in writing. And I, Mr. Reid, am not an amateur."

His pose was relaxed, but his eyes were far too keen, sizing her up, ferreting out her untruths.

"No, you're not." It wasn't intended as a compliment. He folded his arms across his chest, regarding her with unveiled suspicion. "What could so illustrious a figure as the Pink Carnation wish of my humble self?"

Right now, the Pink Carnation wished him to perdition. Jane suspected the effect was both deliberate and carefully cultivated.

Jane seated herself in a straight chair, keeping her voice brisk, businesslike. It was always best to start as one meant to go on. She gestured to Mr. Reid to sit. "What do you know about Queen Maria?"

Instead of sitting, Jack Reid leaned lazily back against the wall. "Other than the fact that she's stark, raving mad?"

Jane wouldn't give him the satisfaction of showing annoyance. "Other than that."

"I don't know, princess," said Reid, his voice silky. "You tell me."

There were times when Jane dearly missed her old headquarters in Paris, where she had carried out her shadowy activities with a well-trained cadre of underlings who followed her orders without question.

But Paris was closed to her now.

Jane kept her voice level. "Queen Maria was meant to take passage on a ship bound for her colony of Brazil."

Jack Reid tipped his hat down over his eyes. "She did. I saw her."

Jane sat a little straighter. "Did you, Mr. Reid? Did you see her with your own eyes? Or do you merely repeat what others have reported?"

Jack Reid let his lids sink down over his eyes, the picture of boredom. "It was a closed carriage. But I certainly heard her. You could hear her from here to the Azores."

It was hard not to feel just a little bit smug. "What you heard, Mr. Reid, was her sister, Dona Mariana. Dona Mariana shares Her Majesty's unfortunate malady."

Jack Reid shrugged. "The Braganzas are so inbred it's a wonder they aren't all barking like dogs. So she wasn't in that carriage; she was in another one. Either way, she's halfway to Brazil by now."

Jane rose from her seat, resting her hands on the table. "Oh? I gather there was some . . . disorder . . . attending the court's departure."

Jack Reid snorted. "Some? It was a rout. I've seen whole armies in retreat with less baggage left behind. But they would hardly forget their monarch."

"Are you so sure, Mr. Reid?" Jane strolled towards the window, giving Jack the option of either following or shouting at her back. "From what I have been told, everyone assumed that someone else had seen to the Queen. Her Majesty, it appears, is not an easy charge."

Reid remained stubbornly where he was. "She's mad and she's violent. There's more than one of her ladies-in-waiting who would happily see her overboard with no questions asked."

"But for the fact that she is the Queen," said Jane, turning to face him across the room. "That still means something."

Reid smiled pityingly. "Does it? I hate to disillusion you,

princess, but royal heads have been known to roll. A monarch is as mortal as any other man. Or woman."

It sounded like a warning. Perhaps it was. But Jane wasn't that easily intimidated.

"It means something to her people. And," Jane added quietly, "it means something to the men who seek to rule those people. In the wrong hands . . ."

She didn't need to say more. Jack Reid gave a low bark of laughter. "Are you telling me that someone spirited the Queen away from the docks? And no one noticed? Try again, princess."

Jane met Mr. Reid's eyes. Between his slouch and her high-heeled slippers, they were nearly of a height. "It was two days before anyone realized that she was missing. By then, it was too late to turn back."

Jack Reid's lips twisted. "I'd always known the Regent wasn't the sharpest knife in the block, but this—this rises to a new triumph of incompetence. I doff my hat to Don John, the man who lost first his kingdom and then his mother. One wonders what he will manage to misplace next."

"They weren't misplaced," Jane reminded him. "They were taken. Both of them."

Jack Reid shrugged, the muscles of his shoulders moving beneath the rough material of his jacket. "I can't imagine anyone will miss her. Her son is probably breathing a sigh of relief. Have you considered the option that he might have got rid of her himself?"

There was something strangely disturbing about that prospect. "You have an odd notion of filial obedience, Mr. Reid."

"Obedience ought to be earned, not given as a right." There was steel beneath his voice, and a vulnerability that he quickly masked by flinging back at her, "Do your parents know where you are?"

"As much as yours do," Jane snapped, and then regretted it.

Reid raised his brows, sensing weakness, probing at the wound. "Ah, but I'm not a gently bred young lady."

He was good. She had to give him that. Very, very good. That was her cue, she knew, to protest, to tell him more than she ought.

But for the fact that she was also good. Very, very good.

"Whatever Don John may feel, or not feel, for his mother as her son, she is also his queen," said Jane coolly. "There are practical as well as personal considerations at work. The Regent will hardly be pleased if the French employ the Queen to set up a figurehead government in Lisbon."

Jack Reid watched her with hooded eyes, but he didn't press the point. "The French already have a figurehead government. It's called the Regency Council."

He was lulling her; he would come back to the attack later. It was a technique she'd used herself.

"The Regency Council won't last a month." Jane had had a week on the boat from London to come to grips with the situation on the ground in Portugal, spending long nights in her cabin reading through one report after another, tackling unfamiliar names, an unfamiliar language. She spoke with more authority than she felt. "You saw what happened in the square. The Regency Council has no authority and Junot has no patience. He'll dismiss them on some pretext before the year is out. The people place no reliance in the Regency Council. But they do in their Queen. If their anointed Queen tells them to bow to the French, what are the Portuguese people to do?"

Jack Reid shook his head. "You're barking up the wrong tree, sweetheart. If Junot had Queen Maria, he'd have paraded her for all to see."

Jane had reached much the same conclusion. She knew General Junot of old, from Paris. He was a man of strong appetites, without the discipline to rule them. Subtlety wasn't Junot's strongpoint. "We don't know who has her. But we need to find out. And get her back."

Jack Reid pushed away from the wall, prowling towards her with the graceful, lazy gait of a tiger assessing his prey. "Tell me one thing, princess. Why should the illustrious Pink Carnation waste her time on a small, regional matter such as this? If," he added, "you are the Pink Carnation."

Jane ignored the one point and focused on the other. "When Paris ran away with Helen, was that a small, regional matter?"

The room wasn't large, and it felt still smaller with Jack Reid closing the space between them. "Queen Maria is hardly the sort to launch a thousand ships."

Jane looked him in the eye, refusing to draw back. "Didn't

she just? If not a flotilla, at least a fleet—a fleet which Bonaparte dearly desires."

She'd made him think, she could tell. Reid paused, assessing her. "Even if Bonaparte gets his hands on the Queen, he can hardly order the ships back from Brazil."

Jane spoke with confidence. This much she knew. "It's not just the ships, not anymore. Bonaparte secured the connivance of the Spanish crown for the invasion of Portugal. He has marched troops across the Spanish border, large numbers of troops. How long before he turns on his allies? How long before he lays claim to Madrid, and from there to the entire peninsula? Bonaparte's goal is a continent under his sole subjection—and Portugal is his gateway."

There was a silence and then Jack Reid put his hands together, clapping once, twice. It made a hollow sound in the high-ceilinged room.

"Very nice," he said mockingly. "All you need is a few draperies blowing in the background and a spear in your hand and you'll be the very picture of Britannia."

Jane stiffened her spine. "Say what you will. If ever I were needed, it's here, now. If we can stem Bonaparte's ambitions in Portugal, we can put paid to his plans for Spain."

Jack Reid's amber eyes were focused on her face, intent. "A large task for one woman acting alone."

"But not for the Pink Carnation." Jane looked the Moonflower in the eye and said deliberately, "I've done more with less."

It might sound like arrogance, but if they were to work together, she needed him to acknowledge her authority. She was a woman and a young one. In the early days that hadn't seemed to matter; she had built her league herself, by trial and error, half by accident. It was a game, and she was the one who determined the rules.

But the game had turned darker somewhere along the way. It had gone from a game of wits to a struggle for survival, where there were no points for cleverness, only for results.

The way to succeed was to show no vulnerability.

I should like to lure you off your pedestal. The voice echoed in her memory, flavored with a lilting French accent, a voice she knew far too well for comfort.

She had ventured off her pedestal once, and found the ground uncommonly hard and rocky.

She would take the high road, thank you very much.

Jack Reid held her gaze. Whatever he saw there, the mockery was gone from his voice as he said abruptly, "Have you ever been to Portugal before, princess?"

"I have not previously had that pleasure, no."

Jack Reid stepped back a pace, folded his arms across his chest. "And your command of the language . . . ?"

Jane raised her chin a little higher. "I speak French, Italian, and German."

"But not Portuguese."

"I purchased a grammar." Jane was aware of how ridiculous it sounded, how painfully inadequate.

"A grammar." Jack Reid adopted a lilting falsetto. "Excuse me, sir, can you tell me the way to the nearest Moorish ruin?"

Even as a schoolgirl, she had never sounded quite that daft. "Did you speak Portuguese when you arrived here three years ago, Mr. Reid? You learned. You learned quickly."

Jack Reid shot her a quick, incredulous look. "Not that quickly. You don't have time to engage in introductory grammar. You have, what? A week? Two at best? If you're to find the Queen before someone else does, you'll need to move fast."

You, not *we*, Jane noticed.

"Which is where you come in," said Jane crisply. "You, Mr. Reid, are to be my mouth and ears. Our first order of operation is to discover whether there were any disruptions to the Queen's domestic arrangements in the days before the fleet departed."

"You mean other than invasion by the French?"

Jane ignored the sarcasm. "Yes. Once the word came that Junot was on the march, someone laid his plans. We need to go to the palace at Queluz to interview the Queen's servants, discover who might have got close enough to move her."

It shouldn't be difficult. The palace at Queluz was within easy reach of Lisbon; she'd checked on her map. She would have to rely on Jack Reid for the interviewing, since her Portuguese was still at the rudimentary stage—she had only had a week, after all—but she could observe their faces, their movements, the little tells that often told more than words.

The Queen's pavilion at Queluz, the palace where she had

been immured since her madness became known, was the obvious place to begin.

"No," said Jack Reid.

"No?" Jane wasn't used to no.

"You're wasting your time at Queluz. Don John picked the palace bare. There's not a tapestry or an armoire left in the building. He took everything but the stones—and that was only because he couldn't find a way to pack them. You won't find anything in Queluz."

He sounded very sure.

"All right, then, Mr. Reid." Jane hated asking for advice, but he was the expert here, not she. "What do we do?"

"Cut your losses and go home."

"I beg your pardon?"

He spoke to her patiently, as to a small child. "I don't know who you are, or what you're really after, but I can tell you one thing: you don't want to be here. This mission is a fool's game." As Jane opened her mouth to protest, he said, "You haven't met Her Majesty. I have. The woman is delusional. She's violent. And above all, she's loud. Once you get your hands on her, you'll have every French troop in Portugal down on you before the Queen can shout, *'Ai, Jesus!'* Your mission is a fool's errand."

"If so," said Jane smartly, "why has no one yet discovered her?"

Jack Reid shrugged. "At a guess? Opiates."

"Ah, yes. Opiates." Among his other dubious activities, Jack Reid had once smuggled opium to a rowdy bunch of bored aristocrats whose Hellfire Club had made a brilliant front for other illegal activities, including a thwarted plot to kidnap the King. "I believe you have some experience of those."

Jack Reid held out his hands, palms up. "Sorry, princess. I'm out of that line of work. So unless you've brought enough laudanum to drug an elephant . . . Queen Maria is about the size of one, and far less amiable."

She had just enough powder in the compartment in her ring to send a man deep into drugged slumber. "That, Mr. Reid, is a chance I have to take."

"A chance you choose to take, princess. Not I." He favored her with a benevolent smile that set Jane's teeth on edge. "My orders were purely observational. That's what they're paying me for, and that's what I intend to do."

"Your orders have changed," said Jane sharply. "When Don John bowed to Bonaparte's pressure and exiled the English from Lisbon, he exiled our agents as well. You, Mr. Reid, are what is left. For good or for ill."

"I see." He rubbed the back of his neck, a studiedly rustic gesture. "Rare commodities command high prices. Do you care to start the bidding?"

She had known he was a soldier of fortune, but it set Jane's teeth on edge all the same. "You're already being paid."

"Not for this."

Jane raised her chin. "I can offer you the accolades of a grateful nation."

"One can't eat accolades, princess. Have I committed a *be-*

tise? My apologies. I ought to have realized that the Pink Carnation is above such base concerns. Myths sup off moonshine and sip drops of dew. There's no need to bother about such base and vulgar matters as food and lodging. Or expensive gowns."

The gown was one of the last of her Paris gowns, refurbished by her own hand. The days when she had money to spare for such things were gone.

More sharply than she'd intended, Jane said, "I shouldn't have thought the man who made off with the jewels of Berar would quibble over the odd tuppence."

"Ah, we come to the point." Jack Reid regarded her with mingled resignation and regret. "Shall we abandon this cock-and-bull tale of missing monarchs? If it's the jewels you're after, you need only say." He cocked a brow. "If you want to charm them out of me, you might try a little harder."

Jane breathed in deeply through her nose. She could hardly tell him that she'd held his jewels in her hand, that she knew exactly where they were kept. It was he, after all, who had precipitated her departure from Paris when he had heedlessly, unforgivably sent the jewels to his sister Lizzy in England, and with them the interest of one of the deadliest spies in Europe. Jane's own sister Agnes had been drawn into the tangle. The girls had been lucky to escape alive, and no thanks to Jack Reid.

He could keep his jewels. They'd cost Jane more than enough already.

Jane drew herself up, exerting an iron will to keep herself

from telling him exactly what she thought. "I have no interest in jewels covered with blood."

"Strong words," said Jack Reid softly. He rested a hand on the wall above her head. "But everyone wants something. What do you want, princess?"

"I want Queen Maria safely in Brazil." Jane could see the flecks of gold in the Moonflower's amber eyes. She could feel his breath against her cheeks, the warmth of his body through his loose clothes. "I want Bonaparte driven back to France. I want England at peace."

"How very touching." Jack Reid pushed away. "There's a tavern not far from the docks. Several of the Queen's former servants have been bunking there. They'd been promised passage to the colonies with their masters, but when there was no room on the ships . . ."

"I see." Jane hadn't realized she had been holding her breath until she let it out again. She felt as she had the first time she had emerged safely from a midnight raid, breathless and slightly light-headed. "Men like to air their grievances. Particularly after the application of a jug or two of wine. The sooner we go—"

"There is no we. I'll go. But I go alone." Jack Reid held up a hand to forestall any protests. "I'm sure you cut a very elegant swath in the salons of Paris, but here? You're a liability."

"As you will," Jane said pleasantly, and had the satisfaction of seeing Jack Reid's brows draw together in disbelief.

Jane held his gaze, keeping her own expression deliberately

bland. Then she drove the knife deeper by saying, "I imagine it will be rather late by the time you conclude your inquiries. You needn't report immediately. Shall we say . . . noon?"

Jack Reid looked at her from under his hat for a long moment. "I'll be there at eleven. Beneath the Arco da Bandeira." He paused for a moment, the door in his hand, before adding helpfully, "You might wear something a little less conspicuous."

The door clanked shut behind him.

The Pink Carnation regarded the closed door thoughtfully. "Mr. Reid," she murmured, "you have no idea just how inconspicuous I can be."

Chapter Three

"Another for my friend!"

Red wine sloshed over the sides of a carafe as the harassed innkeeper clunked it down. The sticky residue on the planks of the table testified to the speed, if not the accuracy, of his service. Everyone was drinking heavily tonight. Word had gone out that Junot was contemplating a curfew after the events in Rossio Square.

"Better drink while we can," said Jack's new best friend, Bernardo, gloomily. The man had once been an undercook in the Queen's palace of Queluz, left behind, as with so many, when the court sailed for the Americas. "In our homes by seven—bah!"

Bernardo spat eloquently, narrowly avoiding hitting the

thinner man next to him, who scooted out of the way, casting the former cook a baleful look. The thin man had been attached in some arcane way to the Queen's retinue and, from what Jack gathered, deeply resented being relegated to the ranks of the forgotten along with Bernardo, the cook, and Javier, the stable hand. Unfortunately, disappointment didn't seem to have loosened his tongue. He nursed his drink in silence, regarding the others with a hauteur not dissimilar to the way the woman who called herself the Pink Carnation had looked at Jack.

For a moment, Jack wondered.... But no. The woman didn't speak Portuguese—she'd admitted this much—and this man had ordered his wine in that language.

Although it didn't take much familiarity with a language to order wine.

Jack shook his suspicions aside and turned back to Bernardo, who, unlike the thin man, was more than happy to air his grievances, especially after a carafe or two of the local vintage, which, from the taste, Jack suspected to be half vinegar and at least a third horse piss, with a slight soupçon of actual wine for piquancy.

Jack had had plenty of chances to sample this particular vintage. Alarico the drunk was well-known at this particular tavern, as he was at most of the taverns along the quayside. People, he had learned, would tell the town drunk what they wouldn't to their confessor. The confessor might impose penance; the town drunk offered absolution for nothing more than the price of a carafe of wine.

It was an easy enough costume to maintain. A wobble here, a waver there. Ragged clothes splashed with wine. A bit of vomit daubed in the hair if one wanted to be really true to the role. And voilà, instant inebriate.

Jack didn't need to see himself to know what he looked like. Ragged hat jammed down low over a horsehair wig, ragged jacket liberally streaked with old wine stains, grime beneath his fingers, and half a day's growth of beard.

Unbidden, Jack thought of his maternal grandfather, the one and only time he had seen him, his blue silk jacket glittering with silver thread, a giant sapphire pinning his silk turban, a knife crusted with jewels at his waist, his mustache elaborately trimmed, radiating wealth and power and scorn.

Jack raised an ironic cup to his grandfather. He'd made clear he thought Jack was the lowest of the low; it was only fair to him to live down to his expectations.

Having made his libation to his illustrious ancestors, he turned his attention back to his work, such as it was.

"When the Queen comes again," Bernardo was saying, his cup listing dangerously to one side, "when the Queen comes again, those sons of dogs will get what's coming to them. Oh, yes, when the Queen comes . . ."

When the Queen comes, indeed. Jack stifled a yawn. Blather and blether and wishful thinking. It sounded to Jack like nothing more than his father's toasts to the King Over the Water, a pointless pledge to a hopeless cause.

Why bother? he'd asked his father once, in his belligerent youth. He'd been reading Rousseau, and saw no point in exchanging one king for another. Stuart or Hanover, it was all one and the same to Jack.

His father had considered the question. *It's a manner of remembrance,* he had said at last. *Your grandparents fled their home for their allegiance to the man they believed their true king. We wouldn't be here but for that. So I toast to the King Over the Water and remember my parents in my heart.*

That was like his father; he had a deep streak of sentimentality that expressed itself in old ballads and useless toasts, and never when it mattered.

The wound was an old one, but it still twinged at times. There was something about that lament "When the Queen comes again" that had dredged up those old stories, long-ago days when his father had sat in his chair, Kat and Alex on either knee, Jack at his feet, and spun tales of a land Jack had never seen, a land as green as Madras was red and brown, shrouded in mist, colder than the coldest day Jack had ever known, peopled by men with hair as red as his father's.

Someday, his father used to say, *I'll take you there.* But he hadn't, had he? And even if he had, Jack would never belong. Nigger brat, the officers in the mess called him. Only when his father couldn't hear, mind, but they called him that all the same.

When the King comes again . . .

Irritably, Jack set his cup down. Either José was pouring it stronger today, or his interview with That Woman had addled his wits. The King hadn't come again, not for his grandparents, not for his father, and neither would Queen Maria. The Queen was most likely halfway to Brazil by now, whatever nonsense That Woman had spouted.

He didn't even know her name.

The Pink Carnation, she had called herself, and it might even be true. There was something uncompromising about her, like a blade made from Seville steel. It wasn't just that she looked like the image of Virtue on a coin, all clear eyes and classical features, head held high, fearless. It was something more. It was the way she had responded when he asked her what the Pink Carnation had to do with such a small, regional manner as this. Jack had met opportunists in his day. He had known more than his share of scoundrels and tricksters; hell, he was one. This woman meant what she said.

Which made her dangerous. Very dangerous.

During Jack's brief stint in the Maratha chieftain Scindia's polyglot army, a former British private—a deserter, a drinker, a wastrel, but a beautiful hand with a musket when he was sober—had told him of the classification of officers.

"There's killing officers and there's murdering officers," he had told Jack laconically. "Your father—now, there's a killing officer. He might get his men killed, but it won't be a'purpose. He's following orders, same as us."

"And murdering officers?" Jack had asked.

Private Jones had given an exaggerated shudder. "They's the ones as *believes*," he had said, and that was all.

The woman who called herself the Pink Carnation believed. She believed enough for both of them. And that was enough to make Jack run straight for Madrid.

So why hadn't he?

There was the money, Jack reminded himself. The Carnation could taunt him all she liked about the jewels of Berar, but he hadn't stolen them for himself, hadn't kept them for himself. The money Wickham paid him, out of whatever shadowy funds, paid for his food, his lodging, and the clothes on his back. Carnation or not, the woman had known the code phrase; there was no getting around it. If Wickham wanted to send him off on a fool's errand, Jack would tug his cap and say, "Thank you very much, sir."

But it didn't mean he had to get himself killed in the process.

Across the room, a group of French dragoons had taken over one of the long tables, shoving the previous inhabitants out of the way. Jack wondered what it was about conquest that did such nasty things to one's disposition. At home, these might be perfectly reasonable men. They probably cheated their tailors and lied to their wives and such other sins to which gentlemen were prey, but he doubted they would muscle their way into a Paris tavern with quite the same swagger, or shove the peasantry out of the way with such lordly insolence.

So much, Jack thought wryly, for *liberté*, *fraternité*, and *egalité*. Fine words to fly on the side of a flag, but not when one was dealing with a subject population.

The dragoons' tempers hadn't been improved by the long and arduous march from France to Lisbon. From the leopard skin on their hats, he could tell these were officers, but their uniforms bore the signs of hard wear, the white breeches mud-stained, the green coats hastily patched, and more than one pair of tall black boots the wrong size for the wearer.

They were young, all of them, from the stripling at the end of the table to the lieutenant with his long locks bragging of his conquests among the women of Almeida. Young and scared and trying to pretend to be neither.

"Your wine is poor as piss!" one of the dragoons shouted, lobbing a charred sardine at José's retreating back.

"Yes, bring more of it!" added another, contributing his own sardine to the fray. "And meat, man! Meat!"

"There might be more of it if you vultures hadn't eaten it," muttered a man at one of the other tables.

In Portuguese, mercifully, or, Jack was sure, there would be a resulting fray that would make the events in Rossio Square look like a tea party.

Bernardo cast a look of pure hatred at the dragoons, his chins dragging down in disgust. "They'll get theirs when the Queen comes back."

"It's a long trip to Brazil." Jack rocked back against the wall, swinging one foot up onto the table. "We'll not be seeing our Queen come again for some time."

Bernardo tapped a finger against the nose. "Not so far as you might think. There's some as say—" He broke off, an expression of drunken cunning crossing his face as he glanced across the room at the French dragoons.

Jack shook his head. "If words were coins . . . Talk is cheap, my friend."

"Not always." Bernardo lowered his third chin into the space where Jack presumed his neck must be. "My wife's sister was a waiting woman in the Queen's apartments. . . ."

It was no use to press for information. Even if the poor, sodden fool had any, pressing would only make him turn mum. The best way to get people to talk was to say nothing at all. So Jack didn't. He merely tipped the carafe over the other man's glass, filling it once more to the brim.

Bernardo nodded his thanks. "Look to the north, she says. Look to the north." And then, almost inconsequentially, "The Bishop of Porto is a good man, they say."

"Yes," said Jack, trying to hoist Bernardo upright as he started to slide down the bench. "A very good man."

It was like wrestling with blancmange. Bernardo's mouth was roughly on a level with the underside of the table. Jack had to lean over to hear what he said.

". . . in force, they say. With banners of gold . . . of gold . . ." Bernardo's mouth opened onto a snore.

Releasing the back of his jacket, Jack gave up the battle to keep him upright and let him sink the rest of the way to the floor.

Banners of gold. A picturesque image, to be sure, but nothing more than any exile might whisper around the fire. To be fair, Bernardo and his kin hadn't been exiled, but their experience was similar. They found themselves strangers in their own homes, yearning after all that was familiar and lost to them.

When the Queen comes again . . .

It was nonsense, all of it, but Jack couldn't quite get it out of his head. Look to the north. A closed carriage. Two days before anyone realized she was missing.

Bernardo's sister-in-law had been one of the Queen's waiting women. If someone had spirited the Queen away, on the very day of departure, they would have needed connivance in the Queen's household, someone to throw together the necessities for the exiled Queen. Including, Jack thought cynically, enough drugs to keep her from shouting down half of Lisbon.

No. He'd heard the stories of life in the Queen's household. It was hardly cozy and chummy. The Queen's mania inclined her to violence; she flung anything that came to hand at her underlings, accusing them of stealing from her, of plotting against her. There was a higher rate of attrition in the Queen's household than in the East India Company's army, and given the number of British soldiers Jack had seen fall prey to cholera, syphilis, and bazaar girls, that was saying something indeed. There were days the Queen banned all of her waiting women from her household entirely, admitting only her confessor.

Only her confessor.

Outside the tavern, Jack could hear the rising and falling chant of monks in procession. Through the half-open door, he could see the palanquin they carried, bearing the carved figure of a saint, gaudily painted, draped in silks and velvet. In his character as Alarico, he clumsily crossed himself as the saint's statue passed, a gesture that would undoubtedly horrify his Calvinist grandparents, the gesture habitual after three years in Portugal. It was hardly anything out of the ordinary. It seemed, sometimes, that every other day was a saint's day. Robed religious of a dozen orders passed through the streets: mendicant friars, prosperous abbots, white-wimpled nuns.

Jack had grown accustomed to it. He scarcely noticed it. Nor did anyone else.

Reaching down, he took Bernardo by the shoulder and shook. The only response was a gentle snore, followed by a much less gentle snore.

That, thought Jack with some asperity, was the problem of *veritas* by *vino*. With enough application of wine, one passed truth and hit oblivion.

Damn, damn, damn. The hint of a memory teased him. In the week before the court had departed, the Queen had acquired a new confessor. Jack was certain. Almost certain. He hadn't paid terribly much attention at the time; he'd been more interested in the rumors emerging about the movements of the French troops marching their slow way through the rains towards Lisbon. But anything to do with the Queen was potentially news, so he'd stowed it away without really thinking of it.

Even in her mania—especially in her mania—the Queen was intensely religious. She swore at her son and mistrusted

her maids, but any man in a monk's robe would have her un-
questioning obedience.

Particularly if he promised her salvation.

It was beginning to take shape in Jack's brain, the outlines
of a plot both daring and bold and so absolutely simple he
couldn't believe he hadn't seen it before.

"—spavined jade." Instinct—and the raised voice of one of
the dragoons—prompted Jack to glance up from beneath his hat.

His younger siblings' mother used to say that one's mis-
deeds always caught up with one, if not now, then later.

In Jack's experience, it was usually now.

Unless he was much mistaken, that dragoon had bought a
horse off him the previous week, in his role as Rodrigo the
itinerant horse trader. Jack had also, in the process, lifted some
rather interesting dispatches out of the man's saddlebags, combined with some rather less interesting bills and billet-doux.
The man had a taste for expensive tobacco, and his mistress
couldn't spell.

Without hurrying or making eye contact, Jack rose casually from his bench, swaying a bit for effect. With any luck, the
dragoon wouldn't make the connection between Rodrigo the
horse seller and Alarico the drunk.

But, just in case, now seemed like a rather good time to
answer the call of nature. Particularly as nature was, indeed,
calling.

Taking care to stay in his role, Jack lurched and swayed
across the room, making sure to wave to acquaintances and

step on the odd foot along the way, all the while calculating the distance to the door and from the door to the alley. One yard, two . . .

And he was in the alley.

But he wasn't alone. One of the dragoons had followed him out. Not the irate one with the illiterate mistress, but the stripling, the one who looked barely old enough to hold his musket, only the shadow of a mustache above his lip, and a weak, pale look to him beneath the regulation hat. He moved tentatively along the wall, as if unsure of the exact etiquette of finding a place to relieve himself.

Jack could have told him that. There was no etiquette. But he moved aside all the same, making room for the boy.

And he nearly jumped out of his skin as he heard the voice of the Pink Carnation say, "There's about to be trouble."

Chapter Four

*J*ack pulled up his breeches in record time.

"What in the blazes are you doing here?" he hissed, his fingers clumsy as he tied his laces.

"Watching your back," said the Pink Carnation equably, which Jack found rather disingenuous, given that his back had not been the part of his anatomy in view.

How in the devil hadn't he realized it was she? Grudgingly, he could see how it had been done. He might have suspected a man or woman alone, but she had entered as part of a group—a group already so inebriated that the addition of an extra to their party had occasioned no comment, in that stage of drunkenness where people came and went and scenes shifted in dizzying ways. The uniform jacket hid a multitude of details; one's eye skated over it, seeing just another French dragoon. The uniform was convincingly battered, as though it had been put through a rough march and then unsuccessfully repaired.

And her face . . . Somehow she'd altered even that. The pure lines of her face were broken, changed by that wispy little mustache and the high stock she wore, pushing her chin at an odd angle. Even her eyes looked different, smaller, darker. Makeup, he could see, now that he looked closely. So skillfully applied that only another master of the trade would know it was there.

She'd gammoned him. Skillfully and thoroughly.

Jack jerked his jacket back into place. "Get an eyeful, princess?"

"Don't be childish." The Carnation dropped her voice, speaking softly in French. "One of the dragoons knows you."

"You mean he knows Rodrigo, the trader of horses," Jack corrected her.

"He says you sold him a lame mare." Even as she spoke, she was going through the appropriate motions, pretending to unbutton her breeches, wiggling her posterior in those tight, uniform pants. If anyone emerged, they would see only two men, each looking straight ahead, answering nature's call.

Jack pulled his hat down over his eyes. "The mare wasn't lame when I sold it to him."

"Be that as it may, he's out for restitution."

"Don't you mean retribution?"

"Given that it's your blood he's after, I wouldn't quibble about the details." Her eyes shifted sideways, meeting his. "He's sent one of his lackeys to lie in wait for you."

"Only one? I'm insulted."

The Pink Carnation wasn't amused. "You haven't seen the lackey."

The lackey didn't worry him nearly as much as the woman standing next to him. Lackeys he'd dealt with before. A blow here, a kick there. He knew how to keep himself alive in a brawl. It was refreshingly straightforward. Unlike the Carnation.

So far, in their brief acquaintance, she'd managed to fool him twice, first as a courtesan, then as a soldier. Jack didn't like it. It made him feel as though his feet were on shifting ground. He was the one who made the ground shift, thank you very much.

She'd claimed not to speak Portuguese, but why should that be any more true than anything else?

Jack looked at her from under the brim of his hat. "I have the information you need—but you know that already, don't you?"

The Pink Carnation neither confirmed nor denied. All she said was, "Not here."

Jack couldn't argue with that. The alley smelled regrettably of piss, not to mention charred fish. "Where, then?"

The Pink Carnation put a hand at the small of his back and shoved him so that he stumbled nearly into the open doorway.

"Follow my lead," she murmured, just before she dealt him a stinging slap across the face.

"Thief!" she shouted in French, so loudly that even Bernardo roused from his drunken stupor, lifting his head and looking about with glazed eyes. "Pig! *Canaille!* I paid you ten livres for a horse and what did I get? Not even a donkey!"

Jack held up both his hands in exaggerated pleading. "Please, I swear, monsieur—" His French was convincingly broken. "It was the best mare—"

She cuffed him around the ears. "I'll have you up before the authorities. Come with me, cretin." The soldiers at the table had half risen to their feet. The Pink Carnation waved them down. "This one is mine," she said, her voice convincingly slurred. "Justice!"

And with that, she placed a boot in his back, propelling him forward into the street. Jack didn't need to feign his stagger as he slipped in the refuse in the gutter. The Carnation grabbed him by the ear, half pulling, half pushing him down the street.

A shadow fell over them as a man stepped out from the alley. Jack hated to admit it but the Pink Carnation had a point about the lackey. He had the physique of a gorilla and the face of a rat. It wasn't a pleasant combination.

But the Pink Carnation breezed past him with all the arrogance of her class. "You may return to your master," she said. "I have this *canaille* in my charge."

And then, just to make sure of the matter, she flipped a coin in the man's general direction.

Leaving the lackey scrabbling in the dirt, the Carnation marched Jack past the tavern, down a side street, and into a narrow alcove between two buildings.

"We're safe enough here. They won't follow."

"Was that quite necessary?" Jack's ear hurt and there was a boot-shaped dent in his back.

"I got you out of there, didn't I?" As the Carnation spoke, she was already stripping off her uniform jacket, revealing a frock coat beneath. She reached into a hole between stones, pulling out a plain black cloak. She swirled it around her shoulders, transforming in a moment from a French soldier to a gentleman out for the evening, her shako hidden beneath a tall black hat.

"You planned that," said Jack flatly.

"I took the necessary precautions." The uniform jacket was whisked away, beneath the cloak. Given what he had seen earlier in the day, she made a surprisingly convincing man. It was, Jack realized, the small details, the way she held herself, the way she walked. She had made a thorough study of her craft.

She might, he thought ruefully, even be the bloody Pink Carnation.

"How did you know the cloak and hat would still be here?" he asked accusingly.

"I took a calculated risk." Her face was completely calm, her hands steady. Jack felt a moment of reluctant admiration. Whatever she was, the woman had nerves of steel. "The streets aren't safe for a lone French officer after dark."

"The streets aren't safe for anyone," Jack corrected. Any large city attracted its share of bandits and cutthroats; right now, with the city seething with resentment, the danger was multiplied tenfold. "I'll see you back to your lodgings."

She didn't argue. Possibly because she was already walking ahead, speeding her pace slightly, as befitted a gentleman being dogged by a drunk.

"Please, sir," Jack whined. "Just a coin, sir." And then, more softly, "You were checking up on me."

The Pink Carnation shook her cloak free of his grasp. "I speak no Portuguese, Mr. Reid. I have a vested interest in keeping you alive." They were at the grille that led to her lodgings. "I'll leave the gate unlocked. Wait ten minutes and then follow."

She swept up the stairs as Jack squatted in the dirt outside, picking at illusory fleas, and deeply regretting the loss of his old contact. Jack hadn't liked the man; he had been one of those round-bellied English merchants, full of his own consequence. The man had never been quite able to hide the faint disdain he felt for a half-caste like Jack, but he had done Jack the supreme favor of limiting his involvement to collecting reports, leaving Jack to get on with his own work as he saw fit.

In the eight hours since the Pink Carnation had arrived at Rossio Square, Jack had been beaten with a parasol, outwitted, and kicked.

This did not bode well for their partnership.

He waited a little longer than instructed, just because. Part caution, and partly because it would be deeply satisfying to make the Carnation squirm. Once roughly half an hour had elapsed, Jack slouched his way up the stairs.

The Carnation had removed her mustache and wig, but still wore the tall black boots and uniform trousers, the white leather clinging to her hips and thighs in a way that made Jack's throat suddenly dry.

She was standing in front of an age-pocked mirror, sponging off the remains of her makeup. Her eyes met Jack's in the mirror. "You said you had information for me?"

Jack removed his hat, tossing it onto the table. "You shouldn't leave the door open, princess. Anyone might walk in."

The Pink Carnation turned, and Jack found himself facing the point of a pistol. It was a very attractive piece of weaponry, chased in silver. It was also primed and cocked.

"If so," she said calmly, "they would have been given reason to depart."

"Off this mortal coil?" Since the dress of the evening appeared to be casual, Jack shrugged out of his odiferous jacket, draping it over a chair. Beneath, he wore only a loose linen shirt over his breeches. "Don't point a weapon unless you intend to use it, princess."

For a moment their eyes met and held, the challenge simmering in the air between them.

And then the Pink Carnation smiled. Just the briefest crease of the lips, but there was something about it that made Jack feel as though he had dealt a blow, only to find himself windmilling through empty air. The Carnation had removed his target and left him flailing.

She set the pistol gently down on the corner of the table, next to the bowl of water with its stained cloth.

"My aim is true enough," she said, "but I prefer to use other means when possible. Littering the ground with corpses is the surest way to attract unwanted attention. You said you had news for me?"

There was nothing so dangerous as charm. Not the obvious charm of the courtesan she had pretended to be before, but this, a wry weariness, agent to agent. The intimacy of her boudoir, the matter-of-fact tone—it was all designed to create an illusion of honesty, to convince him that he had peeled away the layers and come to the core of her.

There were oranges in a bowl on the table. Jack took a knife from his pocket and began to pare one, taking his time over it. He flicked a piece of peel aside before saying, "As much as it pains me to admit it, you might be right. There's a chance—just a chance—that the Queen's gone north."

"Yes?" The Carnation was all attention. "What exactly did your informant say?"

Jack looked at her hard. "You tell me."

The Pink Carnation wrung out her cloth, applying it to the paint beneath her eyes. "It would be disingenuous to say I didn't understand a word of your conversation"—her voice was slightly muffled from her ministrations—"but a word was the extent of it. As you yourself said, Mr. Reid, it takes longer than a week to learn a language. I was there tonight because—"

"Because?" prompted Jack.

The Pink Carnation's face emerged from behind the cloth. "Because even if I couldn't understand the words, I could gauge the man's movements."

It was, Jack was quite sure, not what she had intended to say. "All right, then. There have been rumors afoot that the Bishop of Porto is organizing a resistance. The Queen's servants seem to be operating under the impression that the Queen will come again, and quickly."

"Not from the sea, but from the north?" the Carnation murmured.

Jack nodded curtly. Laid out, it all sounded ridiculous. "I have an idea as to how it might have been done. The Queen acquired a new confessor just before the fleet left. If this man—priest or no—were to hide the Queen in plain sight, as part of a procession . . ."

"Even the French might think twice before disturbing a party of monks—or endangering a holy relic." The Pink Carnation was very still, only the flicker of her lashes betraying the rapid thought going on beneath those fine-boned features. "Once outside the city, they could abandon the procession, change their costumes."

Something about the way she said it made Jack very, very nervous. "We don't know the route they've taken or the manner of their disguise," he said quickly. "They could be halfway to Porto by now. Or stranded in a gorge."

Or dead in a ditch. There were a great number of ditches and no shortage of desperate men looking for a throat to cut.

The Carnation set down her cloth. Her face, scrubbed clean, looked deceptively young and ridiculously fair. "Then we must follow."

For a bright woman, she appeared to have missed the point. "This isn't France, princess. The roads are piss-poor. The terrain is mountainous. It could take weeks to make Porto, only to find the Queen's not there."

The Pink Carnation raised her perfectly tweaked brows. "What else are we to do? Sit in Lisbon and send out pigeons?"

"Yes," said Jack bluntly. "Let's say that the Queen's halfway to Porto. She's safer there than here."

The Carnation rose from the bench, the trousers molding themselves to her legs. "Until the French send reinforcements. Do you really believe they intend to stop at Lisbon? They mean to garrison the whole country—and then invade Spain. The Queen won't be safe until we have her on a boat to Brazil."

What with the other distractions, it took a moment for the

sounds coming out of the Pink Carnation's mouth to resolve themselves into words. Once they did . . .

Jack shook his head to clear it, feeling much as he had the time a mule had delivered an ill-timed kick to his temple. Was the woman mad? That was the only excuse. She had escaped from an insane asylum. No—she was a French plant, designed to be a blight to sensible, hardworking agents.

"Some of us," said Jack caustically, "like to stay alive. I can't vouch for either your safety or mine if we take to the roads."

"That," said the Pink Carnation briskly, "is hardly what I expect to hear from Rodrigo, the seller of lame horses."

"The horse wasn't— Never mind." Jack scrubbed his knife off on a fold of his shirt and stuck it back in his sleeve. It wasn't his fault if certain Frenchmen had never learned to ride.

"You've traveled safely the breadth of the country," said the Carnation, managing somehow to sound entirely sensible. "How is this any different?"

The woman had no idea what she was getting into. Yes, her performance tonight had been without par. She could masquerade convincingly as a courtesan or a French soldier— but could she saddle a mule? Scale the side of a gorge? She was an urban creature, a creature of the drawing room. Oh, all right, and the tavern. But she wasn't accustomed to the type of terrain they would have to travel.

"Do you plan to disguise yourself as a horse?" asked Jack caustically. "Because that's what a horse seller tends to have with him. Horses."

If she had been a man, he would have added certain choice comments about the nether parts of the horse's anatomy. But something about her straight back and direct gaze made the coarse comments shrivel on his tongue. You could put the lady into a French dragoon's breeches, but she was still, unmistakably, a lady.

"You could always go back to England and take ship for Porto," suggested Jack, although without much hope.

"And leave the Queen stranded in the midst of French patrols? No." The Pink Carnation shook her head briskly, as though they were having a perfectly reasonable discussion and not an opium addict's addled dream. "But you do have a point. We'll travel faster by river."

True as far as it went, but she'd ignored a crucial point. "I hate to disillusion you, princess, but the French came to the same conclusion. The Tejo is crawling with French soldiers."

The Carnation smiled benevolently upon him. "Then we shall simply be French soldiers."

Jack spoke without thinking. "No."

"Why not?" The Pink Carnation began ticking off points on her fingers. "There should be no difficulty in acquiring a spare uniform. I've heard you speak the language. Your accent is convincing enough. And I," she added blandly, "have already established my bona fides."

She had intended this all along.

Jack's eyes narrowed on the Carnation's face as the pieces clicked into place. He was beginning to get a sense of how she operated. Like a stage magician, it was all a matter of misdi-rection.

Had she known already that the Queen might be in the north? Possibly. The rest was a charade, designed to make Jack feel important, make him feel as though he were part of a decision-making process that had already been decided.

Deliberately, Jack slouched back against the wall, his eyes traveling from her boots to her breeches and then, finally, to her face. "Is that what tonight's exhibition was in aid of? Es-tablishing your bona fides?"

He saw the Carnation's back stiffen. "Tonight's exhibition, as you put it, saved you from a beating, Mr. Reid."

He would take that as a yes. Jack's lips twisted in a crooked smile. "Only after you put me in the way of one."

The Pink Carnation raised her chin, looking like judge and jury all in one. "You put yourself in the way of one, Mr. Reid. Your way of life is hardly conducive to restful pursuits."

She paraded around a strange city in men's trousers and she dared to accuse him of reckless behavior?

Jack prowled forward. "Which way of life do you mean, princess? Horse trading? Or espionage? Because if it's the lat-ter, there's an adage about pots and kettles that might apply." He paused directly in front of her, looking into her serene, lying face. "I went into this life because I had no other choice. What's your excuse?"

The Pink Carnation stood very still, but he could feel the change in her, a tension beneath the surface.

She lifted her face defiantly to his. "Does the idea of wearing a blue-and-white coat bother you so?" she said coolly, and Jack might have believed it, but for the brittleness of her stand, the watchfulness of her eyes. "You've turned your coat often enough."

"Perhaps I have." Jack waited a moment before adding, "But the coat I wore was always my own. I never pretended to wear any nation's colors."

A shadow passed over the Pink Carnation's clear gray eyes. "It's only another disguise."

"No." Jack's own vehemence surprised him. But as little as he could explain it, he felt it deep in his bones. Perhaps it came of being a soldier's brat. He'd grown up among soldiers, men who took pride in their colors. "It's a symbol—a pledge."

Somewhere in the distance the bells were tolling, calling the monks to compline. Everyone had beliefs, training, unquestioned assumptions that cut deep, so deep they were scarcely aware of them themselves until challenged.

Jack took a stab in the dark. "Would you genuflect at a Roman mass or take their host? Honestly, now."

He watched as the Pink Carnation pressed her lips together, duty warring with conscience. With dignity, she said, "If it were necessary."

Like the seasoned campaigner he was, Jack pressed his advantage. "But you would feel the lie of it. And it would diminish you."

He ought to have felt triumphant. He had won his point. He could tell from her moment's hesitation, from the quick flicker of her lashes.

But he didn't. He felt as he had as a boy, fighting with his sister Kat over a toy horse. He had shoved her. He wasn't supposed to, but she had angered him and he had. Kat was three years older, and knew just how to get under his skin, to taunt him into bad behavior. So he had elbowed her. And he had been left holding the toy horse, with a sick feeling at the pit of his stomach, wishing it back in Kat's hands and himself anyone but who he was.

Maybe it was the way the Pink Carnation was looking at him, as though all of humanity were standing on her shoulders. "I do what I have to do, Mr. Reid. As do you."

"That sounds like a warning."

The Carnation smiled wryly. "Call it instead a reminder. If your conscience will not sit with a blue coat, would you pose as my batman? You need wear no garment but your own."

That wasn't the real problem, and they both knew it. He might be wearing his own coat, but he would be following her orders, playing the game her way. The idea of deliberately placing himself in the middle of the French force felt about as attractive as closing his eyes and plunging his bare fist into a nest of kraits.

He could refuse to go—but this woman represented Wickham, and Wickham was paying the bills.

He could argue; he could insist upon guidelines—no unnecessary risks, no heroics—but what would that be? Nothing but words.

She had him over a barrel and he knew it.

The Pink Carnation was watching him, her expression carefully blank. "Can you be ready by noon tomorrow?"

Noon, afternoon, what difference did it make when one went to the gallows? Jack shrugged into his jacket, pulling his hat down over his horsehair wig.

"It's your funeral, princess."

He just hoped it wouldn't be his own.

Chapter Five

*J*ane's plan hit a snag almost at once.

The Pink Carnation wasn't used to her plans hitting snags. Snags were for other people, people who didn't do their research. But all the research in the world couldn't produce a boat where there was none. When they arrived at the docks, they found the wharf a confusion of French soldiers.

"We're all in the same boat. That is, without a boat," a friendly captain told Jane cheerfully. He seemed very young to be a captain, very young and very raw. His own troop, making for Villa Franco, was already in formation, ready to march. "Everything's been taken by reinforcements bound for Abrantes. You may have to wait a bit, I fear."

"That won't do." Jane mimed youthful distress. She didn't

have to work very hard at the distress. Jack Reid slouched behind her in his role as her servant, and, even if he couldn't
currently say, *I told you so*, she knew he was thinking it. "I'm
to join General Thomières at the fortress of Peniche. I'm his
new aide-de-camp."

"Thomières?" Captain Moreau looked at her in confusion.
"Isn't he still in Lisbon? Thought I saw him at Madame Pin-
to's card party last night."

"He's had his orders," Jane said glibly. And so he had, in
the pouch she had lifted off Junot the day before, in Rossio
Square. It wasn't entirely a lie. Thomières had been ordered to
Peniche. He just didn't know it yet. "I'm to go ahead and secure comfortable lodgings for him—he'll have my head if
there's not a feather bed waiting for him by the time he ar-
rives."

Captain Moreau grimaced in sympathy. "There's nothing
for it, I'm afraid. Unless you want to wait a week."

"We'll have to go by land then." A rain had begun to fall,
not the gentle misty rain of a Shropshire summer, but sharp
and stinging. Jane turned up the neck of her cloak. "Thank
you, Captain."

"Wait!" said Moreau, looking genuinely alarmed on her
behalf. "You don't want to travel alone. The roads are teeming
with bandits. They aren't terribly friendly."

"Bandits tend not to be," agreed Jane gravely.

"You wouldn't be friendly either under the circumstances,"
muttered Jack Reid behind her.

"What was that?" inquired Moreau.

"Nothing," said Jane quickly. "Just my servant. He has a horror of highwaymen."

Captain Moreau glanced dubiously back at the milling men, who appeared to be attempting to move themselves into some sort of formation. Most were without full kit; several had mismatched boots or none at all. Jane had heard that the march into Portugal had wreaked havoc on Junot's forces, but she had had no idea, until now, just how much. Captain Moreau was considerably short of a company. And also possibly a few beans short of a barrel. He reminded her a great deal of an acquaintance back in England who tended, generally affectionately, to be compared to a root vegetable.

"You're welcome to march with us," Moreau offered. "Always room in the mess tent for one more."

In this case, because about half the company appeared to have been lost somewhere en route.

Jane did a quick calculus. They would travel slowly with Moreau. But she couldn't travel as a French officer alone with a servant. Moreau was right; the French had done little to endear themselves on their march from Spain. They would be dead within days. But to adopt any other disguise would be to place herself entirely within Jack Reid's hands.

Reid knew the back roads; he knew the language. Once they veered off the road, away from the familiar, Jane would be at his mercy.

Contact or not, she didn't trust him enough for that. This

was, after all, the man who had betrayed his own people and then, having done so, betrayed the betrayers. He might be in Wickham's pay at the moment, but who knew what he would do should someone on the other side offer more?

"If you're quite certain . . ." Jane shifted aside as Jack made an attempt to kick her in the ankle. Fortunately she had been trained by Miss Gwendolyn Meadows, whose parasol was the opposite of the windmills of the gods. It moved exceedingly swiftly, and Jane had long since learned to get out of the way of it.

There was a muffled yelp as Reid's foot connected with the mule instead.

Jane smiled brilliantly at Moreau. "I would be delighted to accept your kind offer. My servant has my baggage on the mule."

Moreau looked doubtfully at Reid, who was garbed in a rough brown jacket, yet another dilapidated hat pulled low over his head. Reid had abandoned the horsehair, though. His hair was his own, clubbed back in an old-fashioned queue. "He looks a surly fellow."

Jane leaned over confidentially. "I had to hire someone local. My old batman fell ill just north of Lisbon."

Moreau nodded as though that were a story he had heard before. "Just watch that he doesn't cut your throat in your sleep. Some of these local men . . ."

"He came well recommended," said Jane quickly. "And

he speaks some French. Rodrigo!" she called imperiously. "We travel with Captain Moreau and his dragoons. Fetch my trunks."

Reid feigned a look of incomprehension. *"O qué?"*

"Pardon me," said Jane. "I must see to my arrangements."

"Certainly, Lieutenant de Balcourt." Moreau gave a short bow, one officer to another. "I look forward to the opportunity to improve our acquaintance."

"'The opportunity to improve our acquaintance'?" Reid mimicked, as they moved behind a convenient pile of baggage. "What are you doing? We travel faster alone."

"Yes, but we wouldn't have the same opportunity to gather intelligence along the way," said Jane coolly. "We can kill two birds with one stone."

"This lot," said Jack Reid, speaking low and quickly, "is a waste of a good stone. That Moreau is about as much use as an arthritic carrier pigeon. If he knows anything the least bit useful, I'll eat my hat."

"One can never tell what might be useful," said Jane priggishly. "They might have information they don't know they possess."

Reid gave him a look from under the brim of his hat. "Or is it just that you're not accustomed to sleeping rough?"

The bolt struck a little too close to home. Her missions, dangerous though they might have been, had all been conducted against the backdrop of drawing rooms and salons.

But she was country-bred, wasn't she? She had spent her formative years in Shropshire, surrounded by more sheep than people.

Jane drew herself up, feeling the seams of her green jacket scratching her sides. "I'm not afraid of hardship."

Jack Reid regarded her skeptically. "If you say so—Lieutenant de Balcourt." He dwelt mockingly on that aristocratic *de*. "You do realize that this means weeks in their company? It's not a two-day jaunt down the river. What happens if you swill too much port in mess one night and . . . ?"

He made an eloquent gesture that needed no translation.

Jane kept a tight rein on her temper. "I do not, as you so eloquently put it, swill. I assure you I can maintain the deception." Jane didn't let her voice slide back into its normal alto, but kept it a light tenor.

Jack Reid watched her, an ironic smile tightening the corners of his lips. "Have you ever marched with an army before?"

She knew remarkably little of armies on the march. Armies in mess, yes. Officers home in Paris, boasting of their escapades, yes. But she had never had any call before to join an army on the march. "I've remained in the field for months at a time."

"As a man? Among the French?"

Jane looked quellingly at him. "It's always safest to hide in plain sight." She should know. She had spent years in Paris, right underneath Bonaparte's nose, dancing at his balls, dining with his stepdaughter, flirting with his marshals. "We can break off at Santarém."

Jack Reid wasn't willing to let it go just yet. He turned back, his brows drawing together. "What happens when they decide to demand your bona fides?"

"I shall provide them, of course." Her papers were tucked away in a pocket of her cloak: Jean de Balcourt, scion of an old but now impoverished family, seeking to regain favor under the new regime. Lieutenant de Balcourt had made the odd appearance before, although never at such length as this. "Did you think I would be so unprepared?"

Jack Reid fixed her with a long, inscrutable look. "You don't want me to think. You want me to follow."

A dozen retorts rose and died on Jane's lips. That was what he wanted: to draw her into argument, to put her on the defensive.

Loudly, Jane said, "Fetch the mule, Rodrigo. We don't want to keep our friends waiting."

Jack Reid touched his hand to his cap in an ironic salute. "Sir."

He sauntered away, leaving Jane feeling as though she had lost the argument, not he.

Someone had to lead, didn't they? Jane hunched down beneath her cloak as she rode beside Captain Moreau towards the front of the train, Jack Reid somewhere behind with the mule and the baggage. Or so she hoped. She wouldn't put it past him to slope off, evading orders as he had so often in the past.

Did he think she enjoyed making these sorts of decisions? Well, perhaps she did, just a little. At least in the beginning—in the beginning when the work was new and exciting, each challenge a puzzle to be solved. But the more immersed Jane had become in the shadowy world of espionage, the more aware she had become that her actions had consequences. Jane's second in command, Miss Gwen, tended to swash before she buckled, charging off without thought, sword parasol at the ready. Jane's cousin Amy, who had founded a spy school in Sussex, optimistically sent her people into Paris, trusting to Jane to keep them alive.

And Jane had, as best she could.

But that meant taking charge. It meant making decisions based on the totality of the circumstances, difficult decisions, unpopular decisions. It meant keeping her own counsel, even at times when she longed to pour out all her doubts and worries. In order to maintain her authority, she needed to cloak herself in a mantle of omniscience.

Uneasy lies the head that wears the crown, the poet said. He might have substituted "lonely."

The rain dribbled steadily down, the horses' hooves sinking deep in the mire. By the time they made camp, Jane's boots were caked with mud, her cloak a mass of wet wool.

Whatever his other faults, Jack Reid knew how to pitch a

tent. Jane found hers set at the end of a row, close enough to the circle of safety of the camp, but far enough that one might have a murmured conversation without half of Napoleon's officer corps hearing it. Bidding Captain Moreau good night, Jane retreated into her tent, draping her sodden cloak carefully on a hook by the inside of the door.

Jane's thighs and back ached with the unaccustomed exercise. She knew how to ride, of course. She was generally held to have a fine seat. But an afternoon's hunting on a well-trained mare was a very different game from a long march on a bony nag who appeared to have one short leg. It was, Jane thought wearily, rather like being placed in a barrel full of blunt edges and rolled rapidly down a hill. She might have suspected Jack Reid of choosing the nag intentionally, as punishment, but for the fact that all of the other officers' mounts were of similar quality.

Wincing, Jane peeled off her green jacket. Dampness had made darker patches on the wool. It seemed odd to her that with all his other shifts and deceptions, Jack Reid should balk at wearing this green coat.

. . . *You would feel the lie of it. And it would diminish you.*

Fine words from a man who made his life by lying.

But he was right. That was the awful bit. Jane could see her own face reflected dimly in the mirror that "Rodrigo" had propped on top of her shaving kit. It was a face she barely recognized, her own hair tightly coiled beneath a wig of exuberant dark brown hair; the features rendered unfamiliar by the judicious use of paint. In the dim light, in the wavy glass, she might have been looking at a stranger.

Lieutenant de Balcourt, Miss Fustian, Gilly Fairley, the Marchesa Malvezzi, Amelie de Printemps . . . She had been so many people over the past few years, and none of them herself.

Piece by piece, Jane felt herself washing away, like a pebble in a pond, smoothed into featurelessness by the successive waves that crashed over her, until there was nothing left there that was uniquely her own. She wondered dimly what the girl who had first come to Paris five years before would think of the woman she had become. Would she be proud of her achievements? Or would she long after all that had been lost? So very, very much lost. Lost ideas, lost ideals, lost comrades.

Jane pressed the heels of her hands to her forehead. It was important work. She believed that still. She had to believe that. If she didn't, then it was all for nothing, the estrangement from her family, the danger to her friends.

Jane sank down on the camp stool before the makeshift dressing table, her reflected image dark in the uncertain light. She missed her old friends with an ache like a wound. She missed her life in Paris, where she had carried on a double life, to be sure, but under her own name, in her own clothes, in her own skin, with her chaperone by her side to challenge and anchor her. She missed Miss Gwen. She missed her pithy asides and her utterly unworkable plans.

And then Jack Reid had come into her life.

Not in the flesh, not then. It took, thought Jane wryly, a true talent for chaos to upend someone's life from a continent away. But that was what Jack Reid had done. When he shipped the jewels of Berar from India to his younger sister in Bath, it had set in train a series of events that had placed Jane squarely in the path of the most dangerous spy in Europe: the French mastermind known as the Gardener.

She couldn't operate in Paris, not anymore, not now that the Gardener knew who she was. The stakes had been raised with a vengeance. Jane had left behind everything she knew, everyone she loved, going deep undercover with only her wits as company.

And all because Jack Reid had decided it might be amusing to steal a raja's horde of jewels.

"Daydreaming, Lieutenant?" Jack Reid let the flap of the tent fall back down behind him as he walked in as though he owned it.

"What are you doing here?" Hastily Jane yanked her jacket back around her shoulders. As befitted an officer, the shirt beneath was made of fine linen. Too fine.

Jack tossed his hat onto her cot, where it spattered rainwater on her blanket. "We made less than five miles today. At this rate we'll make Porto by spring."

"Don't be absurd. I'm sure we'll pick up speed tomorrow." Jane snatched the hat off the bed and thrust it back at him. "Don't you have somewhere else you need to be?"

"The mule is settled and Moreau's servant is short a week's

pay. Dice," Jack explained helpfully, as he plucked Jane's cloak from its peg and began rolling it into a makeshift pallet.

"How nice for you," said Jane, with heavy sarcasm. Heaven help her, she was beginning to sound like him. She set her hands on her hips. "What are you doing?"

"Insurance." Jack removed a pair of pistols and placed them by the side of the pallet. "Not to mention that it's drier inside than out."

He plunked himself down on Jane's cloak, smiling seraphically up at her.

Jane blinked down at him. She hadn't thought about where he would sleep. She had assumed, if she had thought of it, that the officers' servants would have their own accommodations.

The tent felt very small with Jack Reid in it.

Jane narrowed her eyes at him. "You can't bunk with one of the other batmen?"

"And leave you unprotected?"

There, at least, she was on firm ground. Jane reached beneath her pillow. "I have my own pistols."

"Try not to point them at me," said Jack, and settled back, using his camp bag as a pillow. "Would you mind blowing out the lantern when you're done prinking? I don't like sleeping with a candle lit."

Neither did Jane, but that was beside the point. "What about 'go' and 'away' don't you understand . . . Rodrigo?"

Jack propped himself up on one elbow. The lamplight

picked out the strands of copper in his dark hair, dancing along the lines of his muscles beneath the folds of his shirt.

"Are you going missish on me, princess?" There was a dangerous glitter in his amber eyes. "Because if you are, tell me now and we can abandon this whole bloody charade."

The profanity, Jane had no doubt, was deliberate and designed to shock. "If this is an attempt to provoke me, I can assure you, it will be quite unavailing."

"'Quite unavailing'?" Jack collapsed back on his camp bag, rolling his eyes up at the roof of the tent. "Forget what I said about not pointing those things at me. Put me out of my misery and shoot me now."

Jane resisted the urge to direct a short, sharp kick to the side of the Moonflower's head. "No one asked you to join me."

"Didn't you?" retorted Jack mockingly. "I don't remember being given much choice in the matter. Master."

"In my tent," Jane amended, glaring at him.

It was too cold to strip down entirely, but she'd intended at least to remove her boots before seeking her bed. Jane regarded the recumbent figure on the floor—on her cloak—with tight lips. Missish, he had called her.

If she could endure his presence in her tent, he could bear with her wet feet.

Jack rolled onto his side, looking up at her with an expression of feigned innocence. "Need help with that?"

"I can manage," said Jane, with as much dignity as she

could muster while hanging half upside down. These boots had been designed with a valet in mind. Either that or the leather had shrunk in the rain.

The first boot came off with a pop, nearly conking her erstwhile batman in the head.

Jack dodged out of the way. "Apparently not," he said, and before Jane could stop him he had gripped the other boot by the heel. "Relax, princess. Consider this a basic instinct for self-preservation."

"I thought you had rather a well-developed instinct for that," said Jane tartly. Empires could rise and fall, but the Moonflower always seemed to land on his feet. Generally on the other side.

"If I did, would I be here with you?"

The boot came off easily in his hands, leaving Jane's leg bare but for her silk stockings, rather the worse for wear. Jack Reid's fingers ran along her calf, his thumb digging into the tight muscles, massaging them.

Jane froze.

So did Jack Reid. He snatched his hand away as though burned.

Jane drew her leg back, tucking it behind the other. She could feel the tingles all the way up her shin. "Thank you. For your help with the boot."

Jack Reid rocked back on his heels. "This is only the beginning, you know." He looked up at her, his eyes dark in the uncertain light. "I'm your manservant. I live in your tent. I see to your, ahem, needs. You're going to be seeing a lot of me, princess."

Jane pressed her eyes briefly shut. Of course. Another ploy, another stratagem. She ought to have known.

"We're not going back to Lisbon," said Jane flatly.

"Suit yourself." Jack shrugged, burrowing down into Jane's cloak and tipping his hat down over his nose. From beneath the brim, she heard him murmur, "It's going to be a long march."

By the end of the first week, Jane didn't suspect she had made the wrong choice; she knew it.

It wasn't just the continued presence of Jack Reid in her tent. Captain Moreau's company moved at a rate that made walking seem like a highly viable alternative. The locals regarded them with outright hostility. In his role as Rodrigo, Jack Reid did his best to inquire, subtly, after previous travelers on the road, but his questions were met with blank stares, unflattering commentary, and the odd gobbet of spittle.

"Can you blame them?" said Jack shortly, wiping his face on the back of his sleeve. They had stopped to make camp just south of a village so small that it wasn't even a dot on Jane's map. Jack turned his back, using the heel of his boot to dig one of the tent staves in deeper. "This village has now been ravaged by French troops twice over: once on the march to Lisbon and now on the march back to the border."

"But Rodrigo isn't French."

"Men who choose to work for the enemy are never popular." There was something about the way Jack said it that made Jane wonder whether he was speaking of more than Portugal. But his stance and his expression forbade her to ask more.

They might share a tent, but that didn't make them friends or even comrades. If anything, Jane felt she knew less of her companion than she had when they left Lisbon. He performed the tasks of Rodrigo quietly and efficiently, something she wouldn't in the least have expected.

After that first rather odd night, he hadn't fallen out of his role. Nor had he touched her again.

For which she was grateful, of course. They didn't need complications.

But somehow Jack Reid's compliance made her warier than any amount of argument. That it was compliance and not cooperation, Jane had no doubt. Cooperation implied a degree of agreement, of complicity. The Moonflower was going through the motions of a plan of which he wanted no part, there in body, but withdrawn in spirit.

He was, Jane was quite sure, biding his time. But for what?

"Only three days until Santarém," said Jane, watching her companion closely, "and then we can break off."

Jack didn't respond. His eyes were on the makeshift alley created by the crooked row of tents. "We've got visitors."

Captain Moreau was skipping down the alley, in company

with another man dressed not in regimentals, but in an elegant traveling cloak and well-polished boots.

He must, thought Jane absently, as she scraped her own boot on the board at the side of the tent, have been traveling by carriage; otherwise he could never have maintained that pristine shine.

And then he turned, and all thoughts of boots went out of her head.

No. Her mind was playing tricks on her. It was the mist, dancing in front of her eyes. Or her own guilty conscience, plaguing her with ghosts.

But it wasn't a ghost. She knew that walk, that elegant, graceful gait. She knew the way he furled his cloak, the way he tipped his head in speaking, as though the listener were voicing the most fascinating utterances, even if it was nothing more interesting than "good morning."

Jane made a choked noise deep in her throat. "He mustn't—" she began. And then, rapidly, "Tell Moreau I've a stomach complaint. I—"

But it was too late. Moreau had already seen her. He raised a hand, calling out, "Balcourt! Meet our honored guest—the Comte de Brillac. Monsieur le Comte, may I present my traveling companion, Lieutenant de Balcourt?"

Jane tried to take consolation in her wig and her whiskers. But even horsehair could do only so much. This man knew her in all her guises, or rather, in all her disguises, just as Jane knew him. They had sparred together so many times, each testing the other, enjoying the game despite the deadly seriousness of its outcome.

Jane saw the man's hazel eyes widen in recognition. No disguises there, unless one counted the name, the title he had once sworn to her he intended never to assume.

Surprise was rapidly placed by amusement as he made a polite half bow. "Lieutenant? I hadn't thought to see you turned soldier . . . Jean."

Jane bowed in return, duelists signaling before the commencement of hostilities. "I hadn't thought to see you turned Comte, Chevalier."

The man she had once known as the Chevalier de la Tour d'Argent gave a very Gallic shrug. "When one's Emperor requires . . ."

"How very wearing for you," said Jane dryly. For Moreau's benefit, she added, "My felicitations, all the same."

The Chevalier—no, Jane reminded herself, the Comte now—pressed his hands to his heart. "I shall treasure the sentiment."

Doing it too brown, Nicolas, Jane wanted to say, but couldn't. That was the danger of living in layers: one could never say exactly what one wanted when one wanted.

She nodded instead, politely, correctly, and saw in the Comte's dancing hazel eyes that he knew just how much it had cost her.

Why? Why here? Why now?

But there was nothing to be gained in breaking her role now. Jane held to her composure as Moreau looked from one to the other, like a puppy who had found a new friend. "You know each other?"

Jack Reid was also watching. His eyes were guarded and wary, his hat pulled down low as a shield. He slumped down on a bit of sacking outside the tent and began, idly, to polish a pair of Jane's boots.

"We move in similar circles," said the Comte de Brillac. He handed his gloves and hat to his servant without ever taking his eyes from Jane's. Jane didn't recognize the servant. He must, she thought, be new.

That meant one fewer person in the camp to know Jane. She could be grateful for that, at least.

Small blessings, she mocked herself. Her former chaperone, Miss Gwen, didn't believe in small blessings. Miss Gwen didn't believe in small anything. She could practically hear Miss Gwen's voice saying with a sniff, *Small blessing or large mishap? Dress it up any way you like; it's still no good.*

Miss Gwen, thought Jane wryly, would undoubtedly have taken her parasol to the side of the Comte's head, kicked Moreau in the shins, and even now be riding *ventre à terre*—most likely straight into a gorge.

Jane looked levelly at the Comte. "You have traveled very far from Paris . . . Monsieur le Comte."

The Comte's hazel eyes danced with mischief. "Even Paris occasionally grows dull—when one's friends are absent."

Jack Reid was watching too closely for comfort. Desperately trying to stem the tide, Jane said, "I have heard that one who is sick of Paris is sick of life."

"And perhaps I am." The Comte struck a pose, his hand on his heart. "Not sick, but heartsick."

"Are you quite sure?" inquired Jane repressively. "It might be no more than an attack of indigestion."

Captain Moreau ignored her. "Are you fleeing an affair of the heart?" he inquired eagerly.

Moreau's travel bag included *La Nouvelle Héloïse, Julie,* and a stack of other novels of the multiple-hanky variety. Jane knew because she had searched it.

The Comte de Brillac smiled brilliantly at the captain. "Isn't one always? Such inconvenient organs, hearts, so terribly susceptible to Cupid's dart."

In this case, Jane wasn't entirely sure that Cupid was the relevant culprit. An affair it might have been, but not of the heart.

". . . agony!" Captain Moreau was saying earnestly. "I carried her glove in my pocket for months. At least, I think it was her glove. It might have been her friend's. But it was the thought that counted, don't you agree?"

"Yes, yes, *mon ami*." The Comte de Brillac patted his shoulder, as one might a puppy. "You must tell me at length. Later." Turning to Jane, he said casually, "I trust, Lieutenant de Balcourt, we shall find the opportunity to . . . renew our acquaintance?"

So he didn't mean to unmask her. At least, not yet.

"We certainly have much to discuss," Jane said warily, and Nicolas grinned at her, that open, mischievous grin that had once had the power to disarm her, to fool her into believing that there might be something more between them than policy.

"I shall look forward to it," he said, and moved on, chatting easily with Captain Moreau, as if their discovery of each other here, in this out-of-the-way place, didn't signal impending disaster for one or both.

But it had been like that, from the beginning. Nicolas had always refused to behave as an enemy ought. That had been part of his charm: his ability to appreciate the absurd, his refusal to acknowledge the barriers that ought to separate them.

But one could live on a diet of meringues and champagne for only so long.

Jack Reid unfolded himself slowly from the ground outside the tent. Unlike the Comte, his breeches were liberally spattered with mud; his jacket showed signs of patching. In all the time she had known him, Nicolas had never undertaken a disguise that would render him anything but entirely soigné. Even in the black hood and robe worn by the members of the Hellfire Club, in a drug-fueled orgy, his locks had been arranged just so.

Jack didn't waste time on niceties. "What was that?"

"Don't you mean who was that?" Jane was glad of her false whiskers. They might not protect her from Nicolas, but they might at least hide her blushes. She shrugged, feigning nonchalance. "Call him an old adversary."

And so much more than that. Friend, enemy.

Lover.

"Have you ever heard," said Jane, "of a spy called the Gardener?"

Chapter Six

I had always wondered whether Colin was a spy.

Not seriously. Well, mostly not seriously. I stood there holding his phone in my hand, that horrible, rasping voice echoing in my ears.

Tell him. Bring the box.

I set off up the stairs at a run, aiming for Colin's study. Mrs. Selwick-Alderly had sounded . . . not afraid, precisely. But strained. Very strained.

Mrs. Selwick-Alderly was the most unflappable person I knew. Stiff upper lip didn't even begin to approach it.

I could hear typing from behind the half-closed door of Colin's study. Flinging it open, I said, "Colin?"

My little sister looked up from behind Colin's monitor, her

fingers continuing to move even as she spoke to me. "Outside. He went to check on—something."

Something. Lovely. "Do you have any idea where?"

"You know you're flaking mud, right?"

I flapped an impatient hand in Jillian's general direction. "That's what vacuums are for."

"Don't you mean *Hoovers*?" Jillian had been a little too amused by my attempts to adopt the local lingo.

"Whatever." Right now I had other things on my mind than my sister's *My Fair Lady* impression.

Colin's study had a view back over the grounds. Through the window I had caught sight of a familiar dark blond head making for the abandoned tower on the hill that I had once assumed held family secrets, but that actually held a miscellany of rusting farm equipment and, now, two dozen round tables with folding metal legs. Also some of the wedding presents we couldn't quite figure out what to do with, including the cuckoo clock that sang, for some arcane reason, *"Frère Jacques,"* while a little monk popped in and out of the doorway.

Jillian popped up from behind the computer screen. "If you're looking for Colin, you could always *ring* on your *mobile*."

"Not helpful," I said, and set off down the stairs, making for the garden.

Zigzagging my way past people trying to intercept me felt a bit like being back in the field-hockey unit in gym class, only minus the mouth guard.

"Later!" I called, and, "In a minute!" and, "Is that coffee?"

No, no, mustn't be distracted by coffee, even if Colin's friend Martin, the backup best man (should Nick fail to show up), was carrying a whopping great Costa cup filled with beautiful, life-giving nectar.

Pausing had been a mistake. A man with a clipboard came up to me. "Where do you want the—"

"In a minute," I said, and then spotted my mother. I pointed at her. "Ask her. She'll know."

Resisting the urge to grab Martin's coffee, I hustled towards the tower, which, unlike objects in the rearview mirror, was always farther away than it appeared.

Colin was just emerging as I huffed and puffed my way up the hill. "Did you know you have mud on your—"

"Yes," I said shortly. "It's cosmetic."

Colin looked doubtful but wisely forbore to inquire.

Further explanation appeared to be needed. "Pammy made me do it."

Colin's face cleared. "Ah," he said wisely. And then, "Are you looking for Jillian? She went in to use the computer."

"I know." Resting my hands on my knees, I took a moment to catch my breath. How to even begin to explain? "Someone called on your phone. He wants a box."

"A box?" Colin glanced back over his shoulder at the tower, which was, admittedly, filled with boxes. "What kind of box?"

"You tell me." I straightened, realizing I had omitted the truly crucial bit. "Someone is holding your aunt hostage and he won't release her unless you bring him the box. What in the hell is the box?"

"Did you say hostage?" Colin blinked several times.

I nodded vigorously. "Someone kidnapped your aunt Arabella."

Repeating it didn't help it make any more sense. In fact, it sounded increasingly absurd. But I had heard her; I knew I had.

Rapidly, I said, "It sounds ridiculous, I know, but whoever it was put her on the line. I spoke to her, Colin. She sounded scared." It was time to get down to brass tacks. "What do you have that someone would want that much?"

"I don't—" He broke off, his lips frozen on a denial that wouldn't form.

"You don't?" I prompted. Like George Washington, Colin couldn't tell a lie. At least not a good one. That was one of the things I liked about him. He might clam up from time to time, but he didn't dissemble. Which, considering that he came from a long line of spies and secret agents, was pretty amazing. "You've thought of something, haven't you?"

Colin was wrestling with his conscience. "It's not my secret to tell."

My pulse picked up with the crazy adrenaline rush you get before exams and right before the dentist lowers the drill. "I'd wondered about this. You're a spy, aren't you?"

"What? No." He stared at me like I'd grown a second head. "I'm not a spy. Aunt Arabella is."

Now it was my turn to stare. "Wait, what? Your aunt Arabella is— What?"

"A spy. Agent. Whatever you want to call it." Colin gave a little shake of his head. "Not is. Was. Back in the fifties and sixties. Possibly longer than that. I don't know, really. She doesn't talk about it."

I stood there, my mouth open, trying to reconcile the woman I knew, the one who wore Chanel pantsuits and placed biscuits on tea trays, with all the images conjured up by the word "spy." It was surprisingly easy. Even in her eighties, Mrs. Selwick-Alderly had an athletic grace. In her twenties and thirties she probably could have disarmed a villain one-handed while playing a set of tennis.

Why hadn't I seen it before? Perhaps because, with the arrogance of youth, I had assumed she had always been just what she was: an elegant lady who lunched, a woman of her generation, those bad old days before women seized the day and began hammering at the glass ceiling.

I, of all people, should have known better. Whatever the generation, whatever the circumstances, bright women made their own chances. The more underestimated one was, the easier to infiltrate, to listen, especially to the puffery of men who considered a sweet young thing a harmless audience.

Mrs. Selwick-Alderly was very good at listening. I should know. The first time I'd met her, I'd blurted out my whole life's story.

More than that, she had a Sphinx-like calm that always

made you suspect that she knew far more than she was saying. She doled out information purely on a need-to-know basis, but with the oblique promise of more.

Rather like the Pink Carnation. In fact, very like the Pink Carnation.

"I'm an idiot," I said flatly. "Of course."

She had lived everywhere, traveled everywhere, all around the globe, from hot spot to hot spot, Cyprus, Berlin, Kashmir on the eve of the handover, following her husband, who had something to do with the army.

Unless her husband had been following her, a convenient cover, an excuse. The higher-ups could arrange these things, I'd heard.

I looked at Colin in sudden alarm. "You think it's someone from her past? Then the box . . ."

"Could be anything," said Colin. "Or anywhere."

"Then why would they think you have it?"

Colin held up his hands, palms up. "Your guess is as good as mine."

It wasn't a guess. It was a speed bump in our front hall. "She sent us a wedding present."

"Yes, I know. The Georgian silver service." Colin frowned at me. "No. There's nothing in there except tissue paper. A great deal of tissue paper."

That was a thought, secrets in tissue paper, but I didn't think that was it. "Not that one," I said definitely. "She sent us another present—the Pink Carnation's traveling trunk. It just arrived today."

"Was there a note?" If there had been a light brigade on hand, Colin would have been ordering the charge.

"There was." I dug it out of the pocket of my jeans, somewhat bent but still legible. I handed it over to Colin. "Here. It's all rather oblique."

Lips pressed together, Colin quickly scanned the note. His head jerked up. "Treasure," he said. "She talks about treasure."

I glanced sharply at him. "I had assumed it was metaphorical. You don't think . . ."

"Jeremy," said Colin grimly.

I couldn't blame him. Once he'd said it, I'd thought the same thing.

It was hard to think of treasure and not think of Jeremy. He'd upended our lives a year ago, trying to find the lost jewels of Berar, which, due to a rather tangled chain of custody, had ended their bloodstained career in the bucolic fastness of Sussex, forgotten for two centuries. Jeremy had wanted those jewels badly.

In the end, he and Colin—and I—had all wound up working together to find them, but that was only because Jeremy's grandmother, Mrs. Selwick-Alderly, had twisted all of our arms. It had been truly expert twisting.

Once, I would have been delighted to blame Jeremy for any amount of skullduggery, but now . . .

I bit down hard on my lower lip. "He's been so well be-haved recently."

Forget olive branches; Jeremy had hauled along a whole olive tree. He'd been oozing sweetness and light, up to and including offering to host Colin's stag party. In Monte Carlo. Colin had declined and gone with his best man, Nick, to a series of clubs in London about which I preferred to know as little as possible, given that I presumed they most likely in-volved women wearing a minimum of clothing.

Whatever we needed, Jeremy had offered to provide it. There were plenty of plausible explanations for his sudden burst of goodwill. Concern for his grandmother, Mrs. Selwick-Alderly, who had made it clear a) that she wasn't going be around forever, and b) that she wanted her grandson and great-nephew reconciled before she shuffled off this mortal coil. Belated guilt for the various tricks he had pulled on Colin, including inviting a film crew to Colin's home, and, oh, yes, let's not forget the main one, running off with Colin's mother over Colin's father's deathbed. And, of course, attempting to steal the jewels of Berar out from under Colin's nose, plotting against Colin with Colin's emotionally delicate younger sister, and, most unpardonable of all, wearing black cashmere turtle-necks. In August.

But he had seemed to be trying to make up for all that, with the possible exception of the cashmere turtlenecks, about which he appeared to feel no shame. There had been something almost endearingly puppy-doggish about Jeremy's efforts.

But this was Jeremy we were talking about, a man who had changed his name along with his fortunes, smoothly going from Jamie Alderly to Jeremy Selwick-Alderly because he thought it looked better with black cashmere and champagne flutes. He was a chameleon and, from what I had seen, ultimately self-serving.

Tigers didn't change their spots. Jeremy didn't change his turtlenecks.

Except for other turtlenecks.

I could tell Colin was thinking the same thing. His lips compressed into a tight line. "He's been a little too well behaved."

No. It was the day before our wedding, dammit. I couldn't believe that even Jeremy would be that cruel. "Would he kidnap his own grandmother?"

"If he thought he could get away with it?"

Colin looked so weary that I reached out and cupped his cheek. He hadn't shaved yet. His chin was faintly scratchy against my palm. "But we found the jewels of Berar."

The rubies had been embedded in the cover of a folio edition of the 1806 blockbuster hit *The Convent of Orsino*, cunningly disguised with a layer of brown paint.

"Not all of them."

The sun was shining directly in my eyes. I squinted up at

Colin. "The Moon of Berar?" According to legend, it was the prize of the raja's hoard, a jewel with mystical powers. No one was entirely clear on what the jewel was or what mystical powers it contained, but the very vagueness only made people want it more. "That was just a myth."

"So were the rest of the jewels until we found them."

Fair point. "Where is Jeremy now?"

There were worried lines between Colin's brows. "Your guess is as good as mine."

My family and various assorted friends and relations were staying in the house. Colin's mother and Jeremy weren't. Colin's mother had, as she had informed Colin when invited, already spent too many impossibly dreary years there.

At the time, I'd repressed the urge to do a happy dance. I'd had Jeremy as a houseguest before. If he was going to leave wet towels on the bathroom floor and expect me to pick them up, he could at least leave a tip when he left.

I was joking—sort of—about the tip. I wasn't joking about the towels. Colin's mother was just as bad. The only difference was that in her case it seemed to be genuine obliviousness. In Jeremy's it was a deliberate exercise of power.

Either way, it was a large pile of wet towels.

"They're staying at Chivers?" Chivers House was a country-house B and B about half an hour from Selwick Hall as the Range Rover flies. The stately home of a Victorian magnate, it had been updated with all the mod cons, plus spa, a world-renowned chef, and swim instructors in skimpy swim trunks.

Colin nodded. "They'll be at the rehearsal dinner."

But we didn't know that the culprit was Jeremy, not for sure. "There's no way of tracing the phone call?"

"I'm not a spy, Eloise. I just write about them."

"That's not what I meant." Mostly. "What about the police?"

"We could try." Colin sounded doubtful. "But if the number was restricted—"

"What happened to villains using pay phones?" I groused.

"First they would have to find a pay phone." Taking both my hands in his, Colin gave them a squeeze. "Don't worry," he said quietly. "We'll get this sorted."

I loved him so much that it made my chest hurt. Colin's great-aunt was the closest thing he had to a parent. His father was dead, his mother was a flake, and his stepfather was a rat fink. And *he* was trying to comfort *me*.

"That's my line," I said, squeezing back. There was so much else that could be said, but now wasn't the time, so I settled for "We'll fix this. Together."

And if it was Jeremy, I was personally going to shake him until all his perfectly capped teeth rattled. He couldn't allow Colin even this one day to be happy? As much as Colin claimed to be immune to anything his mother or stepfather did, I knew every betrayal still hurt him, and especially now that they'd supposedly declared an entente. Colin had been happier than he wanted anyone to know to be back on speaking terms with his cousin.

There had to be other possibilities. . . . "Wait," I said, tugging on Colin's hand. "What if your aunt put something else in that trunk?"

"Something else?"

"I don't know." I squinted into the sun. My knowledge of MI6 was limited to old James Bond movies, and somehow I doubted that Sean Connery was a representative example of agent behavior. "Damning documents or old camera film or something else from her own time in the field. When you think of it, it's a great hiding place. Who would look for modern materials in an old trunk?"

I was warming to my own theory, partly because it made sense, but also because I wanted, very badly, for it not to be Jeremy. Not for Jeremy's sake, but for Colin's.

"Just think of it," I said enthusiastically. "Think of the symbolism of it, carrying on the Pink Carnation's tradition, using her trunk. . . . It's just like your aunt Arabella. If we can figure out what this person is looking for, maybe we can figure out who he is and where he has her!"

Colin glanced at his watch. "In the next . . . hour and a half?"

"Or we could call the police."

That decided him. "Where's the trunk?"

"Oh, God. I left it in the hall. I didn't realize—" I grabbed Colin by the arm and began towing him towards the house. Someone tried to cut in front of us with a question about flower arrangements. "Later!" I barked.

"Remind me never to get in your way," murmured Colin.

"Hush," I said, and barreled through the back entrance, dodging the chairs set up in the long drawing room and hurrying through the passage to the front hall.

There were plenty of boxes in the front hall. Most of them were stamped with the Bollinger logo. An hour ago I would have been delighted to see them. Now . . .

My mother was standing in the middle of the fray, counting boxes, to the growing impatience of a man with a clipboard. You don't mess with a corporate lawyer, even a retired one.

I poked her arm. "Mom? Did you see what happened to that trunk?"

"—twelve. You're two cases short," she said to the man with the clipboard. "You mean the trunk you left sitting in the middle of the hall?"

Why did I suddenly feel like I'd been caught stuffing my Barbies under the bed rather than putting them away in the Dream House? "Um, yes. That one."

"Lady—" began Clipboard Man belligerently.

She pointed a finger at him. "Check your truck." He slunk away. To me, she said, "I put it in your room."

I caught myself before I apologized for forgetting to put my toys away. "Thanks, Mom. I don't know what I would do without you."

"Be cheated out of two cases of champagne," she said smartly. "Is that what you're wearing to dinner?"

Since I was still in my jeans, it was clearly a rhetorical question.

"I would change now if I were you," said my father, from behind a bust of Charles I.

"Thanks, Dad. We'll just go do that." I took my fiancé by the hand, and we scurried for the relative safety of our bedroom, one of the few rooms in the house that hadn't been invaded by relatives of various shapes and sizes.

The trunk was there, at the foot of the bed. "Thank goodness," I said, and locked the door behind us before we could be discovered by caterers, florists, or nosy younger siblings with names beginning with J.

Colin knelt by the trunk. "No lock?"

"Try the brass tacks." I hovered over Colin as he gently pressed first one, then another of the tacks, taking care not to do anything to throw off the elderly mechanism. "Maybe there's a pattern to it? Or try pushing them both at once?"

"That's too—" The lid didn't precisely pop open, but something gave a very promising click. "Easy," finished Colin.

"Simplicity is the best deception?" I knelt beside him, remembering our first meeting, when we had knelt beside another trunk in Mrs. Selwick-Alderly's sitting room.

I felt a sudden wash of panic. I couldn't bear the thought of anything happening to her.

"Let's do this," I said, and pushed the lid of the trunk open.

It gave way with a sound very like a groan. Bits flaked from the old leather of the hinges. There was clothing on the top.

Very, very old clothing. I hesitated before reaching in. The fabric would be weak. I should be wearing gloves; we should have acid-free boxes ready. And then I thought of Mrs. Selwick-Alderly's voice on the other end of that phone and dug in with both hands.

"It's a uniform," said Colin, who, being a boy, paid attention to that sort of thing. "French. Hussars?"

The jacket was green, but it appeared to be missing the matching pants. All sorts of possibilities came to mind. A piece of paper fluttered out of the jacket.

Colin caught it. "Papers," he said. "For one Lieutenant Jean de Balcourt, aide to— I can't read it. It's too smudged."

"Jean de Balcourt . . . Jane! It must be one of her aliases." My fingers literally itched to examine that paper. I curled my hands into fists. Now was not the time. "What else is down there?"

Another uniform, this one complete with white leather pants. Assorted gloves. Colin lifted a wooden tray, and beneath that were dresses—dresses that looked as though they belonged in the Met's costume institute, hand-embroidered, delicately tucked and frilled.

And there was still another tray beneath that. "It's like Mary Poppins's bag," I said wonderingly. "All that's missing is a hat stand and a rubber plant."

"Or a Tardis," said Colin, removing another layer. When I looked blank, he said, "Bigger on the inside."

"Okay." It seemed easiest just to agree. "Oh, my goodness."

It was like one of those boxes of chocolates that came in

multiple layers, each one a surprise, richer than the last. This tray held papers. There were maps: maps of Portugal, of Italy, of France. The maps alone . . . I licked my dry lips. Another time. Another time I could go over them.

There were books, too, novels and travel narratives. For amusement? Or some subtler purpose? I felt a pang as Colin set them aside, but our time was getting short. Any moment now, my mother or Jillian was going to come banging on the door, and we weren't the least bit closer to discovering who might have Mrs. Selwick-Alderly and why.

And I still had a face full of dried dirt.

Colin added a small leather journal to the pile. "There's another tray under here."

"Huh?" Telling myself it couldn't hurt, I eased open the leather journal. It was in code, of course, but not the sort of numerical code that would look suspicious to anyone who opened it. No, Jane Wooliston was too subtle for that. It was a code she had worked out with her cousin's sister-in-law, Lady Henrietta Selwick, social events substituting for darker realities.

I spotted the Gardener, pruning the shrubbery. . . .

The Gardener, deadliest spy of his generation.

Well, if one didn't count the Black Tulip. The Black Tulip's body count had definitely been higher. And Gaston Delaroche, agent of the Ministry of Police, who had slid down the charts from third-most-feared man in France to forty-second, although not for want of trying.

Okay, so maybe the Gardener wasn't the deadliest spy of his generation. But he was one of the cleverest.

"Eloise." The strangled note in Colin's voice called me back to the present. "You may have been right."

He was holding notebooks. Modern notebooks. They looked like stenographical notebooks, the sort I vaguely remembered from my mother's office when I was very little, before everything had switched over to computers and dictation had gone the way of the dodo.

I scooted over to him. "These must be your aunt's."

Colin flipped through a few pages of the one on top. He didn't look happy. He tried the next one. Same result.

I took the one he'd set aside. Numbers, letters, and symbols ran riot across the page like something from a mathematician's crazed imagination. They looked sort of like equations and sort of like gibberish. In fact, a lot like gibberish.

Looking increasingly worried, Colin shoved the second journal my way. "Do you have any idea what they say?"

I bit down on my lip. That it was a code of some kind I had no doubts, but it wasn't one I recognized off the bat. Codes weren't really my thing, but I'd been forced by necessity to decipher more than a few. It was a bit like calculus: I didn't particularly enjoy it, but I could do it if I had to.

"It's not any of the classic codes." I hated to say it, but . . . "We'll need a cryptographer."

"Do you have one tucked away somewhere?"

"I have two tax lawyers." My family tended to run heavily towards lawyers. "Not the right kind of code, huh?"

"No." Colin was not amused. Few people are amused by the IRS. "What were the coordinates of the rendezvous?"

"Two a.m. at the old abbey. Donwell Abbey?" The nearest house to Selwick Hall was Donwell Abbey, or, rather, the manor house that had been built on the ground of the old abbey. The remains of the abbey itself had been kept on as a sort of garden folly, a picturesque ruin.

And a very good place for those who chose to lurk.

Colin gave an unhappy jerk of his chin. "Presumably."

I hated the idea of leaving Mrs. Selwick-Alderly where she was. And actually bringing the box to that guy . . . What if it was the wrong box? What if we'd been wrong?

"What do we do?"

Colin's expression was grim. "We go to our rehearsal dinner. After that . . . Donwell Abbey."

Chapter Seven

"Did you say the Gardener?" Jack demanded, hoping to hell that he had misheard. "The Gardener . . . as in *the Gardener?*"

"You know of him, then," said the Pink Carnation, as if it were every day that the devil strolled into camp and demanded a cup of tea. But her hands betrayed her. They were clasped at her waist in a feminine gesture that didn't at all suit the martial garb of Lieutenant Jean de Balcourt.

"Of course I bloody well know of him. I worked for him." The Gardener. The Gardener was there in their camp, in the flesh. This was not good. This was the antithesis of good. Jack considered himself a fairly easygoing sort, a connoisseur of human foibles, but if there were any man in the world whom

Jack hated, loathed, and reviled, it was the master spy known as the Gardener. "But we never met. Everything was through intermediaries."

The Carnation looked at him solemnly. "He won't know you, then. That's to our advantage."

Jean. The Gardener had called her Jean, even though she had been introduced only as Lieutenant de Balcourt.

Jean? Or Jeanne?

A vision of the Carnation as she had been when he first met her, ten days past, flashed through Jack's mind, frilled and flounced and dangerously beautiful in a gown designed to make the most of her charms. A Paris gown. A gown fit for a French count's consort.

"But he knew you, princess." The Gardener had known her in a disguise that would fool most. The Gardener, who had come far from his usual hunting grounds, to this out-of-the-way spot on the edges of the world. "Would you care to explain that?"

That would be the irony, wouldn't it, if, after all these years of successfully evading the Gardener's men, he had blindly followed one into the middle of a French camp.

The woman who had introduced herself as the Pink Carnation looked down the long alley of tents, twin furrows between her brows. "He's traveled rapidly by the looks of it."

Jack folded his arms across his chest. "The Pink Carnation would be a prize worth bearing back to Bonaparte."

"Or the man who stole the jewels of Berar?" the Carnation

shot back, before shaking her head decisively. "No, I don't think it's either of us he's after. The jewels are two years lost now, and I—"

"And you?" Jack's voice was dangerously smooth.

The Pink Carnation didn't quite meet his eye. "The Gardener and I have an understanding."

"An *understanding*?"

The Pink Carnation looked down her nose at him. "So long as certain rules are observed," she said primly, "we do each other the professional courtesy of leaving each other alone."

In a pig's eye. Jack had never known a spy whose motto wasn't live and let die. "How terribly civilized," he drawled.

"Why shouldn't we be?" The Pink Carnation frowned at him. "You're blocking the door of the tent."

Jack held up the flap for her with a flourish. "Spying isn't a gentleman's game, princess. Or," he added pointedly, as he ducked beneath, "a lady's."

In the mirror on the shaving stand, Jack could see the Carnation's teeth dig into her lower lip. "There are rules to war, as to anything else. Enemy officers have been known to take tea between battles."

Jack snorted derisively. "Taking tea? Is that what they call it now?"

"Don't be vulgar." But she didn't meet his eyes.

Did she think he was blind? The tension between his companion and the Gardener could have been felt all the way in

Madrid. Hell, the Gardener had all but taken out an ad in the paper.

The Gardener played tricks. For a moment Jack felt his resolution waning. The Gardener was a master of manipulation; a few well-chosen words and he could have a man convinced the sky was green and the river red. If it amused him to give the impression . . .

But no. Jack came back to earth hard. The woman's averted gaze told its own story.

And if he felt a surge of anger entirely out of proportion to the offense, well, it was anger at himself for being so easily gammoned. He wasn't a boy, wet behind the ears. He should have known better than to have trusted this woman purely on the strength of the code phrase. The code phrase and the clean profile of a goddess on a coin.

Everything had rung wrong. Her insistence that they travel among the French, for one.

And yet.

To say that she had been displeased at the appearance of her supposed lover would be an understatement. There had been a moment, a very brief moment, when she had looked as though she were going to be ill, her face a delicate shade of green that clashed with those damned ginger whiskers.

A good actress could feign many things, but that level of sick disbelief was difficult to counterfeit, even for the most accomplished actress at the Comédie-Française.

There were two roads open to him. Either she was a confederate of the Gardener or she wasn't. In the first case, he strapped her to the chair and ran. Fast and far. Even that idiot Moreau couldn't keep the Gardener occupied babbling on forever.

In the second case . . .

"Either you're a fool or you think I am." Jack stalked over to her. "Anyone who claims there are rules to war is courting a bullet in the back."

The Pink Carnation drew herself up, regarding him with a nice dollop of scorn. "Fine words from the man who refuses to wear the enemy's colors."

"Green has never become me." This show of offended honor might be the sham, the chameleon spy the reality. Jack made a decision—which was not to decide. "Do you want to stand here and spar? Because it's both of our necks you're putting in the noose."

The Pink Carnation looked at him without pretense, her gray eyes more pewter than silver in the dim light. "What do you suggest?"

Jack shrugged, watching her closely. "You could always kill him."

"No." The answer was quick and instinctive. "Just . . . no."

"Oh?" Jack raised a brow, his mind working furiously. If she were working with the Gardener, the logical resort would have been to pretend to consider the plan, to go along with it. He strolled towards her, two steps taking up the space between them in the small tent. The sagging canvas brushed his head.

"You're in the wrong line of work, princess, if you let those sorts of scruples get in the way."

The Pink Carnation held her ground. There were lines of worry on either side of her mouth, but she looked him directly in the eye. "I'm a gatherer of information, not an assassin."

That bolt hit home harder than she knew. Jack pushed the point. "Self-defense is hardly the same as cold-blooded execution."

The Carnation took a deep breath. "Self-defense is a last resort when all other hope is lost." She looked up at him, something wistful in her eyes. "This isn't our last resort."

If she wasn't honest, that was a bloody brilliant imitation of it.

"Just keep telling yourself that when the Gardener takes you back to Paris in chains," said Jack gruffly. He turned abruptly away, pacing as far as the tent pegs would let him. "What's your plan, then?"

The Pink Carnation stood where he had left her, straight and still. Reluctantly, she said, "I believe that the circumstances call for strategic retreat."

He'd be damned if he'd let her gild the lily. "You mean running away."

"No." The Carnation's head came up, her eyes meeting his with a fervor that shook Jack to the core. "If the Gardener is here, it is because he is also on the trail of Her Majesty. We need to get to the Queen before he does."

Brilliant. "I liked it better when I thought we were running away," muttered Jack. "All right. Just how do you propose we do that?"

The Carnation hesitated for a moment, and then said, with what dignity she could, "We go back to your original idea. We travel light and alone."

"My original idea," said Jack, with fine irony, "involved our having time to prepare and provision. And it didn't involve having that cold-blooded bastard on our heels."

The Carnation stiffened a bit at the profanity, but chose not to comment. "Can you get us away?"

"How much time do we have?"

The Carnation glanced at the flap of the tent. "Nicolas— the Gardener—won't be in any hurry." In a quieter voice, she added, "It would never occur to him that I might flee. He will expect me to stay and . . . spar."

Spar. Jack wasn't entirely sure that was what she'd meant to say. Dally? For the Carnation, Jack suspected the two might be one and the same; no sweet nothings for her, but a clash of wits.

Leading, eventually, to a clash of more than wits.

Brusquely, Jack said, "You won't be missed until supper, then. That gives us . . . an hour?"

"More," said the Carnation with quiet certainty. "The Comte prefers to dine late. He keeps city hours, even in the country."

"You know a great deal about the man and his habits."

The Pink Carnation looked aside. "It is—"

"I know," said Jack, with heavy sarcasm. "Professional cour-tesy."

The Carnation winced.

Jack pressed forward, feeling irrationally angry with the world. "All right. But this time we do it my way. You follow my lead. No questions, no arguments."

The Carnation regarded him thoughtfully. "The Gardener doesn't know who you are. You could leave me here. You could go on with the mission alone." Her lips twisted wryly. "That was what you wanted, wasn't it? To be free of me?"

What he wanted? Jack stared at her incredulously, and then he began to clap. "Oh, nicely played. I can't deny that you make a very pretty martyr." He ran a finger along the line of one of her false whiskers, and felt her shiver beneath his touch. "But you might want to remove these before you go to your lion. Pull out your pretty frocks and give him a proper greeting."

Those pink lips opened, but it took a moment for sound to follow. "What are you implying?" she said hoarsely.

"I don't know," said Jack silkily. His finger rubbed against her lower lip. "You tell me."

The Carnation stared at him, frozen, her breath coming hard between her lips. Then she blinked, twice, and yanked away. "Get the horses. If we're to be away before sunset, we need to move now."

Jack's hands dropped back to his sides. He felt as though he'd been running over rough terrain, his breath tight in his chest.

"No horses," said Jack tersely. "We're traveling light, on

foot. All of this"—the rosewood shaving case, the camp bed, the writing table—"stays. Take only what you can carry. And when I say you, I mean you. I'm not your mule."

Exercising great control, the Pink Carnation said, "We don't stand a chance on foot against a man in a carriage."

"On these roads? That carriage is as much of a liability as an asset. And"—Jack smiled unpleasantly at her—"there are other ways to put a spoke in your friend's wheels."

The Carnation was already gathering together provisions with quick, efficient movements. Her head jerked back over her shoulder. "What do you mean?"

"Ipecacuanha," said Jack succinctly. "A lovely little potion from Her Majesty's colonies in Brazil. You've heard of it, I imagine?"

The Pink Carnation's hands stilled on the lid of her writing case. "I've never employed it. It won't—"

Jack permitted himself an ironic smile. "Don't worry. It won't kill him. It will only make him wish he were dead for the space of, oh, six hours or so."

It was a highly gratifying thought. A knife between the man's ribs was an even more gratifying thought, and carried with it its own poetic justice, but the Carnation's words rang ironically in his ears. He was a spy, not an assassin. He had broken with the Gardener over just that principle. He would hardly give the Gardener the satisfaction of breaking his word now.

For a moment it looked as though the Carnation intended

to argue with him. Her knuckles were white on the lid of her writing desk. And then she dropped her head, opening the case with a quick, jerky movement.

"Do what you need to do." And then, softly, "But don't hurt him."

Don't *hurt* him? Jack wrested the vial of ipecac out of the trunk in which he had buried it.

"One day you'll have to tell me how the man managed to earn such tender sympathy," he said, and had the satisfaction of seeing her cheeks flush beneath her false whiskers before the tent flap crashed down behind him.

It took no time at all to empty the ipecac into Moreau's decanter of claret. If Jack spared a moment's regret that Moreau should suffer for his hospitality, it was only a moment. This was war, whatever the woman in his tent might think. In war, innocent people suffered. He should know. He'd seen it firsthand, again and again.

Don't hurt him.

As insurance, Jack slipped off to the makeshift paddock where the horses and mules were getting what grazing they could. He didn't set them all free. That would be too obvious. But if a few horses happened to slip their tether—well, someone's groom must have been careless.

The early autumn dusk was already falling and with it a light rain. Jack was grateful for both. The rain wasn't heavy enough to seriously impede their progress, but it would keep men huddled in their tents. Not to mention dampening the ardor of would-be searchers once it became clear that Lieutenant de Balcourt and his servant had flown.

The Carnation was waiting for him. The lamps had been lit in the tent, a lumpy shape constructed of boxes and bundles placed on the camp stool, where it cast, from the distance, an almost human shadow.

"It is done?" she said, with uncharacteristic hesitation.

She was still wearing her uniform, but had sponged off her whiskers. Without them, her face looked very young and vulnerable, a girl playing dress-up in her brother's clothes.

Not a girl, a woman. A woman with intimate knowledge of the master spy known as the Gardener.

"It's done," said Jack shortly. "Now we need to move. Fast."

"We might have a bit more time than you think." The Pink Carnation did her best to retain her usual poise. "I sent a note to N—to the Gardener, saying I would wait on him after supper. And another to Moreau, informing him that I had a touch of *la grippe* and was keeping to my tent tonight."

It was a good thought, but Jack wasn't going to admit it. A haversack lolled on the cot, stuffed until it bulged. "Is that what you're bringing with you?"

The Pink Carnation's lips quirked. "It seemed easier than carrying the trunk."

Was she trying to be funny?

"I hope you can carry it, that's all," muttered Jack.

He shouldered his own haversack. Unlike the Carnation, he didn't travel with full kit. He was always ready to move on a moment's notice. He didn't need rosewood writing desks and mirrored shaving stands. Kneeling, Jack yanked up one of the tent pegs.

"What are you doing?" asked the Pink Carnation.

"Crawling," said Jack. He peeled back a small section of canvas. "After you."

With one doubtful look, the Pink Carnation crawled. Her white breeches were soon brown with mud. So much the better, thought Jack, forcing himself to be hard. Those white trousers were worse than a beacon.

"No lantern?"

"Not unless you want to be seen."

There wasn't much by way of a moon; the clouds had taken care of that. They pressed forward in grim silence, away from the road, over rocks slippery with rain, up treacherous paths slick with mud and pitted with pebbles. The Carnation staggered and slipped but kept doggedly on, her head lowered, hatless. The rain had slowed, but Jack had led them, deliberately, through a heavily forested region, and the leaves let loose their moisture on the Carnation's bare head, making her hair drip damply around her face, running into her eyes. She had left her uniform hat behind. Sensible if one expected to be seen, not so clever when it came to keeping the rain off.

Jack might have given her his own hat; he raised a hand to his head, and then stopped, as those three little words came back to taunt him.

Don't hurt him.

The path was little more than a goat track, better suited to hooves than boots, particularly if one wasn't accustomed to the terrain. The Pink Carnation stumbled again, catching herself against the jagged branch of a tree. She didn't cry out, but the corners of her lips compressed with pain and her white face went even whiter.

Turning back, Jack relieved the Carnation of her pack.

"You don't . . . need . . ."

"I don't need you breaking your fool neck," said Jack shortly, hefting the haversack onto his shoulder. The Carnation had clearly packed a few bricks, just in case they needed to build their own shelter. Three-story, with a drawing room and space for a music room. "Wickham doesn't pay extra for dead agents. We'll camp at the next clearing."

"Shouldn't we . . . go . . . farther?" The Carnation was shivering so hard she could hardly speak.

"Only idiots would be out tonight." What that made him, Jack wasn't sure.

An abandoned goatherd's hut would have been rather nice about now, but one wasn't going to oblige him by materializing. Instead Jack found a relatively level space between the trees, the ground thickly thatched with pine needles.

"Home, sweet home," he said. "Put up your feet and make yourself comfortable."

He'd expected complaints, protests, demands for an inn

with an en suite chamber pot. The Pink Carnation provided none of those. She turned, surveying her surroundings with a slightly bewildered expression.

"I suppose it's too dangerous to have a fire," she said.

He shouldn't feel sorry for her. It was ridiculous. They wouldn't be in this mess, insufficiently provisioned, wet, hunted, if she hadn't insisted on going her own way in the first place, whether it had been by ignorance or design.

But he did. Her face looked so white and pinched in the meager light, her body racked by chills she did her best to hide.

"More dangerous to die of exposure," Jack said gruffly, squatting on the ground as he cleared a makeshift fire pit. "And, no, no one will see it from here."

He hoped.

He had led them deep into the countryside, well away from the main road. They were, Jack surmised, more likely to encounter curious locals than French soldiers.

The Pink Carnation squatted down beside him, shoving her cold hands into her sleeves. "Which way are we going?"

"North," Jack lied. Not that she had any way of communicating with the Gardener from here, unless she had a carrier pigeon tucked into that bulging bag of hers, but best to be safe.

If she smelled a rat, she didn't say. Instead she scooted a bit closer to the tiny blaze, hunching down into her cloak.

Jack pulled a flask from beneath his jacket. "Brandy?"

The Carnation looked at him in surprise. "Do you— That is, I didn't know. Are Hindus allowed to drink?"

Deliberately, Jack took a long draft. "It's Musselmen who can't drink." He capped the flask and shoved it back in his pocket. "And I'm not."

"A Musselman?"

"Anything." The word came out raw and ugly. Jack had thought himself inured against it, but it still hurt, every time. His father had had him baptized, supposedly, but that was the extent of his theological contribution, theoretically out of respect for Jack's mother, but really, Jack suspected, because it would link Jack too closely to him, this child he had never wanted born of a woman he had never wanted. As for his mother's people, Jack was an outcast, unclean. "I'm neither fish nor fowl, princess. Trust me at your peril."

There was a charged silence. The Pink Carnation raised her hands to her brow and lifted the hair right off her head. The entire dark, sodden mass came off, revealing her own hair, pale and dry beneath, tightly braided.

Another deception.

Jack felt a fool. Here he'd been feeling sorry for her, hatless, when she'd been wearing a hat of hair, dry and snug underneath. He ought to have remembered; he'd seen her in her own hair once before, that day in Lisbon, fine and straight, nothing like the dark curls she had affected as Lieutenant de Balcourt. But she had remained so thoroughly in character throughout their march, never once removing the wig, he had forgotten that the dark curls weren't her own.

It didn't do to take anything at face value with the woman who called herself the Carnation.

She gave her head a little shake as though testing the feel of it. Primly, she said, "We shape ourselves, not the circumstances of our birth. We choose our own course—for good or for ill."

Yes, but she hadn't started life in a leaky ship. Jack rocked back, bracing himself on one hand. "Has your road always run straight, princess? Or have you perchance taken the odd trek down the garden path?"

"If you want to know how I know the Gardener, you could just say so," the Carnation said mildly.

And there he'd thought he was being so subtle. To the devil with it all. Bluntly, Jack said, "Are you working with him?"

The Pink Carnation stared at him across the flames. Quietly, she said, "My loyalties have never been questioned. Can you say the same of yours?"

Maybe it was the contempt in her voice. Maybe it was the way she was looking at him, as though he were a cockroach beneath her heels. Maybe it was two weeks of playing Rodrigo to her lieutenant, fetching her shaving water and saying "yes, sir, no, sir," when all he wanted was to bend her over that camp bed and—

Whatever it was, something snapped.

"Go on," Jack drawled in his most offensive voice. "Tell me what you think of me. Tell me that I'm a turncoat. Tell me that I'm a man without honor. Be honest now. Don't hold back."

She had courage; he'd give her that. There she was, alone with him in the wilderness, lost, vulnerable, and utterly unapologetic.

She looked him squarely in the eye. "I've said nothing more than is true."

"But there's truth and there's truth. Isn't there, *Jean?*" Jack had the satisfaction of seeing her flinch just a bit. "You have your truth. I have mine."

The Carnation was not impressed. "What is true is that you lied. People trusted you—and you lied to them."

"And you don't lie?" Jack looked pointedly at her green uniform jacket. "Everything about you is a lie."

If she sat any straighter, he could use her as a hat rack. "There are . . . compromises we make in the interest of justice. But I have never, ever betrayed my comrades."

The first time he had slipped information to the British, three of his friends had died in battle. He hadn't expected that. When great nations warred, small men suffered. Died. It had seemed so abstract, that information. Such-and-such company to move at such-and-such a time. Words on a slip of paper. Nothing more.

He had forgotten that the point of information was to be used.

And, having committed to his course, he was obliged to do it again. And again. Justice, the Carnation said. Oh, he had believed, initially, in the justice of his actions.

But that didn't change the outcome.

The woman sitting across from him, so smug and sure, had no idea. "Do you want me to grovel and cringe? Yes, I betrayed the men who employed me. But I had my reasons for doing so."

Reasons. The corpses of his friends stared sightlessly up at him, mocking him.

"By reasons," said the Carnation coolly, "I assume you mean coin."

Yes, Jack was tempted to say. *Riches beyond imagining. Dancing girls. Priceless gems.* But that would be a lie, even more of a lie than the green uniform jacket she wore. He had never cared for any of that. He had never desired riches, for all that he had stumbled upon them. Stealing the jewels of Berar had been another way of taking revenge, of thumbing his nose at the man who had stolen his ideals and left him a man with neither a country nor a cause.

"Wouldn't that be nice and simple? No." Jack smiled crookedly. "If you want to know why I did what I did, ask your friend. The Gardener."

Chapter Eight

"*I* can't," said Jane, with some asperity. "He's not here. And he's not my friend."

Her enemy, her lover, but never her friend. Friendship required a measure of trust, and that was one thing, even at the height of infatuation, she had never been able to give to Nicolas de la Tour d'Argent.

Sometimes it seemed to her that everything that had gone wrong, everything that had led her to this moment, here, cold, miserable, unsure, could be dated back to that day in the spring of 1805 when she had first held out her hand to the Chevalier de la Tour d'Argent.

If only she could turn back the clock . . .

But there was no way to do that, and even if she could, what would she do? Stop Jack Reid from sending the jewels of Berar back to England? Jane indulged in a moment's wishful thinking. If Jack Reid had never sent the jewels . . . then her sister Agnes would never have disappeared from her boarding school. Jane and Miss Gwen would never have been summoned from Paris to find her. They would never have met Nicolas de la Tour d'Argent.

And everything could be as it was.

She was being selfish, she knew. If that were so, the Gardener would still be operating untrammeled in England. If she was barred from Paris now, so the Gardener was barred from London. She had accomplished that much, at least. And if Jack had never sent those ill-starred jewels, Miss Gwen would never have met Colonel Reid, would never have had her daughter, Jane's goddaughter, Plumeria. Could she cast that small life into darkness, render it as nothing, merely because she was so petty as to long for the calm certainties of her old existence?

Jane hated herself for begrudging Miss Gwen her happiness. She wanted Miss Gwen to be happy—of course she did. And she owed Miss Gwen so very much.

At times like this, Jane wished she owed Miss Gwen a little less.

"Whatever I may think of the Gardener, for good or for ill, he's hardly Satan, to be blamed for every sin." Jane shifted on the rough ground. It had stopped raining, but she could feel the damp seeping through her breeches. She would have given anything to be anywhere but here. "You made your own choices."

And so had she. As much as she would like to blame Jack Reid for all her current misery.

But she, unlike Jack Reid, knew how to take responsibility for her own actions.

Jack Reid leaned his weight against one arm, his pose lazy, relaxed, but there was something beneath it that made the hairs on Jane's neck prickle. "I'd like to set you an exercise, princess. Imagine, if you will, that you live in a country—your own country, mind!—where you have no rights at all. The law forbids your entering the army, the government, any profession that might suit your interests or talents. And why? All because you were born to the wrong mother. Well? Can you picture that?"

"Picture it?" A slightly hysterical laugh rose in Jane's throat. "I've lived it. I've lived it these past five years."

The confusion on Reid's face would have been amusing if she weren't so entirely beyond amusement, cold and wet and terrified. She'd had two years now—two years of hiding so far from anyone she knew or loved that she'd nearly forgotten herself, two years of bottling her emotions, whistling through her fears.

Jane's hands shook with cold and nervous energy. "What do you think it is to be a woman? If I had been born a man, I might have served my country in the normal way. I might have stood for Parliament or commanded a company. Do you think yourself hard done by, Mr. Reid? You can walk down the street unchaperoned. You can rent a room or sit at a table in a tavern without everyone assuming that you must be a whore."

The ugly word hung in the air between them. On the fire a twig cracked, sending sparks flying into the air.

There was a dark color beneath Jack Reid's tanned skin. "I didn't assume—"

"Didn't you?"

Their eyes locked, held. Jane could feel her hands clench into fists in her lap, the nails biting into her palm, but she kept her spine straight, her head held high. Her reputation was all that was left to her. Once that was lost, she would be fair game. It was unfair, but it was the way the world worked. She had learned that the hard way.

"With every word, with every gesture, you have made clear your opinion of me. And my morals. And why? Because I am a woman alone, doing a man's work. Picture *that*, Mr. Reid. And be grateful for the freedoms you have that I never shall."

Jack Reid's face might have been carved from seasoned wood. Then slowly, deliberately, he doffed his hat to her. "You're fighting for the wrong side, princess. You ought to have joined the revolution."

Someday. Nicolas's voice, urbane and amused, his breath warm against her ear. *Someday you'll realize you're fighting for the wrong side. And when that day comes, I'll be there waiting.*

Don't keep me waiting too long, Jeanne.

"I'm no radical," said Jane flatly. She turned the collar of her cloak up, a small barrier against the world. "And even if I were, the revolution is dead. Bonaparte may claim to be the voice of the revolution, but the only force that drives him is his own ambition."

Jack Reid stared into the fire, his expression abstracted. "I believed in it all once, you know. The revolution, the shining city on a hill, rights for all." He glanced sideways at Jane, his eyes unreadable in the firelight. "When I was sixteen, I ran away and joined Scindia's army. I was recruited by a man named Pierre Perron. You've heard of him, I take it?"

"He was one of Scindia's generals," said Jane warily. "A committed revolutionary."

"A true one. His goal was that the tricolor fly over all of India, in a world where all men were equal. More equal if they were French, but no one's perfect. He meant well. And he was good to me. He took me on as if I were his own. He made me free of his library. He showed me the image of a world made new." Memory softened Jack's features, brought a warmth to his voice that Jane had never imagined he could possess. "He called me son."

It was too much. She didn't want to know this, any of it. There had to be some trick, some ploy. Men like the Moonflower didn't confide without purpose, no matter how cold the wind or dark the night.

"You had a father," said Jane.

The warmth fled Jack's face. "Was that in my dossier? Or are you merely presuming based on the commonplaces of natural science? So I did. For what it was worth."

Jane remembered Colonel Reid as she had last seen him, his two-year-old daughter balanced high on his shoulders, her small fingers tugging at his silvering red hair as the colonel bounced her up and down. The Laughing Colonel, they called him—except when he had cause to mention his second son.

Jane frowned at the Moonflower. "Why are you telling me this?"

Whatever camaraderie there had been between them, it was gone now. "Because," said Jack Reid lazily, "Perron was the one who recruited me on the Gardener's behalf."

"Oh?" Jane affected lack of interest, but the hairs on the back of her neck prickled. If Jack Reid was working with the Gardener still, if this was a complicated plot, now was the perfect time for him to reveal his perfidy—now, when she was isolated, alone, and entirely dependent.

She had, she realized, walked herself right into a potential trap by fleeing with him into the night. In the French camp, on a major road, she might have blended in, found her way back to Lisbon and safety.

But the French camp and the road were miles behind them.

"The work, Perron told me, might be irregular, but it would be for a just cause. Our cause. And it all went well enough for the first year. I remained nominally within Perron's command, but in reality I worked for the Gardener."

Jane moved subtly closer to the fire. A burning brand wasn't much of a weapon, but it would serve in case of need. "Until you saw a shiny case of jewels?"

Jack's eyes met hers, cool and hard. "Until he asked me to murder my mentor."

Jane blinked. "Murder?"

"Perron," said Jack Reid very softly, "had outlived his usefulness. He was too bold in his beliefs, too blunt. He had antagonized the rest of Scindia's forces. There was dissension in the ranks and talk of a potential coup. Battles were lost. Ideals were all very well, but Bonaparte needed results, not rhetoric. He needed Scindia's armies pitted against the British. So the Gardener sent me another assignment. I was to assassinate Perron."

"But . . ." Jane delved into her memory. "Perron lives. He retired to France."

"Yes." Jack Reid kicked a fallen twig back into the fire with the heel of his boot. "Perron lives."

None of this sorted with what she knew about Jack Reid, or what she thought she knew about him. "You refused?"

Jack Reid smiled without humor. "And risk having my own neck on the block? What do you take me for?" He leaned back, clasping his hands behind his head. "I had an unavoidable assignment elsewhere. By the time I returned, Perron had fled Scindia's camp. He had received . . . anonymous information."

There had been something rather unusual about Perron's escape. Jane had marked it as odd even then, but there had been too many other matters demanding her attention.

"Perron fled to the English camp. . . . He was given safe passage to the coast." Jane looked down at Jack Reid as the pieces clicked together. "You saved him."

" 'Saved' is such a strong term." Jack tipped his hat down over his eyes. "Perron was old enough to take care of himself."

If he had professed noble motives, painted a halo for himself, Jane would have been suspicious. But this . . . this had too much of the ring of truth. It would be just like Nicolas to order the dispatch of a colleague who had proved himself a liability. Jane had seen as much herself, with her own eyes.

Perron had lived. And Jack Reid had begun selling secrets to the English.

Jane looked narrowly at him, trying to find his face beneath his hat. "Information for safe passage. Was that the bargain?"

Jack Reid shrugged. "The English paid more. I'm a mercenary, out for what I can get, remember?"

He was sprawled nearly flat on his back, his head propped against his haversack, his hat tipped over his eyes, one foot propped on the opposite knee, the picture of devil may care. But he did care. He cared badly. Jane could hear it in his voice, could read it in his deliberate slouch, in his studied unconcern.

Everything Jane knew about him, everything she had thought she had known—it was turned upside down, on its head. A troubled soul, Colonel Reid had called his second son. Insubordinate, those who worked with him had said. Brilliant but unpredictable.

All true, but from it, Jane had inferred something more. A man without principle, without belief, without honor, his loyalty only to himself. Because what sort of man could turn his back on his father and make common cause with his father's enemies?

He called me son.

Jane stared at the recumbent figure in mounting frustration. "Why?" she demanded. "Why tell me this now?"

"Doesn't every campfire need a story? Remind me next time to tell you the one about the tiger that got away."

"That isn't funny." She prided herself so on her judgment, on her ability to read the hearts and minds of men. And she had been wrong. Utterly, dangerously wrong. And why? Because Jack Reid made a career out of being provoking. Because she blamed him, still, for his carelessness in sending the jewels of Berar to England. Jane snatched the hat off his head. "Do you realize that your stubbornness may have walked us into a trap?"

Jack sat up straight so suddenly that Jane rocked back on her heels with a thump. "*My* stubbornness?" There was a dangerous glint in his amber eyes. The tiger hadn't got away. It was here at the campfire next to her. "May I remind you, Your

Royal Highness, that you were the one who insisted on traveling with Captain Moreau? Against, I might add, repeated advice to the contrary."

Advice that she had ignored, on principle, because he was
Jack Reid, and therefore automatically suspect.

Jane wanted to cry with frustration. "If you had given me
any reason to trust you—"

"What?" Jack's voice was rich with sarcasm. "You would
have placed my judgment before your own? The Pink Carnation who does no wrong?"

He was on his feet now, looking down at her. Jane had
never felt smaller in her life, her legs drawn against her chest,
plastered with mud, Jack Reid standing over her, legs apart,
arms crossed, regarding her with an expression of utter contempt.

"Don't blame me for your own mistakes, princess," he said,
and turned on his heel, stalking past the small circle of the fire.

"Wait." Jane scrambled to her feet, her boots slipping and
sliding against the damp pine needles. She had no map, no
compass. Only Jack Reid. "Where are you going?"

"To cover our tracks," said Jack, without breaking stride.

And he was gone before Jane could follow, leaving her,
foolish and alone, by the dying remains of the fire.

Jack spent the rest of the night laying false trails.

If the Gardener inquired after them, he would discover
that a French lieutenant and his batman had been seen at a

tavern on the road, making rapidly for Lisbon. Should that not suit the Gardener's temper, inquiries in the other direction would ascertain that, in fact, a woman and a man traveling together—the woman with pale brown hair, claiming to be a French noblewoman, the man dressed in local costume—had bespoke a carriage and were headed for the Spanish border.

Trails, trails, trails, and more trails, as tangled as Jack's thoughts, as the sky paled to the chill dawn of December, as gray as the Carnation's face as he had left her behind in the camp.

That had been ill-done, Jack knew. A cad's trick, his father would have said reprovingly, ever the ladies' man, solicitude bred into the bone. And this time his father would have been right.

Jack's conscience gave an unaccustomed twinge. He had been sixteen when he ran away from home, old enough to be on his own. But he could still remember that first night sleeping rough, the desperation and terror of it. He'd stayed awake the whole night, hearing brigands in every footfall, holding with both hands to the bundle of his belongings. And that had been in a city he knew, where he spoke the language, could chart his own course.

You can walk down the street unchaperoned.

Jack had never stopped to think of that before, that there might be others who had been more hard done by than he. For a moment, just a moment, he had seen something in the Carnation, something that spoke to him—and then it had been gone again, locked beneath that haughty mask that reminded him, so forcefully, of the Brits back in Madras, the ones who had looked at him with a sneer on their lips, spoken to him with those same plummy voices, expecting obedience and respect from him all because his mother had been of a Rajput family whose lineage was prouder than any of theirs.

Jack had played them for fools, those men. He had bled them dry, selling the opium they craved for their silly rituals while saying "yes, sir" and "no, sir" and laughing behind his hand while he milked them of information and of coin.

They were so sure of themselves, those English aristocrats. So arrogant. As arrogant as the Carnation, who expected him to say "yes, sir" and "no, sir" and follow her lead, even as she led him into a mare's nest.

Maybe that was why he had done it, why he felt such a need to crack that cool exterior, to make her doubt, question, stop looking at him as though he were beneath contempt.

She hadn't looked at the Gardener like that. For him, she had been all wide eyes and sudden uncertainty.

Nicolas, she had called him.

Jack had worked for the Gardener for years, and against him for as many again, but he had never known the man's name.

For that matter, he still didn't know the Carnation's.

Well, and what did it matter? Jack trudged up the path, yanking on the lead rope of a very cranky donkey. It was unclear whose temper was worse, Jack's or the donkey's.

"If you didn't move so damn slowly, I wouldn't have to pull so damn hard," Jack informed the donkey shortly.

The donkey balked, favoring Jack with a look of scorn remarkably similar to the Carnation's. That was, if the Carnation were covered with gray fur and had long, slightly floppy ears.

Jack prodded at the recalcitrant animal. "You know, meat is scarce here. There is such a thing as donkey stew."

The donkey gave a defiant bray and minced three delicate steps. In the wrong direction.

Yes, decided Jack grimly. Definitely kin to the Carnation.

Another massive tug on the rope, and the donkey was once more headed, reluctantly, in the right direction, towards their makeshift camp. Assuming, that was, that the Carnation was still there.

She wasn't.

The clearing was empty and still, all signs of their presence removed. The Carnation had, Jack noted, not only damped the fire, but done her best to remove all traces of its existence. An experienced tracker would find the marks—she wasn't so expert as that—but he would have to look for them.

This was not good. This was, in fact, the opposite of good. She might, Jack told himself, as he tried to control his rising alarm, have run back to the Gardener. She might, as he had once supposed, be in his pay.

Or she might have blundered into the night, looking for Jack. And if she had, anything might have become of her. The winter woods were full of dangers, especially during the rainy season. Especially for someone accustomed to city streets, to linkboys and sedan chairs.

He could remember her face as he had walked away, pale with alarm, her voice calling after him.

Temper, my boy, temper, his father would have said, so disappointed in him yet again. Disappointed and wary. Colonel Reid had never said anything, but Jack had known all the same—known that his father watched him more closely than he did the others, terrified of finding in Jack's childish tantrums traces of his mother's terrifying rages.

Jack had been only three when she died, but he could remember the storms breaking above his head: fabric rending, furniture breaking, voice ranting, high and shrill. She had been beyond reason in her rages. Jack remembered his father futilely attempting to soothe her, to cajole her, before he gave up entirely, choosing to spend his time instead in the mess with his friends and a bottle.

Jack remembered those years only dimly: hiding during her rages, attempting to tease her into good humor as she lay in a darkened room, her head turned to the wall. And the good times, the times that she would lift him in her arms and spin him around, would cradle him and sing to him and tell him tales of their ancestors, those proud, proud men who had conquered kingdoms that made the East India Company's possessions look petty.

He remembered those years dimly, but he remembered the

sequel very well. He remembered the way his father watched him every time he raised his childish voice in anger, every time he fought with his brother or snatched a toy from his sister. Jack remembered the fear in his father's face, the false note in his voice, so different from the way he spoke to Kat and Alex. It was always there, the fear that Jack would be like his mother, governed by emotions beyond his control.

Jack had proved the contrary to himself time and again. He prided himself on keeping his head, on controlling his emotions.

And then there was last night.

Jack looped the donkey's rope over a shrub, pulling it tight. "Princess?"

"Up here." There was a rustling overhead, and the Pink Carnation dropped neatly down, landing lightly on her feet.

Jack said a prayer of thanks to every god he could remember. "You were up a bloody tree?"

The Carnation looked up at him from under her lashes. Almost apologetically, she said, "I had thought it best to be prepared in case there was . . . unwanted company."

"I won't ask in which category I fall," said Jack dryly.

The Pink Carnation winced, but didn't say anything. There was, thought Jack, something different about her this morning. Something tentative and hesitant.

It must, he decided, be the lack of wig. Without the exuberant dark curls, her own hair escaping in pale wisps from her tightly coiled braids, she looked strangely vulnerable, as though she had lost part of her armor.

She was still wearing her mud-spattered white trousers and the frogged green jacket that shouted "enemy."

Jack seized on that point with relief. "You can't wear those. You'll have your throat slit within the week."

"You instructed me to leave my ball gowns in Lisbon." The Carnation glanced down at her dirty trousers. "I'm afraid this is all I have."

"Here." Jack dug in the saddlebag, thrusting a thick pile of cloth in her general direction. "Take these."

Warily, the Carnation shook out one piece, then another, revealing a thick brown wool skirt, a tight red bodice, and a long-sleeved white linen chemise. The clothes were all sturdily constructed, but well-worn.

"Did you raid someone's clothesline?"

"I leave that to your friends in the French camp. I paid for it." More than it was worth. The region had never been a wealthy one and was poorer still after the depredations of the French troops, who operated under instructions from their Emperor to help themselves as they went.

The Carnation stared down at the brightly colored bodice, her fingers worrying at the stitching on the sides. "I'd thought you'd left me here." She glanced up, her expression wry. "And I'm not sure I'd blame you if you did."

He'd felt easier with the haughty aristocrat. "Put those on," Jack said brusquely. "We need to get moving."

Without argument, the Carnation took the garments and retreated behind a tree. Jack turned his back, cursing himself and her. This new, humble Carnation made him nervous. He didn't want to pity her. Or like her.

"You'll have to travel as my wife," he said, raising his voice so she could hear him.

The Pink Carnation's head popped around the tree. "But I don't speak the language."

Ah, there was the Carnation he knew.

"You'll just have to stay silent, then, won't you?" Jack taunted. "Since you haven't done me the honor of telling me your name, I'll just have to come up with my own. We can call you . . . Jacinta."

The Carnation emerged slowly from behind the tree, shaking out the panels of her skirt. "Flattering, if not entirely auspicious." She filled out that bodice altogether too well. It fit tightly beneath her breasts, cut in a deep square filled in by only the white linen of the chemise, which, in the local fashion, plunged in a deep vee, no more concealing than a fichu. "In Greek mythology, Hyacinth—"

"I know the myth," said Jack shortly. "Did you think I was nothing more than a bazaar brat? I spent three years in a boarding school in Calcutta. They crammed the classics down our throats. It was part of the civilizing effort. As you can see, it didn't take."

The Carnation's gray eyes regarded him levelly. "These are not civil times." More prosaically, she added, "Might it be simpler if we claimed I had been the servant of one of the English factory in Lisbon? If I were a lady's maid from England, that would explain my inability to speak the language."

"That might serve." It would explain not just her lack of Portuguese, but the way she held herself, every inch the aristocrat, even in her shabby clothes. A lady's maid might well ape her mistress's airs. It was certainly better than his plan, as much as he hated to admit it.

The Carnation fingered the laces on her bodice. "I have learned that it is generally safer to stay as close to the truth as one can."

Jack shoved the remains of her uniform into one of the sacks hanging from the donkey's sides. "As you did before, Lieutenant de Balcourt?"

He expected the Carnation to retort in kind. She didn't. Instead, after a moment's internal struggle, she said quietly, "The Vicomte de Balcourt is my cousin. I spent some time living, as a guest, at his house in Paris."

Jack stood, one hand on the donkey's flank, completely at a loss.

The Carnation pleated her fingers together. "Last night you accused me of endangering us both. You were right. I—I do not take advice well."

Jack folded his arms across his chest. "Especially from a traitor?"

The Carnation considered her words carefully. "It was not precisely a point in your favor."

Despite himself, Jack let out a rusty bark of a laugh. "You couldn't speak straight if you tried, could you?"

"I'm sorry." The words shocked Jack into silence. "Is that straight enough for you? You were right. We ought to have traveled your way from the outset." She paused a moment, her lips pressing tightly together. "Had I known that my actions would lead us into the path of the Gardener, I should have chosen otherwise."

As an apology, it left something to be desired, but the fact that she was apologizing at all was amazing enough. It didn't come easily. Jack could see the cost of it in the rigid set of her shoulders, in the lines on either side of her mouth.

But he wasn't letting her off that easily. "Ah, yes," he said, steeling himself. "Your friend Nicolas."

The Carnation took a deep breath that did very interesting things to her bodice. "You asked last night whether I was working with the Gardener."

Jack hastily relocated his attention to her face. "You can understand why it might be a matter of interest to me," he said conversationally.

The Carnation's eyes looked past him, fixed on scenes he couldn't see. In the tone of someone determined to see a bad job through, she said, "The Gardener and I have been, for the most part, enemies. But we did— We had occasion once to come together on a matter of mutual interest. Five months ago. In Venice."

Her lips shut fast, as though she were afraid of saying more.

Jack frowned at her, trying to read that still face, to divine what lay beneath those hastily truncated words. *In Venice.* That there was more to it than that, he had no doubt.

Just how had the Carnation and the Gardener come together?

You can rent a room or sit a table at a tavern without everyone assuming that you must be a whore.

The comment he had been about to make died on Jack's tongue. Instead he said gruffly, "I take it you are no longer . . . mutually interested?"

He could see her weighing her answers, choosing her words. "In Venice," said the Carnation carefully, "one of the Gardener's colleagues, a man with whom he was closely connected, was found facedown in a canal, a knife in his back. The Gardener made great lamentation over him."

She glanced up at Jack, and he could see the reflection of old pain in her eyes, pain and grief, like an echo of an old, sad song.

"But I had seen the Gardener's hand wield that knife. He was not," she added primly, "aware that I had witnessed it."

Jack could picture the scene. A tapestry, richly figured, hanging before the arras in a Venetian palazzo. The Carnation behind. The Gardener, smiling, taking his friend's hand, and, still smiling, driving the knife into his back.

It might have happened like that. Or it might not. It might have occurred on the street, in a crowded reception, anywhere.

But that it had happened, Jack had no doubt. There were

many things one could feign, but not that level of disillusion-ment. He had felt it himself, the day he had opened the Gar-dener's orders and found within the warrant for Perron's execution.

Testing her, Jack said, "There are times when our work turns deadly."

"But neither of us has the stomach for assassination." Her eyes met his. She looked at him without pretense, her pride stripped away. "We did not begin well back in Lisbon. May we start again?"

The scents of dawn were all around them. A cold gray dawn, but dawn all the same. Here, in this abandoned clear-ing, Lisbon felt worlds away, as did the woman he had first met, the colonel's lady in her jewels and curls. From a branch a hardy bird chirped, the only sound of life. Otherwise they might have been the first woman and the first man, before fruit and deceit had conspired to alert them to their own na-kedness.

And that was what he got for actually listening during those mandatory chapel mornings back in school.

Jack shoved aside thoughts of a naked Carnation holding an apple. What she was saying made good common sense. And had nothing to do with that bodice. They had a mad queen to find and a wily adversary to outsmart. Both of those could be accomplished a great deal more effectively if they joined forces.

When was the last time he had worked with someone?

Jack couldn't remember. The very prospect made him deeply uneasy. But what was the alternative? Turn tail and run?

Jack folded his arms across his chest. "All right. But only for the sake of the mission. And you'll have to lead the donkey."

As if it knew they were talking about it, the donkey made an abortive attempt to nip Jack in the backside. Jack swatted at it.

"Good donkey," said the Carnation serenely, not quite managing to hide a smile. Taking the lead from Jack, she inquired, "Does it have a name?"

There was something about that smile that made him want to smile, too. Jack repressed the urge.

"Donkey," said Jack shortly.

"Donkey the donkey?" The Carnation fastened her haversack on the donkey's back. She glanced over her shoulder at Jack. "I have a friend with whom you have a great deal in common. Remind me to tell you about Bunny the bunny."

"Don't get too attached," said Jack. "It's not a pet."

"But surely it deserves a name?" She rubbed the donkey behind the ears, and blast him if the contrary animal didn't follow her, sweet as you please.

Jack shouldered his own pack. "Or possibly just a flower?" he said pointedly.

They walked in silence for a few moments, the donkey ambling amiably along, making great big donkey eyes at the woman without a name. The world was waking up around them, the sun beginning to cut through the clouds, painting rainbows in the mist.

"Jane," she said suddenly.

"What?" said Jack. He'd been plotting their route, weighing the dangers versus the advantages of trying their luck at an inn.

She glanced at him over her shoulder, the sun turning her pale braids to gold. "My name—it's Jane."

Chapter Nine

"Esmerelda," suggested Jane.

They were walking, endlessly, endlessly walking. Jane wasn't sure how many miles and how many potential donkey names they had covered in the past day.

Jack looked back at her over her shoulder. "Do you want him to be laughed out of the pasture? No."

"Perhaps Petunia?" offered Jane.

Jack's only response was a snort.

"Don't restrain yourself," murmured Jane as she limped along behind him. "Be honest. Tell me how you really feel."

The track along which they were currently edging their way had clearly been designed for goats rather than men. Jane caught herself on the donkey's side as she tripped over a large boulder, inconveniently sticking right out of the middle of the track.

She had always considered herself a good walker, country-bred as she was, but she was rapidly learning that a tramp across the Shropshire countryside with tea and a warm fire at the end of it was quite a different matter from scrambling up steep hillsides slippery with ice, the donkey the only warm thing anywhere in sight.

It seemed like longer than twenty-four hours since they had left the French camp, pressing forward, forward, even when Jane's muscles screamed in protest and the leather of her boot cracked away from the sole. She had never known what a blister could be before; her only blisters had been from dancing the night through in thin slippers. The wet leather of her boot chafed against the irritated skin, and Jane had to exercise all her control to keep from crying out. She wouldn't be that weak.

"All right, then. Bonaparte. Boney for short. Descriptive and topical." Talking nonsense was one way to keep her mind off the pain; it was also, Jane realized ruefully, a way of making amends. She had misjudged Jack Reid and she didn't know how to make it right. Being wrong wasn't something to which she was accustomed.

Or, at least, not to admitting it.

Jack's voice floated back along the path. "It's not fair to taunt him just because he's short."

"The man or the mule?" The last word came out as a gasp

as the leather of her boot scraped against her heel. Such a stupid, small, foolish thing to cause so much pain.

"Both." Jack turned, his brows drawing together. "What's wrong with your foot?"

Both Jane and the donkey stumbled to a halt. "Just a blister," said Jane, standing on one foot like a stork. "It's nothing, really."

"Do you intend to hop all the way to Porto?" Jack seized her around the waist, and before Jane knew what was happening she was on the donkey's back, her legs dangling down one side. The donkey was so short, her legs nearly touched the ground.

"Really, there's no need—" Jane made to slide down, but Jack settled a hand on either side of her, holding her in place.

"Why do you think I bought the blasted beast?" The donkey lowered his head, searching for any forgotten grass on the verge. "It wasn't so that he could feast off the fat of the land."

To carry the bags, Jane almost said, but swallowed the words. If she were Jack, she would have done the same. If there were a member of her team who was a liability, she would have taken steps to minimize the damage before the damage happened.

It sliced like a knife to know that he had marked her out as a hothouse flower, and even more that he was right.

Jane pressed her eyes shut against sudden, foolish tears. "I can walk."

"And have you too crippled to curtsy to the Queen?" In a

more serious tone, Jack added, "Broken blisters can fester. What would you rather? Your pride or your foot?"

Common sense warred with pride. Sense won. Jane wiggled among the packs, missing her saddle. Riding sidesaddle was much easier with stirrups and a pommel, but she'd lost enough dignity already without adding riding astride to the list of humiliations. "I can see that there might be difficulties in remaining stealthy while hopping on one foot."

Jack cast her a sardonic look. "So long as it's all for the greater good, then."

He gave the donkey a slap on the rump before taking up the lead rope, settling his pack once more on his back—the pack the donkey might have been carrying—and trudging ahead, silent and sure-footed.

Did she really sound like such a prig?

Jane sat as straight as she could, but the donkey's gait was nothing like that of the horses she was accustomed to ride; nor did her haversack make a satisfactory substitute for a pommel. This was no elegant trot through the park, nor yet a spirited canter through enemy territory. It was a dull, painful plod, every step jarring, a constant struggle to keep from sliding sideways. The donkey started up a steep incline and Jane abandoned her pride altogether and clutched at the animal's neck. There were almost no trees here to break the wind and the sting of a light rain that had turned, the higher they rose, to ice. Only a few twisted olive trees clung to the limestone cliffs, stretching out barren arms as though in supplication.

Ice crunched beneath the donkey's hooves. Abandoning herself to all modesty, Jane wriggled until she managed to inch her leg over the donkey's side, thankful for the full skirt that preserved most of her modesty.

The donkey gave a short bray of indignation as Jane accidentally kicked him in the head.

Jack paused, hitching his pack higher on his shoulder. "What are you doing back there? Calisthenics?"

"At least that would be one way to keep from freezing," Jane retorted, tugging her skirt down over her legs and hoping he hadn't seen too much. "I had thought Portugal was meant to be warm."

The path was wider here. Jack fell back to walk beside her, the donkey's lead looped casually around his wrist. His breath made little patches of white mist in the air. "You've been reading Murphy's *Travels in Portugal.*"

"He made it sound all orange trees and Moorish ruins." And exotic-looking women in low-cut bodices. Jane could vouch for the bodice, but she had yet to see an orange tree.

"In the south," said Jack. "And in the summer."

Midnight gardens scented with orange blossoms, water tinkling through fountains floored in mosaic.

The daydream resolved itself back into stony ground and frost-blasted rocks. Jane hugged her shawl closer around her. "Bonaparte's invasion was ill-timed."

"For him as well." The seriousness of Jack's tone took Jane

by surprise. "He lost a good half of his force in that march to Lisbon. It was poorly done by any account."

"It's Bonaparte's way," said Jane, "to draw a line on a map and tell his men to march by that route, regardless of what might lie in the way. It has a certain brutal efficiency."

"More brutal than efficient." When Jane looked down at him, Jack said, "I shadowed Junot's forces for part of the way. They were dying by the dozen. Men fell in the mud and were looted by their fellows; officers fought one another for dry lodging or a crust of bread. And what they did to those villages that happened to fall within their path . . ." He glanced up at Jane. "Just be glad you weren't there, princess. It wasn't pretty."

"In Paris, I have no doubt," said Jane, "they'll be acclaiming it a triumph." Particularly if they could parade the Queen of Portugal through Paris like the conquered ruler at a Roman triumph. "How long will your potion discommode the Gardener?"

Jack choked on a laugh that rapidly broadened into a grin. "Given the likelihood of his current location, your choice of words is particularly inapt."

Jane gave him a look.

Jack adopted a suitably grave expression, but his eyes still danced, reminding Jane forcibly of her younger brother, Ned, when he was plotting something particularly atrocious. "A day, no more. Enough to give us a fair start."

"I'm not sure 'fair' is quite the word," said Jane.

"No, probably quite foul," said Jack, enjoying himself immensely. "You learn to find humor where you can in this business. Tonight we jest, because tomorrow we die."

"Preferably not tomorrow," said Jane. Once Nicolas knew of her absence, he would move quickly. He liked to give the impression of being a man of leisure, but it was as deceptive as his easy charm. "If both Moreau and the Gardener were ill, they mayn't have noticed our absence."

Jack raised a brow at her. "Would you care to put money on that?"

Jane folded her hands primly on the donkey's neck. "I don't gamble."

Jack cast her an oblique look. "Don't you?"

Jane shifted uncomfortably on the donkey's back. "I prefer to think of it as a series of calculated risks, rather than a game of chance."

Jack tugged his hat down around his ears, saying nonchalantly, "I've heard the same from hardened gamblers—just before they lost their last coin."

Admit it. You like the uncertainty of it. The danger. You're no different from me, Jeanne. . . .

"It's not the same," said Jane sharply. "I do what I do for a purpose. For a cause."

"Winning isn't a purpose?" Jack held up his hands. "All right. All right. Hold your fire."

They trudged on in silence for a few moments, the early winter dusk settling around them, Jack walking uncomplainingly ahead, his pack on his back, his hat jammed low on his head. Annoyance warred with guilt as Jane stared at the back of Jack's head, restless and frustrated. How many times was she required to humble herself? How often did she have to say she was sorry? Somehow, with Jack Reid, she seemed to be always in the wrong.

But she hated, hated, hated beyond reason being so entirely dependent upon him, so painfully aware of her own frailty. She hated that he had to provide her a donkey; she hated that she was, even now, longing for a hot dinner and a warm bed. She had always thought herself strong, but it seemed her strength had been a fragile thing, no match at all for the basic discomforts that the people of these hills dealt with as a matter of course.

Jane patted the donkey's neck. "I imagine Morag will need to rest soon."

At least, she hoped the donkey would need to rest soon. Unfortunately, the animal seemed largely indefatigable.

Jack quirked a brow. "Morag?"

"The landscape," Jane said, the words jolting out as the donkey stumbled over a rough piece of terrain. "It reminds me a great deal of Scotland. The Highlands, that is."

Majestic, and more than a little daunting.

They trudged in silence for a moment. Meditatively, Jack

said, "My father's family came from the Highlands. He'd never seen it himself—he was born in the Americas—but he spoke of it as though it were his home."

Jane had heard Colonel Reid singing the old ballads to his baby daughter, Jane's goddaughter. Scotland might have been in the past, but the faint lilt lingered in Colonel Reid's speech and occasionally, disconcertingly, in Jack's.

Carefully, Jane said, "I've heard many exiles speak so. Home becomes sweeter with time and distance."

She had wanted nothing more than to get away from home, to try her wings in the world. It was only once home was barred to her that she found herself longing for it.

Foolish, Jane knew. Even were matters otherwise, she couldn't see herself settling in Shropshire, going demurely to church on Sundays, listening to her father's lectures on animal husbandry, the greatest excitement an assembly in the nearest town.

But it would have been nice to have the option.

Jack glanced back over his shoulder, his amber eyes unreadable in the twilight. "There's a word for that in Portuguese. *Saudade*. It means . . . something like nostalgia. Missing one's home and friends."

"Do you?" The question came out before Jane could take it back. "Would you go back to India if you could?"

Jack turned away. "Don't delude yourself, princess. I'm no Odysseus. Ithaca can sink into the sea and be damned."

"Your family must miss you, surely."

All she could see was his back as he shrugged, stoically leading the donkey through the narrow pass. "They do well enough without me."

But they didn't. They wanted him back.

She ought, Jane knew, to tell him she knew his family, to tell him that she had been charged with messages for him. But they were, she suspected, not messages he would want to hear. And right now, cravenly, selfishly, she needed Jack Reid's goodwill. Not just for Queen Maria's sake, but for her own survival.

It was a very disconcerting thought.

Jane coughed as a low fug of smoke teased her nose. She seized on the change of subject with relief. "Is something burning?"

"Peat," said Jack, without turning. The smell was strong and very different from the acrid scent of coal to which Jane was accustomed. "It will be dark soon. I know a place where we can stop for the night."

Jane unclasped her frozen hands from the donkey's neck. "I suppose it's too much to hope for an inn?"

She'd meant it as a joke, but it didn't come out that way.

Jack cast her an oblique look. "I doubt it would be what you're expecting."

Jane bit her lip, trying to gather what remained of her wits, feeling as though she had backed herself into a corner and not sure how to climb out of it. "I'm not such a hothouse flower as that." Her voice was hoarse with cold. "Most of the time."

"The inns here are generally just houses with a spare room—or a spare bench." Jack urged the donkey forward, saying conversationally, "An acquaintance of mine secured lodging once, only to discover a corpse in his bed."

"Murder?" Jane did her best to keep her teeth from chattering.

"No, absentmindedness," said Jack. "It turned out that the innkeeper was also the local undertaker. He'd forgotten that he'd left the body in there."

Jane choked on a laugh. "I shouldn't laugh. It's quite dreadful."

"Not as dreadful as a place I stayed once," said Jack blandly, "where the host was also the local highwayman. He held me up on the road—and then attempted to charge me for my lodging."

"Wouldn't it be more efficient to do that the other way around?" They were descending now into a valley, and Jane held tight to the donkey's neck as the animal found its way in the dusk down the narrow path.

"That's what I told him. After I took my money back." Jack led the donkey safely into the valley. "He didn't seem to appreciate my professional advice."

There were four or five houses clustered close together, all low and built of stone. The scent of peat smoke hung heavy in the air.

"Are we stopping here?" Jane didn't know whether to hope the answer was yes or no. She wasn't sure she could get off the donkey. They would have to pry her off in Porto. Or perhaps she would just stay this way forever, frozen, a cautionary tale to other agents.

"If they'll have us." Jack held out a hand to her.

"I'm—I'm not sure I can." Her legs didn't seem to want to move properly. Jane's cheeks burned with cold and humiliation. "I appear to be stuck."

Without a word, Jack lifted her off the donkey's back, staggering a bit as they both got tangled in her skirts. Jane clutched at his shoulders as her numb legs refused to take her weight.

"All right, then?" Jack's hands closed around her waist with surprising gentleness.

Jane was aching in muscles she hadn't known she possessed. Jack, on the other hand, looked no more winded than if he had taken a brief stroll along a pleasure garden.

Trying to hide the effort it cost her, Jane took a wobbly step back.

"Thank you for your assistance," said Jane formally, to somewhere in the vicinity of Jack's shoulder.

Jack gave a curt nod. And then paused. "It's no shame to admit to needing aid."

Jane raised her eyes to his. "Would you?"

She hadn't meant it as a snub. But Jack seemed to take it so. "Let's alert our hosts to the presence of our company, shall we?"

Jane held out a hand to stop him. "What do we do with the donkey? Is there a stable?"

"Yes. It's called the house."

A woman had emerged, wearing a black scarf over her head and the same wide wool skirt as Jane. She was rapidly followed by the man of the house, who greeted Jack with a resonant "Rodrigo!"

A rapid conversation ensued, in which Jane's Portuguese grammar did her very little good. People in real life tended not to confine themselves to such phrases as "Have you seen the pen of the mother of my aunt?" The man's thumb jerked in the direction of the donkey and also at Jane. Jane rather hoped the derisory comments being made were intended for the donkey, and not for her.

After what seemed a very long time, but was perhaps five minutes, they were ushered across the threshold—all three of them.

"What was that about?" Jane murmured, as Jack tugged on the donkey's lead.

"They wanted to know why I had no horses and only this sorry beast. I told them I'd sold them all for a profit and acquired you in exchange. Don't worry," he added blandly. "They were very expensive horses."

Jane looked at him suspiciously. "You didn't really."

"I didn't really." Jack lowered his voice. "I told them that you're the daughter of an English merchant in Lisbon. I'm doing him a favor by getting you to his quinta outside Porto."

It wasn't a bad story. If that was actually what he'd told them. "How chivalrous."

Jack grinned, white teeth showing between red lips. "I

might also have implied that I had other interests in the arrangement."

"All pecuniary, I hope." Jane's sotto voce protest turned into a fit of coughing as a wave of thick smoke assaulted her nose. Through watering eyes, she managed, "Is there something wrong with the chimney?"

"There is none. And we're letting the heat out." Jack kicked the door shut behind them and the smoke rose up and around them, along with a multitude of smells that Jane had never experienced before in quite such intense concentration: cooking smells, people smells, animal smells, and, above it all, the choking scent of burning peat.

The room was small and square, crowded with a confusion of people and animals. A pile of peat burned sullenly against the wall. There was no hearth, no chimney, no windows. Jane's eyes stung with the smoke. A small child tugged shyly at her skirt and then ran away again, hiding behind her brother. Someone brought Jane a stool and a bowl of soup. It was a thin broth, bits of winter-withered vegetables and chunks of bread bobbing on the surface, but Jane couldn't recall anything that had ever looked so delectable.

She murmured her thanks and sat down, hard. After the donkey, the stool that had been provided for her was a miracle of comfort, the stone wall of the hut softer than any settee.

Jack seemed to be everywhere at once, bringing in the donkey, joking with the man of the house, speaking gravely to the lady, turning small children upside down to the delight of all.

Jane stayed where she was, baring her teeth in a smile whenever anyone looked at her.

The woman of the house ladled something into a bowl and handed it to Jack. He made a courtly bow, saying, *"Muito agradecidos, senhora,"* before carrying it off to the corner where Jane sat on her stool.

"I've already had some," said Jane regretfully, resisting the urge to snatch the bowl from his hands. She couldn't remember the last time she had been so hungry, but she wasn't sure the hospitality of the house would stretch to seconds.

"It's not soup." Jack crouched down at Jane's feet, setting the bowl down next to him. "Which is the foot with the blister?"

Instinctively, Jane pulled her foot back. "It's not so bad. Thanks to Daisy."

"Daisy?" Jack held out a hand, and this time Jane put her foot forward.

"Daisy the donkey." Jane gritted her teeth as Jack wiggled the boot off her foot. Her stocking was clinging to her heel, cloth and blood crusted together. "You don't like it?"

"Alliteration is the cheapest form of literary device." Jack bathed her heel with quick, efficient movements.

"Do you have a better suggestion?" Jane just managed to keep her voice steady as he applied the steaming cloth to raw skin.

"Yes." Jack set the bowl aside and drew the brandy flask from his jacket. "Donkey. Or, if you're feeling so moved, 'Ho, you!'"

Jane jerked as he poured the alcohol over her heel. "It seems . . . rather . . . rude."

"You don't get much ruder than a donkey." Jack handed the flask up to her. "You'd best drink some of this, too."

Jane hesitated a moment and then set the flask to her lips. She'd tasted spirits before—it was necessary when masquerading as an officer—but always from a glass. It felt strangely intimate, drinking directly from Jack's flask, placing her lips where his had been.

As comrades did, Jane reminded herself. As comrades did.

She had never had a comrade before, not really. She had had colleagues, yes, and underlings, but not someone in whom she placed her trust, who relied on her and on whom she relied in equal measure. Even with Miss Gwen and her own cousin Amy, Jane had always been very aware of retaining the reins in her own hands. She had never doubted their loyalty, but she knew their weaknesses too well to allow them full control of their missions. When it came down to it, she had never met anyone she trusted as she would trust herself.

Jack patted the wound dry with a clean cloth. One of his cravats, Jane suspected, although she didn't ask. She was enough in his debt already.

Jack's bent head, hatless, was nearly in Jane's lap. Jane stared down at it, indistinct in the smoke, and remembered the last time a man had knelt before her. But for such very different reasons.

She tried to imagine Nicolas bathing her foot, Nicolas taking such care over her, but there were limits even to imagination. Nicolas would have sent his valet. He would never have taken on so lowly a task himself.

Carefully, Jack wrapped the cloth around her foot. "That should give you some relief." He sat back on his heels, looking up at her. "That and the brandy."

She was still holding the flask, Jane realized, and there was considerably less in it than there had been before.

"Thank you." She offered it back to him. The room was unsteady, but Jane knew it wasn't due to the brandy. It was smoke and fatigue and a stomach only partly placated by the *sopa magra*. "I've had more than I ought."

Jack pushed himself up to his feet. His hand settled briefly on her shoulder. "The terrain we covered—it's not easy even for those who know it."

For a moment she thought she might have misheard. Jane blinked up at him. "You are . . . kind."

There were so many things she had expected of Jack Reid. That he would be difficult, yes. Insubordinate, crude, rough around the edges. All of that. But never kindness.

Jack shrugged uncomfortably. "You won't say that when you have to get back on that blasted mule tomorrow." He lowered his voice, even though they were speaking in English. "I have news for you. A party of monks passed this way a week since, heading towards Alcobaça Monastery."

Jane sat a little straighter. "That's hardly unusual, surely?"

"These monks," said Jack, folding his arms across his chest

and leaning back against the wall, "had with them a palanquin bearing a saint's statue of miraculous power."

"Aren't they all?" Jane had been raised to disdain such popish practices. After a year in Italy, she could admire the beauty of the objects themselves, but their worship made her uncomfortable.

Would you genuflect at a Roman mass or take their host?

Jack Reid had been right. He had a talent for finding weaknesses in her she didn't know she possessed.

Jack raised a brow. "A saint's statue of such power that it can speak and move? If you know another such, princess, let me know, and we can make a tidy sum traveling the country, soliciting donations."

"Did you say speak?" Jane tried to control her rising excitement. "Such things could be counterfeited, especially when those watching wished to believe. . . ."

"The saint," said Jack, "called out, *'Ai, Jesus.'*"

Queen Maria's favorite phrase. Her pitiful cries of, *'Ai, Jesus,'* were said to echo along the halls of the Queen's pavilion in Queluz.

But it was a common enough phrase for all that. Jane looked sharply up at Jack. "How do we know?"

"Our hostess's oldest boy heard it. He was most impressed."

"Did he see anything?" Jane was getting a crook in her neck tilting her head back.

Jack settled down on his haunches next to her. "The palanquin was heavily veiled in velvet. The monks blessed him and told him to be off, that the statue was of such great holiness that even to gain the smallest glimpse would burn out his eyes with holy wonder. Or something like that."

"I see." Jane rested her heavy head against the wall, caution warring with instinct. "They would take a great risk, traveling so openly. . . ."

Jack coughed. "A woman I met not so long ago in Lisbon rather forcibly expressed the opinion that it was safest to hide in plain sight. I believe you might know her?"

Jane grimaced. "I'm not sure that woman knew what she was talking about," she muttered. Had it been only two weeks ago? It felt like years. Opening her eyes, she asked warily, "Which saint was this, precisely?"

"Our mother Mary." Jack indulged in a smug smile. "The exact words were, 'Our mother Maria, Queen of us all.'"

Chapter Ten

The Pink Carnation shook her head. "It's too easy."

No, not the Pink Carnation. Jane. If asked, Jack would have guessed at something longer and grander, something that spoke of marble halls and centuries of breeding, a name that served as armor against the world.

But here, in the dim light, with her hair escaping from its braids, her cheeks windburned and her features blurred by the red glow of the peat fire, she looked like a Jane. The brandy had taken some of the tension out of her shoulders, relaxed her as Jack had never seen her relaxed before.

In her red bodice and full skirt, she might look like a shepherdess who had lost her flock, but her voice was still crisp, precise. "Would they really tell people they were carrying the Queen if it were the Queen? It seems sloppy."

So much for Little Bo Peep. And he'd best remember that, Jack reminded himself. Whatever guise she wore in the field, she was still a dangerous quantity. "You're thinking like a trained agent. Don't. Imagine yourself an amateur conspirator."

"That might be too great an exercise in imagination." Jane looked at Jack, her expression serious. "It does change us, doesn't it? What we do."

What we do. Her words sang in Jack's blood like a ballad, the sort where exiles stood on distant shores, where warriors returned from war to find themselves without a home, like the songs sung in the taverns of Lisbon, songs of love and loss. Above all, of loss.

Jack thought of the past five years, of the shifts and evasions, the demurrals and the outright lies. Looking over his shoulder, always. Looking over both shoulders. Never sure who was friend and who was foe, doubting everything and everyone because none knew better than he how false appearances could be.

No, they didn't tell you any of that. They didn't tell you about sleeping with one hand on your pistol. They didn't tell you about the little pieces of yourself that died, bit by bit. They didn't explain what it was to lie even to those closest to you. Which, after a time, became a relative term. There was no close. Even the most intimate relationships became fraught with danger.

Especially the most intimate relationships.

He'd lied to Jane. This hut wasn't a chance-found shelter; the information hadn't been collected at random. Their hostess, Cristina, was one of his informants. If Cristina's husband guessed that Rodrigo the horse trader was more than he seemed, he turned a blind eye. Rodrigo paid generously for his lodging, and if he had an ear for gossip, well, what was wrong with that? There were dozens of houses from Lisbon to Porto where Rodrigo the horse trader was recognized and welcomed, where Jack picked up snippets here and snippets there.

He shouldn't have brought Jane here. With a sudden chill, Jack realized that he was already letting emotion corrupt his judgment. It would have made far more sense to bunk in the rough as they had the night before. But he had looked at Jane, clinging so stoically to the donkey's back, her face white with strain, and had yielded to the impulse to bring her here, where there would be a roof over her head, water for washing, and warm food in her belly.

And, in doing so, endangered Cristina and her family.

No. He'd laid his false trails well. Even if the Gardener found his way here, he'd hardly suspect a humble goatherd's wife. The Gardener ran a very different sort of network.

Even so, though. It had been a lapse in judgment. And Jack thought he knew why.

"It's a living," Jack said brusquely, levering himself to his feet, the wall rough beneath his palm. The fire was burning low and their host and hostess had already retreated to bed. The only bed. "We'd best get some sleep."

A lamb bleated in the corner of the room. The donkey brayed in response.

"If you can," added Jack.

Jane glanced uncertainly around the room. "Where do we sleep?"

Taking her cloak, Jack shook it out onto the floor, gesturing to it with a flourish. "Here."

Jane turned her head sharply. "Together?"

They had shared a tent for the past two weeks. But then they had been master and servant. Not to mention that Jane had been dressed as a man, her hair hidden beneath a wig, her breasts bound flat beneath her green uniform coat.

Now . . . Despite himself, Jack's eyes dipped to the low bodice of Jane's peasant costume. "Flat" was not the operative word.

"Along with a family of six," Jack said dryly. He held out a hand to her to help Jane off the stool. "And your favorite donkey as chaperone."

Her touch seemed to burn as she put her hand in his. A man, Jack told himself—he would just pretend she was a man.

A man in a very low bodice.

"It's nice to know," said Jane solemnly, as she lowered herself onto the cloak, "that the proprieties are being observed."

Jack's thoughts at the moment were anything but proper. Family of six, he reminded himself. Donkey.

"Oh, certainly," he said mockingly. "I'm certain we'll start a trend in the drawing rooms of Lisbon. Donkey as duenna."

As if realizing it was being discussed, the donkey let out an indignant bray.

Jane's lips twitched. "I don't think Dulcibella likes that idea."

Jack dropped to the floor next to her, pounding his jacket into something resembling a pillow. "I don't think it likes being called Dulcibella."

The donkey brayed loudly in agreement.

A sharp comment rose from the large bed in the corner.

"*Perdão*," called Jack, lifting himself up on one arm. "*Perdão, senhor.*"

Jane turned onto her side, her full skirts tangling around her legs, hay crunching beneath her cloak. "What did he say?"

Jack settled back down on the cloak beside her. "He politely reminded us that other people might be attempting to sleep."

Jane's face was only inches from his, her cheek resting on one hand. "I'm guessing that wasn't quite it."

It hadn't been. "I didn't want to singe your tender ears."

Jane's lips quirked ruefully. "I've most likely heard worse."

Because she was posing as a man, Jack imagined she had. It was hard to reconcile the two; even though he had seen her in the role, even though he had seen her pretending to piss against a wall, there was something that seemed to set her apart, untouchable, in the world but not of it.

Jack lifted a finger to her lips. Not porcelain after all, but red and warm. They parted slightly as his finger touched the delicate skin.

"Not from my lips," he said softly.

Jane's eyes dropped to Jack's lips. "No," was all she said, but there was something in her voice that made Jack go hot and cold and hot again.

His finger moved from her lip to her cheek, sliding up her cheekbone, smoothing a fine strand of hair back behind her ear. The room was dim, lit only by the embers of the peat fire, making sensation all the more intense. He could hear the soft sound of her breath, feel her waiting tension.

One movement. That was all it would take. Just the whisper of a movement and those lips would be against his, her body pressed against his, trembling. There was hay beneath Jane's cloak, prickly, perhaps, but soft enough. They could sink down together on the cloak in the warm darkness and—

"What the . . . ?" The donkey butted Jack hard in the backside. He sat up abruptly, glowering at the donkey. "What do you think you are, a goat?"

Jane sat up too, removing a wisp of straw from her hair with fingers that weren't entirely steady. "A chaperone," she said, in a subdued voice. "And a rather effective one."

He was an idiot. A thousand times an idiot. One didn't kiss fellow agents.

Particularly not a fellow agent who might once have been—might, in fact, still be—mistress of the Gardener.

"We should get some sleep," Jack said brusquely. He gave

the donkey a gratuitous shove. "You mind your manners and I'll mind mine."

The donkey released a blast of foul breath right into Jack's face. In the familial bed, the baby began to wail. A sheep took up the cry, bleating its opinion of everyone concerned.

"Good night," said Jane softly. Over the scents of peat and donkey, Jack caught just the faintest whiff of lavender, and the soft rustle of hay as Jane burrowed deeper into the folds of her cloak.

It was going to be a long night.

They were on their way again at dawn, Jane moving gingerly as she rose from her pallet. There was straw in her hair and clinging to the bodice of her dress. She looked, thought Jack grumpily, as though she'd been thoroughly ravished.

"Is there water for washing?" she asked hopefully, making an attempt to coil her braid back into place. The heavy tail of hair flopped promptly back down her shoulder.

"Why? Do you have an appointment at court?" Jack retorted, and then felt like the worst sort of cad. "You're fine as you are."

Jane regarded him skeptically. "I have soot on my face."

"Consider it the latest fashion." Jack felt a glimmer of sympathy as she very carefully wrapped her cloak around her shoulders. She wasn't used to this sort of travel, but she had soldiered on all the same. "This isn't Lisbon, princess. You're going to get dirty."

Jane grimaced at her hands, once so white and smooth, the nails now cracked and dirty. "Truer words . . . ," she murmured. She glanced up at Jack. "When in Rome?"

"I wouldn't know," said Jack blandly. "I've never been."

Jane rolled her eyes, but he saw her shoulders relax.

"Here." Jack handed Jane a chunk of coarse black bread, redolent of garlic and olive oil. "Breakfast."

He half expected her to balk at it, but she didn't. It left him feeling oddly frustrated. It was easier when she lived down to his preconceptions of her.

"We have a decision to make before we leave." Jane took a dainty bite of her bread. Jack watched, transfixed, as her white teeth sank into the dark bread. "Do we make for Porto or Alcobaça?"

Jack swallowed a bite of bread with a throat gone dry. There was something very wrong with him if he found her eating bread erotic.

"Do you really want my advice?" he challenged her. "Or was that just a rhetorical question?"

Jane cast him a wry, sideways glance. "I thought we had both agreed that it would have gone better for us had I heeded your advice before."

Jack opened his mouth to utter a ringing *I told you so*, but the words turned to ash on his tongue. Instead he said grudgingly, "You did the best you could with the resources at your disposal."

"You were the resource at my disposal, Mr. Reid." Jane sat

with her back very straight, every inch the lady, even with straw in her hair and soot on her chin. "It was my duty to use you properly."

Jack choked on his bread.

"Alcobaça," he said desperately. The word came out like a cough. Jack cleared his throat and tried again. "I would make for Alcobaça. Even if the statue was just a statue, it's not far out of our way. And," he added, "you'll have a wash and a proper bed."

Jane plucked a piece of straw from her bodice and regarded it with an arched brow. "I'm not sure I'd know what to do with one, it's been so long."

I can tell you what to do with one.

What in the devil was wrong with him? Clumsily, Jack lurched to his feet. "We'd best go. Time's wasting."

Without waiting to see if Jane followed, Jack hoisted his haversack on his shoulder and strode across the hut to Cristina, who had a baby in her lap and a toddler clinging to her skirts.

"Thank you for your hospitality," he said, and dropped a handful of *reis* into her palm. "My companion and I are very grateful for the food and shelter."

"But this is too much," Cristina protested. The protest was, Jack knew, for her husband's benefit. The pay was for the information as much as the lodging, and for that he had paid fairly.

Jack waved her protests aside. "The pay is commensurate with the inconvenience." He grinned at her. "I would make amends for our donkey."

A hint of amusement showed in Cristina's dark eyes. "It was not the donkey. I wish you luck, Rodrigo."

If he had been a younger man, he would have squirmed. As it was, all Jack could say was, *"Muito agradecidos."*

There was a shadow at his elbow. Jane, not wanting to be left out. She bowed her head to their hostess. Slowly and carefully, she echoed, *"Muito agradecidos."*

Jack opened his mouth to correct her—she had used the male form—and then closed it again.

Cristina tucked the coin away in her bodice. *"Vai com Deus, senhor, senhora."*

It had been a long time since Jack had believed in any sort of gods, but it never hurt to have insurance. *"Fica com Deus,"* he replied politely.

"Go with God?" murmured Jane, as they led the donkey from the hut into a gray dawn that seemed nonetheless very bright after the dark interior of the hut.

"And stay with God." Jack took the donkey's lead from Jane, putting his hands around her waist to boost her onto the donkey's back. "It's customary."

"Somewhat more heartfelt than that, I think." They walked in silence for a few yards before Jane added quietly, "That was generous payment you made them."

Jack wasn't sure which was worse: being caught out in an act of charity, or being caught out in what only seemed like an act of charity. Jack kept his attention on his feet, navigating the uncertain terrain. "These people have little enough. And they'll have less when Bonaparte's men come through."

"So you try to right the balance?"

He could feel her gaze like a knife between his shoulder blades. "Everyone needs a hobby," Jack said flippantly. "It would be boring to be entirely a villain."

He could have told her that he knew what it was to be hungry. He could have told her that he knew what it was to scrounge for coin. Only, in his case, he had brought it on himself. His father might not have been wealthy, but they'd always had enough.

No, it had been Jack's own bloody-mindedness that had sent him out into the streets, on a quest that turned out, in the end, to be as pointless as any of Don Quixote's windmills.

Even then, even when Jack was at his most alone, his most miserable, there had been a home waiting for him, if only he had been willing to swallow his pride and play the prodigal. If he had found pride a sour dish, well, that was his own doing and no one else's. He wasn't going to bow his head and crave his father's pardon, return to a nest in which he had always been the cuckoo.

Even now, the thought of it made his back stiffen and his jaw tense. Eleven years and he was still angry, even if sometimes he had a difficult time recalling just what it was he'd been quite so angry about.

Jane's voice broke into his reverie. "Why did you take those jewels?" Jack turned to find her looking at him with serious gray eyes, her fingers knotted in the donkey's mane. "Don't tell me it was for the money."

"Isn't that the most obvious reason?" Jack deliberately kept his voice neutral. Thief, she had called him, and there was no debating that it was true. He had stolen those jewels as surely as any cutpurse that ever picked a pocket.

"Mr. Reid," said Jane with some asperity, "if there is anything I have learned, it is that nothing about you is obvious."

Jack knew how she felt. He'd been a lot happier when she'd been a society lady in a flounced dress.

And she was that lady still, he reminded himself. Once this mission was over, she would wash her face and put up her hair and be that lady again. They would go off their separate ways, in their own separate worlds.

But for now, they existed outside of time, no one but themselves. And Jack found, as absurd as it was, that he wanted her to think well of him. Even if it was only for now, even if they never saw each other again after Porto. For some absurd reason, her good opinion mattered.

The air was cold and pure, the only sounds the crunch of their progress on the pebbles of the path. Slowly, Jack said, "It's not untrue. I did want the money."

Jane's gray eyes were altogether too keen. "But not for yourself?"

Jack glanced at her from under the brim of his hat. "Has anyone ever told you that omniscience isn't an attractive habit?"

A shadow crossed Jane's face. "Yes," she quietly.

He'd meant it as a joke, not as a jibe. Jack wondered just who had put that bruised look behind her eyes, and found himself inexplicably very much wanting to deliver a fist to that person's nose.

"I wanted the money for my sister." The words came out too loud in the still landscape. "My younger sister, Lizzy."

"Why?"

"She's—" Jack foundered on the words he'd never tried to frame, not even to himself. "She's a half-caste, like me. Her mother was my nurse."

He'd loved Piyali, or thought he had. She was everything his mother wasn't. She'd been soft and warm and tender where his mother had a hawklike beauty, angular and proud. Piyali had sung him to sleep at night, cuddled him through his nightmares.

But apparently he wasn't the only one into whose bed Piyali had climbed at night. George had come first, born two years after Jack's mother had died. And then Lizzy.

As a man, Jack couldn't begrudge his father his consolation. One couldn't say he'd taken advantage of Piyali; theirs had been a comfortable domestic relationship, mutually satisfying. But the boy in him still felt betrayed. Piyali had been *his* nurse; she was supposed to love him the most.

But it was impossible to hate either George or Lizzy. George was a sunny-natured boy, one of life's innocents. Scowl at him and he'd toddle up to you offering a sweet.

And Lizzy—Lizzy was a rogue, like Jack. A rogue with copper curls and, when Jack had last seen her, a deceptively endearing lisp that hid a brain as calculating as the Emperor Aurangzeb's.

Jack's older brother, Alex, was infuriatingly earnest. Well-meaning, but maddening all the same. And it had always been open war between Jack and his older sister, Kat. George was too good for his own good. But Lizzy—she was kin. They were two of a kind.

And Lizzy was vulnerable in a way the others weren't.

Jack cleared his throat. "I wanted Lizzy to have choices. My older sister, Kat—she's full-blood English, and legitimate. But Lizzy— There are men who prey on unprotected girls."

He was making a hash of it, the words clumsy on his tongue. How to explain to someone who'd never seen it just what happened to the half-caste daughters of men who didn't have the power or influence to protect them? Jack had known enough of those men. He'd taken his revenge, in his own way, by bilking them of their coin by overcharging them for the opiates with which they whetted their jaded palates.

But the only sure way to guarantee Lizzy's safety was money. Money meant choices. It meant power.

Jane frowned down at him. "But surely," she said, "your father—"

Jack permitted himself a twisted smile. "My father always means well. Provided it doesn't pose too much inconvenience to himself. He put my sisters on a ship and considered his duty done."

It was Jack who had arranged a place for Lizzy at a young ladies' academy in Bath, and paid for it out of his own pocket. Anonymously, of course.

"But the jewels . . ." Jane didn't look nearly as impressed as Jack had expected. "They aren't the most comfortable thing to possess. You didn't worry about putting your sister in danger?"

"You don't believe all that rot about a curse, do you? There's more danger in being poor. With a handful of rubies in her pocket, Lizzy can do what she likes. She can marry where she chooses. Or not, if she chooses. But she'll be her own mistress." Jack looked fiercely at Jane. "Can you, of all people, deny the power of that?"

"No." Jane's face was as still as the frost-blasted landscape. "I had that . . . once. Or thought I had."

"What happened?"

"How far to Alcobaça?" Jane made as if to spur her mount forward, which didn't work very well when one was sitting on a donkey. Rather than speeding up, the donkey slowed its pace.

"Not far. We should be there within the hour." So much for confidences. It wasn't exactly that he'd expected her to be impressed by his nobility of motive. Except that he had, a little. Jack slapped the donkey on the rump, summoning a jocularity he didn't feel. "If Buttercup here behaves."

Jane raised a brow. "Buttercup?"

"You're the one who wanted to name him." It felt as though a cloud had fallen over the sun, but for the fact that it had already been cloudy when they started out. A gray morning had given way to a gray afternoon. The difference wasn't in the sky; it was in Jane.

"Yes," she said, "but not Buttercup."

Jack yanked on the lead. "You said you were your own mistress once. What happened?"

"It doesn't matter."

"Clearly it does." There was nothing so infuriating as haughty silence. Jack couldn't resist a jibe. "Did your father cut off your allowance?"

"If you must know, yes." Jack had never heard anything like the controlled rage in her voice. "I was disinherited. Disowned. Cast out. Is that what you wanted to know, Mr. Reid?"

No, he wanted to say. It wasn't. But the words seemed to have frozen in his mouth.

The Pink Carnation regarded him with an expression of contempt. But that wasn't what cut to the bone. It was the quiver of her mouth, the glitter of tears in her eyes.

But her voice was utterly controlled as she delivered the coup de grâce. "Thanks to you, Mr. Reid, my family declared me dead."

Chapter Eleven

"Thanks to me?"

That, thought Jane, caught between tears and laughter, was the trouble with staging grand scenes on a donkey. One couldn't ride nobly off into the sunset. High drama turned to low comedy.

"Never mind," she said.

"Never *mind*?" Jack and the donkey both came to a jolting halt. "You tell me I ruined your life and then you tell me 'never mind'?"

Stupid, stupid. She'd always prided herself on holding her tongue and keeping her counsel. It was what kept her—and those who depended on her—alive. Jane made a helpless gesture. "I shouldn't have said anything."

"But you did." Jack wasn't yielding an inch. He planted one hand on the donkey's neck, the other on its rump, his nose an inch from Jane's. "Tell me how I forced your family to disown you. I never set eyes on you until three weeks ago."

Jane pressed her eyes closed, feeling suddenly very weary. "No, but you sent the jewels of Berar back to England."

"What has that to do with anything?" Frustration rang through Jack's voice.

"Fate works in strange ways." Jane met Jack's clear amber eyes and felt, for the first time, a twinge of doubt. She took refuge in trivia. "They say Fortune is a wheel, you know. One person goes up; another goes down."

"Yes." Jack's voice was clipped. "I did have a classical education. Such as it was. Is there a point to this exposition?"

"When you sent the jewels to your sister, you provided her the prospect of freedom. And you took mine away." Jane attempted a smile. "It's really a classic example of Fortune's wheel."

Jack wasn't diverted by abstract musings on the nature of Fortune, which was a pity, because, having begun the conversation, Jane wanted very badly to end it.

He folded his arms across his chest, his stance hard, uncompromising. "Explain."

The donkey brayed.

"You"—Jack poked a finger at the donkey—"quiet. And you"—he looked at Jane, his face carved from granite—"talk. You've judged me already, but I would have thought, under your law, that a condemned man would at least have a right to know the charges leveled against him."

You've judged me already. She had, long ago, long before she'd met him. She'd tried him in absentia and told herself it was justice. But now, now that he was before the bar, all of her grievances felt flimsy and flat, mere paper tigers.

"When you sent the jewels of Berar back to England, you set a train of events in motion. . . ."

Jane could remember that awful night in Paris, the letter from England, delivered by the usual shadowy routes. Her sister and another girl, Lizzy Reid, had gone missing from their Bath boarding school. And Jane had held that crumpled piece of paper and felt a weight like rocks crushing her chest, choking her. She had thought herself very careful in keeping her identity hidden. But no ruse was perfect. There were those who knew. And things slipped out.

If any harm came to her sister, it was on her head.

She had rushed back to England, only to discover that it wasn't on her head at all—that it was, in fact, Lizzy who had run and Agnes who had followed. And why? Because Lizzy's brother had had the ill judgment to send the jewels of Berar to a young ladies' academy.

Looking away, over Jack's shoulder, Jane said distantly, "The Gardener had promised those jewels to Bonaparte. Bonaparte couldn't be allowed to have them. I was summoned from Paris."

It was all true as far as it went. With some rather large

omissions. But to tell the whole story—it was to expose a corner of her soul she didn't want to share. The crushing fear for her sister. The doubt. The questioning.

Not to mention the awkwardness of belatedly explaining her connection to Jack's family.

"I had not previously made the acquaintance of the Gardener. I knew of him, of course, but our paths hadn't crossed." Jane felt Jack stir, and looked him in the eye. "I prevented the Gardener from retrieving the jewels, but at a cost. I learned his identity. And he learned mine."

"Ah," said Jack. That was all. But it was enough. He was a fellow agent; he understood.

"Paris was closed to me." Her league, her web of agents, everything she had built. Jane swallowed hard. "The Gardener professed to have some regard for me, but I didn't imagine that would save me from the Temple prison should I be so bold as to show my face at the Tuileries."

At least, not without certain conditions being met. All she had to do was disown her principles and her country.

A small matter, Nicolas had called it, with his facility for seeing things as he wished them to be.

A small matter to him, but not to her.

"Was that why your family disowned you?" Jack's voice was carefully neutral. "Because of your . . . connection to the Gardener?"

Jane's head snapped up. "No!"

It would have been laughable if the matter hadn't been so

deadly serious. They had danced around each other for years, she and Nicolas, in a double-edged flirtation that was part attraction and part policy, circling, dipping back. There had been nothing in it that would have been seen amiss in any drawing room in London; any impropriety had been purely in suggestion, all the more seductive for being implied rather than acted.

At least, so matters had stood. Until Venice.

Jack held up both hands. "I'm not condemning you for it. My mother was disowned for nothing more damning than being caught in a kiss. And it ruined her entire life. If you met the Gardener because of the jewels and then—"

"It's not that," said Jane hastily. "It's not that at all."

A strained silence fell over them. "Perhaps," said Jack carefully, holding out a hand, "we might continue this conversation more comfortably? It's dashed awkward having Petunia butting me in the thigh every five seconds."

"So it's Petunia now, is it?" said Jane, but she took his hand all the same. It was warm and firm as he helped her down from the donkey, her stiff limbs twinging in protest.

"Would you prefer Columbine?"

"I was thinking . . . Gwendolyn." Jane wrinkled her nose as Jack spread a blanket on the rough ground, tethering the donkey to an olive tree. The sky was beginning to be streaked with pink. "Shouldn't we go on?"

"We can spare ten minutes. We're less than an hour's walk from Alcobaça." Jack produced his flask from beneath his jacket and handed it to her. "Pretend it's tea."

"Strong tea," said Jane, but she drank all the same, the liquid sending a shock of warmth through her. It felt like a bizarre parody of a picnic, a man and a woman on a blanket in the countryside, only the countryside was brown and gray, the refreshments were strong spirits, and the man and woman—

Jane felt a pang for the courting couple of her imagination, young and innocent, in a bucolic setting of hedgerows and grazing sheep, no secrets, no scars.

She hadn't wanted that, she reminded herself. She had left all that without a backward glance. She'd had no patience for rural swains.

But it might be nice, just once, to be able to speak to someone frankly, without reserve.

She hadn't had that sort of honesty with Nicolas. All of their exchanges had been conducted in layers of euphemism and innuendo. It was a battle of wits, with her heart as the prize. Exhilarating at first, but exhausting, too. If one lay down with lions, one ran the risk of being savaged.

Jane looked up at her companion. Jack Reid wasn't a lion. A tiger, she'd thought him at first, barely domesticated. But she was beginning to think she had done him an injustice. Beneath his prickly exterior, she suspected he was more like his father than he knew.

She doubted he would take that as a compliment.

"So," said Jack, and settled back across from her, his booted feet brushing the hem of her skirt. "The Gardener?"

Jane stared at the flask. It was just a simple tube of leather with a tin cap. Nothing fancy. Nicolas had a silver one, engraved with his coat of arms. Not his father's coat of arms, but the one he had designed for himself, when he was still the Knight of the Silver Tower.

Jane took another swig from the flask. The brandy burned her throat. Her voice was husky as she said, "You have it backwards. The Gardener wasn't my lover." She could have left it at that. But some demon of honesty prompted her to add, "Not then."

Jack's hands stilled on the ties of his haversack. He looked at her, his expression unreadable.

Jane hurried on. "It's rather ironic, isn't it? My parents disowned me because they feared the appearance of impropriety. But I didn't become truly improper until I was disowned." She managed a lopsided smile. "It seemed only fitting. Under the circumstances."

She was waiting for him to say something, Jack knew. But the words stuck in his craw. All he could see was Jane and the Gardener, Jane as he had first seen her, polished and poised, garbed in a gown that cost more than his pay for a year, circling in the other man's arms in a ballroom lit by braces of candles.

Jack didn't want to think about it. "You've lost me," he said brusquely. "If it wasn't on account of the Gardener, why were you struck from the family escutcheon?"

Jane's back relaxed just a trifle. Had she expected him to condemn her? He, of all people, had no right. "They didn't approve my going off on my own."

It sounded so ridiculously prosaic after her earlier admissions. "You'd been working as an agent for how long?"

"For three years," said Jane calmly. She appeared to have gathered herself together, cloaking herself in that poise that sat on her shoulders like a shawl of finest Kashmir. "But in Paris I lived in the home of my cousin, my mother's own nephew. He is," she said dispassionately, "a nasty little toad of a man. But he lent an element of respectability. And I had a chaperone."

She looked away, her finely boned profile limned by the golden light of the setting sun.

"A nice setup," said Jack, keeping his voice carefully dry.

A very nice setup, and she'd lost of it because of him. There were a dozen justifications, but the truth of it was that he hadn't thought before shipping the jewels off to Lizzy. He hadn't bothered to think about the unintended consequences, any more than he had when he had run away from the printer's shop at sixteen. It had seemed like a grand gesture at the time, and that had been enough. Enough to turn the Pink Carnation's life upside down and leave her vulnerable to the predations of men like the Gardener.

"You must miss it," Jack said awkwardly.

Jane's eyes met his, and her lips turned up in a rueful smile. "I do. Very much. My parents hadn't minded in the slightest my living in my cousin's household, properly chaperoned, but it appeared they minded very much my traveling on my own through Europe, no matter what alias I employed."

"I can't pretend to know much of gently bred young ladies"—Jack didn't miss her wince at the words—"but couldn't you have traveled with your chaperone? Surely that would have satisfied your parents."

Jane's long, elegant fingers picked at a brown stalk of grass. "When we returned to England to pursue the jewels, my chaperone fell in love with . . . with a man who suited her perfectly. How could I deny her a chance at happiness?"

"Very easily," said Jack bluntly. "Many would."

Jane only shook her head. "Miss Gwen would have come with me, but I would always have known what I caused her to leave behind." After a pause, she added, without meeting Jack's eyes, "She has a daughter now. My goddaughter."

Jack leaned back on one arm. "You might have stayed behind as well. You might have married."

"Who?" Jane's eyes met Jack's. "What man wants a wife who spends her nights crawling through windows, her days studying maps of Europe?"

The image struck Jack forcibly. And not just because of the tight, dark breeches Jane was wearing in his imagination. His father's first wife had been an angel. That was what they had been told. Jack had always pictured her eternally sewing a sampler and singing hymns. His own mother had spent half her life in a darkened room, the other half throwing crockery. And Piyali . . . Her province had been the nursery and kitchen.

His father had had his world; the women in his life had had theirs. Marriage, to Jack, was a house, a set of women's

quarters, a geographical tether entirely unsuited to the itinerant existence he lived.

It had never occurred to him that the shoe might have been
on the other foot. "You might have given it up."

"That was what my parents wanted. They told me there
had been quite enough of gallivanting around foreign parts. I
could come home and wind wool and dance at assemblies—or
I could take myself off."

Jane might have been discussing a night at the opera or the
cut of a new gown, but for the fact that there was a small pile
of shredded grass in her lap, the only chink in her Olympian
calm. The restless movement of her hands told Jack more than
another woman's tears.

She glanced up at Jack, her eyes meeting his. "I don't believe they thought I would."

"Then," said Jack belligerently, "they didn't know you at all."

For a moment, something raw and vulnerable looked out
of her eyes. And then the mask closed down again. "I died of
pneumonia. There's a little stone to me in the churchyard in
Lower Wooley's Town." She arched a brow, inviting him to
share the humor of a situation Jack didn't find humorous in
the slightest. "I could understand cutting off my allowance,
but it was the being declared dead that I found so distressing."

"I'm sorry." Jack didn't know what else to say. "I'm so
sorry."

To be declared dead, officially dead. By one's own parents.
His mind couldn't quite grasp it. Jack had always suspected his

father would have been happier had Jack never been born, but that had never been said, never even been implied.

Come home, his father's letters had read. *Come home when you feel you can come home. Don't feel you can't come home.*

Jack had torn them into shreds and fed them into the fire.

His old home in Madras was gone. His father had long expressed the intention of retiring, eventually, to England. Jack's brother Alex was in Hyderabad, his brother George in the retinue of the Begum Sumroo, his sisters in England. But he knew that he could appear, at any time, on any of those doorsteps, and a place would be found at their tables.

There was no gravestone with his name on it.

It made all of his grievances feel petty and small. "When I sent those jewels—I never imagined—"

"I know," said Jane, but she didn't meet his eyes. "You were only trying to help your sister." With a visible effort, she added, "It wasn't really your fault, any more than it's the fault of a butterfly for flapping its wings."

Jack clung to what small bit of humor he could find. "A butterfly? Really?"

"Would you prefer something more manly? A buzzard, then." She rubbed her hand against her temple, leaving a small streak of grime. There was something strangely endearing about that smudge. With her hair in a braid down her back and dirt on her cheek and brow, she looked painfully young. Only her eyes looked old, old and tired, as she said with an obvious effort, "The truth is that it would have happened anyway."

Jack looked at her doubtfully. "You would have met the Gardener?"

Jane's eyes met his without faltering. "I would have decided the stakes were too high. By operating under my own name, I put my family, my friends, everyone who associated with me at risk." There were lines at the sides of her eyes and mouth that Jack hadn't noticed before, lines engraved there by sleepless nights and hopeless choices. "I had believed that, if I were careful, I could protect them. But I saw agents, good agents, captured. There was a man—an artist—who worked with us who had his fingers broken. It sounds such a small thing, but to him, a man who lived by his brush—"

"You don't need to explain." Jack knew. He'd lived it. He could see them still, the bodies of his friends.

"The Gardener precipitated the decision but he didn't cause it. I could give up the work, or I could go away. Really," Jane said, with a false brightness that broke Jack's heart, "my parents did me a favor—"

He couldn't bear it anymore. He wrapped his arms around her, muffling her words in his chest. "You don't have to be so damned noble," he said into her hair. "Scream at me, rail at me, tell me I ruined your life. I'd rather that."

"But I can't," she said, her voice dampened by his coat. "It wouldn't be fair."

Jack gave a ragged laugh deep in his throat, a laugh that had more in it of despair than amusement, and pulled her closer, resting his cheek on her hair, breathing in peat and lavender. "You're too damned fair for your own good."

"It's only true." Wiggling back, she looked up at him, her hair tousled around her dirt-smudged face. Only her eyes were as he had first seen them, clear, uncompromising. "I don't know what else I could have done, in the end."

Beneath her disguises lay a core, not of steel, but of pure silver. Jack didn't know how he hadn't seen it before. Perhaps because most people were made of baser coin. Himself included.

Jack kept an arm around her, his body providing some small barrier against the elements. He could shield her from the wind, if nothing else. "How did you manage? On your own, I mean."

"It wasn't so very different," said Jane, so carefully that Jack knew it had been very different indeed. "I had connections still. And aliases. The greatest difficulty was the loss of my allowance. Informers tend not to continue informing when one hasn't the coin to pay them. Not to mention gowns, gloves, and fans. I hadn't realized quite how much I'd taken for granted until it was no longer there. It was . . . humbling."

He had twitted her about her expensive Paris gown, her infinite resources. Jack winced at the memory. "What did you do?"

"I found an alternate source of funding," she said obliquely. Jack hadn't realized he'd betrayed himself, but he must have made some noise, or given some sign, because Jane added coolly, "Whatever you're thinking, it was nothing like that."

Jack could feel color suffuse his cheeks. "I never thought . . ."

But he had. Of course he had. And he felt like a cad for it.

"It was my independence I sacrificed, not my virtue." There was a rigidity about her posture that suggested just how much the conversation was costing her. "I sacrificed that later, but not for coin."

"Stop." Jack turned her face towards his, his palm beneath her chin. "Don't talk like that."

"Why not? It's true."

"Because I won't have you making yourself sound cheap. You're not." His own vehemence took him by surprise. "If a man took a lover it would be accounted commonplace. Why shouldn't you? Your virtue lies in your mind, not in what lies between your legs."

He saw her eyes widen, but she said only, "Plain speaking, Mr. Reid."

Despite himself, Jack's lips twisted. "Don't you think, by now, you ought to call me Jack? You could call me Iain if you like, but I'd never remember to answer to it." When she didn't smile in return, he added more seriously, "If either of us cared a fig for the world's niceties, we wouldn't be here."

Jack saw Jane's throat work, that long, graceful throat. "I thought I did. I thought I could have both. I thought I could be both."

He could tell her something about that.

"It's never comfortable belonging to two worlds. You find neither wants you." Gently, Jack tucked a bit of loose hair behind her ear. "For what it's worth, I think you're worth twenty of any of those ladies of supposedly unsullied background. It's an honor to walk beside your donkey."

Jane gave a half laugh. "Are you never serious?"

"I've never been more serious." Some remnant of honor prompted him to add, "If you care for the opinion of a mongrel like me."

Her eyes were silver in the brilliance of the sunset. "I care for *your* opinion."

"More fool you," said Jack, but it came out like an endearment.

His hand cupped her face, so different from that of the woman he had first met in Lisbon, so much more beautiful for all her scrapes and smudges.

He could feel the shift of her chin against his palm as she spoke. "For many things," she said, "but not for this."

And she rose up on her knees and kissed him, tentatively at first, and then not so tentatively at all.

There was a ringing in Jack's ears and a roaring in his blood. He should put a stop to it, he knew. This was . . . He was . . . Something about honor? His world narrowed to the woman in front of him, the silk of her hair beneath her fingers, the warm mystery of her lips against his.

Jack gave up any attempt at rational thought. He'd never believed in fighting losing battles.

They were both still kneeling, sinking down together, Jane in his arms, her body pressed against his as the kiss became more intense, deepened. How could he ever have thought her cold? There was nothing cold about her. She was like a living flame in his arms; her lips burned where they touched. They kissed hungrily, greedily, hardly pausing for air, the cold forgotten, the hard ground forgotten, even the donkey forgotten in a sheer physical need more elemental than breathing.

The ringing was louder now, more clamorous. It wasn't in his head, Jack realized. It was coming from the east, from Alcobaça.

His head spinning, Jack sat down hard on his heels. "Those are bells," he said dumbly. "Real bells."

Jane staggered to her feet, yanking her cloak back up around her shoulders. "From Alcobaça?"

She almost managed to make her voice sound even. Almost. Her chest was rising and falling just a little too fast, her lips red and swollen.

And Jack needed to get his brain out of his breeches if they weren't going to die.

"It's the nearest foundation with bells that size." Jack forced himself to focus on the matter at hand. Survival now, kisses later. Not that he had much hope of kisses later. That had been a one-off, an accident. And— Oh, bugger it. "An attack? It might be an attack. Alcobaça is a rich foundation."

"And Bonaparte's officers are greedy men. Or if someone

discovered the Queen was there—" Jane broke off, a strange expression on her face. "Wait. Do you know what day it is?"

"The day?" Jack wasn't quite sure what that had to do with anything. They needed to plan their next move. If Junot's troops were at Alcobaça— "We left Lisbon on the fourteenth."

"We were eight nights with Lieutenant Moreau . . . and then two since." Jane pressed the heels of her hands to her eyes. "Of course. It's the twenty-fourth of December."

"Of course?" The bells were still ringing, sending out their call of alarm. Jack tried to remember the reports he had rifled, the troop movements Junot had planned. Not that Junot's plans tended to rise to fruition, particularly not on a specific day. He was missing something, he knew, but his brain was too muddled to see it. Confusion made him short. "Is that supposed to mean something?"

"I should say so." Jane looked at him, a rueful smile spreading across her face. "It's not an attack. It's Christmas Eve."

Chapter Twelve

"They don't have tablecloths?"

"It's a pub, Grandma." My fixed smile was beginning to ache around the edges. Festive. We were supposed to be festive. I just had to keep reminding myself of that as Colin and I made the rounds of our guests.

"A what?" My grandmother eyed the scarred wooden tables with disfavor.

How did one define a pub? They just were. "Sort of like a cross between a bar and a diner. Only with less Formica."

My grandmother looked even more pained. "Don't they have any nice restaurants out here, dear?"

"I offered to host the dinner at the Grill at the Savoy," said Jeremy, managing to look both soulful and sorrowful.

My grandmother and Jeremy were getting along like a house on fire. They disliked all the same things. Including informal rehearsal dinners.

"That would have been much better." She patted his well-manicured hand with her own heavily beringed one. "Eloise, why aren't we at the Savoy?"

"Excuse me—Mom wants me," I lied, and ducked away, my attempts to cunningly ferret something, anything, out of Jeremy blocked by the Grandma effect.

As far as I could tell, Jeremy was behaving exactly as usual, but it was hard to be certain. A force field of smarm surrounded him like the shields of the Death Star (*Spaceballs* edition). I wasn't sure what would shake that cool exterior, short of squirting his black cashmere sport coat with raspberry jam.

Hey, it had worked for Lone Starr.

By that point, I was getting a little bit punchy. Everything was proceeding exactly as one would expect. People were being awkward, old family grievances were being aired, and the single members of the bridal party were getting soused.

If it weren't for the empty chair where Mrs. Selwick-Alderly should have been, it would have felt like an entirely normal rehearsal dinner: in other words, full of pitfalls and unresolved family tensions.

We were a small group. Given the huge number of overseas guests, we'd elected to restrict the rehearsal dinner to people actually in the wedding, to keep from having the wedding two times over. Perhaps that was why it felt a bit like five chapters

into an Agatha Christie novel, everyone milling around, looking vaguely suspect.

Where was Miss Marple when you needed her? I'd even
settle for Hercule Poirot and his leetle gray cells.

Not having a sleuth on hand, I took stock of the assem-
blage, particularly the dodgier members. Colin's mother, wearing a dress that was both shorter and cuter than mine, was
currently being occupied by my sister, Jillian. They seemed to
be getting along rather well. I couldn't decide whether that was
convenient or disturbing. If she had a guilty conscience, Colin's
mother didn't show it. She was happily knocking back the
house bubbly, holding forth to Jillian about an art installation
she had just seen that wasn't nearly as innovative as her dear
friend blah blah blah's blah blah blah.

My eyes snaked over to Colin's sister, Serena. When I'd first
started dating Colin, I'd felt sorry for Serena. She wore her
neediness the way her mother wore a little black dress. But my
sympathy had waned when Serena had let herself be bribed by
Jeremy into voting her share of Selwick Hall against Colin.
Behind his back.

I had always suspected that Serena was carrying a torch for
her stepfather. She'd claimed to be mourning the breakup of
her relationship with smarmy archivist Nigel Dempster, who
was now dating Colin's neighbor, Joan Plowden-Plugge, right
next door at Donwell Abbey.

At Donwell Abbey. For a moment, I wondered. . . . Dempster had gone to great lengths to get his hands on the secret

history of the Pink Carnation, believing that a blockbuster non-fiction book could be parlayed into fame, fortune, and a BBC miniseries. The Pink Carnation's trunk had arrived on our doorstep the same day I'd gotten a call demanding a box. And Dempster was, in fact, currently domiciled at Donwell Abbey. Or, if not domiciled, at least staying there pretty frequently.

For fairly obvious reasons, Dempster and Joan hadn't been invited to the rehearsal dinner, although both were on the guest list for the wedding, mostly because both Colin and I liked Joan's sister Sally and one couldn't invite one without the other. Plus, neighbors.

While I might deeply dislike Dempster, it was hard to imagine him carrying off elderly ladies in order to get his book scoop, particularly since he had already been informed, in no uncertain terms, that the family did not intend to cooperate with him and would publish the information themselves sooner than see him profit from it.

Which pretty much washed out Dempster.

Now that I thought about it, it didn't surprise me that Serena had fallen for Dempster. He was very much of the Jeremy type. Both were older men, vaguely metrosexual, self-assured to the point of arrogance. I was fairly sure that Dempster was merely a Jeremy stand-in. Given that Jeremy was, not to put too fine a point upon it, already married to Serena's mother.

Peyton Place had nothing on the Selwicks.

Would Serena be party to kidnapping her aunt? I didn't think so. But if Jeremy were involved . . . all bets were off.

At the moment, Serena was in custody of my best friend, Alex. Thank goodness for Alex, college roommate extraordinaire. There, at least, was one person I could count on unreservedly.

Although I hadn't quite brought myself to tell her that my husband's great-aunt had been kidnapped and it might be spies.

Alex's husband and Colin's best friend, Nick, had entered an involved discussion of something to do with men kicking projectiles for profit and pleasure, which left Pammy, Nickless, to flirt with the only other single man available, Colin's other groomsman, Martin. It was clearly rough going. Pammy rolled her eyes at me in a "shoot me now" gesture.

I gave her a little wave and kept on going. My face was still itching from that mud mask. Pammy meant well, but the road to a blotchy complexion was paved with good intentions.

My eyes slid past Pammy to her companion. Martin. Now there was a dark horse. What if . . .

No. Reality caught up with me. Martin was an accountant. He was about as much of a dark horse as Eeyore. In fact, in his gray sport coat, he bore a remarkable resemblance to the depressive donkey. If he was 008, it was the greatest deception since Sir Percy Blakeney decided to don a floral waistcoat.

That left only two more people: my father and the vicar, who were merrily downing white wine spritzers (my father) and gin and tonics (the vicar) and discussing the intricacies of

BBC costume dramas, in several of which the vicar had been an extra before going all Vicar of Dibley.

"What they really need to do," my father was saying, "is remake *Poldark*."

Looking deeply horrified, the vicar accused him of heresy; the seventies miniseries was the apotheosis of *Poldark*-ness.

"Yes, but the production values . . ."

No, this was not a man who was kidnapping aging secret agents in his spare time. I thought. I hoped.

That was the problem, wasn't it? You never really knew anything about anyone. I was pretty sure I could vouch for my side of the aisle. Even if my father did occasionally, after a few glasses of cream sherry, claim to have worked for the CIA during his postcollege Fulbright year in Berlin.

But, really, if you'd worked for the CIA, would you say you'd worked for the CIA? I thought not.

Jeremy smarmed back over to me. "Where's the lucky groom?"

His tone managed to imply that Colin must have made a bunk for the ferry to France. Or at least to the nearest curry house.

"Dealing with some last-minute details for me." In fact, Colin was phoning all of Mrs. Selwick-Alderly's acquaintances in London, trying to determine when and where she'd been seen last. I decided to take the Jeremy by the horns. "Have you seen your grandmother?"

"She's not here? That's not like her." He managed to look genuinely concerned, but this was Jeremy. Even his name wasn't real.

"Is someone missing?" That was my mother, wearing her harried face.

"Colin's aunt. Don't worry," I said glibly. "There's probably just trouble on the A39."

"Er—" Martin piped up, sidling over to us. "The A39 is in Cornwall."

Okay, maybe not so glibly. I waved a dismissive hand. "All those numbers sound the same to me."

Colin emerged from the corridor with the phone. "Eloise doesn't drive," he explained to Martin, putting an arm around my waist.

I looked up at him quizzically.

He gave his head a little shake.

In other words, no news.

"A fact for which the mailboxes of the world are all grateful," said Jillian.

You splat one mailbox your first time behind the wheel . . . "If God had intended me to drive, he wouldn't have invented taxicabs."

"There aren't many cabs out here, sweetie," said my father.

He and my mother exchanged one of those parental looks. They hadn't exactly come out and said they disapproved, but they had hinted. Broadly. They were worried, they had said, about the pressure living out in the middle of nowhere would place on our relationship. I had pointed out that I had already successfully survived at Selwick Hall, sans driver's license, for months, but they were still worried.

To be fair, my mother would probably have reacted the same way if I'd said I was moving across Central Park to the West Side.

Although they did have taxis there. Or so I'd been told.

We'd been through this before. "No, but there's Colin. I don't even make him wear a little hat. Seriously. It's fine."

Another parental look. It wasn't that they disliked Colin, per se. My mother had reluctantly admitted that he seemed like a Very Nice Boy. But . . .

And there it was. The parental elephant in the room. My parents were convinced that, but for the Colin factor, I wouldn't have dropped out of grad school. The words "abandoning your career to chase a boy" hadn't exactly been used, but they had been implied.

I didn't quite know how to explain to them that I hadn't abandoned my degree; it had abandoned me.

My dissertation, my advisor had said, had read too much like fiction. He'd given me the option of rewriting from scratch, a project that would have taken at least one year and probably two. I'd already been in grad school for six years. Did I want to make it eight?

I might have slogged through, unenthused, for lack of anything better to do. I'd spent my entire postcollege life training to be a historian. What else was there for me?

It was Colin who had cut the Gordian knot. If it sounds like fiction, he'd suggested, why not write it as fiction?

It was crazy. And yet oddly compelling. I'd disappeared from Robinson Hall (aka the history department building), done the bare minimum to teach the classes I was already teaching, locked myself in my studio apartment, and flung myself into the story of the Pink Carnation. The material, as Colin had pointed out, was already there. The people were already alive to me. I'd lived in their homes, read their letters, walked in their footsteps. All I needed to do was add dialogue.

And caffeine. A lot of caffeine.

So, in a way, it was Colin's fault. He'd given me an alternative. By the spring I hadn't been any closer to having official letters after my name, but I did have a manuscript.

I also, miraculously, had an agent. Pammy, who knew everyone and their first cousin, had whisked the manuscript out of my hands and dropped it in the lap—most likely literally, although I hadn't cared to inquire—of the sort of bigwig agent I would never have dared to approach on my own. After a few quick revisions, the agent was now "shopping" the manuscript, which meant that I checked my phone every five minutes and bit my nails a lot while telling myself I really didn't expect anything.

If I had hoped the news might reconcile my parents to my career change, my hopes were unfounded. They hadn't been excited. In fact, they had been extremely skeptical.

I couldn't entirely blame them. Everyone knew that fiction

writing was hardly a stable career. It tended to be associated with garrets, guttering candles, and sneakers with holes in them. I didn't know that Pammy's agent friend would be able to sell my book.

But what I did know? I was far happier here, with Colin, than I had ever been teaching Western civ. And if the novel didn't pan out, well, I'd try something else. Animal husbandry. Or possibly popular narrative nonfiction.

Although I hadn't admitted it, even to myself, that was a large part of why I'd wanted to have the wedding at Selwick Hall. To show my parents just how well my new life suited me, how comfortable Colin and I were.

Great-aunt-napping hadn't been part of the plan.

Predictably, my parents were picking up on the tension, but not the source. I caught another Significant Parental Look.

"I think it's time for us to all sit down," I said brightly, downing the last of my G-and-T. "Anyone want to help with herding?"

With a certain amount of milling and confusion, everyone found their place cards and shuffled into their allotted seats. Colin and I had opted for traditional pub fare: a choice of bangers and mash or chicken tikka masala.

There were speeches. There were always speeches. Martin read conscientiously off a prepared script with jokes in bullet points. Pammy expostulated about embarrassing events that had occurred in fifth grade and really should have been covered by some sort of statute of limitations. Jillian didn't say anything; she was saving her fire for her maid-of-honor speech the following day.

We had moved on to the sticky toffee pudding part of the meal without incident when Colin's mother rose from her seat, clinking her spoon against her glass.

This was not part of the script. I grimaced at Colin. He gave a helpless shrug. Apparently he was as clueless as I was.

"I didn't want my gift to get lost among the throng," said Colin's mother airily, "so I brought it here for you tonight." To the servers, she said, "Sheila, Peter, if you will?"

Colin and I exchanged a look. This was just like Colin's mother. It was always all about her.

"As long as it's not another electric kettle," Colin murmured. We'd gotten eight already.

"Hey, you can never have too many electric kettles." A few more and we could have one in every room in the house, put out little packs of biscuits, and call ourselves a bed-and-breakfast.

I could hear Sheila and Peter in the hallway. There was hoisting and giggling and a clunk that caused Colin's mother to frown and say sharply, "Careful with that!"

I prepared to hate anything that Colin's mother had gotten us. Particularly anything large enough that it required two members of the pub staff to carry in. Four and twenty blackbirds baked in a pie? A pipe, a bowl, and three unhappy fiddlers?

Oh, please, I thought. Let it not be installation art.

It wasn't. Sheila and Peter staggered into the room, each bearing one side of a painting. A very large painting.

It was a good thing Colin had a Land Rover with a lot of room in back.

Colin's mother flicked her wrist at her minions and they dropped the dust sheet covering it.

It was Selwick Hall. I knew, without looking at the signature, who had painted it. Colin's mother was known for intensely detailed paintings, generally of urban areas, featuring dozens of painstakingly crafted little tableaux. "A modern Canaletto," the papers called her.

She had rendered Selwick Hall on a spring afternoon, with the sunlight slanting behind the tower, casting a long shadow across the formal gardens, towards the veranda on which Colin and I were standing, both of us with our elbows braced against the balustrade. I had one hand raised to tuck a bit of hair behind my ear. Colin had both hands in the pockets of his Barbour jacket.

She had caught both of us perfectly.

Mrs. Selwick-Alderly, Colin's aunt Arabella, was there, too, at one of the windows, looking down at us. Pammy was standing on the gravel path by the side of the house, on her cell phone. There was a figure trotting by on horseback, looking covetously at Colin, who could only be Joan Plowden-Plugge. Serena, in the pose made famous by a Fragonard painting, was sitting on the old swing in the garden, the tails of her pashmina trailing behind her as she swung up in the air, her thin face, for once, relaxed and carefree.

It wasn't just the living who had joined us at Selwick Hall. There was a shadowy figure in the window, next to Mrs. Selwick-Alderly, whom I guessed, from the resemblance to Colin, must be Colin's father. A shimmer of paint in the corner of the painting, by the old Roman folly with its statue of Marcus Aurelius, gave the impression of ladies and gentlemen in Regency garb. But just an impression. If one looked too closely, squinted too hard, they seemed to dissolve back into the canvas, nothing but points of light.

Everything was done in miniature, complex and perfect, everyone entirely themselves. But most of all, there was an air of peace and joy that settled across the picture like a blessing.

I really hadn't expected that kind of blessing from my future mother-in-law. I took it as a plus when she remembered my name.

The painting was more than a gift. It was beautiful and unique and heartwarming. It was an investment of time and creative energy that must have taken weeks, if not months of work.

Maybe she wasn't quite so indifferent to her only son as she appeared?

I gave Caroline Selwick-Alderly an impulsive hug. She felt tiny, her bones small and brittle. "This is . . . incredible."

Putting a safe distance between us, Caroline Selwick-Alderley brushed her Guerlain-dusted cheek against mine. "I hope you're happier here than I was."

The "it would be hard not to be" was implied.

I wished I had the nerve to ask what her life had really been like with Colin's father. I had heard only one side of the story, and Mrs. Selwick-Alderly, who had seen first her nephew and then her grandson marry a woman she clearly despised, was hardly an impartial witness.

It was hard to know how to answer that without putting my foot in it, so I merely said, "This is really lovely. Thank you."

It was lovely. At least, on a first glance. As Colin added his thanks to mine, I took a closer look and the shadows began to creep in.

It reminded me a bit of that Holbein painting where a smudge, when viewed at the right angle, resolves itself into a skull. It wasn't just that Caroline hadn't included herself in the picture. It was the way the shadow from the old medieval tower crept towards the house. A dark figure in a hooded robe could be dimly glimpsed behind the tower. The Phantom Monk of Donwell Abbey? It was certainly part of local history, but it seemed an odd detail to include in a wedding picture.

But, most unsettling at all, when one looked at Mrs. Selwick-Alderly in the window, and the faint figure of Colin's father behind her, it became less clear which was the living and which the dead. There was something insubstantial about Mrs. Selwick-Alderly. It felt almost like an ill wish.

With a smile that had lost its warmth, I said, "It was very kind of you to include Mrs. Selwick-Alderly in the picture. I know she would be touched."

No, she wouldn't. She would be skeptical. She had made no

secret that she thoroughly disliked Caroline. I had never heard the term "free spirit" used in a more pejorative tone than when Mrs. Selwick-Alderly spoke of Colin's mother.

Caroline's blue eyes were as hard and shiny as those of a porcelain doll. "She always did think it was still her house. She certainly did everything she could to get me out of it."

The venom in her voice was unmistakable.

No. It was impossible to imagine Colin's slight mother wrestling his aunt into the backseat of a car. Colin's mother looked like she supped on thistledown and dew—which wasn't that far from the mark, except that her version was champagne and cigarettes. Either way, she had the sort of body that worked brilliantly in little slip dresses and high boots.

Mrs. Selwick-Alderly was more of a broad-shouldered 1930s-film-goddess type. It was like imagining Mrs. Peel from the original *Avengers* strong-arming Faye Dunaway.

On the other hand, that Mrs. Peel was pretty spry. . . .

"Are you all right?" It was my own mother, who, if we were going by television references, was a dead ringer for Mrs. Gilmore. She was making her Mrs. Gilmore face right now. Dropping her voice, she said, "If you're having second thoughts . . ."

"No," I said firmly. "No second thoughts."

Just a kidnapped great-aunt. For a moment I toyed with the idea of telling my mother all. I could just see her marching purposefully through the ruins of Donwell Abbey in her Ferragamo pumps, taking the kidnapper by the arm and giving him a good talking-to.

It was a highly tempting prospect.

On the other hand, there had been genuine menace in that voice on the other end of the line. And the truth of the matter was that we hadn't the foggiest idea what, or who, we were dealing with. It could be anyone. Martin might secretly be the grandson of a killer spy Mrs. Selwick-Alderly had seen locked up; Jeremy might be scheming to secure the last of the jewels of Berar; Colin's mother might be settling old scores.

There was no way to find out but to make the rendezvous.

I sneaked a glance at the display on my mobile. It was already pushing midnight. With cocktails and dinner and speeches, the evening had stretched on and on, and no one seemed to be showing much inclination to leave, although the last of the coffee had gone cold, the port had been passed, and the pub staff were yawning.

Jeremy and Caroline were the first to excuse themselves. Coincidence? Or design?

My mother was organizing people into cars. "And Jillian can go with Colin and Eloise."

"Er, Mom, we're going to stick around here for a bit." I tried to signal to Colin with my eyebrows but only succeeded in looking as though Pammy's mud mask had given me a tic as well as spots. "Some last-minute wedding stuff."

Given that my mother knew the wedding preparations better than I did, it was a pretty weak excuse, but it was better than the truth.

"All right." She gave me a warning look. "But don't stay up too late."

What seemed like a century later, but was really only about twenty minutes, everyone had staggered off the premises and Colin and I were leaning wearily against each other, contemplating the rest of our night.

It wasn't the rest of our lives that was the problem; it was the next twenty-four hours.

"Next time," I muttered to Colin, "let's just elope."

He wrapped his arms around me from behind and rested his chin against the top of my head. "Gretna Green or Las Vegas?"

"Blacksmiths or blackjack? Hmm." That was a tough one. "Gretna Green. But only if you wear a kilt."

"Las Vegas it is, then." I could hear the pain in his voice as he said, "This is a hell of a way to begin our life together."

I turned in his embrace, wrapping my arms around his waist. There was something so comforting about the Colinness of him, stable and steady and entirely himself.

"Sickness and health. Thick and thin." I didn't think thick and thin was actually in the marriage service, but it made more sense under the circumstances than richer and poorer. "Better to start out with the tough stuff and then move on to happily ever after by and by. And, hey, think of the story we'll have to tell our kids!"

I could feel his laughter in the movement of his chest and in the snuffle of air against my hair. "That's one way to look at it."

I took a step back, looking up at him. "That's my story and I'm sticking to it."

Colin's lips twisted in a half smile. Taking my hand in his, he said, " 'Doubt thou the stars are fire, / Doubt that the sun doth move, / Doubt truth to be a liar, / But never doubt I love.' " More prosaically, he added, "You're right. We'll get this sorted."

"Together," I said. *Hamlet* might not be the most auspicious of plays, but I appreciated the sentiment all the same.

And it could have been worse. It could have been *Macbeth*.

Taking a deep breath, I twined my fingers through his. "I know we're still a bit early, but . . . shall we head over to the abbey?"

"Why not?" said Colin, and squeezed my hand just a little bit tighter. "Together."

Chapter Thirteen

"Christmas?" Jack looked as rattled as Jane felt. That was gratifying, at least. He smacked his palm against his forehead. "Oh, for the love of—"

"Precisely," said Jane, fighting a crazy urge to laugh. Or possibly to cry. She wasn't quite sure which. She took refuge in trivialities. "And we even have a donkey."

Jack groaned. "After this many years here— I should have realized that was why the bells were ringing."

"It's not surprising you thought first of attack." Jane gathered up the blanket, bundling it briskly onto the donkey's back. She should be grateful for the bells, she supposed. They had kept her from following foolishness with foolishness. "You had battles on the brain."

"That's not what I had on the brain." Jack came up to her side, his tanned face serious beneath the brim of his hat. "Jane—"

Jane ducked around the other side of the donkey, concentrating on loosening his lead. "If we don't hurry, we won't reach the monastery before dark."

Strategic retreat. Which was, as Jack had pointed out to her in the past, just another word for running away. But what else was she to do? She wasn't accustomed to acting on impulse. And that kiss—that kiss had been an impulse. When she had made the decision to succumb to Nicolas's advances, it had been a calculated measure. Jane had told herself that she had nothing left to lose, that society's rules held no more power over her. If her decision to share Nicolas's bed had been driven as much by loneliness as by desire, well, then, that was for herself alone to know. She had chosen the time; she had chosen the place; she had chosen to let Nicolas believe the persuasion was his. Her seduction had been orchestrated with as much precision as any of her missions.

But then, thought Jane despairingly, nothing about this mission had gone as planned. Why should her relations with Jack be any different? There was something about him that seemed to make the best-laid plans go awry. She'd meant to blister his ears and ride off ahead of him in high dudgeon. Instead, she'd bared her soul and kissed him.

Even now, with her lips still tingling from his kiss, she wasn't entirely sure how that had happened. She had always despised those agents who wasted time in useless dalliance, when every moment was of the essence. What were they thinking? she had wondered, feeling happily superior.

She wasn't feeling terribly superior right now.

Jane yanked at the donkey's rope. "Do you want to lead Dulcibella, or shall I?"

They really did need to get to the monastery before dark. The terrain here was gentler than the mountainous region they had crossed the day before, but the roads were still steep and uncertain, dangerous to navigate in the dark. If they delayed any longer, they would be forced to spend another night in the rough.

Curled up together for warmth.

"I can walk if it will be faster," Jane offered.

"And break your blisters again?" Jack followed her around the donkey, absently flapping at it as it attempted an exploratory nibble on his pocket. "What just happened—"

"Happened." Jane had the donkey's rump on one side and a tree behind her back. There was nowhere left to go. Except up. Keeping her gaze straight ahead, she hoisted herself up on the donkey's back. "Consider it a thank-you."

Jack caught her hand. Despite herself, Jane found herself looking at him, arrested by the fierce light in his amber eyes as he said, "You never have to say thank-you like that. Not to me. Not to anyone."

Jane felt a sinking feeling in the pit of her stomach. If he had been importunate, belligerent, defensive, any of those things, she might have brushed it off. But such intensity demanded honesty for honesty.

Jane twitched her hand away. "I didn't have to. I wanted to." She stared straight out between the donkey's ears. "Now can we get on?"

There was a long, pregnant pause.

And then Jack took up the lead and, without a word, urged the donkey forward, onto the path.

It ought to have made her feel better, but it didn't. With a furrow between her brows, Jane watched Jack's back as he trudged along ahead of her, surefooted on the narrow path. She had handed him a weapon. And he had chosen not to use it.

But why should that surprise her? Jane pressed her eyes shut, feeling faintly seasick as she swayed with the motion of the donkey. From the first, Jack had confounded her expectations.

Your virtue lies in your mind, not in what lies between your legs.

Jane scowled at the back of his head. Why did he have to be so maddeningly kind? It made it so very difficult to go on despising him. And if she stopped despising him, she might have to admit that she liked him. Rather a lot. And that she wished, very much, that the bells hadn't begun ringing when they did, that she could be back half an hour ago, in the circle of his arms, feeling so deeply, improbably safe. Safe and cherished.

Stupid, stupid. Jack Reid wasn't the cherishing kind. He was a restless rover who had spent his life cutting off attachments, working alone. And she—she wasn't the sort whom men cherished. Praised, yes. Admired, yes. Set up for display in a prettily contrived glass cabinet, all that. But cherished, no. Men had made Jane extravagant promises, but she'd known it was all part of the chase. They didn't want the reality of her, merely the shell, to set upon a balcony and pay homage. It was about the winning, not the having.

Even with Nicolas.

It's not your body I want, he had said, as they lay together that night in Venice, a gondolier's song drifting through the window. The night was warm, the air sweetly perfumed, Nicolas's chamber hung in silk brocade. Candles guttered on a gilded table, and the remains of the sweet wine they had drunk glowed golden in blown glass goblets. A perfect setting for romance, and yet Jane had felt cold, cold to her core. *It's your heart, your soul.*

Jane had instinctively turned away, taking the fine linen sheet with her. *That would only be fair coin if you were willing to tender your own in return.*

Don't you know they are already yours? Nicolas had said extravagantly.

And Jane had kissed him to keep herself from saying what was in her head, offering him her body instead of her heart. Whatever she had told Jack, the guilt she had felt had nothing— or at least very little—to do with the sacrifice of her virtue, and everything to do with the fact that she had lied, with her actions if not with her words. She might once have fancied herself in love with Nicolas, but it was so long ago that it seemed like a tale told about someone else, a pastel image in a book. By the time she had lain with Nicolas, the glamour had already faded. She had hoped that the joining of the flesh might rekindle that old wonder; she had wanted, so badly, to believe that she could love him.

Familiarity, however, had only made clear that they were less star-crossed than they were ill suited. Nicolas's murder of his colleague had provided her an excuse for leaving; it hadn't been the cause.

It would have been more honorable, if uncomfortable, to have told Nicolas as much. Instead, she had let him go on believing that she had flown out of maidenly delicacy, and that if only he pursued her long and hard enough, she would be his for the winning. There were times when kindness wasn't kindness. Kindness or policy? Jane wasn't entirely sure, but she didn't like herself much either way. She had told herself she had left things as she had to avoid hurting Nicolas's pride, but the truth of it was, as long as the Gardener thought he might still win her, he kept his claws sheathed. He batted at her in play rather than earnest.

There had been reasons, perhaps not good reasons, but reasons for allowing Nicolas to seduce her. She had been curious; she had been lonely; it was a consummation two and a half years in the making.

Jane couldn't think of a single reason, good or otherwise, for kissing Jack Reid.

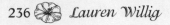

Except that she had.

Jack turned his head. "Almost there," he shouted over the ringing of the bells, which were tolling out their triumphal peal.

"Yes, I gathered that," muttered Jane.

Even without the bells, the monastery was rather hard to miss. From the rise they were descending, it looked as though someone had picked up the Abbey of Clairvaux, plunked it down in the middle of Portugal, and then, while they were at it, added a few wings.

The setting sun turned the limestone facing to gold, picking out the full glory of the Gothic facade. A fitting place, thought Jane, holding tight to the donkey's neck, to hide a queen, if one had a queen to hide. Or so she hoped. Otherwise—

Otherwise they would continue on to Porto, she told herself. As quickly as possible.

There was a party of clerics traversing the courtyard, heading towards the porch of the church. At their head strode a man clad in vestments so rich that he could only be the abbot. A ring glittered on one hand as he gestured to his flock of black-robed companions.

Cutting in front of the group, Jack said something in Portuguese that began with *padre* and involved much descriptive gesturing, if not of the sort that he had used in the hut. From the gestures to the donkey, Jane gathered the prior was being spun a tale of hardships on the road, and most likely lack of room at the inn.

Jane recognized the abbot's type at a glance. His robes had been carefully cut to disguise the effects of one too many generous suppers, but even the excellent line of his robes couldn't hide the fleshiness of his chin and the red lines around his nose.

She had a very good view of his nose. He was currently looking down it at them, taking in their mud-spattered appearance, the peasant clothing, the donkey.

The abbot said something in Portuguese, a very differently inflected Portuguese from Jack's, and Jane didn't need to understand the language to know that they were being told to go around to the back, that the servants would feed them something in the kitchen.

It was true that servants did tend to know everything. And they would be well fed and warm in the kitchen. But there was also the chance that they would be fed and sent on their way again, or given a bed in the stable, like another, far better-known personage in the long-ago past, donkey and all.

Jack bowed, and began to lead Jane and the donkey away, but Jane preempted him by the simple measure of leaning over the donkey's neck and calling in a particularly piercing voice, "Most reverend Father— Oh, dear me, is that the proper form?"

The reverend father stopped in his tracks. He turned, slowly, his surplice blowing in the breeze. *"Senhora?"*

She'd caught his attention, at least. And Jack's. The latter did not look entirely pleased. He was watching her narrowly, his mobile lips set in a hard line.

Jane focused on the abbot, smiling winningly. "Forgive me, Your Excellency. I'm only lately come from England and we haven't much in the way of monks there. Not since Henry the Eighth, you know." She grimaced at Jack, saying plaintively, "Ought I have mentioned that? I've heard it's still rather a sore point."

Jack succumbed to a sudden fit of coughing.

The abbot ventured closer. "You are . . . English?"

His English was quite good. Jane had been counting on that, so near Porto. There were many influential Englishmen with business interests in the region who used this route, or had, before Bonaparte tendered his ultimatum to Dom Joao.

She clasped her hands to her breasts. "You speak English! Thank heavens! You can't imagine the bother we've had. My husband"—she took a moment to simper in Jack's general direction—"speaks a bit, as you can see, but we've been blundering along, getting into such scrapes. And I'm just longing for a hot bath. You haven't a maid to spare, have you? I'm afraid we left mine back in London. It seemed like a good idea at the time. . . . But you see what we are reduced to!"

The abbot's entourage were all staring shamelessly. Slowly the abbot approached Jane, bowing over her dirty hand.

"I bid you welcome to Alcobaça, Dona—"

"Fluellen." Jane shamelessly borrowed the name of Jack's brother-in-law. That Jack wasn't aware he had such a brother-in-law was another matter. Jane pushed that to the back of her conscience. She lowered her voice. "My husband is Welsh, you see. That's why my father didn't approve. Well, that and his serving with the East India Company's army. My father is frightfully high in the instep about that sort of thing."

"High in the—" The abbot was looking justifiably baffled. Good. Jane wanted to keep him that way. The more bewildered he was, the less likely he was to perceive the holes in her carefully constructed story.

"Snobbish. Just because his cousin is an earl!" Jane let that sink in. "He sent me to my cousin, Lady Vaughn, to keep me from marrying my love, but as you can see, we managed to get away despite it. Didn't we, my love?"

She held out a hand to Jack, who squeezed it a little harder than necessary. "Oh, yes, *my love.*"

"But, Dona Fluellen," said the abbot. "How do you come to be in Portugal? And in such times?"

Jane allowed her husband to help her down from the donkey. "It is such a story you cannot imagine!"

"Neither can I," muttered Jack in her ear.

Jane gave his arm a warning squeeze and fluttered her lashes enthusiastically at the abbot. "My father has interests in Porto, you see. He had come to tour the— Oh, goodness, whatever they are. Something to do with grapes?"

"Vineyards?" supplied the abbot helpfully.

"Yes, those. And really to get away from the scandal. He was very cross with us, wasn't he, darling? But I knew, just knew, that if he had time to get to know my darling Johnny-kins, he would adore him as I do. We had the hardest time getting passage over—something about the French?—but I was quite determined, and now here we are!"

The abbot opened his mouth and then closed it again. Taking the path of least resistance, he bowed and said, "You are in good time to share our Christmas meal, Dona Fluellen."

"You are so *very* kind." Jane wrinkled her nose at her travel-stained garments. "I'm afraid I haven't a proper gown. My baggage fell down a gorge somewhere near the Tagus while we were fleeing from a group of French soldiers. They were *most* impolite."

The abbot started to offer her his arm, regarded the amount of mud adhering to her person, and thought better of it. With a sweeping gesture, he ushered them towards an entrance just west of the church. "I am quite certain we can discover something for you, Dona Fluellen."

Clapping his hands, the abbot said something in Portuguese. Lay brothers scattered in various directions, one with the donkey. The expression on the donkey's face, as the brother attempted to drag it in the direction of the stable, bore a remarkable resemblance to Jack.

"Brother Pedro will show you to a room in the northwest wing," said the abbot, and fled before Jane could begin talking again.

Brother Pedro spoke no English, but communicated with Jane by means of exaggerated mime.

Jack, on the other hand, wasn't communicating at all, by English, mime, or otherwise. He walked beside Jane with an insolent swagger that spoke his displeasure louder than any number of words.

Brother Pedro led them through a dizzying series of high-ceilinged chambers, hung with so many paintings of popes and cardinals that their individual features resolved themselves into a blur of red robes. There was a great deal of gesturing, which Jane gathered was meant to indicate prelates of more than ordinary interest.

Brother Pedro paused in front of a particular painting. "Santo Tomás Becket," he said proudly. When Jane merely looked at him, he said, *"Arcebispo de Cantuária? De Inglaterra?"* When that still didn't get a response, he struck a pose and recited, " *'Não haverá ninguém capaz de me livrar deste padre turbulento'?"*

"Turbulent— Oh!" Jane took mercy on him. "Thomas à Becket? How nice. We have him at home. Bits of him, at least. Saints do tend to scatter so."

Brother Pedro eyed her dubiously and reverted to mime.

Meanwhile, Jack had maintained his ominous silence. Jane felt his presence like a shadow beside her. She took his arm, leaning on it as a devoted flibbertigibbet would. "Ought we remind him you speak Portuguese?" Jane murmured

Jack's arm was iron hard beneath her hand. "And ruin the show? Besides, I'm Welsh, remember?" He glanced down at her, his expression inscrutable. "That was very clever. . . . In a single blow, you accounted for both my accent and my complexion."

He did not sound particularly admiring.

"I've heard it said the Anglo-Indian accent is rather like the Welsh. Although you sound more like—" She had been going to say his father. Jane caught herself. "Yourself. You defy categorization."

"Compliments?" Jack smiled lazily down at her, and Jane was reminded of the tiger in the royal menagerie, playing with his prey. "Is that Mrs. Fluellen speaking or Jane?"

"For the moment, the two are one and the same." It was one of the first principles of the game they played: if one didn't live the role, the game was lost. "Do attempt to remember that you're meant to be madly in love."

Jack's eyes glittered like oil paint, bright and opaque. "Am I? Or am I just a half-pay scoundrel who managed to win the affections of a gullible heiress?"

"If you don't mind playing the scoundrel." It came out sounding shrewish and petty. Jane gritted her teeth. She knew better than this. She was better than this. Taking a deep breath, she said coolly, "Yes, that works rather nicely. It gives you room to leer at the serving girls and ask them leading questions."

"Are there serving girls in monasteries?"

"I'd never thought of that. Probably not. I suppose you wouldn't be willing to leer at the novices?"

"I'm not that sort of half-pay officer," Jack said definitively.

"For the good of the Queen?"

"She's not my Queen."

"No, but she is our mission," said Jane quietly. "For good or for ill."

Brother Pedro opened a door. *"Aqui é o seu quarto,"* he said with some relief, began to say something else, gave up, and fled.

"I had expected something more . . . spartan." The room into which they had been ushered had been decorated sometime before the previous century. The materials were sober, but rich: a surprisingly broad bed, a writing desk, a heavily carved chair. The bed was cloaked in crimson damask, as rich as good wine. There was a small door in the corner, which Jane suspected led to a dressing room, where one's servant would sleep.

Or in this case, where either she or Jack would sleep.

Jack shrugged, dropping his hat on the crimson coverlet and turning to examine the books on the writing table. Novels, from the look of it, most likely left by a previous guest. "The monks of Alcobaça are known for having more pipes of wine in their cellar than books in their library. Whether that's true or not, I don't know."

"I imagine we'll find out tonight." Jane regarded Jack's tense back, all lines and angles. She was reminded, incongruously, of an offended feline. And she couldn't blame him, precisely, for being angry. In an attempt at an olive branch, she said, "I thought we might learn more at the prior's table than in the kitchen."

Jack turned abruptly, his face darker than the twisted posts of the bed. "You might have consulted me."

"When?" Jane's hands clenched into fists at her sides. "In the three seconds before the prior began to speak?"

"During that last mile's walk to the abbey, perhaps?"

During that last mile's walk, her mind had been on other things. Jane took a deep breath, knowing herself to be in the wrong, and hating herself for it. "There wasn't— I didn't— The bells were so loud."

Was that the best she could do? *The bells were so loud?*

Jack pressed his eyes shut, making an obvious attempt to get hold of his temper. In a controlled voice, he said, "If you had intended to change the plan, you might have told me. I don't like surprises."

That he was right didn't make it easier.

Carefully, Jane said, "It is very hard to relinquish the habit of command." Particularly when she felt in command of so little right now, not least her own emotions. Snapping her gaze away from Jack's lips, Jane mustered a crooked smile. "Neither of us is very good at working in harness, are we?"

"I prefer not to think of myself as a mule." Jack ran a hand through his tousled hair. "Jane—"

There was a sharp knock at the door. Servants never knocked, but apparently monks did.

"Oh, the devil with it," said Jack savagely, and strode towards the door. He yanked it open. "Yes?"

Brother Pedro shoved a large pile of cloth into Jack's arms, delivered a rapid monologue, and departed, carefully not looking at Jane.

"I think he believes he caught us in the middle of exercising the sacrament of marriage," said Jack dryly. "We are instructed that water for washing is in the dressing room, and we are to be at supper in half an hour. Or something along those lines."

Jack dumped the pile of cloth on the bed, where the garments lolled in a decidedly wanton fashion. It looked like the aftermath of a scene of passion, a silk dress, buttons all undone, tangled with a pair of breeches; silk stockings tumbling, willy-nilly, over the side of the bed; garters flung any which way.

Jane glanced guiltily over her shoulder. It hadn't been like that with Nicolas. There had been no rending of bodices or flinging of garters. Her undressing had been executed as carefully as any lady's maid could desire.

Did that lessen the sin, if there were no corresponding creases in one's chemise?

Hiding her blushes, Jane leaned down and lifted what looked like—and, indeed, appeared to be—a pair of purple plum knee breeches banded in silver and gilt at the knee.

"I believe these are for you," she said, attempting to match Jack's dry tone, as though she handed a man his most intimate garments every day.

Jack took a step back, his brows beetling. Jane was surprised he didn't make the sign against the evil eye. "They can't expect me to wear this."

"Don't forget the jacket." It was plum velvet, thirty years out-of-date, edged with tarnished gilt embroidery tortured into fanciful swirls and rosettes. Some grandee of a previous generation had left his court clothes behind. Either that or the abbot had exhumed a premonastic costume of his youth.

Jack looked deeply horrified. "You must be joking."

"I might be, but I don't believe the abbot is." Since Jack appeared to be frozen with a raw fear that neither death nor danger had previously induced, Jane draped the garments over the screen in the corner on his behalf, adding to them a heavily embroidered white silk waistcoat and a pair of silk stockings, only lightly munched by moths. "Here. Put these on. You can't sit at the prior's table in all your mud."

"It might be mud, but at least it's not purple," retorted Jack, but he retreated behind the screen all the same.

"Consider it imperial," replied Jane, and felt a pang of longing for her old chaperone, Miss Gwen, and her fearsome purple parasol. For Miss Gwen, imperial and imperious were generally one and the same.

Only she wasn't Miss Gwen anymore. She was Mrs. Colonel William Reid.

Jane glanced at the screen behind which various bumpings and mumblings could be heard. It had seemed so sensible, back in Lisbon, to avoid the entire tangle of admitting she knew Jack's family. Jack's relationship with his father was, by the latter's own admission, fraught. Jack was more likely to comply with orders if he thought of Jane as an arm of Wickham, an agent, impersonal.

And Jane had wanted the armor that came of being the Carnation and only the Carnation. To tell him about Colonel Reid and Miss Gwen, of her sister Agnes's friendship with Lizzy, of her little goddaughter, Plumeria, all the tangled ties that bound her to his family, struck too close to the heart of her, to whatever there still was that was Jane rather than the Carnation.

That, of course, was before she kissed him by the roadside.

Grimacing at herself, Jane snatched the remaining garments off the bed and retreated to the dressing room.

The dress was, mercifully, not of the same vintage as Jack's borrowed ensemble. Good. It was very difficult to creep stealthily in three-foot-wide panniers. The dress was several years out-of-date and musty, but it was of silk, with slippers to match. The rich fabric had been heavily embroidered by someone with a taste for lopsided carnations. Pink carnations.

Chance, Jane told herself, untying her heavy wool skirt and letting it drop to the floor. The carnation was a popular flower in Portugal.

The dress had been made for a smaller woman. The bodice squeezed in a way that would, Jane thought wryly, look very fashionable in Paris. But beggars couldn't be choosers. Loosening her hair from her braid, she twisted it into a knot at the back of her head, using some of the water from the basin to dampen the ends into curls around her face.

The curls wouldn't curl. Giving it up as a bad job, Jane tied her locket around her throat, and, suitably armored, went forth into the bedroom and promptly tripped over her too-small silk slippers.

There was a grandee waiting for her, a grandee in a purple plum velvet coat, his brown hair brushed into a queue, his arms folded across his chest. The light of the candles glittered off silver and gold embroidery.

There ought, thought Jane, to have been orders on the man's chest and a sword by his side. This was a man who could sweep through the halls of St. James, who threw down a winning hand of cards without a second thought, who danced with duchesses and sneezed at dukes.

"I look like I'm impersonating an aubergine," said Jack, tugging irritably at the fall of lace at his throat.

"No," said Jane, going without thinking to shake out the lace and settle it back in its proper place. "You don't."

She glanced up, and saw that he was looking down. And down. Jane froze for a moment, her hand against Jack's chest, the embroidery scratchy against her palm. There had been no gloves with her dress, and no fichu.

Jane could feel a flush rising in her chest. She took a hasty step back, resisting the urge to tug at her bodice. She had worn lower décolletage at the Tuileries, without a hint of embarrassment. And used it, too, to her own advantage.

"Are we— Shall we go down to supper?"

Jack made a leg, an elegant, old-fashioned bow that wouldn't have been out in place in Versailles. Instinctively, Jane sank into the matching curtsy, feeling dimly as though she had been presented with a changeling.

"Where did you learn that?" she asked, trying desperately

to bring this man back to the Jack she had known on the road, the workaday Jack in his battered hat and shapeless jacket. "At your boarding school?"

Jack glanced at her from hooded eyes. "No. My father."

Now was the time to introduce the topic of Colonel Reid. But Jane's tongue seized on the words. "He must be . . . he must be very charming."

"He is." Jack held out an arm, lace ruffles dripping from his sleeve. His hands looked oddly bare. He ought to have rings: great rubies set in gold, curiously carved cameos, massive signets. "Shall we to dinner . . . darling?"

Chapter Fourteen

A different lay brother appeared to escort them to the dining hall.

They had undoubtedly scared off poor Brother Pedro, thought Jack grimly, shaking back the fall of lace that was tickling the back of his fingers. The lace he could do something about. Jane's ungloved fingers on his arm, her bosom pushed to proximity just beneath his nose—those were another matter. Jack could feel sweat gathering in the small of his back, beneath the heavy velvet.

Bloody court clothes. There was no way he was creeping the corridors in these. Anyone could see that silver-gilt embroidery a mile off, not to mention that it weighed more than the bloody donkey.

If Jane had only waited five minutes, they might have hammered out another plan, thought Jack irritably. She glanced up at him, all innocence in the candlelight, and Jack smiled back with his teeth, the sort of smile a fortune-hunter might give his prey.

Since that was the role she had assigned him.

"I feel like a trained monkey," he muttered. "All I need is a cap with a feather."

"That wouldn't go with the ensemble at all." They paused as the lay brother rapped at a door. Jane looked up at Jack, and there was something in her eyes that Jack couldn't quite read. "I think you look . . ."

She paused, searching for the right word.

"Yes?" Jack prompted, hating how much it mattered to him.

The door opened before Jane could complete her thought.

"Welcome, welcome." The abbot moved forward with the practiced grace of a politician, ushering them into a small dining parlor. Small, that was, by the standards of the monastery. It would have made four of the hut they had stayed in the night before. "I trust you found the accommodations to your liking?"

"We are not to dine in the refectory?" Jack drawled, casting an "I told you so" look at Jane.

Jane blinked dewily at the abbot. "I had so hoped to see the workings of an establishment such as yours, sir. I had heard that the refectory is so very impressive."

"Perhaps tomorrow," said the abbot. "Tonight is one of our

great feasts. I had thought you might be more comfortable with your fellow travelers."

"In other words," muttered Jack in Jane's ear, "contain the heretics."

In his absurd clothes, he had been belled as surely as any leper. As Alarico, he might have mingled with the servants, questioned them, perhaps even slipped into the refectory in the guise of a lay brother in a borrowed robe. If the Queen was, indeed, at the monastery, the abbot had very effectively closed off any chance travelers who might not be so chance.

The abbot led them to the table, too long for a mere four place settings. "You are only four at table this evening." He looked pointedly at Jack and Jane. "Most remain home with their families at this season."

"We had so hoped to be in Porto with my father for Christmas," murmured Jane, dabbing at her eyes with a scrap of lace. "Christmas isn't Christmas without family."

Jack glanced sharply at her, feeling a pang of guilt. That last hadn't been altogether fiction. He had, in his annoyance over purple velvet, neatly managed to shove aside the root of his discomfort.

It was the being declared dead that I found so distressing. . . . There's a little stone to me in the churchyard in Lower Wooley's Town.

Not my fault, Jack told his conscience, but his conscience wasn't having it. His conscience didn't like him terribly much right now. He didn't like himself terribly much right now.

And the plum velvet wasn't helping.

Jack shook back his ruffles and tried to look sufficiently jaded as the abbot led them to the table, where two men occupied a space designed for at least ten. One was tall and spare, garbed in a deep-burgundy coat that contrasted with his fantastically embroidered silk waistcoat. Next to him, Jack's plum velvet seemed positively restrained. The man's hair was white, a particularly luxuriant white, worn long in a way that evoked philosophers of old, or Prospero, alone in his island kingdom with his book and his staff.

It was, Jack thought, a very deliberate effect. The man's appearance was as carefully choreographed as a production of the royal opera in Lisbon.

Seated across from the taller man was a little mouse of a man in shades of rusty black: rusty black coat, rusty black hair, rusty black eyes. Jack half expected him to start gnawing on a crust with a pair of long front teeth.

He didn't. But he did regard Jack and Jane with beetled brows that might have benefited from a bit of a brush and a trim.

"We have only two other travelers with us this evening," said the abbot, hurrying the introductions along with the air of one determined to see to the niceties under trying circumstances. "Senhor and Senhora Fluellen, may I present to you the Marquis de la Mare"—the taller man rose, bowing gravely—"and Mr. Samson, who has recently come from inspecting a glass manufactory in which he has an interest. Monsieur de la

Mare has been with us for a week. Mr. Samson"—a faint expression of pain crossed the abbot's face—"arrived yesterday. He has been delayed by damage to his conveyance."

"And a terrible journey it was, too! Terrible! Terrible!" Mr. Samson's eyebrows quivered. "The roads—disgraceful! And then to be stranded *here*—"

The abbot's lips tightened. "I assure you, Mr. Samson, my men are fixing the matter as rapidly as possible." Before the man could launch into continued complaints, the abbot added, "I am afraid I must leave you. If there is anything you require, do not hesitate to ask."

One monarch, presumed missing? Jack held out a chair for Jane, doing his best not to twitch with impatience. Shut into this room, with these two, his chances for reconnoitering were slim.

It would have to wait until after supper. Being heretics, they would presumably be excused from the midnight mass. There was that, at least, thought Jack reluctantly. Had he remained Alarico, he wouldn't have had the opportunity to prowl the grounds while everyone else was at their devotions.

He took his seat across from Jane as she said to de la Mare, with the most delicate suggestion of alarm, "You are French, sir? I had not been aware that the French had come so far north as this."

The marquis smiled benevolently at her. Or, rather, at her décolletage, where her gold locket dangled enticingly in the valley between her breasts. "You have nothing to fear from me,

Madame Fluellen. I have been away from France longer than Bonaparte has been in it. I am a student of the world."

And, apparently, of female anatomy.

"I have never before seen an establishment of this size," said Jane, looking up at de la Mare beneath her lashes. "Even the palace of St. James cannot compare."

The marquis poured rich red wine into Jane's goblet. "It has been said of Alcobaça that its cloisters are cities, its sacristy a church, and its church a basilica."

In other words, a perfect place to conceal a missing monarch and her entourage. Jack's eyes met Jane's across the table.

She lifted her goblet, turning the stem about in her fingers. "*Do* tell me more, Monsieur le Marquis."

If the man was really a marquis, then Jack was the Prince of Wales.

"The origins of the monastery stretch back into history. . . ." The so-called marquis prosed on about mystical chalices and wonder-working saints and the endowment of this or that monarch.

Jack caught only bits of it. Mr. Samson, taking advantage of his own captive audience, was holding forth on the manufacturing of glass, the laziness of the local population, and those terrible thieves of customs inspectors in England, none of which impeded his shoveling course after course of rich food into his surprisingly spare frame.

Across the table, candlelight glimmered off the silk of Jane's dress, casting interesting shadows across her face, highlighting the hollows beneath her cheekbones, the deep valley between her breasts. It was almost impossible to recognize in the poised lady across from him the woman with whom he had traveled on the road, her hair in a braid and soot on her cheek. But then there would be the tilt of her chin, the quirk of a brow, and there she was, like a smile glimpsed from behind a veil, all the more tantalizing for being only partly seen.

Illogically, Jack wished the road had gone on longer, that Alcobaça had been farther away.

If the Queen was at the monastery, then their association was almost finished. They would have to get the Queen to the coast, to the rendezvous—and then?

Jack thrust a forkload of food into his mouth, although he couldn't have said, with any assurance, what he was eating.

"... locked." Jack forced his attention back to the marquis, who appeared to have abandoned fairy tales about miracle-working monarchs and returned, at long last, to the present. "Water damage, they say."

"Water damage?" Jack swallowed a mouthful of rice flavored with spices and mixed with seafood. "To what?"

"The hall of the novices." Jane narrowed her eyes at him, but her voice remained dulcet. "Monsieur de la Mare was just telling me about their lovely art collection. I do so hope it hasn't been hurt by the wet, don't you? A Titian is a terrible thing to waste."

"It is, indeed, a terrible thing to lock away from the world," agreed de la Mare gravely. "His mastery of the tones of the flesh . . ."

Jack cleared his throat. Emphatically.

Monsieur de la Mare raised his eyes from Jane's throat in a leisurely fashion and gave a very Gallic shrug. "I had hoped to be granted admission, but alas. They have it locked tighter than the lips of a virtuous woman."

"It is very odd that you should say so, Monsieur de la Mare." Jane affected a puzzled expression. "Most of the virtuous women of my acquaintance never cease speaking. Lecture, lecture, lecture, that's all they do. I have two aunts who are both terribly worthy and neither ever stops to take breath."

The marquis lifted a brow to Jack, man-to-man. "Perhaps it is that they have nothing better to do with their lips?"

Jack didn't want to think what Jane might be doing with hers. Or, rather, with his.

"The novices," he said, pulling his brain back up from his breeches. "What of them?"

De la Mare waved a dismissive hand. He wore, Jack noticed, three rings, one enameled with the figure of a skull, another incised with strange symbols. The third looked like a signet, but Jack had seen enough trick rings to be able to tell when a neatly hidden hinge masked a secret compartment. "There is, as you can see, no dearth of beds in the monastery. They have been housed elsewhere until the roof may be repaired."

"How terribly inconvenient for them," said Jane.

"Living in the lap of luxury . . . ," Mr. Samson interrupted his steady consumption of Christmas supper to sputter through a mouthful of excellently baked cod. "I don't know how you can stomach it. Hooded robes, wonder-working saints—it's enough to make a man sick!"

"And yet, *mon ami*," said de la Mare lazily, directing his gaze to the empty platters surrounding Mr. Samson, "you seem to have stomached a great deal."

"Wonder-working saints?" Jack interjected quickly, before Samson could retort. "Do they have those hereabouts?"

Samson snorted. "I had the ill fortune to pass one on the road here. Wonder-working, my knee! The only wonder was how quickly they forced us into the ditch. Took my muleteer a full hour to dig us out again. An hour, sir!"

"What is an hour?"

"Time is money," said Samson testily. "Not that I would expect you to understand, Mr. Dellymeer."

De la Mare waved a dismissive hand. "Not being entirely occupied with getting and spending, my mind has room to entertain larger possibilities than, for example, the price of glass."

Their sniping was almost a little too well choreographed. A broken carriage might be easily arranged. And such seeming rivalry could conceal a very effective partnership.

Jack rescued a lace ruffle before it dipped into the green sauce on his cod. He wasn't reconciled to the plum velvet, but he was willing to admit that Jane's change of plan might have had its merits.

Including, but not limited to, the décolletage on that dress.

"Glass . . . I do miss my looking glass," mused Jane, effectively ending the argument before it could begin. "*Such* a favorite. It broke on the road. Do you believe, Marquis, that I shall have seven years' bad luck?"

De la Mare sketched a courtly gesture. "The bad luck is the mirror's, for losing its power to gaze on that fair face." To Jack, he said, "If I were thirty years younger, *mon ami* . . ."

"You would be back at Versailles," riposted Jack. He raised his glass to the other man. "Presumably."

If the man had ever seen Versailles, he was Louis XVI.

On second thought, make that Louis XIV. Decapitation had never been among Jack's career goals.

The marquis raised his own glass in a barely perceptible toast. "We are, I think, both men of the world." The white brows lifted. "But there is more than one way to make one's fortune."

"There is also," said Jack, "more than one way to lose it. Do you play at cards, monsieur?"

"Frequently—but not on the night of our blessed Savior's birth. Some other time, perhaps." De la Mare rose from his chair with an ease at odds with the white of his hair. "I hear the bells calling me to mass."

"Papists," sniffed Samson. "I'm to bed."

"Bed," drawled Jack. "What an excellent idea. My dear?"

If he sounded possessive, well, that was part of the role, he told himself. That was his story and he was sticking to it, no matter how amused Monsieur de la Mare looked.

"Ah, to be young again," said de la Mare, smiling benevolently upon Jack and Jane in a way that made Jack want to use his head as a nutcracker. "To be made immortal with a kiss. Until tomorrow, my friends."

Bowing, he exited in the direction of the church. Mr. Samson, muttering his own good-nights, went the other way, in the direction of the guest rooms.

Which proved, thought Jack, keeping an arm looped lightly around Jane's waist, absolutely nothing.

Other than the fact that Jane fit very nicely into the curve of his arm.

"It didn't work very well for Dr. Faustus," murmured Jane, stepping away. "But then, they never do learn, do they?"

Jack blinked at her. "What are you talking about?"

"The quotation. It was from Marlowe's *Doctor Faustus*. 'Sweet Helen! Make me immortal with a kiss—'"

"'Her lips suck forth my soul; see where it flies!'" Jack finished the quotation for her and wished he hadn't. He shoved his hands in his pockets, where they wouldn't be tempted to reach for her. "I knew that. I'm not entirely illiterate."

Jane looked quizzically at him. "I never thought you were."

He was behaving like an ass. In purple velvet. "Despite my low origins?"

"Your origins aren't low. In fact—" Jane broke off, evidently thinking better of whatever it was she was about to say.

Somehow, that hurt worse than any of the names flung at him by the boys at school. That she would begin to defend him—and decide she couldn't.

"I'm illegitimate, princess." The sooner she remembered that, the better. "And a half-caste."

Jane's eyes were silver in the candlelight. "You are what you choose to be. It's not the circumstances of your birth that matter; it's what you make of them."

It sounded like a quotation. "That's not Marlowe."

"No." She turned on her heel and Jack realized that, beneath her cool facade, she was as angry as he was. "It's a paraphrase of something a wise man told me earlier today." She looked back at him over her shoulder, every word a challenge. "Unless you didn't really mean it?"

She had him tied in a rhetorical knot. "The circumstances aren't entirely the same," Jack protested.

"No." In her white silk, she looked like an avenging angel, minus the flaming sword. "My actions were of my own doing; your situation was determined before you were born. Which of us is more to blame?"

Jack suspected that was a trick question. In fact, he was quite sure that was a trick question.

"I'm not going to win either way I answer this, am I?" he said.

Jane pressed her eyes very tightly shut. "Is that all you can say?"

"I'll take that as a no, then?" said Jack.

Jane muttered something that he didn't quite catch. The word "mule" appeared to be involved. Somehow he didn't think she was talking about Buttercup.

"If de la Mare is to be believed," said Jane crisply, taking off across the room with rapid strides, "something is secured in the chamber of the novices."

"Most likely the novices." Jack had to hurry to catch up with her. "I'm more interested in what Mr. Samson said about the party that passed him on the road."

Jane slowed slightly, just enough to give him time to open the door for her. "You believe our bird has flown?"

Birds. Always birds. Jack rolled his eyes at a stretch of elaborately painted ceiling. "You've been working for Wickham too long."

Jane glanced at him sharply. "Why do you say that?"

They were both as jumpy as . . . extremely jumpy things. Jack gave up. He paused at the base of the stair leading up to their rooms. "I meant no disrespect to our esteemed employer. The man has an alarming propensity for avian metaphors. If I have to hear about one more eagle landing . . ."

The corner of Jane's mouth twisted reluctantly. "Not terribly imaginative, is it? But more impressive, I suppose, than 'the hedgehog has molted.'"

"Do hedgehogs molt?"

"I haven't the foggiest." She looked up at him, her expression serious. "Will you come with me to the hall of the novices?"

Jack's instinctive protest died on his breath. It meant something that she was asking, not ordering. "It might be a trap, you know. A way to smoke us out."

Jack's instincts told him that anything de la Mare said

should be taken with enough salt to preserve a school of cod. There was something decidedly off about the man. Again, fish came to mind.

Jane frowned, tapping her fingers against the stair rail. "That smoke works both ways. If we're smoked, so is he." She glanced up at Jack, her expression carefully neutral. "And there are two of us."

There were any number of ways Jack could respond. He could shrug and say, *You're the one in charge.* Or the ever-popular *If that's what you want.* Disclaim responsibility, shove off any possible blame, keep himself free and clear of entanglements.

In short, take the easy way out. The same way he always did.

"Yes, there are," Jack said, and felt as though he had just crossed some impossible gorge, and slammed hard against the other side. Trying for sangfroid, he added, "But do you mind if we change first? That dress of yours, while fetching, is more than a little bit conspicuous."

"We're in a monastery," said Jane, smiling up at him in a way that made Jack's chest swell just a little. "We should have no difficulty finding robes."

Except that they did.

"They couldn't be Dominicans?" Jack grumbled.

The trouble with the Cistercians was that they wore white. Difficult to keep clean. Even more difficult for creeping around late at night.

There was a brief but spirited debate as to whether two

people skulking in dark cloaks were more or less conspicuous than two novices in white robes attempting to get back into their rooms. A novice might not stand out in a field of novices, but one certainly would in a dark corridor, particularly as all good novices were meant to be at mass, celebrating the miracle of Christ's birth, not wandering up forbidden stairways into locked rooms.

In the end they went with the cloaks, which also had the benefit of being both there and theirs.

Jane, who appeared to have gotten rather detailed directions out of de la Mare, led the way. She moved silently down corridors and up stairs, noiseless in her soft slippers, blending effortlessly into the shadows. The halls through which they passed were abandoned, the inhabitants all being occupied with the Christmas mass. Another might have grown careless, might have relaxed her efforts.

But not Jane.

She was really, Jack had to admit, quite good at what she did. It was like watching a prima donna go through scales: a level of virtuosity so extreme that it gave the impression of being effortless.

The hall of the novices was located up several flights of stairs, in a suitably secluded location. Presumably, Jack supposed, so the novices wouldn't be tempted to sin. Either that, or to protect that art collection about which de la Mare had waxed so lyrical.

There was also a rather large lock on the door.

Without losing a moment, Jane dropped to her knees, setting her candle down beside her and drawing a leather case from her pocket. The case contained several pieces of metal, all linked by a bar at the top.

Jack shielded his candle with one hand. "You have a lock pick?"

A quick twist and a click. "Don't you?"

His wasn't nearly as elegant. She had the deluxe set of twelve picks; his contained only four. "Well, yes. But . . ."

"I can also hit a target three times out of four, sketch a pretty scene, and cover a cushion in *petit point*." Jane rose to her feet, opening the door with one smooth motion. "Shall we?"

Jack followed. There was really nothing else to do—other than apologize, and he wasn't entirely sure he knew how.

"Is there anything you can't do?"

"Name a donkey." Jane held up her candle, illuminating the room. The light glimmered off rich tones of red and blue, including a lush woman wearing a great deal of hair and very little clothing. "I think we've found de la Mare's art collection."

"And his Titian." Jack moved his candle a little closer to the painting. The warm light moved across the woman's skin like a lover's touch, bringing a flush to cheeks and breast.

It was, he supposed, a Magdalene, although her rapture didn't look entirely religious. Her lips were lightly parted, her head tilted back expectantly. Her hair, unbound, snaked down her back and around her breasts. Light brown hair, tinted golden in the candlelight . . .

The Magdalene's hair was a riot of curls, but Jack found he was imagining straight hair instead, fine, straight hair, released from its braid, fanned out across the red brocade coverlet of the bed downstairs.

"I don't think that's really a Titian," said Jane, regarding the painting critically. "Although the flesh tones are very fine."

"Yes," Jack managed. "Very fine."

He walked rapidly to the other side of the room, where a very understanding Madonna nursed her infant and regarded him kindly. A heavily embellished golden cup, studded with precious stones, stood on a table covered with a cloth embroidered in yet more gold.

Jack tilted his head to look up at the ceiling. "I don't see any signs of water damage. Do you?"

"Not in here. But we haven't examined the cells." Raising the candle, Jane indicated a row of doors.

Tentatively, she pushed open one of the doors. The room was a narrow rectangle with a cot, a crucifix on the wall, and a window that was nothing more than a slit in the stone, set well up by the ceiling, where it could provide a certain minimum of light, but no distraction.

She looked back over her shoulder at Jack, raising a brow. "Locked doors within a locked door. No windows."

Jack looked back the way they had come. "Up several flights of stairs, well isolated."

Jane rapped her knuckles against the whitewashed wall. "Thick walls."

Jack voiced what they were both thinking. "The perfect place to hide a missing queen." There was just one problem. "If they were here, they're not here now."

There were shades to silence. Jack knew them all. There was the waiting silence of the pursued: frozen, barely breathing. And then there was real silence, the silence of emptiness. There was no hastily hushed scuffle, no abbreviated sneeze. Their whispers echoed off bare walls and empty rooms. The complex was deserted.

"But they left quickly." Jane was peering into yet another room. A blanket lay rumpled on the cot, the weave far too fine to belong to one of the novices. "Someone slept here, and recently."

Jack paused on the threshold of another room and let out a low whistle. "Someone did more than sleep here."

"What do you . . . Oh." Jane stopped short, pressed against Jack's side in the narrow doorway.

The cell was a disaster. Shards of porcelain littered the floor. A piece of paper had been trampled where it fell. A woman's lace veil lay forgotten, crumpled in a corner.

"The Queen is known for her violent rages." Jack gave a short laugh. "And we're trying to put her back on her throne, God help us."

Jane squeezed past him into the cell, stepping carefully around the larger bits of debris. She had to right a table before she could set her candle down on it. "We're trying to keep Bonaparte off it. That's not at all the same thing."

Jack shrugged. "One monarch is much the same as another."

"Don't say that." Jane turned sharply, porcelain crunching beneath her heel. "You sound like Nic—"

She didn't need to complete the name. The way her lips snapped together told Jack more than enough.

Her former lover. The Gardener. In the air like a ghost between them.

"Did you love him?" Jack hadn't meant to say it. The words just came out, hard and fast, like bullets.

Jane turned away, making a pretense of examining a glove left crumpled on the cot. Her hand trembled slightly as she lifted the leather. At last she said, "Would it justify my actions if I said I did? Or make my fall worse if I said I didn't?"

"I never thought of you as fallen." If he could have taken back his words, he would. He didn't want to know the answer. Particularly if it was yes. Gruffly, he said, "Never mind. I had no right to ask."

"No," said Jane distantly, and Jack thought she was agreeing with him that no, it was none of his concern, until she added in the same detached voice, "I didn't love him. I'm not quite sure what that makes me—but no. I didn't love him."

"It makes you a woman of sense." Jack felt light-headed with relief. Relief for what, he wasn't quite sure. "Not to be taken in by that snake."

Jane shook her head ever so slightly. Her face was averted; all Jack could see was the curve of cheek and chin. "I had thought, for a time, that I might. . . . He was clever and fascinating and so very sure of himself. So very sure of me."

All the things Jack wasn't. Some of his euphoria faded. "Why not, then?"

Jane's voice was low. "Because I knew him. I knew the manner of man he was—is." She looked helplessly at Jack, deep hollows beneath her eyes, old lines at the corners of her lips. "How can there be love where there is no trust?"

Jack was put in the very odd position of simultaneously wanting to punch the Gardener for being such an unworthy human being—and wanting to thank him for being such an unworthy human being.

"You can trust him to take care of himself," Jack said dryly.

It occurred to Jack, as he said it, that the same might be said about him. It was not a very flattering reflection.

Jane looked at him for a long moment. "Nicolas," she said, "might have acquired a donkey. But he would have ridden it himself."

The only sound in the room was the singing of a nightingale somewhere through that slim, high window.

And then, from the other side of the corridor, the scrape of metal in a lock.

Chapter Fifteen

They both acted instantly, without words. Jane snuffed the candle, plunging the room into total darkness. Jack drew the door closed, leaving it open the merest sliver.

Taking care to avoid the telltale crunch of broken crockery, Jane crept forward until she was kneeling beside him. She felt Jack's arm come around her, drawing her against his side. If he'd had a pistol, he would have leveled it at the crack in the door. Since he didn't, he did what he could do: he angled his body, using it as a shield between Jane and whatever lay outside.

It was an odd sensation, being protected. Jane might have been offended, but for the fact that the movement was so automatic.

The darkness was total, intensifying other sensations. The

warmth of Jack's skin beneath the fine fabric of his borrowed shirt. The faint scent of peat that still clung to his hair, the tinge of port on his breath that Jane could feel more than hear him breathe, her own chest moving in tandem with his. She had wound up, somehow, on her knees, with a hand pressed against his chest, another on his shoulder, frozen in tableau as they waited to see whether the sound would come again.

For a moment, nothing. Nothing but Jack's heart beating beneath her fingers, his arm curled around her waist.

And then it began again, the creak of careful footsteps. Jane tensed in Jack's arms, mentally cataloging the possibilities. She could tell, from Jack's waiting stillness, that he was doing the same. That table, the one on which she had placed the candle. It was small enough and sturdy enough to use as a weapon. The walker in shadows had them penned, but they had the advantage of a half-closed door.

And there were two of them.

Of course, at the moment only one of them could see what was going on. Jane leaned forward just a little, trying to get a glimpse through the opening in the door. Her body pressed full against Jack's, and she felt his quickly contained, restless movement before one hand clamped down on her waist, and another found her mouth, pressing a finger against it in the universal gesture for silence.

Jane tried to banish the erotic thoughts the pressure of his finger against her lips conjured, images of nipping, licking, biting.

She blinked rapidly, and recalled her attention to the matter at hand. Not Jack's hand, she hastily amended. They were penned like rabbits in a snare; one would think she could make herself concentrate just a little bit more effectively instead of behaving like a debutante meeting her first rake.

She had never once allowed Nicolas to impede her concentration.

And what that said about her, or Nicolas, was another matter entirely. *You let your head rule your heart*, he had chided her. He hadn't been amused when she had taken it as a compliment.

I don't know whether it's that you're English . . . Nicolas had been on the bed, stretched out against the crimson brocade.

Or? Jane was in her dressing gown, her hair unbound down her back, frowning over a letter. Nicolas had wanted her to come to bed, but there was work to be done.

Or just incapable of true passion.

It had been designed to sting; Jane knew that. To sting and to goad, to force her to prove him wrong.

Mmm, she had said, feigning abstraction, the one thing guaranteed to deflect his carefully crafted barbs. *Go to sleep. I'll be along presently.*

She had won that round, but his words had stung all the same. She had heard them before, from others—from her cousin Amy, who had considered all well lost for love, and didn't in the least understand why Jane shouldn't do the same; from her chaperone, who sniffed, and said such self-containment wasn't natural, and, mark her words, one day she was going to fall and fall hard. The fact that a chaperone was meant to be discouraging rather than encouraging such behavior fell on deaf ears; Miss Gwen was interested in trouble, not propriety.

And then Miss Gwen, too, had counted the world well lost for love.

There goes all the world but I, and I am sunburnt.

She wasn't sunburnt. She was frostbitten. Cold through and through. An ice maiden, one of her swains in Paris had called her admiringly.

She wasn't feeling terribly icy at the moment. She was painfully aware of her own body in a way she had never been before, as if a limb, previously asleep, had been woken to pins and needles. Her nipples pebbled against the bodice of her gown where her chest pressed against Jack's, every breath, every movement rendering the sensation more acute.

She could feel the prickle of hair through the fabric of her shirt against her palm, and couldn't stop herself from wondering what it would be like to slide her hand up beneath that shirt.

The footsteps were closer now, the light brighter. There was the sound of something clanking, metal against stone, and with that clink Jane's brain cleared.

She was fairly sure she knew who was there. And why.

De la Mare? Jane mouthed against Jack's finger, and felt his chin against the top of her head as he nodded.

Moving very, very carefully, he shifted a little bit to the right, making room for Jane in front of the crack in the door. Jane's lips felt swollen where he had touched; she licked them, trying to recall her mind to her work. De la Mare. If she wasn't mistaken . . . She eased cautiously into the space Jack had vacated.

"Vacated" was too strong a word. He had moved as far as he could, his back against the wall, one leg pulled up, the other stretched out to the side. Concentrating on de la Mare, Jane moved into the space between Jack's legs, setting her eye to the crack in the door.

He had the chalice. The cabochon-cut jewels glimmered sullenly in the light of de la Mare's lantern. But it wasn't the jewels that seemed to interest de la Mare.

Jane leaned forward, and felt Jack shift uncomfortably behind her.

Taking a thin piece of paper and a stick of charcoal, de la Mare placed the paper against the side of the cup and began briskly rubbing with the charcoal. He repeated the operation on the other side, the scratching of the charcoal unnaturally loud in the silent room.

With a nod of satisfaction, he folded the sheets, tucked them carefully into a leather wallet, and slipped the wallet beneath his jacket.

Was it her imagination, or did his eyes flick towards the row of cells?

Imagination, Jane told herself. Imagination and the glint of the lantern light. Hopefully.

She stayed where she was, pressed against Jack, feeling his breath warm against the back of her neck as de la Mare took an unconscionably long time examining the paintings in the chapel. It felt like an age that he stood in front of the Titian, examining the brushwork—at least, Jane decided to give him the benefit of the doubt and assume it was the brushwork— before he took himself and his lantern back through the door, plunging the room once more into darkness.

They were both too well trained to move immediately. It could be a trap. There was nothing to do but wait, feeling Jack's chest rise and fall behind her, his leg mirroring the curve of hers, his thigh hard against her own. Nothing to do but wait as the silence stretched on between them, broken only by the high, clear voice of a nightingale singing its own tale of love and loss.

The minutes stretched on, agonizing, endless.

"He's gone." Jack's voice sounded rusty and hoarse. He shifted awkwardly, but it was enough to send Jane scrambling off his lap. "What in the devil was that in aid of?"

"Not the devil." Her legs were cramped and she appeared to be tangled in her own skirts. "Calling him went out of fashion a century ago after all of those amateur diabolists got flung into one of Louis the Fourteenth's dungeons."

Jane put a hand down to lever herself up. It landed on something warm and hard that tensed when she touched it.

Jane snatched her hand away from Jack's thigh. "You haven't a flint, have you? It's rather dark."

Jack's voice sounded rather strangled. "No." He helped her up by the simple expedient of wrapping both hands around her waist and lifting. "What have diabolists to do with anything?"

"They haven't." Jane felt unaccountably muddled. She blamed it on the darkness. She wasn't used to such complete darkness. In Paris there was always the low glow of the street-lamps, the haze of coal smoke turning the sky purple and or-ange. "You're quite sure you haven't a flint?"

"That," said Jack through gritted teeth, "was not a flint."

If she couldn't see, it meant that Jack couldn't see either, which meant he couldn't see the color staining her cheeks.

"De la Mare was after the cup," Jane said rapidly. "Weren't you listening at dinner? He was waxing lyrical about a mysti-cal chalice in the monastery's collection. Apparently it has words from the kabbalah graven around the base."

Jack was feeling his way along the wall; Jane could see him only as a slightly darker shadow. "It all sounded like so much gibberish to me. Nothing but a passel of— Ow."

"What was that?"

"My foot. At least, it used to be." Jane followed the sound of hopping. "Mind the wall. It kicks back."

"You walked into the wall?" For a man who had navigated treacherous ravines on a moonlit night, Jack was being unusu-ally clumsy.

"It's dark!" As if realizing how foolish he sounded, Jack lowered his voice. "Sorry. It's been a long night. I don't like de la Mare showing up like that. It's too pat to be coincidence."

Ordinarily Jane might have agreed, but she had a different theory. "I don't think we have anything to fear from Monsieur de la Mare. His eye is on the philosopher's stone, not a lost queen. He's an alchemist."

"In this day and age?" Jack successfully located the door, wrenching it open. Torchlight, blessed torchlight, filtered dimly up from the lower reaches of the stairs.

"Sir Isaac Newton believed, and not so long ago." Everything seemed subtly distorted and out of proportion. Jane blinked, trying to help her eyes readjust themselves. "You must have seen stranger things in your travels."

Jack preceded her down the stairs, keeping a practiced eye out for would-be assailants. "'There are more things in heaven and earth, Horatio'?"

Jane wrinkled her nose at his back. "I'm not sure I would go that far. But just because I don't believe doesn't mean de la Mare doesn't. The power of belief can be as real as the thing itself."

"Or," suggested Jack, looking back over his shoulder, "it can provide a very good excuse for odd behavior."

He held out a hand to help her down the final step. Jane's ungloved fingers tingled where they touched his.

She hastily walked ahead, towards the guest wing. "Possibly. But if it is as you say, why is de la Mare still here if the Queen is gone?"

Jack caught up with her as one wing joined the next. "To set a snare for the Pink Carnation?"

"Subtle," said Jane with approbation. "But possibly a little too subtle."

Jack raised a brow. "Is it?"

He didn't invoke the Gardener's name. He didn't need to. They both knew what he meant.

Nicolas never chose the direct route when a twisty one would serve.

"I don't know," Jane said at last. "The scene in the cell might have been staged; de la Mare might have been set in place to drive us there. But it all seems terribly chancy. And to what end? If they were trying to herd us someplace, wouldn't there have been a note?"

"Badly coded?" Jack acknowledged her point, holding open the door of the bedroom. "'Your Majesty, your devoted subjects await only your presence'?"

"Something of that sort." A servant had lit a branch of candles on the writing table, and another on the table by the bed. Light shimmered across the silk brocade of the coverlet, glimmering an invitation. "I feel as though there's something we're missing, but I'm too tired to think what."

Jack flung himself down in the chair by the writing table, stretching his legs out in front of him. "In between telling me more than I ever wanted to know about the manufacturing of glass, Samson said that the wonder-working saint was making for Peniche. In some haste."

Jack tried and failed to smother a yawn, his head dropping back against the carved wooden back of the chair.

He looked so weary, thought Jane with a pang of tenderness. They were both tired, but it was Jack who had borne the brunt, who had taken the late watches, who had walked while she had ridden.

She wanted, so very badly, to cradle his head against her shoulder, to stroke his hair until the lines of worry and fatigue disappeared from around his eyes, to lean her cheek against the top of his head and close her eyes, and not think of anything at all.

Jack stirred in his chair, suppressing another yawn.

Come to bed, Jane almost said, but the words might be taken the wrong way.

"You are sure he said Peniche?" she said instead, perching primly on the end of the bed.

Jack opened his weary eyes, looking at her with bleary resignation. "He was very specific about all of his trials and tribulations. In excruciating detail."

Jane traced a pattern in the brocade with one finger. "General Thomières was assigned to garrison Peniche—but his orders were delayed." She should know. She had been the one who had removed them. She had had a particular interest in the disposition of that fortress. "There was previously a Portuguese garrison in place."

"Loyal to the Queen?" Jack had sunk so low in his chair he was practically perpendicular.

"Presumably." There was a pattern there, if only she could see it, something dancing just out of reach. "Our marines have taken the island of Berlengas, just off the coast of Peniche. That's where I was to deliver the Queen, once I located her."

Jack cracked open an eye. "Hence the loss of Thomières's orders? Nicely done."

Jane shook her head. "A delay of a few days, no more. He might have reached Peniche by now."

"But it's a close-run thing." Jack levered himself upright in the chair. "If time was of the essence . . . Do you think Wickham dispatched another agent?"

"It's not impossible." Wickham hadn't been entirely keen about contracting the mission to the Pink Carnation. And Jane couldn't blame him. She knew she wasn't best qualified. But there had been other considerations and other debts to be paid. And she hadn't realized then, in the relative comfort of Wickham's office in the Alien Office, just how ill qualified she was. "None of us is indispensable. Or it might not have been Wickham at all. There's also Admiral Sir Sidney Smith. He was the one who lost the Queen. He's better known for acts of daring than calm good judgment."

"You think he might have attempted to redeem his honor by coming back for her?"

"Abandoning the rest of the fleet to his second in command? Possibly."

Jane had never had much respect for Sir Sidney, who had made much of his romantic escape from the Temple prison several years back. As far as Jane was concerned, it wasn't the escape that counted; it was the fact that he had been caught in the first place. But that was Sir Sidney. Flashy. Showy. Careless of his life and those of others in the pursuit of yet another flattering engraving in the illustrated papers.

Yes, she could imagine Sir Sidney landing at Peniche, sending someone to summon the Queen, and walking right into the teeth of an incoming French garrison.

If the Queen was in Peniche. If this wasn't all an elaborate trap.

"What do you say, princess?" Jack's jaws cracked on a yawn. "Do we take the bait and make for Peniche?"

"I think," said Jane carefully, "that right now you make for bed."

"I've slept in worse than this chair."

"In a French dungeon?" The chair was angular and unyielding, and Jack was already beginning a slow slide towards the floor. "Come to bed. I promise not to seduce you."

A slow grin spread across Jack's sleepy face. "If you put it that way . . . what's the point?"

Jane yanked down the covers. "For heaven's sake. You're too tired to commit any improprieties."

"Is that a challenge?" said Jack, but he ruined it with yet another massive yawn. He plopped down on top of the coverlet, his head hitting the pillow with an audible thump. "A pillow. How decadent."

Jane leaned over his prone figure. "You might be even more decadent and try sleeping under the covers instead of over them."

"And run the risk of getting used to it?" He turned his head on the pillow, looking at Jane with a seriousness that was more disconcerting than any of his banter. "The covers are yours. Enjoy."

Was he trying to preserve her modesty? Given what he knew of her past, that was as noble as it was foolish.

Or, she realized, with a feeling like lead in her stomach, he might be trying to preserve his own.

Jane's cheeks flamed with sudden color. "Take your cloak, at least," she said abruptly, shaking it out over him.

It was silly to feel rejected. Jack had more sense than she. They were colleagues, partners. Anything else would only muddy the waters. And the waters, thought Jane with wry humor, were more than muddy enough already.

It was more comforting to think that than that he didn't desire her.

The problem had always been quite the opposite. She had never doubted she was beautiful, as society measured beauty. She had been told so again and again, in poetry and prose. She knew how to fend off advances, but when it came to encouraging them, she was remarkably inexperienced.

They had been on the road too long; that was all. She was tired and lonely—and if Jack had wanted to kiss her, he would have. She had certainly provided opportunity enough.

There was only one conclusion. He didn't want to. *Quod erat demonstrandum*.

There were times when it was deeply unpleasant having a

logical mind. One by one, Jane snuffed the candles until all the light that was left in the room was the subdued glow of the fire in the brazier.

As she navigated her way around the edge of the bed in the darkness, she heard Jack's voice rise sleepily from the depths. "There's a saying in Portuguese. *Amigos de Peniche.*"

Jane peeled back the coverlet. It felt like heaven sliding into a real bed, on a real mattress, beneath a real blanket. The weight of Jack's body tipped her towards him, her blanket and his cloak a barrier between them.

"What does it mean?"

She could feel Jack's exhalation of breath as he shifted, turning on his side, away from her. "False friends."

Chapter Sixteen

"Wakey, wakey, princess."

Jane blinked blearily up at him. "Is it morning?"

"Almost."

"Almost" by a rather broad margin. The sky was just beginning to turn from black to gray. The nightingale still sang the last ragged notes of his song.

Jack hadn't slept well. He found that particularly irritating, given that he prided himself on sleeping anywhere. But anywhere didn't usually include next to Jane, on a mattress that sagged. A blanket between them wasn't nearly barrier enough, not when Jack dozed, only to dream of lavender, and woke to the reality of Jane against him.

Jane had slept the sleep of the exhausted, her head pillowed on Jack's shoulder, her hair tickling his chin. One hand stretched out across Jack's chest. He had never seen her like that before, all her watchfulness dissolved in sleep, relaxed, trusting.

How can there be love where there is no trust?

It was exhaustion, Jack told himself bluntly. That was all. She was tired past endurance. And this was a real bed, not the makeshift pallet of the previous night.

But Jack had turned all the same, making a cradle for her of his arms. Rest, true rest, was rare in their line of work. It was seldom one could sleep deeply, secure in the knowledge that someone else was on watch. Especially someone like Jane, who took everything on herself.

She could be high-handed. Could be? Ha. She was. Autocratic, dictatorial, domineering. But never beyond reason. That, Jack realized, was what made all the difference. She might be accustomed to acting unilaterally, but she wasn't beyond explaining her reasoning, or, when it came to it, admitting when she might be in the wrong.

She would never fly into rages like his mother, never retreat someplace he couldn't reach her.

Where in the devil had that come from? Jack tried to push the thought aside, but once there, it didn't quite want to go away. Jack could remember slinking up to his mother, never sure if she was going to greet him with a kiss or a cuff. Or, on that final day, with a knife in her breast.

Did she die because I was bad? Jack had asked his nurse,

thinking of the broken clasp on a necklace, of singing too loudly when he had been told to be quiet, of half a dozen other minor infractions.

But she had only held him closer, humming to him.

His father, when cornered, had sighed, and said only, *She wasn't a happy woman, your mother.*

But all Jack had taken from that was that he might have made her happy—they both might have made her happy—and they had failed. Love was terrifying. It brought with it the uncertainty of trying to please another person, trying to understand another person, the mechanisms of whose mind were, by their very nature, opaque.

In the end, it just wasn't worth it.

But when he looked down at Jane's pale profile, serene in sleep, Jack felt some of that old fear leaching away. It was impossible to imagine Jane behaving in any way that wasn't fundamentally fair.

Stabbing oneself in front of one's three-year-old son wasn't fair.

She wasn't a happy woman. For the first time, Jack thought he understood some of what his father had meant. There were some so locked in their own minds that they couldn't get out.

And that hadn't been his fault, or his father's, or anybody else's. It just was.

Jane had stirred in her sleep, burying her head deeper into his chest, and Jack had felt an almost painful feeling of tenderness. In sleep, it seemed rather incredible that a collection of bones and flesh could contain all the things that made her Jane, the sharp mind, the wary humor, those flashes of vulnerability that made her achingly, endearingly human.

What was he going to do next, write sonnets? Jack hastily turned his back, yanking open the curtain. "Time to be back on the road. Our friends of last night are most likely what they seem, but if they're not—why make it easy for them?"

Jane regarded him blearily. She looked damnably appealing, warm and flushed from the layers of blankets, a crease on her cheek from the pillow, her hair escaping in wisps from last night's coiffeur. "We're leaving? Now?"

Jack couldn't blame her for sounding doubtful. The sky was charcoal gray and distinctly uninviting.

The bed, on the other hand . . .

"As soon as you can dress." Jack tossed a pair of breeches, a shirt, and a jacket on the coverlet. "I liberated these from the poor box. Don't worry—I left a donation in return."

"I wasn't. Worrying." Jane rubbed her fingers against her eyes, a gesture Jack found strangely endearing, so different from her usual polished poise. "I take it this means a change of role?"

"Anyone looking for us will be looking for a woman and a man," said Jack defensively, "not a man and a boy."

"I wasn't arguing." Jane wiggled off the side of the bed, her white satin gown tugging up to reveal a flash of ankle and calf. Jack turned aside as she stepped into the breeches, pulling them up beneath her skirt. "How far to Peniche?"

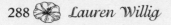

"Under good conditions? A day."

The wind rattled the casement window, followed by the ominous clatter of hard-driving rain. "In other words," said Jane, twisting to try to reach the buttons on the back of the dress's bodice, "two days."

Her contortions were doing very interesting things to the already tight bodice of the dress. Jack had to clear his throat before he could speak. "Do you need help with that?"

"These gowns were designed with a maid in mind," said Jane ruefully, and turned her back to him. The view from that angle was . . . well . . .

"I don't think it was a maid they had in mind," Jack muttered.

"What?" Jane turned her head slightly, her hair brushing the backs of his fingers.

"Nothing," Jack said quickly.

Jack backed up as the dress slid down over Jane's shoulders. There was just a fleeting flash of bare back as she yanked the rough cambric shirt over her head, but—

"I'll go see to Marigold," he said, and fled.

The weather was his ally. The rain was ice-cold, hard where it struck Jack's face. The winds had risen, making walking difficult and talking harder. There was no energy for anything but pushing against the elements as Jack, Jane, and their donkey struggled through the town and to the west.

From the other side of the donkey, Jane gasped something that sounded like "bath."

"What?" Jack shouted back.

Jane turned to look at him, the brim of her hat flapping around her face. "I should have had one while I had the chance."

Jack tugged his hat further down around his ears. "We're getting one now," he shouted back.

Jane wrinkled her nose at him, but didn't retort. She was too busy pushing against the wind, bent nearly double in her attempt to forge forward, her boots making squelching sounds as she dragged one, then the other, out of the mud.

Jack made a quick decision. "We'll take the main roads. They should be fairly deserted today."

Jane clutched the donkey's side, using it for balance. "Because of the weather?" The words came out as a gasp.

"Because it's Christmas morning."

She stumbled, catching herself just in time. "I'd forgot." Jack couldn't see her face, just her profile beneath the hat. "Everyone will be with their families."

A family she didn't have. Because of him.

"Those blisters aren't healed yet," Jack gruffly.

"Won't it look odd if I'm riding?" It had been one thing when she was posing as a peasant woman; dressed as a boy, she would be expected to bear her share of the load.

"To whom?" said Jack, and Jane had to admit he had a point. There was no one in either direction. Unless . . . No. That flash of black was a crow's wing, not someone lurking by the side of the road. She was fairly sure. "There's no point in your crippling yourself. We'll make better time if you ride."

He was lying, she knew, but it was a kind lie. Jane accepted Jack's hand as he helped boost her, again, onto the donkey's back.

"Thank you," she said.

And that was lie, too. She would rather walk. At least the pain in her heel, the struggle against the elements, provided a distraction. Clinging grimly to the donkey's back, the rain dripping down her face like tears, there was nothing to do but think.

Right now, back at home, they were probably walking from the house to the church in the village, Agnes squealing while Ned menaced her with mistletoe, her mother peering myopically back at them and murmuring something about not muddying her slippers, her father too busy reciting the reading to himself to notice.

There had been the year that Ned had decked the sheep, and her father had been so furious. And the year that Jane's cousin Amy had accidentally set fire to her frock poking at the Yule log. Miss Gwen in church, glowering through the gospels and singing louder than anyone else during the hymns.

But that wasn't now. Jane caught herself up short before she could tumble too far down that particular path. What was the word Jack had taught her the other day? *Saudade.* A kind of nostalgia. Nostalgia was, by its very nature, about something that no longer was.

It was a pleasant sort of pain to imagine that everything meandered on exactly as it had been, to jumble together a decade's worth of memories and paint them into the definitive picture of Life as It Had Been. But it was as much a fiction as any other fairy story. They weren't all there in Lower Wooley's Town. Amy was married and living in Sussex; the last Christmas that Jane had spent home in England hadn't been in Shropshire at all, but in Kent, at the principal seat of Amy's husband's parents, the Marquis and Marchioness of Uppington. There had been a spot of bother with spies getting into the mince pies, but Amy had dealt with the matter in her usual, inimitable fashion. In other words, with a great deal of difficulty with a side of French farce.

Everyone had scattered. Jane's older sister, Sophia, was long since married, with four children in Gloucestershire. Miss Gwen had her Colonel Reid and little Plumeria. The church in Lower Wooley's Town had been spared Miss Gwen's insistent descant for some time now.

The world moved on. When Jane had left for France all those years ago, the words "home" and "family" had had a very specific meaning; they were constants. But they weren't, not really. Homes changed; families changed. The house where she had been raised wasn't her home anymore, and hadn't been since early 1803. Jane wouldn't know what to do with herself there, any more than they would know what to do with her.

Was that better or worse? Jane didn't know.

What she did know was that she heard the sound of hoofbeats on the road behind them. Not the plodding footsteps of the mules usually employed to lead travelers down these roads, but a horse, moving rapidly.

She was off the donkey in an instant and at Jack's side, aching heels forgotten. "Someone—"

"On the road behind us." Jack finished for her. He was already urging the donkey off the road, onto the verge, into a scrum of fallen rock and low shrubs.

As a hiding place, it was distinctly inadequate, but to try to lead the donkey up the hill would render them even more conspicuous. Jane frowned at the road, saying urgently, "He'll see our tracks."

It wasn't the sort of thing she had ever had to worry about in Paris; there were too many people muddling about the streets for one set of footprints to stand out.

Jack hunkered down behind a shrub, one hand on the donkey's lead. "There's nothing for it." He glanced quickly at Jane. "If someone was following us, he'd be stealthier."

Jane wasn't reassured. "Unless his orders were to sweep in and shoot." To shoot Jack, that was.

It would be a brutal but effective strategy. Take them by surprise. Shoot Jack. Grab her.

"If so," said Jack grimly, extracting a pistol from his belt, "he's in for a surprise of his own."

He cocked his pistol, training it on the stretch of road ahead of them. Jane turned a wary eye to the slope on their other side. It would be a classic distraction: a lone rider on the road, while others slithered down the slope behind them.

The hoofbeats were louder now. The rider was almost

upon them. Jane glanced at Jack's profile, his face alert, his hands steady on the pistol.

There was no reason for the Gardener to come after them, she told herself. No real reason. His goal was the Queen.

The Pink Carnation would be a prize worth bearing back to Bonaparte. Jack had said it, and he was right.

She and the Gardener had a truce. Noninterference on neutral ground. But Jack's words gnawed at her all the same, making her jumpy, making her glance over her shoulder. How long would Nicolas maintain their truce if he decided it no longer suited him to keep it?

The horse's rapid hoofbeats slowed as the rider approached, falling from a canter to a trot, from a trot to a walk. He was nearly level with them now.

The horse slowed and stopped, and the rider swung down from the saddle.

Jane didn't need to hear Jack's quick, indrawn breath to know that he had recognized the rider, too. She didn't dare turn to look at Jack—couldn't do anything but wait, like a rabbit in the field as the dogs drew near.

Chapter Seventeen

*R*emoving his hat, Mr. Samson gave it an irritable shake, sending water skittering down the brim.

Samson was still dressed all in rusty black, from his old-fashioned hat to his many-caped cloak. He moved, however, like a far younger and sprier man than Jane had recalled him being. Or, that was, than he had given the impression of being.

Jane didn't dare look at Jack. Any movement might dislodge a pebble, or even worse, excite the donkey's attention. The last thing they needed was a betraying bray. Stillness, she had learned long ago, was her best weapon. Samson might look like he was alone, but if he was, in fact, an emissary of the Gardener, there might be men even now waiting to pounce, concealed among the rocks as Jack and Jane were concealed.

Samson's nose twitched. Reaching into his pocket, he removed . . .

A handkerchief.

Jane's throat was dry; it hurt to swallow. She watched as Samson removed the commodious handkerchief from his pocket, dabbing irritably at a patch of mud on his sleeve.

A pretense? Possibly. Her back ached with maintaining her position; her neck was stiff and her nose was beginning to itch.

Having completed his ablutions, Samson reached into his saddlebag and removed a map, turning it this way and that and muttering something to himself. It sounded like, "blasted uncivilized . . ."

Samson consulted his map. He partook of a dry biscuit, complaining to himself about the dryness of it. And then, creaky and cranky, he mounted his horse and trotted down along the road, in the direction of Peniche.

A small shower of pebbles sifted down to the road. The donkey, freeing itself from Jack's hold, was nosing along the ground, searching for a few strands of dry winter grass.

Slowly, Jack lowered his pistol, his eyes still trained on the road. "He seems to have gone."

"I don't like 'seems.'" Jane straightened, arching her aching back. She had evaded far worse in Paris, in London, and in Venice. She had slipped past assassins, waited out enemies, but she had never felt exposed there as she did here. "I thought Samson was traveling with a muleteer."

Jack slid his pistol back into his belt. "He seems the sort to dismiss minions."

Jane rubbed her sore neck with two fingers. "And then travel back in the direction he came?" All of their information about the religion procession moving towards Peniche came from Samson. A trap?

She jumped as Jack's hands closed around her shoulders, rubbing the sore muscles. "He couldn't very well move on towards Lisbon. Anyone would be able to tell him that the French are moving north. It would be logical to go back."

Jack's hands were warm and sure on the back of her neck. Jane's head dipped forward, allowing him better access as she tried to hold on to rational thought. "Towards Peniche?"

"Towards Porto," said Jack easily. "If you were Samson, wouldn't you go back to the heart of the English community? Or what's left of it?"

It was too hard to think with Jack's thumbs digging into her shoulder blades, turning her muscles to mush.

Twisting away, Jane put a safe yard of ground between them. "There's too much that doesn't ring true. Why slow just when he reached the end of our tracks? Why stop here? I don't like coincidence," she said belligerently.

"Neither do I." Jane had expected an argument. Jack didn't give her one. Taking the donkey's lead, he handed it to her. "Are your blisters up to a brief walk?"

"Brief" was a misnomer. Jack's route led them north and then west and then south again, doubling back and around.

There were no paths here, just trails. Jane clung grimly to the donkey for balance, but she didn't dare ride. The terrain was too steep; even the donkey was having trouble picking its way. The mist turned to mizzle and the mizzle to rain, sluicing down beneath her collar, soaking through her boy's clothes.

"This was not what I meant when I said I wanted a bath," she muttered through clenched teeth. If she didn't clench them, they would chatter.

Jack's hand was at her elbow, helping her over the scree. "We're almost there."

"Where?" Jane squinted into the twilight, which had fallen barely perceptibly, gloom darkening into more gloom. Her eyes ached from staring at the path at her feet. All of her ached.

"There." Jack pointed ahead and Jane caught a glimpse of white stucco walls and red-tiled roofs.

She stumbled. "A town?"

"Caldas," said Jack, as though it should mean something. "Caldas da Rainha."

"S-s-surely—" It was hard to sound sensible with one's teeth rattling. "S-s-surely we would be s-s-safer in the rough?"

"And have you take a chill?" The tone was the old mocking one, but there was real concern there. "That's more of a threat at the moment than Samson."

Jack moved sure-footed through the deserted marketplace, around a statue of a medieval monarch, past a church along whose pale sides dark stone pillars climbed like moss, until they reached an imposing building of yellow stucco, in the baroque style of the previous century.

Bypassing the main door, he rapped at a smaller portal on the side. "We'll stay here for the night."

"What is this place?"

"This," said Jack smugly, "is a thermal hospital. Or, in layman's terms, a hot spring. You did say you wanted a bath?"

"I— A hot spring?"

"A rather famous one." Jack held up both hands, palms out. "Don't get too excited. The waters smell like the pits of hell. But they're said to be therapeutic. And they're hot."

Hot. Never had a word sounded quite so seductive.

A gatekeeper holding a lantern opened the door. From his blistering tone, Jane gathered that they were not within operating hours for new admissions.

A rapid conversation in Portuguese ensued, of which Jane understood very little. The glint of a coin being passed from Jack's hand to the other man's, however, required no translation. Nor did the man stepping back from the door and gesturing them forward before taking a quick look, first this way, then that, and locking it firmly behind them.

Jane Wooliston desperately wanted a bath; the Pink Carnation wasn't so sure. It felt like a terrible indulgence.

"Do we have time?" Jane said doubtfully. There was, after all, a queen to be saved.

"We have to stop for the night somewhere, don't we?" When he saw her hesitate, Jack propelled her forward with a hand against her back. "Don't think about walking out now. I already paid the gatekeeper."

As they followed the gatekeeper down the corridor, Jane could smell a whiff of rotten eggs. She didn't care. It was water. And it was hot.

Every inch of Jane was plastered, head to toe, with mud. There was mud under her hat and between her toes. Her clothes itched. Her hair itched. Even her eyes itched. The idea of submerging herself in hot water, even if it did smell like Satan's own eau de cologne, was utter heaven.

They paused in front of a large wooden door, which appeared considerably older than the facade of the building. The gatekeeper fumbled at his waist for the key, muttering softly to himself.

Jack was right. They were no use to anyone if they fell ill. The Gardener, if he was looking for them, would never think to look for them here. What agents worth their salt stopped at a spa? It was absurd. And therefore safe.

Or as safe as one could be.

Jane tucked a mud-stiffened strand of hair behind her ears. "Well, then. In that case . . ."

Jack's eyes were amber beneath the brim of his hat. "Happy Christmas, Jane."

"But I don't have anything for you." Jane looked away from the light in his eyes, feeling strangely flustered. "Ordinarily I would have embroidered you a pair of slippers, but . . ."

"It's not a quid pro quo." Jack shoved his hands in his pockets, leaning back against the whitewashed wall as the door-keeper fitted a massive key into the lock. "In any event, don't thank me; thank Queen Leonor. She was the one who founded the hospital."

The door creaked open into total darkness. Jane caught another strong whiff of rotten eggs.

She looked at Jack. "You don't take gratitude well, do you?"

"No better than you take a gift." Lowering his voice, Jack added, "If it makes you feel better, I'd thought the Queen might have stopped here. This place is a favorite with the royal family."

Jane kept an eye on the gatekeeper's back as she murmured, "Was that what you were asking?"

The gatekeeper touched his candle to the single torch that sat in an iron bracket against the wall, illuminating a large, stone-walled room, taken up almost entirely by the rectangular bath in the middle. A narrow wooden walkway banded the pool on all four sides, with a shallow set of stairs leading into the water.

"Part of it. If the Queen came this way, she didn't stop to take the waters, although he did confirm that a miraculous statue passed by. He was rather grumpy about it, too—apparently when wonder-working statues make their way through, fewer people feel the need to take the waters."

Jane put a hand to her mouth as she crossed tentatively over the threshold. "I can see why. You weren't joking about the smell."

"It's good for you. Or so they say. I make no warranties."

Jack remained in the doorway, surveying the room with the air of one who had seen it before, which, Jane assumed, he most likely had. "This is one of the older baths."

The stone ceiling arched up above their heads, punctuated only by two holes, which might have been for light or ventilation or both. In the dark it was hard to tell. Mist rose from the bath, wreathing the windowless stone walls in an air of mystery.

"It feels like something out of—" Jane had nearly said *something out of one of Miss Gwen's novels.* "Something out of a horrid novel."

"The specter-ridden castle of Otranto?" Jack offered blandly. "Or perhaps the vaulted dungeons of the Knight of the Silver Tower?"

Jane glanced sharply at him. She didn't think he knew that was his own stepmother's novel, but . . . "You've read *The Convent of Orsino?*"

"I've read a great many things. Amarantha was a ninny, but I liked the battle with the flying monkeys."

Amarantha had been, although it pained Jane to acknowledge it, very loosely based on her. "Amarantha was placed in difficult circumstances," she said primly.

"Amarantha didn't have the nerve to admit she was attracted to the Knight of the Silver Tower, so she just sat there wringing her hands and waiting to be rescued."

"She had been placed under a spell!" Jane realized she was objecting a little too vehemently. "And maybe she had reservations about the knight's character."

"And maybe you're reading this just a little too closely? Ah, *obrigado*," Jack said to the gatekeeper, while Jane bit her lip and told herself to stop being an idiot.

Jack couldn't know that *The Convent of Orsino* was something she took very personally indeed. The novel had made Miss Gwen's fortune, the fortune that was even now funding Jane's missions. But it had also held up Jane's life to her own eyes, albeit in a distorted mirror. A very distorted mirror.

In Miss Gwen's version, it was the wise chaperone who was needed to free the beautiful but rather wishy-washy Amarantha. Amarantha, who personified virtue and grace and all sorts of other lovely, albeit bland things, fell prey to the fatal attraction of the Knight of the Silver Tower. She remained in his thrall, in his doomed castle, neither yielding to him nor with the strength to pull herself away, until her brave chaperone came to her rescue.

The Gardener's name, before he persuaded Bonaparte to bestow upon him his dead father's title, had been the Chevalier de la Tour d'Argent.

The Knight of the Silver Tower.

It was, Jane knew, a highly romanticized and fictionalized history. But it stung all the same.

She hadn't been in his thrall. Not for long, in any event. And she certainly hadn't needed Miss Gwen to rescue her from her fatal attraction. It had taken only time spent with Nicolas: not stolen moments in a ballroom exchanging quips, but stretches of time working together, sleeping together. The more she had known him, the harder it was to convince herself that she might love him.

Or, for that matter, that he loved her. That he loved the idea of her, Jane had no doubt. The Gardener and the Pink Carnation: what more fitting match? He wanted to display her on his arm, to deck her with jewels. That their principles clashed, that they had found it difficult, if not impossible, to work together, that was something Nicolas dismissed with a wave of his hand.

Probably, thought Jane grimly, because Nicolas had assumed that she would retire from active work and grace the head of his table.

She had left him in Venice with nothing more than a note. Would he go to the trouble of trying to bring her back by force? Or would he assume that their paths would eventually circle back together, as they always seemed to do? That was more in keeping with the man Jane knew.

Unless he had decided to speed the process by sending a lackey along to find her trail.

Jack and the gatekeeper appeared to have arrived at some sort of agreement. More coins passed from Jack's hands to the gatekeeper's, along with the large, age-blackened key.

The light of the gatekeeper's lantern receded down the hallway, leaving Jack and Jane alone in the dimly lit bathing chamber.

Jack lounged against the open door. "According to our genial host, it seems the hospitality of the house might also stretch to bread and cheese and a cup of mulled wine. No Christmas puddings, though, I'm afraid."

"I should have been very surprised if there had been one." Jane's damp shirt prickled against her back. Feeling suddenly awkward, she nodded to the key. "Is that the only key?"

"So he claims." Jack's fingers brushed hers as he passed her the heavy key, his eyes meeting hers, the reflected torchlight warming them to the color of sherry. "You won't be disturbed."

"What about you?" Next to Jane, the water gleamed an invitation, reflecting the reddish light of the single torch. "You're not planning to bathe?"

Jack made an ironic bow. "I wouldn't wish to intrude on your privacy."

The bath was large enough for the entire Regency Council, three French hens, and a partridge in a pear tree. The room was dark, further obscured by the steam rising off the water. Once under the water, there would be nothing to be seen, just her bare shoulders emerging from the pool, and she showed more than that to the world every time she donned an evening dress.

"After weeks of sharing close accommodations," said Jane, not quite knowing what she was doing, "I hardly think that's a consideration."

"Yes," said Jack, "but there was the donkey to ensure your virtue."

They looked at each other and Jane knew they were remembering the same thing: the night in that hut, the straw crackling beneath her cloak, their faces a whisper away. Jane could feel the tingle starting in her fingers, moving up her arms.

"There's no need to be so noble," Jane said. "You must be sore, too."

"What gives you that idea?"

Jane raised a brow. "The fact that you're walking like a bowlegged old man?"

"The bath is your Christmas present."

"And I choose to share it." Turning, Jane retreated to a dark corner of the room, her frozen fingers fumbling on the unfamiliar lacings of her breeches. Just for good measure, she added, "You smell like donkey."

"*I* smell like donkey?" But she could hear the sound of mud-soaked cloth dropped with a splat. Jane paused with her fingers on the ties of her shirt. She could go into the water with it on. Invalids bathed in shifts, after all.

But did it matter? The dark created its own shield. And, when it came down to it, she had already been stripped bare in all the ways that mattered. She had never told anyone before of her affair with the Gardener; Miss Gwen might have suspected, but she had never dared ask. And yet . . . and yet she had told Jack Reid. Told him and then kissed him.

Mere nudity was nothing next to that.

Jane's fingers lingered on the neck of her shirt. With one swift, decisive movement she peeled it up over her head. Naked, she turned and strode gracefully towards the steps that led down into the pool.

Chapter Eighteen

$\mathcal{J}$ack did his best not to look as Jane descended into the pool.

He couldn't help it. No matter how he tried to keep his eyes locked straight ahead, they insisted on straying to the side, catching glimpses of Jane moving deliberately forward, Jane stepping down into the pool, Jane with water lapping at her calves like a latter-day Aphrodite. The steam from the pool wreathed her body, hiding and revealing, making her descent more tantalizing than any courtesan's practiced dance.

Jack sank a little deeper in the water, grateful for the darkness, grateful for the murkiness of the water.

He didn't think Jane had been making that sort of offer when she invited him to share her bath. At least, he amended,

it was safer to assume she hadn't been making that sort of offer. Now he had only to convince his body of that.

Disdaining the wooden planks set out for the invalids, Jack
had seated himself firmly on the pool floor. It wasn't deep,
after all. He plunked his arms down on the wooden walkway
banding the bath. Relaxing. They were meant to be relaxing.
If he told himself that often enough, he might even believe it.

The water slapped against the side, the sound awakening
all sorts of lascivious echoes in Jack's imagination, as Jane settled herself carefully into the water.

From the corner of his eye, he could see her as she lifted her
arms to pull the last of the pins from her hair, shaking the
thick mass free with an unconscious gesture that made Jack
swallow with a throat gone very dry.

"I'll . . . just see if our host has left the wine," he said, and,
rather than pass Jane on his way to the stairs, he hoisted himself up over the side of the pool by the strength of his arms.

He wasn't sure whether he hoped she was looking or hoped
she wasn't. Flashing one's backside in the air wasn't generally
the accepted way of attracting a lady, unless one were a monkey.
Jack had spent time with monkeys. He didn't want to ape them.

Wrapping his shirt around his waist as a makeshift loin-
cloth, he scuttled crablike to the door, where a jug of steaming
wine and a plate of *biscoitos* were waiting.

Jack poured the mulled wine into two goblets. Crouching
by the side of the pool, he handed one down to Jane. "Refresh-
ment."

"Thank you." She leaned her head back against the side of the pool to look up at him, and Jack's breath caught at the sight of her, her hair dark with wet around her pale face, snaking down around her unbound shoulders. The way she was looking up at him brought her breasts up out of the water, so he could just almost see . . .

"You're welcome," Jack said brusquely, and thrust a *biscoito* into her other hand. "Have a biscuit."

Discarding his shirt, Jack dropped back into the pool. At the other end. It seemed safer that way. But the pool that had seemed so large in concept was a great deal smaller with Jane in it, a goblet in one hand, a biscuit in the other.

Turning her head, Jane said, "Thank you for my Christmas present. It's much better than yet another pair of embroidered slippers."

But for him, she might have been spending Christmas with her family, not in a sulfur-smelling tub with a mad Frenchman in pursuit.

Jack took a long swig from his goblet. The wine had been heavily sugared; the taste of cloves cloyed against the back of his throat. "It isn't the Christmas you would have had at home."

For a moment, all was still except for the gentle lap of water in the pool, the drip of condensation along the walls. Then Jane said quietly, "What was that word you told me about? The one for nostalgia?"

"Saudade?" The muscles in Jack's arms were tightly corded as he propped them against the side of the pool.

"*Saudade,*" Jane repeated, tasting the word on her tongue. "Longing for people and places past. But that's the point. They're past. They don't exist anymore. Not really." She turned, and Jack could feel the faint ripple of water bridging the space between them. "It's the exile's dilemma. The home they yearn for is never the home to which they return. If they return."

"Would you return? If you could?" Jack's voice felt hoarse and rusty. Sulfur and cloves, he told himself, sulfur and cloves.

Jane tilted her head back against the side of the pool. Distantly, she said, "Miss Gw— My former chaperone concocted a plan to bring me back from the dead, should this war ever end. I would be introduced as a distant cousin and presented into society."

Jack's reaction was immediate and negative. "People wouldn't recognize you from your old life?"

Jane sank a little deeper in the water, her long hair trailing in ropes around her. "I was raised in the country. There is no one in London who would know me—other than those who already know."

He should be glad for her, Jack knew. But he wasn't. He hated the idea. He hated the idea of Jane disappearing back into her old world, lost under gloves and bonnets and airs and graces, nodding and smiling to the overbred who didn't realize that she was more than a graceful figure in a fashionable gown.

Would any of them know how she could switch roles at a

moment's notice? Decipher a complicated code on sight? Face down a French spy without turning a hair?

No. And if that was the way Jane wanted it, Jack told himself, that was the way Jane wanted it. It wasn't his choice to make. Hell, he'd done enough damage in her life already, before he'd even known her name.

Carefully, Jack said, "So you could go back."

"No."

"What?" Jack forgot that he was supposed to be averting his eyes and turned and stared. "I thought you just said . . ."

Jane sat up straight, shoving her wet hair back over her shoulders. "I might be able to go back, but that doesn't mean I could."

Jack did his best to make sense of that, although it was very hard to make sense of anything with a half-naked Jane in front of him. "I'm missing something," he said at last.

"It doesn't matter if no one recognized me. *I* would know." Jane leaned forward, a sheen of water glistening on her bare shoulders and chest. "My deceptions here—they're for a purpose. They have an end. I play a role for a few weeks, or even a few months, but at the end of it—I'm still myself. Can you imagine living a lie for the rest of your life, pretending to be someone you're not? Watching yourself disappear, piece by piece?"

Her lips were moving, but it took a moment for the words to resolve themselves into meaning.

Pushing the words out of his dry throat, Jack said, "I am familiar with the concept."

Jane gave one brisk nod, a gesture so entirely Jane, and so utterly at odds with her garb or lack thereof. "Could you imagine going on being Alarico or Rodrigo?"

"Or Johnny Fluellen?" Jane was right, of course. He had at one point toyed with the idea of remaining in Portugal, marrying, bearing children, sinking into the landscape. But he couldn't. He would be lying to his neighbors, his wife, his own children. He couldn't do that. "No."

The word sank into the silence between them.

Jack could hear a faint creak as Jane leaned back against one of the wooden planks. "You understand, then."

Heaven help him, he did. When he had met Jane, he had assumed that she had everything she lacked: a cause, a country, a family. That when the mission was over, she would return . . . somewhere.

He had never imagined that she might be as lost as he.

"If you won't go back to England," said Jack quietly, "then where?"

"I don't know." There was something almost hypnotic about the movement of the water, the rising of the steam, the patterns traced by the torchlight. "Have you ever thought of returning to India?"

The red light on the surface of the water twisted and changed, became a spill of blood twining down the folds of a sari of crimson silk, a red uniform jacket, a series of pennants waving in the breeze. A series of memories, and none of them good.

"At that rate," said Jack flatly, "I'd rather remain Alarico. There's nothing in India for me."

"The Gardener no longer has the power there he did." Jane turned on her side to look at him, her hair falling over one shoulder. "You could go back to being a soldier."

"I never wanted to be a soldier." The words came out before he could think better of them. Jack shrugged. "That was my father's province. And my little brother, George. He always liked playing at soldiers."

"What about you?"

Jack's lips twisted in a wry smile. "I looked down on it. Anyone could hack with a sword. I was going to be a philosopher king and right the world's wrongs. Or at least govern a small district."

He remembered how smug he had been, how sure. He had hated that boarding school in Calcutta, but there had been a purpose to it. He was going to rise in the ranks of the East India Company's administration and show everyone: Alex, Kat, his father. . . . They would see.

Only they hadn't seen. He had.

"But—I thought . . . The laws . . ."

"Didn't come into effect until I was already old enough to have expected otherwise." Jack could taste the old bitterness at the back of his throat.

He had been ten when Cornwallis had put out the first of

the series of regulations that stripped him of any future in his own country; he hadn't learned of it until he was thirteen. His father had kept it from him, although whether from hope that it would change, or fear that Jack would fly into a rage like his mother, Jack was never quite sure.

It was one of the boys at school who had told him, taunting him. And Jack had gone to his father—only to discover that what he had been studying for, working for, those past three years didn't exist. Not anymore.

Jack stretched out his legs in the water, concentrating on the stretch of his muscles, the rough bottom of the pool against his skin. "I think my father hoped it was all nothing, that the laws wouldn't be enforced, or that someone would find a gap in them. Unfortunately, Cornwallis was too good a legislator for that."

It had cost his father, he knew. In a very real sense. That school in Calcutta hadn't been cheap, and his father had never been particularly plump in the pocket. That he had kept Jack in it for years longer than he had to . . . well, it was either a kindness or a very real aversion to any kind of unpleasantness. Or a little bit of both.

"What did you do?" Jack was dimly aware that Jane had moved closer, that she was only the breadth of a board away.

"My father took me out of school in Calcutta and apprenticed me to a printer." Jack could still remember the humiliation of it. He shrugged, feeling the water ripple around him. "As much as it pains me to say it, I believe my father meant well. It was the best he could do for me under the circumstances. He thought I'd be happy among books and tracts. Better that than some other trade. And a trade was all that was open to me."

"But you weren't happy."

"I was furious." Jack could smell it still, the ink and glue. He'd slept in a room with a press, on a pallet on the floor. He'd hugged his grievances to himself; his father might be an officer, but his mother had been a princess. He had convinced himself that he was owed better, that he would have better. "I ran away to find my mother's people. I thought—I hoped . . ."

In retrospect, it felt so hopelessly naive.

Jack looked up at Jane, his lips twisting in a humorless smile. "I spun a fairy tale for myself. I had a dream that my mother's father would welcome me with open arms and proclaim me his heir. Oh, there were all sorts of versions of the tale. In one version I would burst onto the scene just as he was being menaced by a man-eating tiger and save him single-handedly, with nothing but a small dagger."

He looked at Jane, inviting her to share the humor of it, but she wasn't laughing. Her gray eyes were clouded with sympathy. "Oh, Jack," she said.

"You haven't even heard the best of them. My favorite was the one in which he announced that he had had men scouring Madras, searching for me, that he had been looking for me since I was a baby. And lo, all the kingdom was filled with rejoicing."

Jane winced at the sarcasm in his voice. "What really happened?"

"What you would expect. He threw me out on my—" Jack caught himself with a cough. "Let's just say he threw me out. Or rather, he had me thrown. He wasn't going to sully his jeweled fingers doing it personally. He had retainers for tossing out the rubbish."

Jane's fingers brushed his arm, just a light touch, no more substantial than the water around them. "Jack. I'm so sorry."

Jack smiled a crooked smile. "Don't look so grim. It was to be expected. He'd disowned my mother. As far as he was concerned, I didn't exist. It was rather embarrassing for him to be reminded that I did."

Jane's hand rested lightly on his arm. "Pride makes people do foolish things."

Jack looked at her, at her shadowed gray eyes, and thought of that tombstone in a little graveyard in England.

His hand closed over hers. "Shall we raise a toast to the dispossessed? We've been disinherited and survived."

Jane glanced down at their joined hands. All Jack could see was the water-dark fall of her hair as she said, "What about your father? Surely he would be glad to have you back."

"The prodigal son returneth?" There was nothing like a mention of one's father to kill the mood. Particularly in his case. Jack removed his hand, leaning back against the wall. "My father's married again. He's started another family. He's good at that." One family disappoint you? Have another one!

Jack knew he wasn't fair, but he wasn't interested in being fair. "I doubt he'll be breaking out the fatted calf."

Jane pressed her lips together, looking far more perturbed than the situation warranted. "I wouldn't be so sure of that."

Jack rolled his head sideways. "You don't know my father."

Jane moved back a little. She cocked her head, looking across at him. "I do, actually."

"What?" Slowly levering himself up, Jack squinted at Jane in the darkness.

She sat pale and still as a statue at the center of a fountain, carved of marble and moonlight. "When I said my chaperone fell in love? Jack—that man was your father."

Chaperone . . . father . . . what? Jack stared at her, trying to make the individual words coalesce into meaning.

"Was?" he said.

"*Is* your father," Jane corrected herself hastily. "He's very well. Thriving, in fact."

Thriving. Jack didn't know what to say. Jane knew his father. His father was thriving. Jack felt as though he were caught in a bad dream.

Without his breeches.

"He misses you terribly."

And with that, the paralysis that held Jack broke. "My father married your chaperone."

"My former chaperone," Jane corrected. Jack wasn't sure whether that was supposed to make it better. Biting down on her lower lip, she added, "Your sister is my goddaughter."

That certainly didn't make it better.

"And that makes us?" Jack bit out.

"Nothing," said Jane hastily. "Absolutely nothing. The relationship is a sentimental, rather than a legal, one."

His father could tell the world something about sentimental rather than legal relations. But he'd gone legal this time. He'd married the woman. Jane's chaperone. Jane's former chaperone.

Who apparently hadn't been doing much of a job of chaperonage if she'd been so busy canoodling with Jack's father that she'd failed to notice that Jane was forming an attachment with a dodgy French spy.

One would think, thought Jack, breathing in the smell of hellfire and brimstone, that Jane might have found, oh, five minutes over the past three weeks to share this small piece of information. That she might, during those many nights they had shared a tent, have somehow managed to mention that she knew his family a damned sight better than he did.

What had he told her? Jack couldn't remember. All those times he had mentioned his father, and she had sat there and let him go on. No wonder she knew his bloody dossier so well. She'd had it from the source. Plenty of people knew his father—the man did get around—but it wasn't as though Jane and his father had just nodded to each other at a regimental ball.

She was his sister's bloody godmother, for heaven's sake.

Jack tasted bitter gall and wormwood. Or maybe it was just mulled wine meeting sulfur. He didn't really care.

"Why in the *devil* didn't you tell me this before?" The words exploded out of him.

Jane sat very still, self-containment around her naked shoulders like a cloak. "Did it matter?"

Ask a stupid question . . . Jack gave her a withering look. "What else don't I know?"

"Your sister Kat is married," Jane said rapidly. "To a man named Fluellen—Tommy Fluellen. They live in Wales." When Jack didn't smile, she kept going. "Your new sister's name is Plumeria. Plumeria Jane Amarantha. She's nearly two years old. And very clever."

The pride in Jane's voice as she spoke of Plumeria grated on Jack like salt on raw wounds. He'd known he had a new sister, but he hadn't even known her name. All right, he hadn't wanted to know. It hurt less if he didn't know.

But Jane—Jane didn't just know the bare fact of her existence. Plumeria was a person to her. She knew her. Knew her and loved her and was proud of her.

Who in the hell named a child Plumeria? It was worse than Iain.

"What about Lizzy?" Jack ground out. "I assume you know Lizzy?"

"Yes, I know Lizzy." Lizzy. Not "your sister Lizzy." Not Elizabeth. Just Lizzy, with an easy familiarity that told Jack more than any number of words. "Lizzy is well. In fact, she's more than well. She's the toast of the town. She's rejected offers from three viscounts and the heir to a marquisate."

She'd let him go on, telling her about his grand plans to rescue his little sister, when all the while . . . "You're joking."

Jane didn't know when to quit. Her lips curved with private amusement. "I'm afraid I'm not. She's really quite incorrigible."

The last time Jack had seen his sister, she'd been six years old.

"With a dowry such as she has, I'm not surprised," said Jack, his anger seeking any target it could find.

"It's not her dowry." A wrinkle zigzagged between Jane's brows as she looked at him, silently reproving. Reproving. Him. "Lizzy's conquests are of her own making. Or do you rate your sister so low?"

Jack could feel his temper rising like the steam off the water. "I rated her high enough to steal for her, as you may recall."

"You might have spared yourself the trouble." Jane lifted her chin, back in full princess mode. At the moment, Jack hated her and the world. "No one knows about the jewels. Your father set them aside. For you."

"He had no right."

"To what? To look out for your interests?"

"To disregard my wishes!"

"You weren't there to express them."

No, but Jane had been there. Jane, and his sisters, and this woman he'd never even met, his new stepmother.

Jack folded his arms across his chest, saying tightly, "My invitation to the wedding must have been lost in the post." A muscle throbbed in his jaw. "If they'd let me know I'd have sent a gift. A few rubies, perhaps."

Rubies that he might, apparently, have saved himself the trouble of stealing. Everything he'd done had been for nothing. Lizzy hadn't needed him, didn't need him. They none of them needed him.

Why would they? They had Jane.

Jane pressed her eyes shut, taking a long, deep breath. "Don't," she said quietly. "You're only making yourself unhappy."

Jack brushed her hand aside. "*I'm* making myself unhappy? I'm not the one who's been hiding the fact that she's a member of my bloody family!"

The profanity was deliberate. Jane's back stiffened. "When was I meant to tell you? While we were fleeing from the French camp? While we were inspecting the hall of the novices?"

"What about when you were sharing the details of your affair with the Gardener?" It was a low blow, but Jack was beyond caring. "You found the time to kiss me. You couldn't have taken two minutes to say, 'Oh, by the way, I'm your sister's bloody godmother'?"

Jane's face was very white in the torchlight. "This," said Jane distinctly. "This is why I didn't tell you. Because I knew your reaction would be . . . strong."

What she really meant was "irrational." He wasn't irrational. He wasn't his bloody mother.

"No," said Jack, breathing heavily through his nose. "That's not why you didn't tell me. You didn't tell me because knowledge is power. And you like having that kind of power."

"That's——" She broke off, biting her lip.

"Absurd?" Jack turned his shoulder, deliberately shutting her out. His voice rich with scorn, he said, "Don't lie to yourself. The Pink Carnation always has to know more than everyone else, don't you, princess?"

"And you always have to be more disaffected!"

The frustration in Jane's voice made Jack turn. If she could have spewed fire, it would have been coming out of her nostrils. She hit the water with a flat palm, the sharp report making Jack jump. "Won't you get through your thick skull that there are people who love you? Who miss you?"

She rose to her feet, entirely unconcerned with her own nudity, too angry to care. Her hands curled into fists at her sides.

"Haven't you spent long enough feeling sorry for yourself, Jack? You have a family who want you." She pushed her hair back with both hands, taking a deep, shuddering breath. With difficulty, she said, "You have someone to go back to."

She turned away, but not before Jack saw her face twist out of kilter, like the exaggerated lines of a commedia dell'arte mask, comedy melting into tragedy. She stalked towards the stairs, but not quickly enough to hide the fact that Jane, his unflappable Jane, was doing her damnedest not to cry.

"Happy Christmas," she flung back over her shoulder.

"Oh, hell." She always had to have the last word. Ignoring

the fact that he wasn't wearing breeches—or anything else, for that matter—he strode after her, catching her by the shoulder. "Jane."

She wouldn't look at him. She simply shook her head, not turning.

"Jane." He gave her a little shake. "I didn't mean— Oh, *hell.*"

In a strangled voice, Jane said, "It's the sulfur."

"It's not the sulfur."

Jack felt like a heel. Worse than a heel. He was the lowest of the low, the slimiest form of slime to crawl the underbelly of the earth.

Her eyes were pressed shut as though, through sheer strength of will, she might stop the tears from falling. But they leaked out all the same, slow, painful tears that cut Jack deeper than any number of heaving sobs.

Jack brushed ineffectually at the tears with his thumb. "Do you want a family?" he said hoarsely. "You can have mine. They'd probably prefer you to me."

Jane's swollen lids fluttered open. "Stop belittling yourself." She looked up at Jack, looking so hopeless that it tore at his heart. "They love you. It's you they want, not me."

"I want you." Jack hadn't meant to say it. It just came out. But once it was out there, he didn't know how to take it back, particularly since his body appeared to have recalled that they were both wet and naked and standing all too close for comfort. "What I mean is— Oh, hell."

Jane took a long, shuddering breath that made her chest do things that reduced Jack's mental capacity by a considerable degree. "You don't need to try to make me feel better."

"I don't need to— What?" The air was cold. The water had been warm. There was a pair of very pointy nipples in very close proximity to Jack's chest.

His name was Jack, wasn't it? He couldn't quite recall.

With difficulty, Jane said, "You don't need to pretend to be attracted to me." While Jack was still trying to make that make sense, she took a step back, towards the stairs. "I would rather be alone than pitied."

There were a great many words that didn't seem to mean what Jane thought they meant. "You think I'm *pretending* to be attracted to you?"

Jack would have laughed if he hadn't had a very uncomfortably large pretense making itself felt just below the waterline.

"It's not that it isn't kind of you. . . ."

"Kind?" Jack didn't know where to begin. "I've spent the past few weeks doing my damnedest to keep my hands off you. And if you think it's been easy, then you're deluding yourself. Even when I didn't like you, I wanted you. You're very wantable."

"Wantable?" A flicker of amusement lightened Jane's face. "Is that a word?"

"Desirable, then." No, that wasn't fair. "More than desirable. You're . . ." He was in too deep to dig himself out, so why not be hanged for a sheep as for a lamb? Jack tried to shove his hands in his pockets before he realized he wasn't wearing anything. "You're wonderful. You don't need me to tell me you're beautiful. You can see that when you look in your mirror."

Jane looked ruefully down at her cracked fingernails. "Not so much right now."

"Especially right now," said Jack firmly. "And you don't need me to tell you you're brilliant. All of the agents you've outwitted can attest to that. But you're also"—a smudge on a cheek, a tentative glance, a wry smile, high-handed, fair-minded, maddening, intriguing—"you."

Which, roughly translated, meant a million times too good for him. And now, on top of it, she was his sister's godmother.

Jack waved his arms helplessly in the air. "Why in the hell do you think I slept on top of the covers last night?"

Jane took a tentative step forward. "But when I kissed you—"

"I wasn't going to take advantage!" Since that might have come out just a bit too forcefully, Jack modulated his tone. "I know I haven't always led the most honorable life, but that doesn't make me a complete cad."

"No." There was something in Jane's face as she looked at him that made the breath drop in Jack's chest. "It doesn't."

"We have to work together," said Jack rapidly. "How could I make any kind of advance, knowing you might be in a position where you might not be able to say no? It wouldn't be fair to you."

Jane took another step forward, the torchlight glimmering off her wet body. "Your scruples do you credit."

"Do they?" Jack said hoarsely, trying to remember what they were. "I should go. Now."

"No." Jane slid her hands up his chest, to his shoulders. Her arms wrapped around his neck, her chest pressing against his. "No, you shouldn't."

Chapter Nineteen

*I*ntellectually, Jane knew Jack was right. This was folly. They were so close to the end of the mission, to finding the Queen, to bringing her home.

But for once in her life, Jane didn't want to be led by her head. She wanted this moment, this one little moment here in the darkened bath, with the steam rising up around them, veiling them from the world, for no other reason than that she wanted it. Than that she wanted him.

So she slid her hands up his chest to his shoulders, and felt his muscles tense beneath her touch, his breath catch in his throat. His hands came around her waist, pulling her close with a jerk that should have knocked the air out of her had she been concentrating on such a mundane and wasteful thing as breathing.

Breathing, at the moment, seemed highly irrelevant.

One hand twining in her wet hair, Jack lowered his lips to hers—and stopped.

"This isn't a thank-you for the bath, is it?" he asked darkly, his lips hovering centimeters from hers.

"If," said Jane shakily, "I had wanted to thank you for the bath, I would have embroidered you a pair of slippers. With carnations."

Jack's face broke into a rogue's grin. "In that case . . ."

The world spun dizzily as Jack swept her up in his arms, rather an impressive feat given that they were nearly the same height. But then, she had just had a firsthand view of those shoulder muscles. Fieldwork, thought Jane vaguely, did keep one fit.

"What are you doing?" she demanded, clasping her arms around Jack's neck to keep from falling. The water lapped around Jack's legs and her dangling feet.

"Not saying 'you're welcome,'" he said, and carried her up out of the bath.

Afterwards, a very long time afterwards, they lay together in the warm dark, on a makeshift pallet constructed of their cloaks, both tired, neither ready to sleep.

To sleep would be to invite morning. This intimacy between them was too fragile, too new, too bound to this particular place and time. Silently, Jane willed the planets to realign themselves, the sun and moon to stop their circling, to leave them just a little more time together like this, suspended between dusk and dawn.

Jane ran her finger along a line of puckered skin just below Jack's collarbone. "Where did this come from?"

"Malpura." Jack stared up at the ceiling, tracing lazy circles on Jane's bare back with one hand. "It was my first time on the field. We ought to have had the advantage of surprise, but our cavalry jumped the gun and tipped them off. The left wing, where I was, was crushed. The Rajput cavalry sliced right through us. We lost hundreds of men in a matter of minutes."

"But not you." Jane tried to imagine what that had been like, standing there on a battlefield, watching a trained band of warriors streaming down at you, the men around you writhing, dying, doing everything you could to keep yourself alive in the melee.

For some men, this was what they craved; it was what they had trained for, what they had wanted.

But not Jack, who had wanted to be a philosopher king.

Jack's lips twisted. "It was luck, not skill. I had no idea what I was doing. I scarcely knew one end of my musket from the other. That they were putting men like me in the field gives you a fair idea of why it was such a rout. After that," he added, looking up at Jane, "I decided it wasn't enough to be lucky. I drilled with that damned musket until I could fire it in my sleep."

"What about fencing?" Jane inquired, with professional interest. Well, maybe not entirely professional. The muscles in his arms hadn't been acquired merely by hoisting a musket.

"Saber," Jack corrected. "Although I can wield an épée if necessary."

Jane rested her head against that thin line where the Rajput sword had missed its mark. "We can have a bout someday."

She could feel Jack's lips against her hair. "Why does it not surprise me that you know your way around an épée?"

"Like you," said Jane, her fingers exploring the area around his ribs, "I decided it wasn't enough to be lucky. I prefer to rely on my wits when possible, but there are times when a length of steel is far more effective."

"You would win," said Jack bluntly. "I learned to hack, not to duel like a gentleman."

"I have never been entirely sure there is anything gentlemanly about duels," said Jane, smothering a yawn. "It's merely a temper tantrum by more civilized means." There was another ridge of hardened skin beneath her fingers. "What was this one?"

Jack lifted his chin slightly to look down. "That? Oh. Ujjain. Another defeat." He smothered a yawn of his own. "I'm not giving you a very good idea of my fighting prowess, am I? I ought to be bragging of the battles I've won and the number of enemy strongholds I've taken."

Jane propped herself up on one elbow. "You're alive. Isn't that prowess enough?" A glint in Jack's eye made her cheeks color. "On the battlefield, I mean."

"Mmm," said Jack, but he let it go. Lifting a strand of her hair that had fallen across his chest, he twisted it around his finger. "Have you seen battle?"

"No." It felt odd to be admitting it. She had thought she had lived an adventurous life, but in this, she was so much less versed than he, so much more sheltered. "This is the closest I've come. My work is generally conducted well behind the scenes, where the decisions are made."

"Or," Jack said dryly, "where rulers like to believe the decisions are made. There's always a difficulty in translation. Look at Junot's march. It made sense to Bonaparte on a map. It was a disaster in practice. A better general would have redirected his men."

"A better general wouldn't have lasted so long in Bonaparte's service." Jane had spent three years as a member of the consular retinue. She had seen firsthand Bonaparte's temper tantrums when his subordinates disputed his judgment. "Bonaparte admires talent, but he admires loyalty even more. He doesn't take well to being disobeyed."

"That's going to trip him up sooner or later," said Jack, with professional detachment. "One man's experience goes only so far. A good leader knows enough to know that he can't be an expert at everything."

"Very wise," said Jane softly.

"I try," said Jack, and Jane wondered whether he was thinking, like she, that it was a pity that he would never have a chance to try, to put those theories into practice.

Resting her head against his chest, Jane tried to imagine a different Jack, a Jack whose life had followed the path he had expected, a Jack who rose through the East India Company's service, who might, even now, be administering a small district. Mentally she erased the weather-browned skin, the scars, the battered brown jacket and breeches, the shapeless hat with its drooping brim. In their place she clothed her make-believe Jack in a crisp cravat and somber hat. That Jack's hands were pale and soft and stained with ink; there was a pursed look to his lips.

Jane wasn't entirely sure she would have liked that Jack. There was something rather smug and prissy about him.

Rather as she had been before the jewels of Berar had worked their curse and sent her world crashing down around her.

She had never really thought of it that way before. Had she been that smug? That sure of herself? Unwillingly, Jane remembered a few choice words from Miss Gwen, delivered in a darkened drawing room.

A line from Shakespeare drifted through her head. "Sweet are the uses of adversity. . . ." She wouldn't call adversity sweet, per se—there had been a great deal of bitterness in that particular cup—but it had brought her and Jack to where they were, here, together, all their scars laid bare.

If the course of their lives had run smooth, they wouldn't be here. She would be in Paris still, in the Hotel de Balcourt, clad in the latest fashion, cameos at her throat and wrists, fluttering her lashes behind her fan at yet another tedious general, playing a game that had long since begun to lose its challenge.

The jewels of Berar would be . . . well, goodness only knew where. If Jack hadn't stolen them from the ruins of Gawilghur, someone else would.

And Jack would be somewhere in India, wearing crisp white linen and a well-brushed hat.

Drifting in and out of sleep, Jane dreamed that she was back in her bed in the Hotel de Balcourt. Her hair was washed and braided, the linens of the bed pressed and spotless. And she reached out in sudden panic, because Jack was gone and she was alone and everything had been nothing but a dream.

Until she felt his arms close around her, pull her back against his front, one heavy leg settling over her hip. And Jane drifted to sleep, feeling strangely comforted that she wasn't at the Hotel de Balcourt after all.

When she woke again, it was to Jack leaning over her, his lips touching her temple as he smoothed the tangled hair away from her face.

"I hate to wake you," he said, his breath warm against her ear, "but we only have the room until dawn. We're not meant to be here. Officially."

Jane scrubbed the backs of her hands against her eyes. "Which means we have to leave—unofficially?"

Jack sat back on his heels. "Something like that."

He was dressed already, back in the old brown breeches and jacket. The torch had burned out, but a faint light trickled through the opening in the ceiling. Jane was suddenly very aware of her own nudity. She appeared to have far too many limbs, all of them bare. Hastily, she scrambled to a sitting position, yanking one of the cloaks up to her chest.

"You've fed the donkey?"

"And acquired food for us." He handed Jane a slightly stale biscuit. "The remains of our host's Christmas feast."

"You seem to have thought of everything." Jane tried to hold the cloak in place and wiggle into her breeches at the same time, a maneuver that Jack watched with some interest.

"I could just go away if you like," he said.

"You needn't bother." Dropping the cloak, Jane yanked the shirt over her head, feeling like an idiot. "It's nothing you haven't already seen."

Her usually well-behaved hair was a mass of snarls. Jane tried to draw her fingers through it in lieu of a comb and stopped short, grimacing.

"Here. Let me." Jack came up behind her, gently separating the worst of the tangles. Quietly, he said, "If I had intended seduction, I would have brought you someplace with a proper bed. Not to mention better-smelling."

Jane had had a seduction with a proper bed and sweet-smelling perfumes. Of the two, she would take rotten eggs and a hard plank floor any day. That wasn't what was making her cranky.

Wincing as Jack tugged at a knot, she said reluctantly, "You needn't protest so much. I know your intentions were honorable." That hadn't come out as she'd intended. "Or, rather, not dishonorable."

She bit her lip against the urge to elaborate. Assuring him that she didn't expect a proposal would only make matters worse, by implying the contrary. They both knew that this was what it was.

"Thank you," said Jane smartly, and snatched the long rope of her hair away from Jack. "Have you seen my hat?"

The day dawned, miraculously, bright and clear. Jane would have preferred rain. It was easier to skulk beneath one's hat brim in the rain. It didn't help that she kept catching Jack watching her, a little furrow between his brows, as he loaded the bags on the donkey.

"Ready?" he said, and held out a hand to help Jane mount.

Looking at him in the pale morning sunlight, Jane saw for the first time the dark circles beneath his eyes. They were both running low on sleep, but it was Jack who had borne the brunt of their trek, walking for miles while she had swayed along on donkey-back.

Not that he had shown any signs of fatigue last night.

Jane stepped hastily back, waving Jack in the general direction of the donkey. "My heel is feeling much better. If you would like to doze for a bit, I can lead Hippolyte."

Jack let his hand drop. "Hippolyte? Not Hyacinth or Hydrangea?"

Jane tried to smile, but it came out crooked. "I would say we've moved well past flowers, wouldn't you?"

The sunlight picked out the strands of copper in Jack's dark hair. "Is Hippolytus much of an improvement?" he said, his voice carefully neutral. "As I recall, he came to a bad end."

Jane took a deep breath, forcing herself to look Jack in the eye. "He was accused of a crime he didn't commit. His own father condemned him."

She wasn't talking about Hippolytus anymore and they both knew it.

"Jane." Jack rested both hands on her shoulders. Jane had to stiffen herself against the urge to lean into that touch, to bury her head against his shoulder and wrap her arms around his waist. Even if he did smell like rotten eggs. But then, so did she. "I committed my crimes. I took those jewels. I passed information to both sides."

"Are you trying to scare me away?"

Jack let out his breath. "I'm trying to be honest."

Jane pressed her eyes shut. Honesty: another word for "this wasn't meant to be."

Turning away towards the gate, she said in a distant voice, "How much farther to Peniche? We'll make better time now that the weather is clear."

"Jane." Jack's hand reached the gate before she could, holding it closed. "Wait."

There was barely room to turn. Jane was caught between Jack and the gate, his proximity awakening a distracting mélange of memories from the night before.

"Yes?"

Jack said something sharp and emphatic in Portuguese that Jane had a feeling she was better off not having translated.

He fell back a step, a muscle working in his cheek. "If circumstances were different—if I were different—I would be the first man under your window with a lute."

If she were a different sort of woman, she would have stamped her foot.

Not being the foot-stamping sort, Jane merely set her teeth and said tightly, "You don't understand at all, do you? I've had men under my windows with lutes. I don't want a lute. I don't want sonnets. I don't want bows or flowery compliments. None of those mean anything. I want . . . I want someone who notices that my blisters need binding."

Jack perked up. "Are your blisters bothering you again?"

"No! Yes. But that's not the point."

What was the point? Jane wasn't sure. Or, rather, she was fairly sure she didn't want to be sure.

This was ridiculous. They had a queen to rescue, didn't they?

Wrenching the gate open, Jane strode briskly forward. "If anything goes wrong in Peniche, there's a boat waiting off the coast of Berlengas. There's a signal. I'll show it to you."

"You're going the wrong way." Jack caught up with her in a crooked alley between houses, tugging a reluctant Hippolyte behind him. "Why should anything go wrong?"

Aside from her going the wrong way?

They retraced their steps past the marketplace, Jane trying to put a finger on her feelings. "It's what you said . . . about *amigos de Peniche.* There's something I don't like about this. Something smells wrong."

"Lingering eau de hot spring?" When Jane didn't return Jack's smile, he said, "That saying dates back to Sir Francis Drake."

Jane couldn't quite explain it. Something was niggling at her, something she had missed. Why would the Queen leave Alcobaça in such a hurry? Why go to Peniche rather than continuing on to Porto?

Amateurs, Jack had said, and that much was true. Amateurs were unpredictable.

"All the same," said Jane slowly, "it's foolish to charge in without thinking through all the contingencies. If there's one thing I've learned, it's that nothing ever goes quite as planned."

She glanced up to find Jack's eyes on her face. "Once we have the Queen—"

Something about the way he was looking at her made her feel like a girl at her first assembly, waiting breathlessly to be asked to dance. "Yes?"

"We bring her to this boat you mentioned?"

Jane swallowed her disappointment, giving a short, businesslike nod. "It's called the *Bien-Aimée.* The captain is named Lord Richard Selwick—he was formerly the Purple Gentian."

"Formerly?"

"It's a long story." There was no more time for stories, long or otherwise. Jane shoved that depressing thought aside, forcing herself to concentrate on the matter at hand. "The signal is two longs and a short, followed by two shorts and a long."

"That's all? What about a signal for distress?"

"That," said Jane dryly, "generally consists of waving one's arms about in the air and shouting loudly."

"It won't work," said Jack dismissively. "It's miles to Berlengas. They'll never see a lantern from the coast."

Did he think they hadn't thought of that? "There's a lighthouse. With any luck, the keeper is amenable to bribes."

Jack frowned. "It's chancy."

"Do you have a better plan?" Jane stalked forward, the road hard beneath her thin-soled boots. "Everything is chancy. Life is chancy."

"Jane." Jack caught her arm, the momentum swinging her around to face him.

"What?" she demanded. "What?"

Whatever he had been about to say, Jack thought better of it. "Do you think we're walking into a trap?"

"I'd prefer that we not," said Jane. She felt suddenly very tired. They were both behaving like children. Like spoiled children.

This was why one didn't allow oneself to embark on affairs of the heart, not while on mission. The Purple Gentian had blundered into a trap because he was busy mooning over Jane's cousin Amy. As for Miss Gwen— No, Jane didn't want to think that closely about her chaperone and Jack's father. Suffice it to say they had allowed themselves to become distracted while on mission and leave it at that.

And Jane had watched, superior and slightly scornful, knowing she had the sense not to tumble into that particular trap.

Nicolas had been different. She hadn't been in love with Nicolas.

"Jane?" Jack waved a hand in front of her face. She was staring. She hadn't realized she had been staring. "Jane? Are you all right? You've gone green."

"Just thinking," Jane said quickly. "About Peniche."

Jack did not appear entirely convinced. "What about it?"

Jane tried to remember what she'd been thinking before inconvenient topics like love got in the way. "Amateur conspirators make me nervous. They're unpredictable. It's a weakness."

Jane's steps faltered as an idea teased at the edge of her consciousness.

Slowly, she said, "The Gardener is very good at exploiting weaknesses."

Jack looked at her sharply. "You've thought of something. What?"

"What if it was a trap, but it wasn't meant for us?" She couldn't believe she hadn't seen it before. "Amateur conspirators use simple codes. They're painfully easy to copy. It would be child's play to infiltrate their organization and find the key."

Jack's eyes met hers. "And once he had it . . ."

"He wouldn't even need to go after them. He could just sit in comfort and wait for them to come to him."

"It's brilliant." His voice was warm with admiration, and not for their old adversary. "You're brilliant."

Jane made a self-deprecating gesture. "It's only a theory."

Jack had already gone into full planning mode. "If Thomières did arrive in Peniche as planned, how many men will he have?"

"A full battalion, plus a detachment of artillery. Oh, and fifty dragoons." She'd nearly forgotten the dragoons.

"So . . . three hundred—odd men? I don't want to underestimate our mutual talents, but that might take more than a saber and an épée."

"I left my épée in Paris," said Jane. "And my pistols in Santarém."

She didn't miss the épée, but she did regret those pistols. Not that a pair of pistols would be terribly much use against an entire French battalion, however travel-weary or battered.

They couldn't hope for much by way of reinforcements. The island fortress of Berlengas was held by a handful of British marines. Richard might have brought five men, six at most.

Jane looked up at Jack, bracing herself for objections. "We haven't the resources to storm the castle . . . but we can infiltrate from within. *I* can infiltrate from within." Quickly, Jane added, "If the Gardener isn't there, I can pose as a distressed Frenchwoman. And if he is—"

Jack's arms were folded across his chest; his features might have been carved out of granite. "All right."

Chapter Twenty

"*I* 've had more experience— What?"

"All right," Jack repeated. Hippolyte emitted a bray of protest as Jack strode forward, his pace forcing the reluctant donkey into a trot. "If we find a French garrison there when we arrive in Peniche, you go in."

Jane hurried to catch up with him. "You're not going to argue with me?"

The frozen earth was hard beneath the soles of Jack's boots. "Would I like to single-handedly storm the fort, rout the entire garrison, and present you with a queen on a platter? Yes. Do I stand a chance? No. You do." Relenting, Jack slowed a bit, looking sideways at Jane. "Do I like it? I'd rather be pounded with a mallet and roasted over hot coals."

"One seldom roasts over cold coals." Lightly Jane touched Jack's arm. Softly she said, "Thank you."

"For what?" He could feel her touch like a brand. "For stepping back and letting you do all the work?"

"No." She looked at him under the brim of her hat, seeming painfully young in her boy's garb. "For trusting me."

He could brush it off, make it less than it was. "I would sooner trust you than anyone," said Jack gruffly. *"But."*

"But?"

"We don't leave anything to chance." Jack tramped grimly forward. "We need a strategy before you go in. A plan. And we're going to make bloody sure we've thought through every last contingency."

Something that would provide him with a spurious sense of control while the woman he loved surrendered herself to her former lover.

Jack glanced sharply at Jane. Loved? He hadn't meant loved. He'd meant—

Loved.

Damn.

Jane, mercifully, didn't seem to notice that he felt as though he'd just been kicked in the head by the donkey. "Even the best-laid plans go awry."

Striving for normalcy, Jack said, "I believe the phrase you're looking for is 'aft gang agley.'"

Love? No, no, no. That wasn't part of the plan. That wasn't part of any plan. Jack tried to conjure the image of Jane as he'd first seen her, frilled, jeweled, and dismissive in a rented room in Lisbon, but, while he could recall the picture of her, he couldn't recall the animus that had gone with it. He knew too much of her now; he knew that beneath that supercilious poise lay a deep desire to do right, an earnestness that rendered her infinitely vulnerable. The spoiled society beauty he had met in Lisbon didn't exist, any more than the peasant boy trudging beside him.

There was just Jane, quick, clever, earnest. Passionate.

"You read Burns?"

"What?" It took Jack a moment to realize what she was saying. "No. My father used to read me Burns."

It was one of those memories he'd chosen not to remember: taking refuge with his father late at night, after the others were in bed, his father reading the verse by the light of a single lantern, his voice deepening into the rolling Highland brogue that had belonged to Jack's grandparents in a misty green land far, far away.

It was easier not to remember that. It was easier to remember only the unhappy hours.

"I'm sorry I didn't tell you sooner that I knew your family," said Jane quietly.

There was so much he wanted to ask, but to do so would be to admit that he wanted to know. That he cared.

Jack shrugged. "It wasn't relevant to the mission. You did what you needed to do. And we," he said firmly, pushing aside any thoughts of what they'd done, "need to find that Queen and get her out. Get you both out," he corrected himself. "So. How are we going to do this?"

Jane eyed him sideways, but didn't push the topic. "It's really very simple. I go in. I ask for Nicolas."

"And if he's not there?"

"I pretend to be a distressed Frenchwoman lost on the road," said Jane promptly. "I have the white silk gown from the abbey. If I claim to be under the Comte de Brillac's protection, no one will molest me."

Jack didn't need her to spell out what was meant by "protection." "In other words," he said, folding his arms across his chest, "you'll pose as Brillac's mistress."

"The easiest roles are those with a touch of the truth." Jane's pale eyes met his, rueful, questioning.

Jack bit his tongue. Hard. It wasn't fair for him to condemn her liaison with the Gardener, any more than it would have been fair for him to pretend that there had been no one before her, or that none of them had mattered in their way, at their time. They were neither of them youths just out of the schoolroom.

"Just so long as it's only a role," muttered Jack, and then felt like a cad. "Fine. You go in. You ask for the Comte de Brillac. And then?"

Jane looked away. "And then," she said, "I imagine Nicolas will offer me a glass of wine."

Hippolyte gave an indignant bray. Jack loosened his stranglehold on the donkey's lead. "If the Queen's not there," he said, his voice flat and hard, "you get out. You get out quickly."

"Agreed. And if the Queen is there?"

Jack frowned. "You won't be able to shift her on her own. She's a large woman. The odds are that she'll be heavily drugged."

"Rendering her limp, and thus even harder to move." A faint smile crossed Jane's lips. "We could take a leaf from the conspirators' book—you and Richard could infiltrate the fortress, disguised as priests."

Jack raised a brow. "Richard? Not Lord Richard?"

Jane looked him quizzically. "Lord Richard is married to my cousin Amy. He's like a brother to me."

Not that Jack had thought otherwise. Not really. Oh, the hell with it.

Jack shoved his hands into his pockets. "Irritating as all hell, but always there to watch your back?"

Jane smiled ruefully. "Precisely. We can only hope he hasn't brought Amy. She is in a delicate condition, but I'm not sure that will stop her from wanting to swing through the window on a rope and single-handedly confront the Gardener."

"If he's busy delivering a baby," said Jack bluntly, "he won't be chasing you."

"All the same, I would prefer my next godchild not be born in a French fortress." She winced, and said hurriedly, "I don't know whether Richard has the appropriate clerical garb on board, but it shouldn't be too hard to come by."

Jack reluctantly dismissed the plan. "Two priests dragging the limp body of the Queen through the courtyard might arouse attention."

"Could we lower her by rope?"

Jack tried to recall what he knew about the fortress of Peniche. "The windows on the seaward side aren't large enough."

Jane grimaced. "Had I known it would come to this, I would have commissioned a plan of the fort. The fort is old; it was constructed over successive generations by multiple architects. There must be some forgotten entrance or exit, something discreet, something a new arrival wouldn't necessarily have found."

They walked in silence for a moment. Half to herself, Jane said, "It's a pity it's such a small garrison. If it were larger, you and Richard might slip in disguised as members of the detachment of dragoons. But with a force this size, after traveling together for so long, a newcomer will stand out. Unless we wait until after dusk?"

While Jane sat in her white silk gown, sipping wine with the Comte de Brillac.

Sipping wine . . .

Hippolyte nearly ran into Jack's back as he stopped short. "Is the Queen in the custody of Thomières or the Comte de Brillac?" he asked abruptly.

Jane looked at him quizzically, but she answered readily enough. "I would imagine the comte. He would want the credit."

"Thomières doesn't outrank him?" The plan Jack had in mind was contingent on the Gardener's being the orders that would count.

"Perhaps on paper," said Jane thoughtfully, "but I doubt Thomières would dare to countermand him. There are times when self-preservation is more important than protocol."

Ordinarily the Gardener's power would have annoyed Jack; at the moment it worked in their favor.

"So," said Jack, his eyes meeting Jane's, "if the Comte de Brillac were to sign an order for the Queen to be moved, it would be obeyed?"

Jane's breath caught in her throat. "An order specifying that the Queen was to be transferred—to the fortress of Berlengas, perhaps?"

Jack smiled smugly. "How well can you imitate the comte's handwriting?"

"Well enough." Jane's face fell. "But I'll need his seal. They won't honor his orders without his seal."

It wasn't the sort of seal one could counterfeit. Jack knew that seal of old. It had signed the orders directing him to kill his mentor—and, he was sure, the order commanding Jack's own death.

"There are opiates in my bag," said Jack. "Enough to give the Gardener some very interesting dreams. Can you get them into his wine?"

"After Santarém," said Jane wryly, "he might not be so eager to take food from my hand."

Jack grinned. "I'd forgotten about that. Zounds, that felt good."

"Not for Nicolas," said Jane.

Jack's grin broadened. He couldn't help it. It was childish, but the thought of the Gardener bent over a chamber pot just made his day.

"Can you carry it off—despite that?"

Jane thought seriously about the question. "Yes," she said at last. "As odd as it seems, he may not have connected me with his stomach upset."

"Even though you ran?"

Jane glanced wryly up at him. "I've run from him before. It seemed easier than continuing to say no."

It was hard not to feel just a little satisfied by that. Jack tried to focus on the matter at hand. "Hell hath no fury like a man scorned. If it's not safe—"

"Nicolas," said Jane wearily, "believes that flight is merely an invitation to pursue. It is a game to him."

"It's not a game to me." Had he said that out loud? Jack hastily backtracked. "Er—the Queen, I mean. Saving the Queen."

Jane cocked her head. "Didn't you once say this was a fool's mission?"

"Yes, but we're the fools assigned to it." Oh, hell. Who was he deceiving? To the choppy waters of the ocean, Jack said brusquely, "And I don't want anything to happen to you."

The air smelled of salt. The irregular shape of the fortress was already in sight across the spar of land that joined Peniche to the mainland. Jack could feel time slipping away from them. He wanted it back.

Weeks and weeks they had had together, but it felt like minutes, too quickly gone. What had they done with that time? Jack willed the waters into the distance, willed the stones of the fortress to crumble and fall away into the sea. Let Rome into Tiber melt and let the road roll on and on.

But it didn't. The stones stayed firmly in place, closer now, and a gull cawed over the waters.

With unspoken agreement, they turned off the road, into a copse sheltered by large boulders. Hippolyte grazed among the thin stalks of winter brown grass. Plucking off her hat, Jane shook her hair free. It sifted down around her shoulders, the color of winter wheat in the sunshine. Jack's hands tingled at the memory of it, the feel of it against his palms, sliding through his fingers.

Jane took the white silk dress from her pack and shook it out. In another minute she would be back in her gown, back in her role, ready to confront the Gardener in his den, leaving Jack wondering and waiting.

He couldn't let her go. Not like that.

Jack braced his hands against a boulder. "Jane. About last night . . ."

Jane's hands stilled on the dress. Without looking at him, she said carefully, "Is this really the time?"

"We might not have another time." Jack took a step forward, and then caught himself.

Nicolas believes that flight is merely an invitation to pursue. He didn't want her to feel caught or cornered. But he needed her to know—

Abruptly, Jack said, "We never discussed—if there should be a child . . ."

It wasn't what he had meant to say.

Jane ducked her head, hiding her face from him as she carefully smoothed out the folds of the gown. "You needn't worry. My courses—it would be highly unlikely."

The jerkiness of her movements might be attributed to embarrassment. Jack was a little surprised. Jane wasn't generally missish about the practicalities.

The word left a bitter taste on his tongue. Practicalities. He shouldn't be talking about practicalities. He should be telling her that she hung the moon in the sky, or that her eyes were the same color as some flower or other, or some such romantic drivel that didn't even come close to how he felt.

"Nevertheless," Jack persisted doggedly, "if there should be consequences, you're not on your own."

It might not be what he'd intended to say, but he meant it. The idea of any child of his out in the world on its own—no, no, and no.

That was a lesson, Jack realized, he had learned from his father. Who, no matter the circumstances, no matter the inconvenience to himself, the demands on his purse, the ribbing of his messmates, had never denied any of them.

Jack had never thought of himself as emulating his father—in fact, he had very determinedly attempted not to—but in this, the old boy had a point.

Jane glanced at him sideways. There were fine lines between her brows. "You would abandon your post?"

"Rather my post than you," Jack said gruffly. "Or our child."

The words seemed to echo in Jane's ears. Her hands tightened on the white gown, crushing the material between her fingers. Slowly, carefully, she set the dress aside, drawing in a long breath through her nose.

She had never particularly pined after a child of her own. Yes, she enjoyed her goddaughter and the children of her friends, but her time with them had never awakened any burning maternal desires in her breast. In her line of work, a child would be worse than an inconvenience; it would be a disaster. Jane had seen what happened to other agents. The obvious discomforts of pregnancy were the least of the matter. How could one make clear choices knowing that one's child might be taken as hostage? It was a vulnerability, a potentially fatal vulnerability.

Once the war was over . . . Yes, perhaps. Jane had never devoted much thought to the prospect. The idea of a child was something vague and distant, something for a misty and decidedly unlikely future.

But in Jack's voice, the concept became very real indeed. Jane could smell the downy head, feel it cradled in her arms. *Our child.*

"I should—I should change," said Jane. Just because Jack was willing to accept the responsibility didn't mean he wanted it. He cared for her, that much was clear, but as a friend, a comrade. To delude herself that it was anything more would do them both a disservice. "Will you stand watch?"

"Eat something first," said Jack, thrusting a bit of bread and cheese in her general direction. "I don't want you drinking with that bastard on an empty stomach."

"I shan't lose my head." Jane nibbled obediently at the cheese, which tasted a little bit of cheese and a great deal of lint.

She set it aside. Her stomach was unsettled, and not at the prospect of seeing Nicolas.

"Unless he drugs you before you drug him." Jack's expression was grim. "Maybe we should go back to that plan with the priest costumes."

"I have the advantage of surprise." Jane jammed a pin in her hair, dressing it as best she could without comb or mirror. "I have a sleeping draft in my ring. I'll empty it in his cup— and I'll make sure he drinks it. And then . . ." She paused to hunt for another pin.

Jack handed it to her, his movements tense. "Then?"

"Then," said Jane, "the Gardener and the Queen shall depart for the island of Berlengas."

She and Nicolas were of a height. His clothes would fit her well enough. While she wouldn't want to attempt the impersonation for an extended period of time, Jane was confident that she could fool the odd sentry.

Jane jammed the final pin in her hair. "It will be more convincing if the Gardener accompanies his hostage. Look for us at the fortress of Berlengas by sunset." Before Jack could argue, she said, "The *Bien-Aimée* is too conspicuous. If you sail it into harbor, they might fire on you."

"So we're just to sit there on Berlengas, waiting for you?" Jack looked more mulish than the mule. "We could take a dinghy."

"And do what? Masquerade as my coachman?" The Gardener didn't know Jack, but that didn't mean he wouldn't be in danger. "It will arouse less suspicion if the Gardener's usual coachman takes us to the docks. The fewer people involved, the better our chances. You know that as well as I. It's safer this way. For all of us."

Our child.

There was no child. Resolutely, Jane reached for the white gown.

"What about the docks?" Jack turned abruptly to face her, pebbles crunching beneath his boots. "You'll need a boat. And a boatman."

"Can you sail a boat?"

"No, but I can hire one and pose as crew."

"Do fishing boats have crews?" The fact that Jack looked as blank as she did was argument enough against the plan. He had posed as a seller of horses, not a sailor. "It's how far to Berlengas? An hour? More? It makes no sense for you to go back and forth."

"All the more reason for me to stay here."

"And be captured? It makes more sense to gather reinforcements and wait for a signal." Turning her back, Jane yanked the white silk gown over her head. She bent her head forward. "Will you do up my buttons?"

Reluctantly, Jack stepped forward. "I don't like this," he muttered.

Jane shivered as Jack's knuckles brushed the tender skin at the nape of her neck. "It was your plan."

Jack did up the last button. His hands rested, far too briefly, on her shoulders. "I still don't like it."

"It's our best chance." Jane turned to face him, not sure what to say now that the moment of parting had come. There was only a yard of frostbitten ground between them, but it felt like much more. Tentatively, Jane said, "If I need help, I'll signal."

"If I don't hear from you by sundown," Jack countered, "I'll come after you."

"Nicolas won't hurt me. He fancies himself in love with me."

"Would you be willing to wager your life on that? The man's a ruthless bastard."

"Quite literally. You didn't know? His mother cuckolded the Comte de Brillac with an Englishman." She was drawing this out, Jane knew, putting off the moment of parting. "Nicolas has his reasons for being what he is."

Jack folded his arms across his chest. "Don't start feeling too sorry for him."

"I shan't leave him in custody of the Queen, if that's what you're worried about."

"I'm not worried about the Queen." Jack jammed his hat down over his head. "Just—be careful."

Jane started to put a hand out and then thought better of it. She stood there as primly as a schoolgirl in her too-tight gown, her neck turning blue with cold. "You as well."

"This," said Jack succinctly, "is ridiculous."

And without another word, he reached out, pulled Jane to him, and kissed her until her ears were ringing and her neck was no longer the least bit chilly.

"Don't take any chances," he said gruffly.

Jane's hands were clutching the collar of his jacket. She forced herself to let go. "No more than necessary."

"No more than necessary." Jack rested his forehead against hers, breathing in deeply. His arms closed around her, cradling her close. "Come back safely to me," he whispered.

And then he was gone.

Jane watched him as he strode away, just another man and his donkey, heading for the harbor.

It hadn't been an *I love you*, but it had certainly felt like one.

Nicolas, Jane reminded herself. She would need all her wits about her to deal with Nicolas.

Strange to think that once her palms would have tingled and her chest would have felt tight at the prospect of sparring with Nicolas, part fear, part anticipation. Now there was no titillation, just grim resolve.

But she couldn't let him see that. He would need to see her equal parts eagerness and apprehension.

Amarantha, thought Jane wryly, still in thrall to the Knight of the Silver Tower.

Little did the knight know that his silver armor had lost its lure. Perhaps Miss Gwen should write a sequel, thought Jane wildly. Something about a moonflower.

She didn't need to ask directions to the fort. The large, irregular structure was hard to miss. The windowless stone walls were rather a giveaway. There was a gate set into the forbidding stone wall, manned by a bored French soldier who looked like he would far rather be playing cards.

He stood up a little straighter as Jane approached, shouldering the musket he had left carelessly propped by the side of the door.

"Yes?" he demanded insolently, his eyes lingering on the flesh exposed by Jane's bodice.

In flawless and very aristocratic French, Jane said, "Tell Monsieur le Comte de Brillac that he has a guest."

"Er . . ." It was clear the guard didn't know what to make of her. "Do you have papers?"

Yes. In a trunk somewhere on the road to Santarém.

Jane drew herself up, doing her best imitation of the Dowager Duchess of Dovedale in a snit. "Take me to the comte. At once."

"But—"

"You may tell him," said Jane, flicking at a smudge of dirt on her sleeve, "that his fiancée is here to see him."

Chapter Twenty-one

I held tightly to my fiancé's hand as we picked our way carefully across the midnight grounds of Donwell Abbey.

We didn't dare light a flashlight; that might alert our adversary to our presence. The idea was to outsmart the kidnapper. If we were already here when he arrived, crouching in darkness, we might get the jump on him and wrest Mrs. Selwick-Alderly away before he knew what was happening.

It wasn't much of a plan, but it was all we had. Further proof, if I'd needed it, that Colin was telling the truth about not being MI5, 6, or 23. In the spy novel he'd been writing, his hero generally defeated the villains with more firepower than cunning. Since the largest weapon at our disposal was a tractor and the only firepower a few leftover fireworks from Guy Fawkes Day, we'd been forced to default to simpler means.

I was to do the distracting; Colin would do any wresting required. Brute strength was more in his line than mine.

We had come prepared. Sort of. In the car I'd changed my high heels for sneakers. They didn't do much for my DVF knock-off wrap dress, but they were much more practical for traversing the uneven terrain around the ruins of the old monastery, as I had learned the hard way on a previous occasion. I also had a sheet, with holes cut out for eyes. If worse came to worst, two could play at being the Phantom Monk of Donwell Abbey.

Even if I looked less like a phantom monk and more like Casper the Friendly Ghost.

Right now, in the darkness, with the remains of the old abbey looming up ahead of us, it was far too easy to believe in real ghosts. Colin had told me some of the old tales when I had first come to stay at Selwick Hall: a restless spirit, searching for his lost love, seeking revenge on the men who had driven them apart.

Most of the abbey had disappeared over time, looted by locals who had used the stones for sheds and cow byres. But there were still a few walls intact, rising jaggedly against the night sky, punctuated by the empty arches of windows.

Or were they empty? My imagination conjured specters in the shadows. The night was full of strange rustlings and mur-murings, the calls of unfamiliar birds and the too-loud beating of my heart.

This was really not how I'd intended to spend the night before my wedding. But we were together, I reminded myself, leaning against Colin's side and breathing in the familiar, comforting smell of him. And maybe, just maybe, this would all turn out to be a massive misunderstanding or a prank, nothing sinister at all.

Something crackled loudly and I nearly jumped into Colin's arms.

A crisps packet. That was all it was. The abbey might give the impression of being lost to time, but according to Colin it was a very popular destination for local youth, for all the obvious purposes.

"The old refectory?" I murmured to Colin, and felt him nod against my hair.

He paused, taking my hands in his. "Ready?"

I hefted my sheet. "As ready as I'll ever be." The whole thing felt more than a little unreal.

"Not exactly how you thought we'd be spending tonight, is it?" It was too dark to see his face, but I could hear the smile in his voice.

"I'm with you," I said simply. "That's a plus."

Colin pulled me forward into a quick, crushing embrace. "I love you," he murmured.

"I love you, too." I pulled away just far enough to grin at him, high on love and nerves. "Maybe we should—I don't know—get married or something."

Colin grasped my hand, the one with his ring. He'd given

it to me last year, on my birthday cupcake. I'd had to lick off the icing before he could put it on my finger. Because nothing says lasting love quite like buttercream frosting.

"Refectory?" he said, and I followed him through the treacherous ruins, skirting sinkholes that might once have been the monks' fishpond or the results of a ten-year-old searching for treasure.

The refectory was the only room that had retained all of its walls and some of its roof. It might look like something out of one of Mary Shelley's nightmares, but it was the best place to ambush our quarry.

Unfortunately, someone else appeared to have had the same idea.

"You're early." A man stepped out of the shadows. His Phantom Monk costume was much better than mine. The cowl fell in long folds around his face, and a remarkably accurate-looking rope circled his waist.

What was less accurate? The gun in one hand.

Don't ask me what kind of gun. The only weapon I'd ever handled was a Super Soaker. All I knew was that this one was metallic and dangerous and pointed squarely at me.

I hadn't been expecting a gun. One doesn't, really, any more than one expects kidnappings the night before one's wedding. In the back of my head I think I had assumed all along that the malefactor was Jeremy. And Jeremy, for all his other sins, was reasonably harmless.

This man wasn't looking particularly harmless.

"Where's the box?" he demanded.

It was too dark to see his face, but I knew that voice. "Dempster? Nigel Dempster?"

It was like pulling the mask off the zombie, only to discover that he was really the owner of the amusement park and he'd have gotten away with it, too, if it hadn't been for those pesky kids and their dog.

I should have guessed when he'd said "box." If anyone was as obsessed with the Pink Carnation as I was, it was Nigel Dempster. He'd dated Serena to get to those papers and, when that failed, took up with Colin's neighbor, Joan.

I'd been so relieved at Dempster's distracting Joan that I hadn't inquired too closely into any ulterior motives he might have had in dating someone next door to Selwick Hall.

But who would have thought that he cared quite that much? I had certainly never imagined that Dempster, with his carefully groomed hair and immaculate sport coats, would go to the lengths of kidnapping an elderly lady.

Attempting to suck up to said elderly lady, yes. Plying her with tea, yes. Holding a gun on us? No.

Which just goes to show that you never know.

Even now, with the gun pointing straight at me, it didn't quite compute. I know death is supposed to concentrate the mind wonderfully, but it was having the opposite effect for me. My ear itched. One of my sneakers was laced too tightly. And I felt strangely indignant at being put to all this trouble by Dempster—Dempster!—of all people.

Adding a little gravel to his voice, Dempster growled, "Where is it?"

"Where is my aunt?" Colin countered. Slowly, carefully, he eased away to my right, attempting to draw Dempster's fire.

"Safe." Dempster wasn't drawn. He kept the gun pointed right at my chest. "But you won't be if you keep moving."

"Isn't this a little bit extreme?" My Casper sheet was bundled underneath one arm. I hitched it a little higher. "If you had wanted access to the Pink Carnation's trunk, you might have just asked. Instead of, you know, holding a gun on me the night before my wedding."

"I don't know what you're talking about," said our assailant, affecting a deep voice with a faint and entirely unbelievable accent.

"Oh, come on." In my own defense, if it were a Russian mobster or an unknown assailant of any extraction, I would have been behaving myself nicely, but this was Dempster. I'd seen the man fall to pieces over a broken nail. He was more metro than sexual. If that gun was even loaded, I'd be very surprised. "What else? You've been angling for those papers for years. Is it worth this"—I jabbed a finger in the general direction of his firearm—"for a book deal?"

Colin gave me a discreet thumbs-up as he edged to the side, towards a convenient piece of loose coping.

"This isn't"—Dempster had forgotten he was meant to sound French—"about a book deal."

Huh. I believed that just about as much as I believed those

were real streaks of silver at his temples. The man's oft-repeated master plan was to soar to notoriety as the first person to unmask the legendary Pink Carnation. Interviews in the *Guardian*, opinion pieces in the *Times*, a BBC miniseries . . .

It would be a bit like finding the real Robin Hood, only with fewer tights. The fact that the Pink Carnation was a woman provided extra bonus points. The media would be all over that and, by extension, all over Dempster.

"Intellectual curiosity, then," I said generously, pretending to believe him. "Look, as long as Colin and Aunt Arabella agree, we'd be happy to open our archives to you."

As a distraction, it was working rather nicely. Or maybe not. Dempster glared at me down the barrel of his gun. "Just bring me that damned box!"

"Right now? Wouldn't you rather sit down and go through the papers with a cup of coffee and a Danish?"

"Cherry or cheese?" murmured Colin. I had the feeling he was getting a little punchy.

"I don't like Danish," snapped Dempster.

"Pain au chocolat?" I offered.

"I don't need catering," said Dempster tensely. "I just need those papers."

I exchanged a glance with Colin. "The trunk is in the Land Rover." It wasn't, actually, but if we moved Dempster out into the open, we might have more of a chance.

"Fine." Dempster pointed the gun at Colin. "You. Go get it. She"—damn, the gun was back on me—"stays with me."

"The box is heavy," I said cunningly. "It takes two people to lift."

"I don't need the whole box. I just need those notebooks."

"Don't you mean those papers? The Pink Carnation's papers aren't in notebooks; they're loose."

"I don't give a damn about the Pink Carnation!" Dempster did his best Rumpelstiltskin imitation. "Who cares that much about nineteenth-century spies?"

"I do, actually." I frowned at Dempster. "I thought you did, too."

"That was what you were meant to think. That was what you were all meant to think." He waved his gun in exasperation. "Would it have killed you to have given me access to those papers?"

All of this weapon waving was making me nervous. "Er— if not the Pink Carnation, then why do you want the family papers?"

"Because," he said, his voice as nasal and overenunciated as ever, "your aunt killed my father."

My eyes slid towards Colin's. He gave a little shake of his head. He had no clue either.

"Mrs. Selwick-Alderly killed your father?" I said. Keep 'em talking. That was what they always did on TV. Of course, on TV there was usually backup coming. I was our backup.

It was not a reassuring thought.

"Well, what do you call it when someone leaves you a loaded gun and the threat of exposure?" said Dempster testily.

" 'Blow your brains out and we'll keep it quiet.' What sort of offer is that?"

"That depends," said Colin quietly, "on the nature of the offense."

"You sell a few little secrets to the Russians . . ." Dempster jabbed the gun at him. "It was all your bitch of an aunt's fault. He made a run for it and it all came out. Stories in the papers, boys whispering behind my back at school. She ruined him. She ruined *me*."

"Of course," said Colin quietly. "I should have realized. The Dempster Affair."

"The what?" I felt like I was missing something.

Colin kept an eye on Dempster as he explained. "In the seventies. I was only three or four. It was all over the news. A very senior MP was passing sensitive information to the Russians—"

"Supposedly passing information to the Russians," Dempster corrected him.

I didn't want to make trouble, but . . . "Have you ever considered—just for argument's sake—that your father might actually have been conspiring with the Russians?"

"Of course he was!" said Dempster impatiently. "The tuition at Saint Anselm was absurd."

"So," I said slowly, "what you're saying is that Mrs. Selwick-Alderly was doing her job and your father got caught red-handed."

"Oh, no," said Dempster, a thin smile pursing his lips.

"Quite the contrary. An excitable woman overstepped herself and accused a man of sterling reputation. A man who was then hounded to death by the media. And naturally her superiors covered it all up. MI5 doesn't like to admit when they get it wrong."

There was something that didn't quite add up. "But you just said . . ."

Dempster looked altogether too pleased with himself. "You see, those notebooks are going to reappear—in a slightly edited form. And the author of them will be found, tragically, dead by her own hand. Out of remorse. For framing my father all those years ago."

Okay, I was scared now.

Colin was standing very, very still, like a tiger poised to strike. "Where is she?" he asked quietly.

"Still alive. For the moment." Dempster looked impatient. "There's no point in killing her until I know you have the notebooks."

It made a mad sort of sense. If she'd hidden them elsewhere, he would need her to tell him the location.

"Do you remember any notebooks?" I said to Colin. "I was focusing on the nineteenth-century documents."

"Nice try," said Dempster. "I know they're in there. They have to be—"

He paused at the sound of a footfall on the stone. Our backs were to the entrance, so I couldn't see her, but I knew that cultured, hesitant voice. "Nigel? Who are you—"

"What in the—" Colin whirled around as his sister hesitated on the threshold, a raspberry pashmina trailing over one shoulder, peering into the murky interior.

"Insurance." Dempster reached out and dragged Serena into the room, mashing her back against his chest, the gun against her temple.

Part of me hoped that Serena would secretly go ninja and truss him with her pashmina. If Mrs. Selwick-Alderly was a spy, why not Serena?

But she didn't.

Serena clawed at the arm holding her, trying desperately to catch her balance as her high heels scraped back against the cracked stone flags of the floor. "Nigel— What . . . ?"

I could have cheerfully strangled Dempster then and there. The rat fink must have told Serena that he missed her, that he wanted to see her. There was nothing like a sibling's wedding to make a single woman feel vulnerable. And what more romantic place than the ruins of an old abbey on a moonlit night?

I stared at Dempster in disgust. "Oh, right. Go ahead. Pick on people who aren't strong enough to fight back. She weighs, what, half of what you do?"

Serena's eyes were beginning to bulge a bit as Dempster's arm clamped down over her neck. "I need those papers and I need them now."

And that was when my phone started ringing.

Brring-brring! Brring-brring! The sound echoed against the jagged stone walls, metallic and insistent.

I bit my lip. "Um, I'll just ignore the call, shall I?"

"Pick it up." Dempster held Serena in one arm, pointing the gun at me with the other. "No tricks."

Slowly, carefully, I clicked the green button and held the phone to my ear.

"Hello?" I really hoped it wasn't my mother.

It wasn't. "Eloise!" I only vaguely recognized the Southern-inflected male voice. "It's Jim. Jim Landry."

"Oh, hi, Jim." I kept one careful eye on Nigel and the gun in his hand. From the corner of my eye I could see Colin starting to inch forward.

"I know it's a little late to be calling—"

"It's two in the morning." Inch, inch, freeze, like a game of red light, green light, one, two, three.

"It's— Oh, crap. You're in England, aren't you? I forgot. Did I wake you up?" Before I could answer, he said, "It's just that we have an offer! And I wanted you to know straight-away."

"An offer?" Serena squirmed weakly against Dempster's hold. Which might have been a good thing if I hadn't been worried that any sudden activity might jar his trigger finger.

"For the book!" My agent's voice crackled merrily across the transatlantic divide. "Aren't you excited?"

"Yes, very excited." Or I would be excited, if I didn't have a crazed archivist strangling my future sister-in-law.

Jim was still talking. "—two-book deal, world English, we retain the foreign rights—"

I appeared to have missed several important points, like the name of the publisher and the amount of money involved, all of which would be much more relevant if I lived to see the morning. How many bullets did a gun like that hold? I smiled weakly at Dempster as I said to Jim, "That's great. Great."

"—a preempt," Jim was saying. "I know we could have tried for an auction, but I think, under the circumstances—"

My circumstances were looking increasingly grim. Serena gave a little gurgle as Dempster jerked the gun in my general direction, indicating that it was time to wrap it up.

"Uh, Jim? Can I call you back tomorrow? Or maybe Monday? I'm supposed to be getting married tomorrow," I added apologetically.

"And I interrupted your beauty sleep!"

If only. I did my best to curtail the avalanche of apologies and congratulations. "Yes, yes, I'll absolutely show you pictures—no, we won't be leaving for our honeymoon until Tuesday. We wanted time to clean up first. What? Oh, Istanbul. Okay, sure, we'll look for that restaurant." Dempster was going to shoot me any minute now. "Er, Jim, I really have to go."

I would have asked him to call the police for me, but a) he was in the wrong country, and b) I couldn't think of any way to do it subtly, without Dempster noticing. Because, let's face it, there was no way to explain that we were being held in the ruins of an old abbey by a crazed archivist without some pretty damning explanations.

I clicked the end-call button, cunningly keeping the phone

in my hand. If I could only remember the number of the British equivalent of 911, maybe I could dial it without Dempster seeing.

"So," I announced to my future husband, my almost-sister-in-law, and our assailant. "I've got a book deal!"

"Wonderful news, my dear!" The voice came from one of the gaps in the wall. One navy blue court shoe stepped firmly through the aperture, followed by a leg in a slightly rumpled blue trouser, a matching white-braided blue jacket, and, at last, a sleek silver head. "I'm so very proud of you."

Dempster jerked around, his gun pointing wide. "You! How did you—"

Taking advantage of his confusion, Colin yanked Serena by one arm, pulling her free of Dempster's grasp, while I flung my Casper sheet over his head, smothering him in five yards of off-white cotton blend.

Dempster flailed wildly, tripping over the edge of the sheet. The gun skidded across the floor. A hand shot out. I stomped on it, wishing I were wearing stilettos instead of sneakers.

I needn't have worried. While I was looking about for a weapon, Mrs. Selwick-Alderly, without missing a beat, removed her shoe and conked Dempster neatly over the head.

Dempster dropped like a stone.

Mrs. Selwick-Alderly fitted her shoe back on her foot. "I'm so sorry, my dears," she said. "I'd meant to be here sooner, but I'm not as fit as I used to be."

Chapter Twenty-two

"Y ou're not Jane," said the brunette standing on the deck of the *Bien-Aimée*. She cocked her head, looking Jack up and down with hazel eyes that tilted up at the corners. "And you're certainly not the Queen of Portugal."

"Is Lord Richard Selwick on board?"

The *Bien-Aimée* had been a surprise, and so far not a pleasant one. It was a rich man's pleasure yacht, and the woman on the deck seemed ordered to match in her fashionable traveling dress. Jack had bad feelings about this. Very bad feelings. Hell, he had bad feelings about all of this. He had bad feelings about climbing aboard a strange boat. He had even worse feelings about leaving Jane behind, in Peniche, at the dubious mercy of a man not known for mercy.

"I need to speak to him."

The brunette sighed. "Always Richard."

"What about Richard?" A man bounded up on deck, a floppy lock of blond hair descending over one eye.

"I've been instructed to give a message to Lord Richard Selwick," said Jack, eyeing the other man dubiously. He looked like an overgrown golden retriever, not like the former leader of a sizable spy ring.

On the other hand, he also didn't look like a minion of the Gardener, so there was that. The man in front of Jack had that pink-cheeked, beef-fed look that no impostor could hope to ape. And that was a biscuit in one hand, not a gun. Jack smelled . . . ginger?

"I saw him a moment ago." The blond man peered up into the rigging as though expecting the mysterious Lord Richard to drop like manna from heaven. "I can't think where he's got to." Belatedly recalling his manners, he held out a hand to Jack, saying affably, "Hullo. I'm Miles Dorrington. This is my wife, Lady Henrietta. And you are . . . ?"

"Trying to find Lord Richard," said Jack tersely.

He devoutly hoped he was on the right ship. He appeared to have stumbled onto a pleasure cruise for aristocratic lunatics.

He should have known something was wrong when he was piped on board by a man dressed like the popular misconception of a seventeenth-century buccaneer, complete with frogged frock coat, a parrot on his shoulder, and an entirely gratuitous use of "arrrr" and "avast."

If this was Jane's rescue party, he'd have been better off storming the fortress with the damn donkey.

Jack tried again. "Is Lord Richard here?"

"Anything you can tell Richard, you can tell us," said Lady Henrietta with a confidence that Jack was far from feeling.

"Tell me what?" said another man, emerging on deck.

"I don't know." Crumbs scattered as Miles waved his biscuit. "He won't tell us."

The newcomer stepped forward, assuming command with an air of easy assurance. And thank goodness for that, thought Jack irritably. Here at last was someone with whom he could speak reasonably. "I am Lord Richard. And you are . . . ?"

"The Carnation sent me," said Jack. Old habits died hard. No names. Only necessary information. Especially when time was wasting. "She's gone into the fortress of Peniche to retrieve the Queen."

"Er . . ." Miles Dorrington spoke indistinctly around his biscuit. "Isn't Peniche in the hands of the frogs?"

"Yes," said Jack tersely. That was rather the point.

And so, at the moment, was Jane.

"Jane's been captured?" Lady Henrietta surged forward like the statue on the prow of a ship.

"She's gone in," Jack corrected shortly. "Voluntarily."

"And you let her?" Lady Henrietta's eyes were as wide as they could go.

A dry cackle came from the hatch that led to the nether regions of the yacht. "Have you ever seen anyone 'let' Jane do anything?"

A parasol emerged first, a purple parasol, the point hitting the deck with a force that made Miles jump. The newcomer strode forward, blindingly purple skirts swishing around her legs. Jack had never seen that much purple all in one place before. It was like being assaulted by an aubergine.

"If Jane is there, it's because she chose to be there," said the newcomer definitively. Jack wasn't sure whether to appreciate or resent her support. "Jane does or she doesn't. I would as soon try to yoke an aardvark."

Lady Henrietta cocked her head. "Does one yoke aardvarks?"

"No," said Jack shortly, putting an abrupt end to what might otherwise have become a fascinating and largely pointless discourse on natural history.

The woman in purple subjected Jack to a critical inspection. "You must be Jack. Jane succeeded in part of her mission, at least." And then: "You don't look at all as I expected."

"Fewer horns?" said Jack tersely. "If we could return to the matter at hand, Jane is currently attempting to extract the whereabouts of the missing Queen of Portugal from the Gardener."

That, at least, had some effect. Miles Dorrington stopped crunching his biscuit. Lord Richard Selwick looked grave.

The woman in purple's nostrils flared. "*He* is here?"

"I hate that man," muttered Lady Henrietta.

"That," said the woman in regal purple, "is hardly an original sentiment." Turning to Jack, she said, "You allowed Jane to fall into *that* man's clutches?"

"What happened to 'no one lets Jane do anything Jane doesn't want to do'?" said Jack testily.

If there was anything less appealing than defending an unpopular plan, it was defending someone else's unpopular plan, especially since he was beginning to have serious second thoughts about it.

Now—now that he was away from Jane—he could think of a dozen objections, a dozen other ploys they might have tried, none of which involved Jane seducing her way into the confidence of Jack's mortal enemy. This, Jack thought grimly, was how the snake must feel once the fakir stopped playing his tune, when it awoke to find itself suspended on a bit of rope, with no idea how it had gotten up there, and a dim sense that this was a very bad idea indeed.

Jack glared impartially at each of the others in turn. "Don't you think I'd have gone in myself if I had the choice? I dislike it as much as you do. But there's nothing to be gained by standing about beating our breasts. There are plans to be made." He looked hard at the woman in purple, daring her to challenge him. "If you value Jane's life."

There was silence and then the woman in purple thumped her parasol against the deck. "Well, well," she said, in a way that made Jack feel like a schoolboy caught out in an infraction. "Well, well."

"No," said Jack, "it's not well. It's bloody awful. But it was the best we could do under the circumstances."

"What do you need from us?" said Lord Richard.

Jack decided embracing the man on first acquaintance might be a bit much, so he confined himself to a quick nod of gratitude.

"Jane has until sunset to bring the Queen to São João Batista fort. If she hasn't arrived by then, we're to go after her. Subtly," said Jack, with a hard look at Miles Dorrington, who had bounced up on the balls of his feet.

Dorrington subsided.

"Why so long?" asked Lady Henrietta.

"Because," said Jack tightly, "Jane needs time to gain the Gardener's confidence, drug him, and forge orders in his name."

Put that way, it sounded mad. No, it *was* mad.

Lady Henrietta exchanged a look with her husband.

The woman in purple shrugged. "Dull, but serviceable. *I* could have come up with something far more interesting."

Jack was beginning to feel more than a bit beleaguered. "We have reason to believe that the Queen is being held in the fortress of Peniche. Jane felt strongly that the most expedient way to get her out was to—"

"Seduce the Gardener?" offered Miles Dorrington, taking a healthy bite of his biscuit.

"Enter the fortress," said Jack, fixing him with a basilisk stare. Stubbornly refusing to turn to stone on the spot, Dorrington went on placidly munching his biscuit. "Jane was insistent that the Gardener would treat her with all courtesy."

Nicolas won't hurt me.

Jack only wished he felt as sure.

"Hmph," said the woman in purple. "That man is about as courteous as an asp."

"I know," said Jack shortly. "But—"

"Did I hear voices?" A newcomer wandered up out of the hatch, holding up a hand to shield his eyes from the afternoon sun. His eyes fell on Jack and he stopped short. "Jack? Jack!"

The man's face lit up like a hundred candles, until it was brighter than the sun glinting off the red and silver of his hair.

Jack froze. "Father?"

He had to be imagining things. But if he had imagined his father, he would have imagined him as he had seen him last, eleven years ago. This man wore those eleven years in the lines in his face and the silver streaks in his red hair. His athletic form had thickened with age, although he carried the extra flesh well. But mostly the restlessness that Jack remembered was gone. This man seemed settled. Happy.

Jack didn't know what to say or do. He wasn't prepared for this—for whoever this was. Perhaps, he thought wildly, he had fallen asleep in the hot spring and was having one of those dreams where one went from waltzing with an aardvark to rewriting Dr. Johnson's dictionary, all the while being late for some very important appointment that one would get to if only one were wearing breeches.

"Father?" he repeated.

"My boy," said his father, his voice thick with emotion. The next thing Jack knew, he was being enfolded in a massive embrace that squeezed the breath out of his chest and made him see spots.

For a moment Jack was four again, five, six, seven, running up to his father, being tossed up in his arms, lying in wait at the window so he could be there before Alex and Kat, so he could be first.

Extricating himself from his father's embrace, Jack stumbled back a step. "What are you doing here? Aren't you meant to be—" Jack couldn't for the life of him remember where his father was meant to be. "In England?"

"I came to see you, of course." His father clasped his shoulders, holding him at arm's length, looking him up and down. "You've grown."

"It's been eleven years," said Jack numbly. "Of course I've grown."

What in the devil was his father doing on Lord Richard's yacht? Vaguely, very vaguely, Jack remembered Jane telling him that his father had married her chaperone. Her former chaperone. But surely she would have mentioned a little detail like his father lying in wait for him on Lord Richard's yacht, wouldn't she?

Jack frowned at his father. "Jane didn't tell me you would be here."

"Jane didn't know," Jack's father said hastily. He glanced at the woman in purple, who was smirking fondly at Jack's father in a way that filled Jack with darkest foreboding. "We wanted to surprise you."

Jack looked from his father to the woman in purple. He thought he knew what was coming and he didn't like it. "We?"

His father slid his arm through that of the woman in purple. He cleared his throat. "Jack, may I present my wife, your new—"

"Felicitations." If his father thought he was going to call this woman mother, he had to be mad. But then, that was his father, wasn't it? He always saw the world as he wished it to be. It was stupid, at Jack's age, to feel disappointment. Jack nodded crisply to his new stepmother. "Congratulations, madam. Had I been informed, I would have sent a gift."

"That didn't sound terribly celebratory," whispered Lady Henrietta to her husband.

"We didn't know where to reach you," said his father apologetically. The woman in purple—Jack's stepmother—squeezed his father's hand, a gesture that made Jack see red.

"You certainly seem to have found me out now." Which raised an interesting question. How in the hell had his father found him?

A boat, Jane had said. His stepmother was her former chaperone. Jane had known he would be here. Hell, Jane had led him here.

Jack looked hard at his new stepmother. "You said something about Jane succeeding in part of her mission. What did you mean?"

"You, of course," said his stepmother dismissively.

Before Jack could say anything, he was bowled sideways by a small female moving with great velocity.

"Jack! Jack, Jack, Jack!" His sister Lizzy flung herself at him, momentarily stunning him. Or maybe that was just the large wooden object she was holding banging into the side of his head.

Jack gave his sister a quick, reflexive squeeze before turning to glare at his father. "You brought *Lizzy?*"

"How could I miss the return of my favorite brother?" said Lizzy, smiling winningly at him, and Jack realized, dizzily, that she wasn't the little girl he remembered. The wild red-brown curls were the same, but the missing front teeth had grown in and the rest of her had grown up.

He wasn't prepared for this. He wasn't prepared for any of this. In his head, Lizzy was still perpetually six years old.

She's rejected offers from three viscounts and the heir to a marquisate. Jane had told him, hadn't she? But Jack hadn't believed it. It had been a story about someone else, not his Lizzy.

"Lizzy is in training," said his stepmother grandly.

"For what?" demanded Jack. He noticed for the first time that the object in her hand appeared to be . . . "And why is she holding a crossbow?"

"Because I'm too small for a longbow," said Lizzy patiently. "Don't look so alarmed. I haven't hit anyone by accident in months."

"Hasn't hit anyone on purpose either," murmured Miles to Lady Henrietta.

Lizzy narrowed her eyes at him. "Is that a challenge?"

"No!" said everyone in unison.

Lizzy dismissed them all as irrelevant. Flinging her arms

around Jack's neck, she gave him another bone-shattering hug. "I have missed you. I'm so glad Jane brought you back."

Like his father, Lizzy appeared to take his presence entirely for granted.

Brought him back. Jane had brought him back. Step by step, piece by piece, she had led him to this place, to this boat. The quest for the Queen, the clues along the way, all of it turned on its head, tilted sideways, transforming into something barely recognizable.

He had only Jane's word that the man they had met in the camp near Santarém had been the Gardener. The Comte de Brillac might have been just that, the Comte de Brillac, no one in particular.

No. Jack shoved aside the crazy thoughts buzzing through his brain. It was too elaborate a ruse. If Jane had been commissioned to bring him home, she might have accomplished it through simpler means, not a wild-goose chase through half of Portugal.

He tried to conjure Jane's image, but instead of the woman he had left in Peniche, he saw the one he had first met in Lisbon, her Sphinx-like smile, that moment when she had removed her false curls, showing a deception beneath a deception.

No, Jack told himself again. Not Jane.

To his father, Jack said in a taut voice, "Is there anyone else here for this charming reunion? Do you have Kat tucked away in the hold? Is Alex clinging to the rigging?" He forced himself to voice the words he could barely stand to think. "Is the Queen of Portugal truly at large?"

"Of course." His stepmother thumped her parasol against the deck. "Would we lie to you?"

"I don't know. Would you?" Anger filled Jack, all the more frustrating for being without a target.

His father made soothing noises. "Everything you've been told—whatever you've been told—it's mostly true."

Only his father could utter that "mostly" with such an air of guileless sincerity.

"Mostly true," Jack repeated dangerously. "Mostly?"

His father looked imploringly at his stepmother, who stepped in, literally, between them. "The Queen of Portugal disappeared during the royal departure. The Pink Carnation was dispatched to discover her whereabouts." She looked at Jack as though he were a field mouse caught in a snare. "While she was here, it was only efficient for Jane to retrieve you."

"Retrieve me." As if he were a misplaced piece of luggage. Jack was not feeling warm and filial sentiments towards his new stepmother. "What was she meant to do, deliver me trussed and bound onto the ship?"

"Wouldn't that be a bit gratuitous?" Everyone turned to look at Miles Dorrington, who held up both hands in self-defense. "Why would you truss and bind? Surely one would do."

"You," said Jack's stepmother, advancing purposefully, "are not helping."

Miles Dorrington ducked behind his wife.

"Nothing like that," said Jack's father reassuringly. "We merely hoped that she might persuade you. . . ."

"Persuade me," Jack said flatly.

Jane, kissing him in a field by the road. Jane, picking her way gingerly down those steps into the water, the torchlight glimmering over her naked body. Jane, pressing up against him, her arms around his neck.

No. No. Whatever else he believed or didn't believe, Jack wouldn't believe that.

"Is it so wrong," said his father quietly, "for a man to miss his son?"

Oh, no. No, no, no. His father wasn't putting this on him.

"If," Jack gritted out, "if the threat is real, then why in the devil does no one seem the least bit concerned that your former charge, madam"—Jack looked pointedly at his stepmother—"is currently in the custody of the Gardener and three hundred Frenchmen?"

Lord Richard clapped a hand on his shoulder. "We are. Deuced concerned."

"But we know Jane," put in Lady Henrietta. "Her plans always go as planned." She exchanged a glance with her husband. "Well, almost always. But that wasn't her fault." And then, as if it explained everything, "She is the Pink Carnation."

She wasn't just the Pink Carnation. She was also human, very,

very human. She made mistakes, she doubted herself, her heels blistered, and her hair snarled. Couldn't any of them see that?

"She's not invincible." Jack tried to banish the images of what might be happening even now, but they crowded around him. Sunset. He had promised her until sunset. "If something goes wrong, we need to get her out."

Miles Dorrington looked thoughtful. "I say, we could raise the Jolly Roger and storm the fort as pirates. While they're panicking, you sneak in and retrieve Jane."

"Too many cannons," said Jack tersely. "You'll be blown to splinters before we can get inside. Next?"

Lizzy raised her crossbow. "I could—"

"No," said Jack and his father in unison. When Jack had finished glaring at his father, he said, "Jane and I discussed this. If she's not back by sundown, Lord Richard and I"—Jack nodded to the blond man, who nodded back—"will go after her disguised as dragoons."

Lord Richard quickly took charge. "I'll see that my men acquire the relevant uniforms."

"No," said Jack's new stepmother.

"No?" Jack looked narrowly at his stepmother. "What do you propose, then?"

His stepmother paced decisively down the deck. "Richard"—Lord Richard leaped agilely out of range of her parasol—"will stay and mind the *Bien-Aimée*. If Jane isn't back by sundown"—Jack's stepmother regarded him imperiously—"you and *I* will go after her."

"Gwen is very good at rappelling down walls," said Jack's father, looking at his bride with gooey eyes. "Up them, too."

"We're not rappelling," said Jack. If there was anything he hated, it was rappelling. It was as showy and useless as swinging through windows on ropes. "We're going through the door."

"I've known that girl since she was born." His stepmother stalked towards him, parasol point glinting. "I've protected her from more assailants than you've had hot suppers. If you go, I go."

"How lovely," said Lady Henrietta brightly. "You can get to know each other."

Miles Dorrington prudently lifted his wife by the waist and deposited her out of parasol range.

"We don't know that she'll need rescuing," said Jack, staring down his new stepmother. "The plan might go as planned."

His stepmother snorted. "With the Gardener? I'll go get my pistols."

And she departed, leaving Jack with a sick feeling at the pit of his stomach as he tried not to contemplate what the Gardener might be doing with Jane right now.

Chapter Twenty-three

Candlelight slid sensually across silver candlesticks and brocade draperies, picking out the silver threads woven into the sapphire blue satin.

The candlelight was rather unnecessary, considering that it was still broad daylight outside, but it did set the mood nicely. And to be fair, thought Jane generously, the window slits were rather small.

Bathed and perfumed, Jane sat primly on the edge of a divan. The divan had clearly been designed for sensuous lounging, but it wouldn't do to make it too easy. Nothing would make Nicolas more suspicious than to find her too eager for his embrace.

It hadn't surprised her—not entirely—when she hadn't

been brought immediately to Nicolas. After her announcement at the gate, there had been a brief flurry of junior officers running forth and back, which had resulted in Nicolas's valet being sent, bowing and scraping, to escort Jane to a small and stony chamber, in which a steaming bath was waiting, along with a selection of lotions, oils, and perfumes.

Jane had been reasonably certain she would remain unmolested, but she had propped a chair against the door all the same. It wouldn't stop it from opening, but it would give her fair warning and time to grab a wrap.

There had been a gown waiting for her as well. Jane decided not to inquire how Nicolas came to be traveling with women's garments. She preferred not to know. Although, under the right circumstances, he would make a rather pretty girl. Jane considered the question with professional interest. If she could masquerade as a man, why not a man as a woman?

It was easier to focus on abstract speculation than to fret about what was to come, or where Jack might be now.

As Jane donned the sheer undergarments, the silk stockings, the embroidered garters, the lace-edged chemise of finest French lawn, she hoped fervently that Jack had stayed true to his word and was, even now, climbing the ladder to the *Bien-Aimée*.

She wasn't sure that Jack would entirely approve of the methods she intended to use with Nicolas.

Nicolas's valet knocked respectfully before coming in. The

chamber in which she had bathed had been small and barren; the chamber to which she was escorted was not.

Nicolas always did know how to set the scene for a seduction. Jane recognized the candlesticks and the drapes. She had no doubt that she would also recognize the linen on the bed, should it come to that.

But it wouldn't. Jane touched a finger to the bezel of her ring. The white powder contained within was designed to act quickly.

Nicolas, mercifully, preferred to seduce slowly. There would be wine and sweetmeats, barbed repartee and gestures that were almost, but not quite, caresses. Jane began running sums in her head. Ten minutes, fifteen perhaps, to get the glass of wine into his hand. Another half an hour for the drug to do its work. A fifteen-minute margin for error.

An hour, then.

It had been at least an hour since she and Jack had parted ways, possibly more. Just time enough for him to have reached the *Bien-Aimée*. The sun set early in December. It would take them an hour to sail to Berlengas, slightly more if the sea were rough or any complications ensued. That left her, Jane determined, roughly two hours to incapacitate Nicolas, forge the orders, and see the Queen onto a boat.

There was no decanter of wine in the room, no platter of sweetmeats, no goblets ready for filling. Nicolas, Jane thought wryly, had taken precautions. A setback, nothing more. Had he been careless, she would have mistrusted him more.

They had always been on their guard with each other, even when they had been at their most intimate.

It was the opposite of the way she felt with Jack: stripped bare, unguarded.

The door opened and Nicolas made his entrance, as theatrical as any thespian. He paused in the doorway, perusing Jane with a faint smile on his lips. Then, doffing his hat, he swept an elaborate bow. "Do I understand that you are about to make me the happiest man on earth?"

He was dressed for riding, in breeches, boots, and an impeccably cut coat. Which meant . . . absolutely nothing. He might have been riding or he might have been lounging in the next room in a brocaded dressing gown.

Jane rose to her feet. "My apologies, Nicolas." She held out a hand to him, her smile not entirely feigned. She might despise him in absentia, but it was hard, in person, not to feel a little fond of Nicolas. Which, given all he had done and all she had seen him do, was saying a great deal. "I had to say something to make them let me in."

Her former lover delicately raised her hand in his. Turning it over, he pressed a kiss against her palm, looking up at her from under his lashes. "Your beauty alone would open any doors."

"There are some doors," said Jane, gently retrieving her hand, "which are best left closed."

Nicolas made a gesture behind his back to his lackeys, who crossed the room in procession, depositing trays and platters on a table. To Jane, he said softly, "My offer still stands."

Jane wondered sometimes whether Nicolas realized how much he was a creature of that same ancien régime he claimed to deplore. Servants weren't people to him; he was perfectly content to play out his love scenes before them, as if they were nothing more than wardrobes or chairs.

Serenely, Jane seated herself on the divan, arranging her skirts modestly around her legs. "As does my reply."

"Circumstances have changed." Nicolas flicked his wrist, indicating that his entourage should close the door behind them. He knelt beside the divan, taking Jane's hand in his. "Has it not occurred to you, my dearest Jeanne, that I can make you a countess?"

Jane looked down at their joined hands. He wore two signets now: his own sigil and that of the Comte de Brillac. His supposed father's arms, which he had sworn he would never wear.

Jane looked directly at him. Honesty was always the best illusion. "I have no desire for titles. I never have."

Nicolas rose smoothly to his feet, a dimple appearing in one cheek. "Nor for riches or fame. My dear Jeanne—so charmingly incorruptible." He didn't touch her. That would be too crude. But his look was the equivalent of a touch. "Or . . . almost incorruptible."

And that, thought Jane grimly, was what she got for feeling sorry for Nicolas. She wasn't the only woman to have been lulled by that dimple, only to feel a knife in the ribs. A metaphorical knife, in her case, but a knife all the same, designed to belittle her, to weaken her.

Your virtue lies in your mind, not in what lies between your legs.

Taking strength from the memory, from Jack, Jane folded her hands in her lap. "I do not perceive myself as in any way corrupted."

Nicolas glanced down at her, his eyebrows quirking. "Is that a compliment or a repudiation?" He strode across the room to the decanter his servants had left, Venetian glass, costly and rare. "Wine?"

"Yes, please," said Jane demurely.

It would be too obvious if she offered to pour. She had never played Ganymede to his Jove. It was a deliberate choice, another tactic in the constant maneuvering for supremacy between them. To play the servant would be to cede a point.

Which, in this case, was rather a disadvantage.

Her best chance, Jane decided, was to drink, lightly, of her own wine before drugging it. A circumstance would arise, she had no doubt, in which she might offer Nicolas her cup.

Leave a kiss but in the cup, the poet said. It wasn't a kiss she had for him.

She smiled up at Nicolas as he handed the goblet to her, his fingers lingering, ever so slightly, against hers. "I should like to think that I have made something more of an impression than that."

Nicolas's tone was light, but there was something in his eyes that made Jane feel like a cad.

"Indelibly," said Jane, matching his insouciant air. She

feigned a sip of her wine. It was claret, not port. It was, she thought, very like Nicolas to travel with his own cellar into a region famed for its wines. "I shall always think of you as a friend."

"Only a friend?" Nicolas arranged himself flatteringly at her feet. It was, Jane knew, a standard tableau, the young swain at the feet of his love.

She could speak her lines, or she could change the dialogue, throw him off balance. "Said the amorous shepherd to his love? Do get up, Nicolas. I've come to you on a serious matter."

"What could be more serious than love?" But he rose all the same, drawing a chair to rest beside the divan. "If not for my so charming person, why are you here?"

While his eyes were fixed on her face, Jane turned her hand over her cup, releasing the hidden catch in her ring. "I've come for Queen Maria," she said calmly.

Nicolas stared at her for a moment, his eyebrows rising to his carefully curled hair, and then he began to laugh. His laugh was one of his more charming attributes, a light tenor, and entirely unfeigned.

"Only you, my Jeanne. Only you."

"Then you do have her?" Casually, Jane swirled the glass, letting the powder dissolve in the strong claret. "Would you consider releasing her into my custody? She can be of no use to you."

"On the contrary, she is a great deal of use to me." Nicolas

cast her a heavy-lidded look that lacked some of its usual smol-
der. It was too practiced, too pat. "She brought you to me."

"Flattering, but not, I think, the whole story." He was up
to something; of that Jane had no doubt. "Just what is the
Queen worth to you, Nicolas?"

"Shouldn't I be asking the same of you?" It was a duel
without swords. "To place yourself within my power . . ."

"Within the terms of our agreement," Jane reminded him.

"Ah, yes." Nicolas leaned back in his chair, his glass of wine
dangling between his fingers. "Our agreement."

"An agreement which has held good for longer than most
treaties," Jane reminded him, feeling, for the first time, a fris-
son of unease. She knew that cat-with-the-cream look of old.
It did not bode well.

"Two years?" Nicolas's fingers brushed hers, just at the tips.
"They have been two good years, have they not?"

Jane wasn't sure she would call them "good," precisely. They
had certainly been educational.

"Two and a half years," she said crisply. Two and a half
years since she had met Nicolas, since she had struck off on her
own, since they had, of necessity, brokered their odd entente.
"I trust the agreement still holds?"

"But of course." She mistrusted Nicolas the most when he
was his most accommodating. "In all of its particulars."

Jane narrowed her eyes. "We engage not to interfere with
one another on neutral soil."

It had seemed the most expedient solution. She was barred

from France, Nicolas from England. But outside of those bounds, they afforded each other the mutual courtesy due to fellow professionals.

"On neutral soil," Nicolas agreed, holding his glass to the light to admire the rich red of the wine. Gently, he said, "But Portugal is now French soil, my love."

"Tell that to the Regency Council," Jane said, leaning sideways along the divan in the pose popularized by Madame Recamier.

Nicolas looked at her with a peculiar glint in his hazel eyes. "I imagine," he said, "that General Junot is telling them something to that effect even now."

Jane abandoned her languid pose. "Really, Nicolas, you can't be serious." She swung her legs down to the floor, yanking her skirts with them. "We operated as allies in Italy. By that sort of argument, Italy was far closer to being French soil than Portugal. You haven't even got around to conquering the entire country yet."

"In Italy," said Nicolas quietly, "you had not yet fled from me."

His eyes held hers, for once devoid of merriment.

"My work in Venice was done," Jane prevaricated. "I was needed elsewhere."

"Did you stop to think that I might need you?" His voice was light, but there was something beneath it that wasn't light at all. He set his cup down on a small table. "You may understand why I might be somewhat reluctant to let you go."

Jane set her glass next to his. Straightening very slowly, she said, "Would you have me against my will?"

"Would you be so unwilling?"

He was in breach of their agreement, but even so, Jane felt a slight twinge of guilt. She had played with his emotions. Not intentionally, perhaps, but she had used him all the same.

Striving for a middle ground, she said, "I shouldn't enjoy being taken back to Paris in chains."

Nicolas smiled a little grimly. "The only chains in which I wish to drape you are ropes of pearls and strings of rubies."

Jane lifted Nicolas's glass from the table. "A golden chain is still a tether." She looked at him regretfully over the rim of the glass. "I've told you before. I have no desire to be the toast of any court."

Nicolas took the other glass, holding it aloft. She had done her work well. There was no sign of the drug in it. The powder had dissolved completely. "Not even that of His Royal Majesty, King Louis the Eighteenth?"

Jane looked at him sharply.

"Oh, yes," said Nicolas, enjoying the effect. He set the glass down on the table, undrunk. "There have been negotiations."

This might merely be a ploy. Or it might not. "Can he offer you better than Bonaparte?"

"Bonaparte gave me my father's title, but not his lands." Nicolas's face was carved into harsh lines, his knuckles white on the arms of his chair. "I want it all. Every hectare of ground, every painting, every candlestick. And if there's any sort of hell, I want *him* to look up and see me enjoying everything that was his."

Jane had known Nicolas long and well enough to know that he referred to the Comte de Brillac, his supposed father, the man who had acknowledged him publicly, to save his own reputation, and alternately neglected and abused him in private.

She knew only pieces of the story, those pieces that Nicolas had allowed her to know. Jane suspected that in this, the truth was probably grimmer than he had permitted her to see. He wasn't a man who liked to expose his weaknesses.

From everything Jane had heard, the old comte had been a brute and a bully. It had galled him no end, apparently, to see his older sons, his own sons, received at court without enthusiasm, while the cuckoo in his nest had been feted at court and welcomed at every salon.

The comtesse had been dead by the time revolution had broken out—some said by her husband's hand. The comte and his two older sons had gone to the guillotine, wrenched out of hiding, denounced by an anonymous source.

Nicolas had maintained a good pretense of grief. He had come to England with the other émigrés, feigning filial sorrow well enough to fool even the heir to the French throne. He had quickly become an intimate of the French court in exile at Hartwell House in Buckinghamshire, playing cards with the Duc de Berry, all the while weaving his web of agents and informers.

The court at Hartwell House had been particularly miffed when news of Nicolas's duplicity had come out.

"You have lied to King Louis before," Jane pointed out. "Why should he welcome you now?"

"His Majesty," said Nicolas, "said much the same thing. He seems to believe he needs an earnest of my good intentions. A gesture that will render me persona non grata at the Palace of Saint-Cloud."

He lifted the drugged glass of wine, turning it this way and that.

Jane watched him closely, revolving these new possibilities. There was no denying that Nicolas was an accomplished liar. But one thing she could trust in him: his self-interest. His allegiance to the revolutionary regime had always been driven more by revenge than conviction.

Nicolas, not Jack, was the real opportunist, for sale to the highest bidder.

Nicolas was also, Jane thought practically, a snob. He might sneer at his father, but when it came down to it, what he wanted—what he had always wanted—was to be feted by the very same society his father had attempted to deny him.

"An irrevocable gesture," said Jane. "Such as, perhaps, stealing a queen?"

Nicolas smiled at her, the roguish glint back in his eye. "Check and mate."

He lifted the glass to his lips to drink.

"Wait." Jane stilled him with a hand on his wrist.

Hoping she was doing the right thing, Jane removed the glass from his hand and set it firmly down on the table.

"I have a proposition to put to you."

"Words that warm the farthest reaches of my heart." The honeyed words lacked conviction. It was cupidity rather than Cupid driving her former lover now. "What terms?"

"I have reinforcements waiting on Berlengas." There was no harm in telling Nicolas as much; he must know that the English held the island. "Write the orders. Have the Queen delivered there."

"Who are these reinforcements?" Nicolas's pose was relaxed, but his eyes betrayed him.

Revealing any information was always a gamble. Perhaps, Jane realized, Jack had been right when he accused her of gambling. She preferred to think of it as weighing the probabilities, but what was that but another name for a game of chance?

Jane looked the Gardener in the eye. "Lord Richard Selwick. And his crew."

"Ah." Nicolas sat back in his chair. "You interest me, strangely."

"I had thought I might."

It wasn't just that Lord Richard had the influence to press Nicolas's case with King Louis. Nicolas had his own private history with the Selwick family.

He tapped his fingers lightly against the arm of the chair. The sigil of Brillac glittered in the candlelight. "But it was not Lord Richard Selwick with you at the abbey, was it?"

There was no mistaking the blade beneath the velvet of the Gardener's voice.

Jane raised a brow, keeping her voice lightly amused. "You are well-informed. As always."

"Where you are concerned, I leave no stone unturned. Who was he?" They weren't playing anymore. The game had turned serious.

Jane leaned back against the divan, feigning an ease she didn't feel. She ought, she thought grimly, to have let him drink the drugged wine. Working with Nicolas was always much more dangerous than working against him, perhaps because it was never entirely clear where the one left off and the other began.

"Do you tell me the names of all of your agents?" Her pearl earbobs swayed, heavy and rich, as she leaned forward. "Such as, for example, your man at the abbey?"

"Ah." Nicolas sat back, propping one ankle against the opposite knee. "But he wasn't my man."

"Whose then?" Jane took another gamble. "I assume Mr. Samson isn't his real name."

"His real name is Rene Desgoules." Nicolas rose abruptly from his chair, pacing towards the narrow slit of a window. He left the glass of wine behind him.

Jane rose, too, moving behind the divan, resting her hands on the gilded rail. "Why tell me that?"

Unless, of course, it wasn't true. A falsehood designed to create the impression of honesty. What was a name, more or less?

Nicolas looked back over his shoulder. There was a fraught pause, as the candles guttered in their silver holders and a seagull cawed outside the window. "I told you. He's not my man."

Jane wouldn't have believed him under any circumstances. It became ever more difficult to do so when the door crashed open and the man himself appeared in the doorway. He tripped over Nicolas's walking stick and, kicking it aside, stalked into the room.

"I had to hear it from the guards downstairs," he complained in rapid French flavored with the distinctive accent of Marseilles. "Why didn't you tell me you had her?"

He might no longer be Mr. Samson, merchant, but the tone of grievance was the same.

"As you may have noticed, Desgoules," said Nicolas calmly, "the lady and I were having a private conversation."

"Lady?" Desgoules spat eloquently. "Put her in chains and have done with it."

Nicolas's face froze into an expression of aristocratic hauteur. "She is my captive, Desgoules, not yours."

"I speak not for myself," said Desgoules, drawing himself up, "but for Fouché."

The captive in question moved quietly towards the door. Desgoules used his foot to kick it shut, oak crashing against stone.

As the reverberations died away, Jane raised the swordstick she had scooped up from the floor, the point sharp against Desgoules' throat.

" 'Every hectare of ground, every painting, every candle-stick'?" she quoted, without turning to Nicolas.

"You are a rather valuable commodity," said Nicolas apologetically. "Wouldn't you rather I benefit than this creature?"

"Shoot her! Why don't you shoot her?" Desgoules was quivering with impatience, but not quite brave enough to make a grab for the swordstick. "You're taking too many chances. You always take too many chances."

"Not this time," said Nicolas, and there was a curious note to his voice. Out of the corner of her eye, Jane could see the glint of silver. Nicolas's pistol, elaborately chased, a masterpiece of art.

But still deadly.

"Drop the pistol," said Jane levelly, "or I shall run Monsieur Desgoules through."

"Will you?" said Nicolas reproachfully. "Will you truly?"

Beads of sweat stood out on Desgoules' forehead. His eyes darted sideways, making him look more than ever like a rat in a trap. "Take the shot, man! Take the shot!"

Nicolas let out a light sigh. "If you insist," he said, and pulled the trigger.

Chapter Twenty-four

The acrid scent of powder filled the air.

Jane jerked sideways, out of the way, but she needn't have worried. Desgoules' mouth opened in a silent expression of shock. His hands went to the hole in his chest before he dropped, heavily, to his knees, and from there, facedown on the floor at Jane's feet.

Jane froze, the swordstick clenched in her numb hand. "You shot him."

"Did you think I was going to shoot you?" Calmly Nicolas set down his pistol, waggling his fingers in a bowl of rose-scented water to remove any nasty traces of powder. "I told you. He wasn't my man."

The blood throbbed in Jane's temples. "No. He was Fouché's man." The pieces clicked into place. "You wanted me to kill him for you, didn't you?"

Nicolas shrugged, dabbing his hands dry on a piece of linen embroidered with the arms of Brillac. "It would have been convenient—although it did seem unlikely."

If pushed . . . if cornered. . . . Jane had never killed, in self-defense or otherwise, but she knew that someday the necessity might arise. And it would haunt her.

Nicolas knew that, too. "Two birds with one stone," Jane said tightly. "Eliminate your enemy and—"

"And?" Nicolas prompted, looking far too amused for a man with a corpse at the threshold of his room.

And win a point in the game between them. Prove to her that she wasn't as virtuous as she had thought. Streak blood on her hands. Render her vulnerable.

How had she ever fancied herself in love with Nicolas?

Jane found herself desperately wishing she had Jack there with her, a strong presence at her back.

Rapidly, she said, "Fouché suspected you, didn't he? He sent Desgoules with you to make sure you didn't abscond with the Queen."

Nicolas spread his hands wide in a gesture of graceful assent. "And now there is no obstacle to our departure." Catching sight of the narrowing of Jane's eyes, he added quietly, "He was not a very nice man, Desgoules. He would have done far worse to you without blinking an eye."

Jane's eyes dropped to Desgoules' fallen form. Somberly, she said, "Don't pretend this was on my behalf."

"But wasn't it?" Nicolas raised a brow. "Why would I betray my Emperor but for the chance of your hand?"

It was, as far as Jane could tell, still entirely unclear who was betraying whom. "You forget," she said, "the small matter of a thousand hectares, a dozen Fragonard paintings, and a very old grievance."

"Ah, yes," said Nicolas, the corner of his mouth twisting up in a grin that had little humor to it. "That as well."

There was the sound of heavy footfalls approaching the door.

Before Jane could say anything else, Nicolas leaned his head out the door and shouted, "Guards! Guards! We have an enemy in our midst!"

An ensign skidded, breathless, to a stop outside the door. His eyes widened as he saw the man crumpled on the floor, the slow stain of blood seeping out beneath him.

Bonaparte was calling up young soldiers now, more and more soldiers to fill his endless armies. This soldier looked no more than sixteen, and his complexion turned a delicate shade of chartreuse as he stared at what was most likely his first dead body.

It took him a moment to find his voice. "Monsieur . . . Monsieur Desgoules—"

"Was a traitor," said Nicolas, with well-feigned woe. "I caught him in the act of ransacking my dispatches. He has been suborned by the English. When I accused him of his perfidy, he attacked my fiancée, holding my own sword to her throat."

The ensign stared with wide eyes at Jane and the sword cane in her hands. Jane tried to look like someone unaccustomed to handling a blade.

Nicolas put a comforting arm around the younger man's shoulders. Pushing him towards the door, he said rapidly, "My position here has been compromised. Have a carriage prepared and my royal guest fetched from the next chamber. It is necessary that I take her to a place of safety at once."

The young soldier blinked. "But . . . General Thomières. Surely I should . . ."

Nicolas looked at him sternly. "Do you want to be responsible for a valuable prize falling into the hands of the English? Quickly now! There's no time to be lost. I have it on good authority that the Pink Carnation is on his way here even now. Yes, the Carnation," he said, as the young soldier paled. "You understand the seriousness of the situation? Question everybody. Trust nobody. And fetch me a swift carriage and a good bottle of claret."

"Sir, yes, sir." The soldier scurried off, glancing over his shoulder to make sure the Carnation wasn't behind him.

"Trust nobody," said Jane, watching Nicolas as he seated himself at his writing desk, penning something in a quick, elegant hand. "Excellent advice."

"He won't take it." Nicolas dusted sand across the paper,

then held it up to inspect it before dripping red wax on the folds and pressing it with his seal. "A note for Thomières. The Queen is being transferred to a safe place pending voyage to France."

The sword cane was still in Jane's hand. She touched the blade to the sealed note. "Give me one reason why I should trust you."

Nicolas smiled winningly. "Because my heart is at your feet?"

It wasn't his heart at her feet, but a murdered operative. That, in its own way, was better assurance. Fouché wouldn't take the death of one of his picked men lightly. The tale of subornation might fool a young soldier; it might even fool Thomières. But it wouldn't pass muster with Napoleon's spymaster.

"It's not your heart I need," said Jane, "but a swift carriage. Quickly now."

But she kept the sword cane in her hand as she followed her old adversary to the door.

"She won't come that way."

Jack's stepmother stepped out beside him on the large terrace in front of the fortress. All around them, the setting sun painted the sky a brilliant red and purple that only accentuated the jagged cliffs of the isle of Berlengas, jutting out into the sea around them. The wind had risen, slapping the waves into a frenzy. Whitecapped, they dashed themselves against the base of the narrow causeway that connected the Forte São João Batista with the island.

"I know that," said Jack quickly, but despite himself, his eyes turned again to that narrow and twisting stone bridge, the shadows playing tricks on him, presenting him with the image of a carriage, the echo of horses' hooves against the stone.

His stepmother was right: anyone would be mad to attempt the bridge at dusk in a high wind. Under the very best of conditions it would be dangerous. And these were not the best of conditions.

If Jane came at all, she would come by sea.

"She will come," said Jack fiercely. "She knows what she's doing."

His stepmother furled her parasol, tucking it under her arm. "Most of the time." Before Jack could retort, she added in a voice like vinegar, "I care about her, too, you know."

Jack looked down at the cracked paving at his feet. The last thing he wanted was to have a discussion about his emotions with the woman who had married his father—who, for some bizarre reason, everyone, with the exception of his father, persisted in referring to as "Miss" Gwen.

It didn't seem to bother his father. In fact, his father was as happy as Jack could ever remember seeing him.

It was very odd thinking of one's parent as a person. Even odder being introduced, in one fell swoop, to his father's new life: a wife, a family, albeit a rather amorphously connected

family. Miles Dorrington had attempted to explain how everyone was connected, but Jack would have needed a chart to map
it all out, and frankly he just wasn't that interested.

He was more concerned about what was happening with
Jane.

The urge to turn his back until his stepmother went away
was strong, but the urge to talk about Jane was stronger. "You
were her chaperone?" Jack said, the words half lost on the wind.

"Chaperone, second in command." Miss Gwen rested her
parasol point on the ground, frowning out to sea, her eyes
searching the waters that separated them from the mainland.
"I've known her since she was born."

"Was she always . . ." Jack stuck.

"Maddeningly omniscient?" Miss Gwen gave a sharp bark
of a laugh. "Yes. Even as a child. Oh, she hid it well. The girl
had good manners. She knew when to keep her mouth shut in
adult company. But if you made the mistake of asking! The
vicar," she said with satisfaction, "never questioned her about
her catechism again."

Jack's throat worked as he looked out across the waves.
"How much of a chance do you think she has against the Gardener?"

Miss Gwen didn't belittle or make light of his concerns.
"The man's twisty; I'll give him that. And there was a time . . .
There was a time when he might have been a danger to her."
She looked shrewdly at Jack. "I take it that is no longer likely
to be a concern."

Was he wearing a sign on his chest? Jack felt like a raw youth caught mooning beneath a girl's window.

"Jane isn't the only one who is maddeningly omniscient," Jack muttered.

"Where did you think she got it from?" But Miss Gwen's gloat was short-lived. Her eyes narrowed on a speck on the horizon. Leaning forward, she jabbed her parasol at the water. "There! Don't you see it? Look again."

Her eyes were better than his. All Jack could see was a pale streak against the dark waves. Slowly it resolved itself into a boat.

"It might be a fishing boat," said Jack, his voice rusty.

"At this time of night?" Together they craned to see.

Navigating the choppy waters with the skill of long practice, the skipper moored the boat at the base of the fort. Two flights of long stairs led up to the platform. As Jack watched, a lithe figure in boots, breeches, frock coat, and curly brimmed hat swung out of the boat, saying something to the skipper in passing.

It might be Jane, as planned, dressed in the Gardener's clothes. It was supposed to be Jane dressed in the Gardener's clothes. Jack cursed the uncertain light that played tricks with his eyes. He couldn't make out features from this distance; the figure looked like a dressmaker's doll.

The figure glanced up at the fort and lifted its hat ever so slightly.

The caw of the gulls and the splash of the waves thrummed in Jack's ears. "There's something wrong."

He couldn't say how he knew, but that wasn't Jane. She wouldn't have lifted her hat; she would have waved. The height was right, as was the general build, but the movements were all wrong.

"That's not Jane."

"No," said his stepmother, leaning as far over the side as she dared. "*That* is Jane."

Holding his hat with one hand, the man that wasn't Jane held out his hand to someone else on the boat.

She stepped out of the boat gracefully, holding up the long skirt of her gown with one hand. The white gauze of the gown glimmered even in the fading light, turning her into something out of myth or fancy, the Lady of the Lake rising to give Arthur his sword.

Only the hand she was holding, Jack was quite sure, belonged not to the mythical king of the Britons, but to Britain's great enemy, the Gardener.

"*Him*," said Miss Gwen.

Jack couldn't have agreed more. Miss Gwen drew the hidden sword from her parasol, holding it at the ready. Jack cocked his pistol, pointing it at the top of the stairs.

A useless gesture, he knew. He couldn't fire without risking hitting Jane. He could only hope the Gardener wouldn't realize that.

There had to be a pistol in the Gardener's hand, behind Jane's back. That was the only explanation. Why, otherwise, would she be climbing the stairs with him so easily, so gracefully, one hand resting on his arm with an intimacy that made Jack's finger tense on the trigger?

Jane stepped onto the platform, the wind flattening her sheer skirt against her legs, teasing little wisps of hair out of her topknot. The sleeves of her dress were long and tight, entirely impractical for combat. Pearl earrings glimmered in her ears; her hair had been bound up with a gold fillet. She smelled of rare perfumes and expensive lotions.

"Miss Gwen! Jack." There was no gun at her back. Looping her skirt over one wrist, Jane dropped the Gardener's arm and moved forward. "As you see, we have arrived."

The scent of her hair wafted behind her: not lavender, but French perfume, a scent for seduction. Jack had liked it better when she smelled of sulfur and donkey.

Jack kept his pistol trained on her companion, who was watching them with a slight, mocking smile playing around his lips. The Gardener gave a slight bow. "Miss Meadows. Mr. . . . ?"

"It's Mrs. Reid now," growled Miss Gwen.

The Gardener raised his hat. "My condolences to Mr. Reid."

"Colonel Reid," Jack said tersely. To Jane, he said, "What in the devil is *he* doing here?"

The Gardener strolled forward. He held his hands up so that Jack could see he was unarmed. "You have the advantage of me, sir." He considered Jack critically. "You are not, I think, a Selwick. Who are you?"

The Gardener's seal swam before Jack's eyes, red as the setting sun, red as the blood of good men.

"I," said Jack, "am the Moonflower."

That, at least, discommoded the Gardener. He narrowed his eyes against the stinging wind. "I thought I had you killed in Calcutta."

"You certainly tried." Jack leveled his pistol at his old adversary. "Allow me to return the favor."

"Wait!" Jane blocked Jack's shot with her body. Slowly he lowered his pistol as she said rapidly, "We have a truce in place. The Gardener has given us the Queen. He wishes to . . . reconsider his allegiances."

The only thing the Gardener was going to reconsider was his grip on this mortal coil. The man was entirely without morals. He was as slippery as a snake, which frankly did a disservice to reptiles everywhere.

And this was the man whom Jane was bringing into their midst?

Jack looked at Jane incredulously. "And you believe him?"

Jane ignored him. To her former chaperone, she said, "The Queen is in the boat. If you could call someone to take her to an appropriate chamber?"

Miss Gwen gestured imperiously with her parasol to one of the sentries on the battlements, part of the detachment of British marines who were holding the island of Berlengas.

Jack kept one eye on the Gardener, who was watching them all with detached amusement. "Are you sure it's the Queen in there? He might have the bottom of the boat packed full of grenadiers."

Jane gave him a quelling look. "The only thing in the bottom of that boat is fish. I checked."

"Pity." Miss Gwen gave a little smirk. "I was hoping for men in loincloths."

Jane eyed her former chaperone askance. "They're French, not Greek. And it's December."

And Jack still didn't like it. He circled Jane, pacing closer to the Gardener. There was a trick; there had to be a trick. "He might be sending his men after us."

The Gardener raised his brows, enjoying himself just a little too much. "You could shoot me before they get here."

"Excellent suggestion," said Jack, and cocked his pistol.

Chapter Twenty-five

*J*ane applied pressure to Jack's arm. He grimaced and dropped his pistol.

"Stop," Jane said, trying to stare down two bristling men at the same time. "Both of you."

"Why?" demanded Miss Gwen, retrieving the fallen weapon. "It was just getting entertaining."

"You," said Jane, "were not meant to be here."

Even as she said it, she realized it was a pointless objection. Miss Gwen would be where Miss Gwen wanted to be, whether one had invited her or not. And that wasn't the main concern. It belatedly occurred to Jane that she had done exactly what she had promised Jack she wouldn't: she had changed the plan without telling him. Again.

Circumstances had demanded. But that seemed a somewhat weaker argument here, with Nicolas inflaming Jack's temper just by being himself and Miss Gwen happily fanning the flames for her own amusement.

Silencing her former chaperone with a look, Jane turned to Jack, who was rubbing his wounded biceps. "It's all right," she said quickly. "Nicolas is working with us now. For the moment."

The twilight played tricks with Jane's eyes, blurring Jack's features, but she could see his throat work, feel the tension in his shoulders as he said tersely, "Do you trust him?"

Jane pictured Desgoules, sprawled on the floor. "I trust him to look out for his own interests."

"In that interest," said Nicolas, in an amused voice behind her, "might we go inside? I am rather fond of this hat. I have no desire to make a sacrifice of it to Poseidon."

He offered an arm to Jane, but dropped it as Miss Gwen prodded him in the back with Jack's pistol, making him stagger. "All right. But don't try anything funny."

Nicolas glanced back at Miss Gwen. "Is that really quite necessary?"

"Yes," snapped Miss Gwen, and prodded him again.

Nicolas rolled his eyes at Jane, inviting her to share in the ridiculousness of it. There had, it was true, been a time when she might have smiled back. Right now Jane wished him to perdition.

"We accomplished our mission." Jane took Jack's arm as

they followed Miss Gwen and Nicolas to the door in the wall, walking half bent over against the force of the wind. "We have the Queen. Surely that is cause for satisfaction."

"Satisfaction, is it?" Jane could feel the muscles of Jack's arm tense, hard as iron beneath her fingers. "You smell like a French brothel."

Was that really to the point? "At least I don't smell like donkey."

Jack glowered at Nicolas's back. "Why is he here?"

She had already explained this. Twice. "Because," said Jane, as Jack stood aside so she could precede him through the door, "it was easier to move Queen Maria with his connivance than without it."

She would have liked to tell Jack the whole story—Desgoules, the crosses and double crosses—but Jack's expression was hard as the rock of the fort. "And what was the price of that connivance?"

It took Jane a moment for the meaning of those words to sink in. It was like a stiletto blow; one didn't realize one had been stabbed until after the blade was already in place.

Jane struggled with a feeling of betrayal. Sharply, she said, "Not what you're implying."

The wind slammed the door sharply shut behind them.

Jack thrust his fingers into his hair. He had, Jane realized, lost his hat, probably on that windy platform above the sea. "I was worried about you." The words came out half apology, half accusation. "And I don't trust him."

"Few do." There was no reason for her to feel this bewildered or hurt. But she did. Jane tried to keep her voice level. "But you might have trusted me."

"I did. I do." The correction was just a moment too late. The words came up out of the pit of Jack's chest, ragged and raw. "I hate the thought of you together—working together."

She couldn't change her past any more than he could. "It was for the best. Should I have risked your life and Richard's to spare your feelings?"

It was the wrong thing to say; Jane knew it the moment the words were out of her mouth. Jack jerked back as though he had been slapped. "Oh, certainly, don't let my tender emotions get in the way of your mission."

He reached to tug down a hat that wasn't there and clutched at empty air.

"I didn't mean it that way. I—" Jane stopped, flustered, all too aware that both Miss Gwen and her former lover were watching them with considerable interest. "Shouldn't someone be seeing to the comfort of Her Majesty?"

Jack took a step back, away from her. "I'll go. I don't seem to be needed here."

But you are, Jane wanted to say, but Nicolas spoke first. "Yes, do, Moonflower. Jeanne—"

He was interrupted by a new voice, a voice that rang off the stones of the guardroom to the fort as only a trained lyric soprano could.

"*You*," said Henrietta, regarding the Gardener with the

sort of venom usually reserved for people who ignore the queue at lending libraries. "What are you doing here?"

The Gardener doffed his hat. "Lady Henrietta. How lovely to see you again."

Jane couldn't echo the sentiment. It wasn't that she didn't love Henrietta; Henrietta was like a sister to her, or at least the closer kind of cousin. But she wasn't exactly the person Jane would have chosen for a sensitive mission to a French-occupied country.

And where Henrietta was . . .

"Hullo! Did I hear voices?" Miles careened into his wife's back.

Catching sight of the Gardener and his wife's Medusa stare, Miles prudently backed up a step.

"Does anyone have any port on hand?" Miles inquired of no one in particular. "And perhaps a biscuit."

Lady Henrietta plunked her hands on her hips. "You're going to feed him?"

"No," said Miles, hiding behind his floppy hair. "For me. I feel in need of fortification."

He wasn't the only one in need of fortification. Jane's simple plan was turning into a French farce.

In an undertone, she said, "What are Miles and Henrietta doing here?"

Jack's face was as closed as the pages of an uncut book. "Don't ask me. They are your people."

"Don't worry," called out a voice from the balcony. "I have him in my sights."

Lizzy gave a cheerful wave, making the crossbow wobble drunkenly.

"Not all my people," said Jane.

"Ah, yes," said Jack. "That. Did you ever think to mention that you were assigned to retrieve me? Trussed, not bound."

Colonel Reid ventured out beneath the balcony. "Lizzy, my love, why don't you put that down and join us?"

Jane turned resolutely away from Lizzy and her crossbow. "I never—" Jack gave her a hard look. Jane reconsidered her answer. "Well, yes, I was meant to ask you to visit your father, but certainly not against your will."

"No," said Jack, his eyes opaque as centuries-old amber. "You had only to persuade me."

The memory of the hot spring wavered between them, the smell of sulfur, the mist in the air.

"Not like that. Never like that." Jane gathered the remaining shreds of her dignity. "I never wanted— Miss Gwen asked me to convey the request. I was of two minds. I didn't know you. And when I did know you . . ."

Jack folded his arms across his chest. "What?"

"It wasn't my choice to make."

They stared at each other for a long moment, all the noise and commotion around them fading to nothing. A muscle pulsed in Jack's cheek.

Jack gave a short, sharp nod. "Thank you."

Jane felt as though she had been through a wringer. Limp with relief, she said, "I had thought we would have more time—time to tell you myself, before—"

"Jane? Jane!"

"What?" Both Jack and Jane turned at the same time.

"If you don't mind my interrupting your no doubt fascinating private conversation," said Richard, lifting a blond brow, "there have been some inquiries as to why our guest is not bound."

"Or trussed," contributed Henrietta.

"I have," said Nicolas, spreading his arms wide, "attempted to explain, but your comrades, my love, seem reluctant to listen. I would prefer not to have rope marks on this coat, if it is all the same."

"There must be some shackles in the dungeon," said Henrietta darkly.

"Rust stains," said Nicolas politely, "are very difficult to get out. My valet would be most cross. And one does not like to encounter Gaston when he is cross."

Miles nodded knowingly. "Valets, eh?"

"Don't worry," said Lizzy brightly, dancing into the chamber in a peculiar costume that was part Robin Hood and part Paris frock. "I have my crossbow."

Nicolas regarded the costume appreciatively. "That is a most unusual ensemble, mademoiselle. But becoming."

"I know," said Lizzy. "And I still have my crossbow."

Nicolas bowed his head in acknowledgment.

"Does anyone have any rope?" demanded Henrietta.

Jane felt a headache coming on. She wished they would all just go away, and preferably take Nicolas with them. "No rope. Our guest"—she gave Nicolas a hard look, willing him to behave himself—"is not bound because Monsieur le Comte de Brillac has expressed a desire to become our ally."

Miss Gwen snorted. "Oh, is that what he's calling himself now?"

Miles looked at Miss Gwen with interest. "Do you mean the count thingy, or ally?"

Nicolas stepped into the middle of the room with the grace of a born performer. "Both, I assure you, are true. The title of Comte de Brillac comes to me from my mother's husband. Ally, I hope, is a title I may earn." He bowed towards the door, where four marines were staggering beneath the burden of an unconscious Braganza. "May Her Majesty Queen Maria be the first token of my good intentions."

"Rather a large token," muttered Miles.

"The size of the token," said Nicolas, with a courtly bow, "is a representation of the sincerity of my commitment."

Or of Queen Maria's fondness for *biscoitos*, but Jane decided not to press that point.

"Monsieur le Comte de Brillac," said Jane, raising her voice to drown out further commentary from her unwanted entourage, "has offered his services to His Majesty King Louis the Eighteenth. Which means"—she was all too aware of Jack's silent presence beside her, his arms folded uncompromisingly across his chest—"that our interests are now aligned."

"I'll believe it when I see it, missy. Snakes don't change their scales, no matter how many times he"—Miss Gwen poked her sword parasol in the Gardener's general direction—"changes his name. What has it been? Four names so far? Five? It's getting hard to keep track. Make up your mind already."

"I have." Nicolas affected a convincing gravity. "When the Bourbons have been restored to their rightful throne, I shall return to my lands at Brillac and devote myself to rebuilding all that has been shattered."

"Noble sentiments," said Richard, his voice hard.

"Oh, for heaven's sake, read between the lines," said Miss Gwen. "He wants Louis the Eighteenth to give him his land back. It's not the least bit noble."

"Noble, ignoble, does it matter?" Nicolas was his most maddening when he was his most philosophical. "All of us are creatures of both dark and light. If one does a good deed for a dark motive, does the motive matter?"

There was a time when Jane had found those sorts of musings a sign of an elevated intellect. Most likely because Nicolas had usually been looking smolderingly at her while he uttered them. Right now, the philosophy and the smoldering both grated on her nerves.

"Fine," said Jack, speaking for the first time. "Put him on a boat and ship him to Louis. He has what he wants; we have what we want."

"Not quite everything," said Nicolas. He paused for dramatic effect, waiting until all eyes were on him before turning and looking at Jane, an intimate, heavy-lidded look designed just for her—and his audience. Holding out both hands to her, he said in a voice designed to carry, "It is traditional, is it not, for an alliance to be sealed with a marriage?"

Taking Jane's hands, he drew her forward, into the center of the room, where everyone could have the best possible view.

Jane's hands were cold, cold as ice. She drew them away, frozen with the wrongness of it. "Nicolas—don't. Please."

She cast an anxious glance over her shoulder at Jack, who was doing his best impression of a stone boulder.

Nicolas tugged on her hand, claiming her attention. "Surely now," he said softly, smiling up at her in a way that would once have made her all fluttery, "there can be no obstacle to our union."

"Aside from good taste and common sense," said Henrietta hotly.

"He's not bad-looking," commented Miss Gwen. "If you like reptiles."

Dropping to the floor at Jane's feet, Nicolas drew the signet from his finger. Not his personal signet, the one he used as the Gardener, but the sigil of the counts of Brillac.

Once, a very long time ago, Jane had imagined this moment, had imagined a world in which she and Nicolas might be together.

That, however, was before she had known him.

And before she had known Jack.

"Well, my Jeanne?" Nicolas said whimsically, proffering the ring. "Will you make me the happiest of men?"

Gold glittered in the torchlight. On the edge of the circle, Jack turned on his heel and stalked off.

Yanking her skirt away, Jane said sharply, "Did you really believe that making a public spectacle of me would change my answer?"

From the side of the room, there was the faint click of a door closing.

The dimple was very apparent in Nicolas's cheek as he smiled up at her. "I live in hope."

"Don't," said Jane crisply. "Not on that score."

"That," said Henrietta, "in case you didn't notice, was a no."

Nicolas rose easily to his feet. "I prefer to think of it as a 'perhaps later.'"

"It was a no," said Jane, and turned on her heel, not sure whom she wanted to shake more: Nicolas for refusing to take no for an answer, or Jack for walking away.

Jack had made his way through a door at the side of the armory, not out to the drilling ground and battlements, but into one of the many cells that honeycombed the side of the fort, once home to monks, now used as storerooms. Jane let herself in without bothering to knock. She found Jack standing by the narrow slit of a window, surrounded by burlap bags of meal, staring out to sea.

He turned as she entered, barely visible in the dusky room. "Am I to wish you happy?"

Jane stopped short. After all these weeks together, everything they had shared. "That's all? That's all you have to say?"

Jack pushed away from the window. "What am I meant to do? Duel for you?" He jerked a thumb back in the direction of the armory. "He would win."

"I never asked you to duel for me!" She would do her own dueling, thank you very much. Jack of all people should know that. Jane's nails dug into her palms. "I'm not a prize to be won or a parcel to be handed back and forth."

Jack held up a hand. "I never said—"

No, he didn't, did he? Tight-lipped, Jane advanced on the man she had foolishly allowed herself to grow to love. "You never say anything. Because if you did, you might have to admit that you care. It's easier just to turn around and walk away. Just like you've walked away from everything."

She could tell she had hit home by the way Jack stiffened. "I didn't precisely see you saying no to him, did I?"

It was cold in the small room, icy cold, but Jane didn't feel it. "Because you didn't stay to see it!"

Jack's fingers closed around her shoulders. Jane could feel his labored breaths, the ragged movement of his chest. "You show up looking like *that*—wearing his dress, his jewels, his perfumes. What in the hell am I supposed to think?" He released her, stepping back. "My congratulations, Countess. You'll make a beautiful ornament at the court of Louis the Eighteenth."

Jane had always prided herself on her ability to retain her poise, even in the most grueling of circumstances. But she was frustrated, humiliated, hurt, and just plain furious.

Jane poked Jack in the chest with her index finger. It felt good, so she did it again. "Would you like to know just how many times I've told Nicolas no? By last count, approximately thirty-seven. Not that it's any of your concern. You see, he, like you, seems to believe that I don't know what is best for me."

Jack grabbed her hand before she could poke him again. "He can give you everything I can't. He can give you riches, titles, a place in the world."

Jane jerked her hand away. "I have my place in the world! I made it myself, with my own hard work." And error, a great deal of error. She braced her hands against Jack's shoulders, holding herself away to look at his face. "Have I ever—ever—given you any indication that I desire titles or riches?"

"Not in so many words, no . . ." Jack's fingers itched to close around her waist and draw her close. Everything that had seemed so clear ten minutes ago was murky and blurry. He knew he had a point, but he was no longer entirely sure what that point was. He retreated a step, his back hitting the whitewashed stone of the wall.

Jane stalked forward, cornering him. Jack could feel the rough stone biting into his back as Jane glared at him, her chest right beneath his nose. "I don't want to be placed on a pedestal. I don't want to be the ornament of anyone's court. And I certainly don't want a lute beneath my window!"

She had told him that, hadn't she? Jack was beginning to feel rather less sure of himself. The Gardener, that proposal, felt very far away, and Jane was very near.

Jack reached up to tuck a loose strand of hair behind her ear. The perfume was growing on him. "How are your blisters?"

It didn't work. "They sting," said Jane shortly. "But I didn't mind that. I didn't mind any of it. As I would have told you if you had only *listened*."

Jack pressed his eyes shut. Somehow he had gone from being noble and wronged to just being wrong. He wasn't quite sure how that had happened. "I thought you wanted a bath and a proper bed."

"There is," said Jane dangerously, "a vast difference between wanting a proper bed and requiring coronets on my sheets. Did it ever occur to you that I didn't care what sort of bed it was as long as you were in it?"

The words rang through the small room. Jack's throat felt sore, swollen. He couldn't seem to force words out, even if there had been any words to say. Jane's chest was rising and falling rapidly, her bosom swelling distractingly over the low neckline of her white gauze gown.

"Jane—" Jack managed, but it was too late.

Jane jerked away, knocking over a bag of meal in the process. "I don't need another man to put me on a pedestal. I have enough of those already." She wrenched open the door to the drilling ground, the sky flaming red and orange behind her. "Congratulations on a successful mission, Moonflower."

And the door slammed, taking with it Jane and the last of the light.

There was a creaking noise from the other side of the room. Jack whirled, reaching for a pistol that wasn't there.

His father peered around the door, assured himself that Jack wasn't armed, and then stepped inside. "I don't think that went very well, my boy."

"No, really?" There was a lump in Jack's throat the size of a cannonball. He could go after Jane—but whatever he said only seemed to make it worse. And what did he have to offer her, after all? A besmirched past and an uncertain future. "Because you've done so very well with women."

His father closed the door behind him, carefully navigating the fallen bag of meal. "I've made my share of mistakes. Your mother among them."

This day just kept getting better and better. Jack punched the wall, which did nothing to the wall and a great deal to Jack's hand, none of it good. "Lovely," he said, through the pain in his knuckles. "Everyone wants to be the product of a mistake."

His father seated himself on a cask of nails. "You were never a mistake, Jack. Never."

"Oh? That's not what I heard." Servants gossiped. Especially in the zenana quarters, where gossip was a way of life. "What does it matter?" Flippantly, Jack quoted Marlowe: "'That was in another country, and besides the wench is dead.'"

"You don't mean that."

Jack was sick of it. He was sick of his father making excuses for him, excuses that were their own form of condemnation, worse than any tirade. "Why not?" he shot back. "Don't tell me you haven't thought it."

Jack's father stared down at his hands, the same broad, capable hands that had lifted Jack on the back of his first pony, steadied Jack's hand on the quill, teaching him his letters. "Your mother and I were ill-suited. We knew that. We tried to make the best of it, in our own ways—"

Best. Jack remembered his mother lying listless in a darkened room, his father sneaking back smelling of spirits after spending yet another late night in the mess. They had both sought escape in their own ways. And he had been caught in the middle of it, lurking in the shadows, longing for affection.

His father shook himself out of his reverie. "It was a bad match and there's no denying it. But neither of us doubted for a minute that we loved you."

Jack gave a short, sharp laugh. "She killed herself."

"Not because of you." Jack's father leaned forward, his hands resting on his knees. "If anyone was to blame it was me. I couldn't give her what she wanted. Whatever that was. She wasn't a happy woman."

The understatement of the century. "Is that meant as an excuse?"

"Consider it an explanation. I'll always bear the guilt of your mother's death on my conscience, lad. There are times I tell myself it would have happened anyway, and times I wonder what I might have done to save her. I can't go back and do it again. If I could"—his father spread his hands wide—"I would have taken more care of you."

That wasn't what Jack had expected. He had always assumed that if his father could go back and do it again, he would have eliminated Jack's mother from his history entirely. And, with her, Jack.

Jack's father looked at him earnestly. "We were both too wrapped up in our own unhappiness to think what we were doing to you. And for that, I beg your pardon."

It felt very wrong to see his father humbling himself before him. Jack tried to shrug it off. "You did the best you could."

"Not well enough." His father seemed determined to have it all out. "I never rose high enough to have real influence. I couldn't fight for you when you needed me."

Jack's eyes prickled. From the residue of gunpowder, of course. "You taught me to fight my own battles. I'd say that was well enough."

Jack's father nodded towards the door to the battlements. "Why did you abandon that one, then?"

And that was what came of letting his father get beneath his guard.

Jack feigned nonchalance. He'd learned that trick long ago: pretending he didn't care, pretending what he didn't care about couldn't hurt him. "You're the one who told me that some battles aren't meant to be won."

"I said a great many foolish things in my youth." Jack's father cocked his head. "You're not holding it against Jane that Gwen asked her to bring you home? I didn't know," he added quickly. "Not until the plan was in motion. And by then—"

"I don't imagine many people say no to Mrs. Reid," said Jack dryly.

"Not within range of her parasol." His father grinned at him.

Reluctantly, Jack found himself grinning back. Even at his angriest he had never been entirely proof against his father's charm. It was part of the reason he had stayed away so long.

"She meant well, you know." His father's expression sobered. "You've been a hole in my heart, and there's no mistaking that. I hope . . . I hope you can see your way to coming back with us, even for a little bit. There's a little girl who would very much like to meet her brother Jack."

It was crass manipulation, but it was alarmingly effective.

"I'll think about it," said Jack brusquely, and was surprised to find that he meant it. There was something dangerously attractive about the world his father was offering him: a home, a family, a new sister. Jane. "Although her godmother might not be too happy to see me there."

His father rested a hand briefly on his shoulder. "Some women, my boy, are worth fighting for."

Jack resisted the urge to make a sharp comment about those who weren't. His mother had been an open sore between them long enough.

Hating himself for being so vulnerable, Jack said hesitantly, "What if I can't make her happy?"

His father steered him towards the door. "Happiness isn't a gift you can give. It's a task you work on together."

There are two of us, Jane had said to him back in the monastery.

And they'd done rather well at being two, until Jack had opened his big mouth.

He paused, his hand on the doorknob, looking back at his father. "What am I going to say to her?"

It was the first time in a long time that he'd asked his father for advice.

Clapping Jack on the back, his father swung open the door. "Have you considered telling her that you love her?"

Chapter Twenty-six

A cannon made a very uncomfortable seat.

It was, however, the only seat available. Jane perched on the barrel of a cannon, staring blankly through the embrasure at the roiling waters of the Atlantic. At least, she knew it was the Atlantic, and based on the strength of the wind she assumed its waters roiled. She couldn't actually see much of anything. The sun had set, leaving her darkling, the enclosure behind her lit only by the scattered light of a few torches that did little to illuminate the vast swath of water beyond the range of the fort.

Somewhere on the other side of the fort, Jane knew, lay Peniche and its lighthouse. But that was behind her. Only the cold waters of the Atlantic lay ahead, as murky as her future.

Oh, for heaven's sake. Jane shifted uncomfortably on the

barrel of the cannon, which had the dual disadvantages of being both cold and damp. She should never have agreed to read the draft of Miss Gwen's next book. She was starting to think like her ninny of a heroine.

The sun would rise tomorrow, as it always did. She would board the *Bien-Aimée* and sail back to England to prepare for her next adventure, wherever that might be.

And Jack would remain in Portugal, doing what he did best: avoiding everyone who might possibly care about him.

What was it Miss Gwen had said? Reptiles didn't change their scales. They did, actually. They shed their old scales and grew new ones. But that didn't mean that Jack was going to change his ways.

Jane leaned her head against a rough bit of brickwork. She couldn't say that she hadn't been warned. She'd known what Jack was before they began working together.

But she hadn't known all the other things he was: the kindness, the fundamental decency of him. Beneath the layer of deliberate devil-may-care, his moral code was as stern as hers, and he was, she realized, a great deal better at seeing to the needs of others.

She tried to remember the frustrating bits, the moments when they had clashed. But all she could remember was Jack adapting to her change of plans. Jack taking charge when her plan had failed. Jack challenging her, making her think more carefully, and then, when she'd charted their course, covering her back without question. Caring for her.

When she was with him, she felt the weight of being the Pink Carnation lift off her shoulders. She didn't have to be perfect. She didn't have to have all the answers. Because Jack was there with her.

Well, he wasn't going to be with her much longer, and she would just have to get her head around that, Jane told herself bracingly. There was work to be done, arrangements to be made. Misplaced monarchs didn't just transport themselves. While she didn't think the French had the sea power at hand to successfully storm the fort, it was very lightly manned. The sooner Queen Maria was on her way to rejoin the Portuguese fleet, the better.

There was the sound of smashing crockery and a cry of *"Ai, Jesus!"* from one of the second-story windows.

The opiates with which Nicolas had dosed the Queen appeared to be wearing off.

She should go, Jane knew. She should make sure that Nicolas wasn't baiting Henrietta and that Miss Gwen hadn't run anyone through with her sword parasol.

But she didn't. She didn't want to face them just yet: Miss Gwen's smirks, and Nicolas's practiced gallantry, and Lizzy's youthful enthusiasm, and Miles's and Henrietta's obvious delight in each other.

There was someone walking, soft-soled, across the clearing. Not Miss Gwen. Her progress was a staccato tapping. Nor any of the others; Jane knew their various treads as she knew her own.

She might have turned or made some sign, but she didn't

trust herself. Instead she stayed where she was, a monument on a pedestal, staring blindly out to sea, painfully aware of every step, every breath, as Jack joined her in the narrow embrasure. She didn't need to see him to know he was there; every sense was attuned to him, to the soft brush of his coat against her dress, the faint scents of sulfur and donkey that aroused memories that were not generally associated with either of the items in question.

Jack leaned a hand against the cannon barrel by her hip. Conversationally, he said, "I hear that the eagle nests only once."

Time tilted backwards. Of all the things Jack might have said, nothing could have disarmed her so. There was a seductive promise to it, the idea that they might start again, wash the slate clean, forge their partnership anew.

The salt spray stung Jane's eyes. Rustily, she answered, as Jack had all those weeks ago, "The eagle sometimes nests in uncommon strange places."

Jack leaned back against the curved side of the embrasure. "Where will you go now?"

Not *I'm sorry.* Not *Stay with me.*

Jane looked out over the choppy waves. In the night sky, the stars were just beginning to emerge, offering guidance to the sailor and light to the lost.

"I was thinking . . . Russia, perhaps. The court speaks French." She glanced at Jack over her bare shoulder, earbobs dangling heavily from her ears. "And I hear the Tsar has an eye for a beautiful woman."

Jack shoved his hands in his pockets, watching her with shadowed eyes. "You'll travel all that way alone?"

Jane made a brief, dismissive gesture. "I can hire a maid."

"That's a long way to travel with only a maid for company."

"Who says I won't find company along the way?" Jane knew it was childish as soon as the words were out of her mouth. And what was the point of making him jealous? He'd already made his position clear. Striving for normalcy, she said briefly, "Amy and Richard have a school for spies. I'm sure there is someone they can spare for me."

"There is another option." Speaking rapidly, Jack said, "Have you ever considered traveling with a husband? I hear they can be rather useful for acquiring donkeys and binding blisters."

Jane could feel the cold metal of the cannon barrel beneath her palms. "A feigned one?"

"No." Jack kept his hands in his pockets, his back against the wall, but Jane felt his gaze like a touch, pinning her in place. "A real one. Bell, book, candle, or whatever it is you use."

"Generally special license." This hurt too much. She couldn't play this game. Baldly, Jane asked, "Are you volunteering for the position?"

Gently Jack took her hands in his. He didn't kneel; that would have put his nose against her knees. The words tumbled out like scattershot: "I would offer you testimonials, but I haven't any. It's not a role I've attempted. I don't know if I'll be any good at it." His hands tightened on hers. "But I do know that wherever you go is where I want to be."

Jane looked down at their linked hands, fighting against an irrational desire to fling her arms around his neck and go with him wherever he wanted to go. It didn't work like that. In one of Miss Gwen's novels, perhaps, but not in real life. "You—you might think that now—"

"I do," said Jack. "I wouldn't have said it otherwise."

"But what about five years from now?" What about the next time she changed the plan without telling him? What about the first time he saw her flirting, on mission, with another man?

Even as she thought it, she knew the answer. Jack's temper might flare for a moment, but he would always, always, in the end, see her side of it. He always had.

That wasn't really what she was afraid of. As to what she was afraid of . . . Jane seized on the least of it. "I don't mean to give up my work," she said belligerently.

"I wouldn't expect you to." Jack's thumbs made little circles around the insides of her wrists, warming her through. "I'm not asking you to be an ornament. Or stand on a pedestal. I'm asking you to slog through the mud with me, blisters and all. If you'll have me."

Jane tilted her head, feeling a little quiver of hope, like the first faint light of dawn. "No lutes?"

"No lutes," Jack promised, his lips spreading into a grin that warmed her through to her core. The grin turned cocky. "Unless you want them. You're welcome to serenade me, if you like."

He was giving her space, Jane knew. Space to make her

decision. Playing for time, she said, "I'm better on the piano-forte than on the lute."

The tenderness in Jack's eyes as he looked at her made Jane's knees wobbly. "I didn't know you played the pianoforte."

She played the pianoforte very well. She played the harp indifferently and sang not at all. "There's a great deal we don't know about each other."

"Would a lifetime be time enough to learn?" Jack squared his shoulders, his face serious, intent. "I mean it, Jane. I'm not walking away this time. I've found my nest."

Jane's lips twisted up in a crooked smile. "And the eagle nests only once?"

Jack wasn't smiling. "This one does."

The stars seemed to stand out more brightly in the sky; the cries of the gulls were louder. Every detail, every line of Jack's face stood out with unnatural clarity.

No matter how long she lived, no matter what she saw, this moment, Jane knew, would remain complete in her memory, every word, every sound, every gesture. The world might not quite stop spinning on its axis, but it seemed, for the moment, to rest.

Until the door of the armory banged open.

"Jane!" Lizzy burst out the door into the enclosure. "Jane! Are you— Oh."

"Go away," said her brother. "We're busy." Turning back to Jane, he said, "While we're on the subject, my father thinks I should tell you I love you."

High romance descended into farce. Jane felt more than a little giddy. "Do you?"

Jack regarded her ruefully. "As it happens—yes."

Jane twined her fingers through his. "That's not much of a declaration."

"You wouldn't let me bring my lute." Jack's eyes were very bright in the darkness. Without turning, he tilted his head sideways. "Also, we have an audience."

Their audience appeared to have grown. Miss Gwen stalked out in pursuit of Lizzy. "Elizabeth! Where are— Hmph." Catching sight of Jack and Jane, she prodded Lizzy in the back with her parasol. "Inside! Now."

Lizzy attempted to squirm away. "But—"

"In!" snapped Miss Gwen.

The door slammed shut behind them.

Jane looked up at Jack, her eyes dancing with laughter. "Do you think they're really gone?"

"Have you met my sister?" said Jack darkly. He cast a hunted look over his shoulder, saying rapidly, "I give it five minutes before she comes back. Possibly less. Do you?"

Jane blinked. "Do I what?"

Jack hunched his shoulders, his brows drawing together. "Love me, damn it."

What is love? Jane had asked Nicolas, when he had professed that emotion, unasked. It hadn't been coyness. It had been a genuine question.

She knew what the poets said of love; she knew what great

men and women had sacrificed in the name of that elusive emotion. Towers had toppled; fleets had been launched. But Jane had always wondered if they had all felt a bit sheepish about it afterwards, if what they had lauded as love was merely, in fact, the grip of a strong infatuation, lust fueled by inaccessibility. The prize, when won, lost its luster; infatuation turned to indifference. The famous beauty had a shrill voice; the great lover stinted his servants. Love was a chimera, an ideal.

Maybe you just aren't capable of feeling it, Nicolas had tossed back at her, one of those golden barbs that cut deeper than she had ever allowed herself to acknowledge.

But he had been wrong. And so had she. Love wasn't an ideal; it was messy and muddy and fraught with inconsistencies. It was a hard arm around her shoulders when she slipped and might have fallen, a reluctant nod in the middle of an argument. It was the slouch of Jack's shoulders and the crooked line of his smile. It was knowing that whatever hardships befell them, they would stumble through it together.

"Do you know," said Jane, feeling rather like an astronomer who had spotted a new planet in the skies, "I'm fairly sure I do?"

Jack rested a hand on either side of her hips, a wolfish smile spreading across his face. "Fairly sure?"

"Extremely sure?" Jane said breathlessly, clutching at his shoulders for balance.

Jack nuzzled her neck. "I'm not giving up until I get absolutely certain."

"Oh, hullo! Er, never mind." Heavy footsteps retreated back in the direction of the fort, along with a faint whiff of ginger.

Jack banged his forehead against Jane's shoulder. "Can't a man propose in peace?"

Jane made the mistake of glancing towards the armory. Lizzy appeared to be jostling with Miss Gwen for space at the window. Colonel Reid was ineffectually attempting to shoo them both away.

"But we might miss something!" Lizzy's voice floated across the drilling ground.

Jane wrapped her arms around Jack's shoulders, resting her cheek against the top of his head. "Apparently not," she said apologetically. "It could be worse. They might be trying to help."

Jack groaned. "How long does it take to get a special license?"

Jane slipped down off the cannon, her body sliding against Jack's. "There's no hurry," she said. "We have a lifetime, after all."

Jack's hands closed around her waist. He looked at her through one eye. "I take it that's a yes?"

"Yes," said Jane, and, heedless of the cries of the Queen and the crowd jostling at the window, sealed her answer with a kiss.

The eagle had found its nest.

Chapter Twenty-seven

One year later . . .
Constantinople, 1808

A woman's shrill scream rent the air.

Janissaries rampaged down the normally forbidden Golden Way, the Sultan's private passageway through the harem, shoving eunuchs and slaves out of the way. The sound of agitated cries and footfalls echoed off the domed ceiling and tiled walls of the privy chamber. All was in disarray.

Rumors were everywhere. The rebels had sacked the city; the Sultan was dead. The Sultan was alive and enacting terrible reprisals. The Sultan had murdered his brothers and was killing their concubines.

No one quite knew what was true and what wasn't, but no one wanted to be there to find out. The history of the Ottoman sultans was too bloodstained to take chances, and Mustafa IV was not known as a kind or generous man.

"Assassins!" someone screamed, and a rampage began, people running first this way and then that, some by accident, others by design.

In the confusion, no one noticed when yet another Janissary threw a screaming slave over his shoulder. She was Georgian, with the fair hair and gray eyes of her people, but her ordinarily well-tended skin was streaked with ashes, and her garments were torn and dirtied.

"You got Mahmud safely away?" muttered the Janissary, as he bore the slave girl off down a narrow stone staircase, away from the fray.

"Only just." The slave girl lay in a seeming swoon, her mouth close by the Janissary's ear, her lips hidden by her white veil and the large flap of his uniform hat. "The assassins were already there. I tossed ash in their faces. Naksidil Sultan got Mahmud up to the roof of the third court while I held them off."

"Do you know where he is now?"

"Hidden in a furnace beneath the baths of the Valide Sultan." The slave girl spoke with absolute confidence.

This plan had been weeks in the making. The slave girl had worked closely with Naksidil Sultan, Mahmud's mother, who spoke beautiful, lightly accented French. Some whispered that it was because she was French, kidnapped by Barbary pirates on her way home to her native Martinique. Whatever she had once been, though, Naksidil Sultan had become a force to be reckoned with within the harem, fierce in her defense of her son.

Tonight, Mustafa IV had sent assassins to kill his half brother, Mahmud. He hadn't reckoned with Mahmud's secret allies.

"Oh, bother it." The Janissary checked as he caught sight of a large cluster of eunuchs, but as they seemed more occupied in fleeing with whatever loot they could carry than impeding his progress, he brazenly went on.

"And you?" the slave girl murmured to her captor. "Did you bring Alemdar Mustafa Pasha?"

The Janissary permitted himself a smug smile. "He is proclaiming the new Sultan as we speak." It hadn't been easy herding the leader of the rebel forces, but when it had been explained to him that a palace coup was in progress and he could be in or out, the rebel leader had chosen in. "I assume you have the new Sultan's assurance?"

"That no treaties will be signed with France? Yes."

Napoleon had had his eye on an Ottoman alliance for years. But right now the new Sultan owed a far greater debt to someone else: the Pink Carnation.

The Pink Carnation smiled wryly up at her husband. "Whether he'll honor it is another matter."

Outside the Gate of the Girls, a covered palanquin waited to convey them to the port at Yenikapi. The curtains swished closed around them. In the confusion of the night's events, one palanquin leaving the palace would hardly be noticed.

The Pink Carnation glanced through the slit in the curtains, a worried line between her eyes. "Do you think we were right to interfere?"

"Mahmud can't be any worse than Mustafa." More seriously, the spy known as the Moonflower added, "Between Mustafa and the rebels, there was going to be bloodshed; the most we could do was try to prevent it. You saved at least one life tonight. More than one. Well-done, Mrs. Reid."

Jane's fingers twined through her husband's, clasped and held. "I did have some assistance."

Jack grinned down at her. "I try to make myself useful."

The sun was beginning to rise over the Bosphorus, turning the sky to an imperial display of purple and gold, the light dancing between the waves that lapped at the quayside. At the end of the quay, a boat waited for them, and in it a new set of instructions, of papers, of disguises.

"Shall we?" said Jane, and together they sailed off into the sunrise.

Chapter Twenty-eight

"The Pink Carnation was also married from Selwick Hall," said Mrs. Selwick-Alderly, as she adjusted one of the bobby pins that held my antique-look veil in place.

My eyes met hers in the long mirror. For an eighty-year-old woman who had been kidnapped, escaped her bonds, and felled her attacker, she looked pretty good. It was either makeup or good bones. My money was on good bones.

This, I decided, boded well for Colin's and my future children.

I was still feeling more than a little sluggish, but a pot of strong coffee and the makeup man had worked their magic. Ten layers of foundation had dimmed the dark circles under my eyes, and various arcane tints and powders had provided the illusion of healthy color. No one looking at me would guess that I had been up until four in the morning.

Or, if they did, they would probably assume it was because I was tying one hundred tiny ribbons onto our favors. The truth was far too bizarre for anyone to even begin to contemplate.

The incident would never appear on any official record. Not the sort open to the public, in any event. No one had wanted to call the police. Instead, Mrs. Selwick-Alderly had borrowed my cell—I mean, my mobile—to make a discreet call to persons unknown. Said persons unknown had shown up about an hour later and removed the unconscious Dempster and our sheet.

I had decided it was wiser not to ask who they were or where they were taking him. There were some things you just didn't want to know, especially at three a.m. the morning before your wedding.

By the time we had staggered back, the sky was beginning to look suspiciously light, and I was beginning to wish that I had taken my mother's advice and had an evening wedding, like normal (translation: American) human beings.

But it was my wedding day and the sun was shining, which isn't something you can take for granted in England, even in June. The lark was on the wing and the snail was on the thorn; the marquee hadn't collapsed yet, the vicar was only mildly hungover, and I was buoyed by a swelling sense of well-being that owed a little bit to coffee and a great deal to a sense that the world was just as it was meant to be.

I hadn't seen Colin yet. Adhering to tradition, we'd decided that would be bad luck, so he and my father were busy
tying their bow ties elsewhere. My mother and Jillian were
currently under the heavy hand of the makeup man and the
hair woman, respectively. Grandma had wanted to make sure
that no one stole her front-row seat, so she had gone in early to
stake her claim and her cane, with Jeremy in attendance.

Pammy was prinking and Alex was assuring Serena that
she didn't look fat in her dress, which left Mrs. Selwick-Alderly
momentarily in charge of care and management of the bride,
i.e., me.

She gave my veil a final tweak. "Very nice, my dear."

I stepped back to take a look. We were in the library, one
of my favorite rooms of the house, which had been comman-
deered for the occasion as robing room. It looked much as it
usually did, the only jarring notes the large three-sided mirror
that had been plunked in the center of the room and the in-
congruous clutter of hair dryer, brushes, and makeup cases
where my laptop usually sat. Light slanted across the carpet
through the long windows, creating the sort of radiant effect
that generally takes a great deal of fiddling with filters and
lenses.

I wish I could say that my dress was a Regency reproduc-
tion or, even better, one of the Pink Carnation's own. But that
would have been a bit much, even for me. I wanted Colin to
know I was marrying him, not some historical daydream.

So my dress was Vera Wang, cream-colored satin with a

waist cinched in with a bow and a full skirt. There was, however, a design of beaded flowers on the strapless bodice. It
struck me as a subtle nod to what had brought me and Colin
together.

It was also the one dress on which Jillian and my mother
had both agreed.

We will not even discuss the wedding dresses that Pammy
had attempted to make me try on. Leopard print and tulle do
not go together in the same garment.

"What happened to the Carnation's wedding dress?" I asked
curiously.

"Wedding dresses then weren't what they are now," said
Mrs. Selwick-Alderly. "I imagine the material was cut down
and reused. But we do have one of her wedding presents. A
silver tea set."

Rather like the very large, very heavy silver tea service currently sitting on our dining room table. "*That* silver tea set?"

Her eyes meeting mine in the mirror, Mrs. Selwick-Alderly
adjusted one discreet silver earring. "It was a wedding gift
from Lord and Lady Vaughn. It was left behind with Amy
and Richard. Jane and Jack didn't have much use for a full tea
service on their travels."

Their travels. That had a ring to it. I twisted slightly, the
lace of my veil brushing my cheek. "Where did they go?"

"It might be simpler to tell you where they weren't." Mrs.
Selwick-Alderly gave a little tweak to my veil. "We'll never
know the whole of it, but I've always suspected that they had

a hand in putting Mahmud the Second on the throne of the Ottoman Empire in 1808. From there, they went to Russia. As I'm sure you know, that particular venture didn't go very well for Napoleon."

No. No, it hadn't. Although it had worked out rather nicely for Tolstoy, half a century later.

"Where did they go after the war was over?" It was a wishful-thinking sort of question. I didn't really expect her to know.

But Mrs. Selwick-Alderly answered without hesitation: "They settled in Brazil. I did a bit of work there," she added modestly.

I didn't ask what kind of work. After last night it seemed safer not to know. At least for a hundred years or so, at which point it might be my great-great-grandchildren inquiring into Mrs. Selwick-Alderly's secret activities, wondering over such quaint costumes as minidresses and bell-bottoms.

The mind boggled. Over many things.

"They settled in Brazil?" It wasn't so much that it was Brazil, per se, as that I hadn't really thought of the Pink Carnation and the Moonflower settling anywhere. One expected them to sail off into a glowing sunset, à la an Errol Flynn movie. "Why Brazil?"

"The Portuguese crown owed them a few favors," said Mrs. Selwick-Alderly. She seated herself in a large cracked leather chair. "Although I think King John came to regret his largesse later on. Jack and Jane were instrumental in Brazil's War of Independence."

"I gather that is basically what it calls itself?" My knowledge of Brazilian history was limited to my friend Carrie's dissertation-in-progress, which focused on the German community in Brazil post–World War II.

"Brazil had been governed by the Portuguese crown," Mrs. Selwick-Alderly explained patiently. "Jack and Jane backed the move to make Brazil an autonomous constitutional monarchy. Jane learned to speak Portuguese, of course."

"Of course," I echoed.

What was the little matter of a language barrier? Both Jane Wooliston and Jack Reid were the sort who would eventually take charge wherever they landed and fight for what they believed to be right.

I wondered what their children had been like. I suspected that if I opened any textbook on Brazil, I would find them staring out at me. One couldn't imagine that the offspring of the Pink Carnation and the Moonflower would lead placid lives, any more than their English cousins had.

"There's a book there," I said.

"More than one, I should think," said Mrs. Selwick-Alderly with a faint glimmer of amusement. She rose from her chair, taking the largest bouquet from the row the florist had left on one of the scarred old tables. "But all in good time."

"Thank you." The bouquet was heavier than it looked, weighing down my wrist. It required two hands to hold properly.

I caught a glimpse of myself in the long mirror, veil, bouquet, and all, and knew that Mrs. Selwick-Alderly was right.

Perhaps someday I would write the Pink Carnation's love story. But right now I was more interested in my own.

"Are you ready?" My mother bustled into the library, wearing a lime green silk suit and matching shoes, Jillian close behind in pale green chiffon.

Pink might have been more appropriate for the Carnation, but green went much better with my hair. I was sure that Colin's ancestors would understand.

"Everyone is downstairs," said Jillian. In an undertone, she asked, "What were you and Colin up to last night?"

I shot a sideways glance at my aunt-in-law. I could tell my mother's ears had perked up. "You'd never believe me if I told you," I muttered.

Downstairs, the bridal party had assembled in what had once been a music room, but had devolved, over successive, less musical generations, into a sort of den.

My father was fidgeting with his tie. Pammy was admiring her face in a small handheld mirror. Alex was giving last-minute instructions to her daughter, my flower girl. The page boy we had borrowed from one of the Canadian branches of the Selwick clan.

Through the curtain that had been hung over the music room door, I could hear a fanfaronade of baroque music.

My mother sent the first wave through. I could hear the requisite oohs and aahs as my flower girl minced down the aisle, carefully portioning her petals.

Alex followed her daughter, followed by Pammy, who mouthed something to me before she disappeared behind the curtain. It sounded like "More rouge!"

I was not putting on more rouge.

As Serena made her way up, I felt her thin hand clasp my wrist.

I couldn't tell whether green wasn't a good color for Serena or if it was the aftereffect of being held at gunpoint by her ex-boyfriend, which admittedly could make anyone feel a little queasy. Her long brown hair was as shiny as ever, but her face was nearly as green as her dress.

I put a hand on her arm. "Are you all right? If you need to sit down—"

"I'm fine." She didn't look fine, but I decided not to argue. The last time we'd had this sort of exchange, I'd wound up holding her head over a toilet bowl, and I was due in front of an altar in approximately three minutes. "I just wanted to say . . . I'm sorry. For everything."

"It's okay," I said, giving her a quick hug. "And that's your cue."

In fact, it had been her cue a few times already. Jillian, whose bouquet was larger and whose dress was longer to mark her elevated status as both maid of honor and Great and Mighty Younger Sister (which ranked a few steps higher than Oz and well above grand poobah), whispered, "What was that about?"

"I'll tell you later," I murmured, and chivvied her out onto the runway.

Which left me. I peeked through the curtain. From my vantage point I could just make out Colin, his blond head shining in the light from the French windows.

The vicar winked at me. I hastily pulled my head back through the curtain.

My father held out an arm. "Ready?"

"Ready," I said, flexing one foot beneath my dress. My heels were very, very high. Not as high as Pammy's, but there was some serious leverage going on.

"If you have any second thoughts . . ." my father murmured.

"No second thoughts." Except possibly about the shoes, which were going to get very uncomfortable very quickly.

About Colin, on the other hand, I had no doubts at all. If he and I could face an armed archivist together, we were ready for anything. Up to and including diapering and midnight feedings.

Eventually. I had some books to write first.

The music changed, swelled. My father opened the curtain and we stepped through, into the bright light of the drawing room. Old friends and new acquaintances were a happy blur on either side of the aisle, the line of Colin's groomsmen a gray smudge against the pale walls.

Only Colin stood out distinctly. Because in the end, that was what this was about. The two of us.

He held out a hand to help me up the two steps onto the makeshift platform, and the words of the ceremony washed over me as I held his hand, dust motes drifting around us in the sunlight.

It was hard not to think of the first time I had entered this room, nearly two years ago. It had been autumn then. Colin was an inscrutable albeit attractive stranger in a green Barbour jacket. And I was going to finish my research, write my dissertation, go back to the States, and fling myself into the academic job market. My world had been coffee soaked, rain gray, November cold.

November would come again and rain—it was England, after all—but my horizons had opened and expanded in ways I could never have imagined.

Once, I thought I knew exactly what I was doing. Now I hadn't a clue. But I had a book and I had Colin, and I had learned to take the unexpected in stride. The future lay ahead of us, uncharted and full of possibility, and I gave silent thanks to the Pink Carnation for turning my plans upside down. If she had been any less elusive, I wouldn't be here.

Colin's eyes met mine in one of those moments of perfect well-being.

Solemnly, the vicar intoned, "Do you, Eloise, take—"

Which was, of course, when Pammy's mobile began bleating, making the entire bodice of her dress vibrate.

The vicar lost his place in the service as Pammy dug in her bodice, muttering, "Sorry, sorry . . ."

Three out of four groomsmen looked as though they were ready to start drooling. Jeremy was too busy fixing the set of his cuff links to be distracted by vibrating cleavage.

My mother, who had never liked Pammy, took a death grip on my bouquet, which had been handed off to her. My father took a death grip on my mother.

I couldn't look Colin in the eye. If I did, I was going to lose it laughing, which isn't necessarily how you want to precede that all-important "I do."

"Hey!" Pammy had managed to fish her phone from her bra and was waving it triumphantly in the air. "It's Jim! He says he got you a book deal!"

"You got a book deal?" said Jillian, from her place at the front of the row of bridesmaids. "Yay!"

Unsure what to do, some of our guests began clapping, but it quickly died out as they glanced around and saw that other people weren't.

"A reading from the Book of Eloise?" murmured Colin, sotto voce.

The vicar winced a little. I had a feeling the sunlight shining right into his eyes wasn't doing much for his hangover. "As wonderful as that is—and it is wonderful news—we do have a bit more to get through. If you don't mind, that is?" he said to Pammy, with dangerous politeness. "Pamela?"

"Huh?" Pammy, scrolling through her five hundred other texts, glanced up at the sound of her name. "No, no, of course."

With grim determination, my mother marched over and confiscated Pammy's phone.

"Thank you," said the vicar, lifting his eyes heavenwards. "Now. Do you, Eloise—"

"I do," I said quickly. Pammy had three mobiles. I wasn't taking any chances. Goodness only knew which part of her was going to start vibrating next.

The vicar looked taken aback for a moment, and then decided to go on. "Do you, Colin—"

"I do."

"Your eagerness is touching," muttered the vicar. "But I'd prefer if you'd wait for your cue. Now. If I might proceed—"

Pammy's bouquet began to quiver.

I couldn't help it; I leaned against Colin, chortling softly into his morning coat. " 'Man and wife—say man and wife.' "

The vicar buried his face behind the Book of Common Prayer. "It's like trying to conduct the wedding in *The Princess Bride*."

"But without the speech impediment," Jillian pointed out helpfully, from where she was trying to keep my mother from strangling Pammy.

"There's gin in the marquee," I said to the vicar.

"Good," he muttered. He raised his voice to a boom of Old Testament proportions. "Now if everyone could silence their phones and return to their places . . ."

As we walked back down the aisle to the triumphal strains of Handel's Water Music and the vibration of Pammy's third mobile, my husband murmured, "I never did have a chance to say congratulations. On your book."

"Well . . . we were rather busy last night." I glanced up at him. "You don't mind?" Colin was still hard at work on his own book.

"I'm proud of you," he said seriously. Before I could get too teary-eyed, he added with mock severity, "And I expect a mention in the acknowledgments."

I beamed up at my husband, light-headed with joy and lack of sleep. "For you—a paragraph."

We exited through the French doors, climbing towards the tower, enjoying the few moments of privacy before the bridal party streamed out behind us and our respective families closed around us again. The marquee lay below us, and the mushroom village of tiny tables that had been set out for the cocktail hour. We would take pictures up by the old tower while our guests got started on the serious drinking.

But for the moment, it was just me and Colin.

I bent my head so that he could take the pins from my veil without taking my hair with it. "Have you thought of a title for your book?"

The sun was warm on my bare head, and the grass smelled fresh and sweet. "Well . . . I like *Pride and Prejudice*, but that's already been taken."

Colin thought about it for a moment. *"The Convent of Orsino?"*

"Also taken." I could just imagine Miss Gwen rising from the grave, parasol in hand, to defend her territory. Miss Gwen gone zombie was something we could do without. "Something with Pink Carnation in the title?"

The rest of the bridal party were beginning to make their straggling way up the hill. I had a feeling that my choice of a

photo spot was not universally popular, especially for the pho-
tographer.

A faint smile played around Colin's lips. *"How the Pink
Carnation Stole Me Lucky Charms?"*

I had been introducing Colin to the classics of American
culture.

"Not funny." Okay, it was pretty funny. I liked that Colin was
making an effort to learn my language. I'd have him making
Bueller jokes in no time. *"The Pink Carnation's Secret History?"*

"No," said Colin, looping an arm around my waist as our
respective families joined us at the crest of the hill. *"The Secret
History of the Pink Carnation."*

From our vantage point, I could see all of Selwick Hall
spread out before me, everything clear and sparkling in the
morning sunlight. For a moment, just a moment, I could have
sworn I saw the image of a young woman in a long dress in
one of the library windows. And then it was gone, just another
trick of the light.

"You know," I said, leaning my head against his shoulder.
"You might have something there."

I could hear the smile in Colin's voice. "Of course I do," he
said. "I have you."

Acknowledgments

I've been living with the Pink Carnation series for a very long time. As my little sister would say, "All the feels, all the feels." Theoretically, I knew the time had come for the series to end. But when it came to putting words on paper? I put this book off. And I put this book off. And I would have put this book off even longer, but for the fact that my agent, editor, and publisher were all getting justifiably antsy and pointed out that there actually needs to be a manuscript for a book to get published.

So many thanks to my agent, Alexandra Machinist, and my editor, Danielle Perez, for holding my hand when I got angsty, prodding me when I dragged my feet, and for being very, very generous with extensions. Thank you to the best of all possible book doctors, Claudia Brittenham, Brooke Willig, and Sarah MacLean, who talked me through plot crises and helped me over the rough spots. Also, to my husband, who helped me puzzle out the Portuguese, plotted distances on maps, and generally dealt with the practical bits. (And only once suggested just sticking everyone in a TARDIS as a much easier travel alternative to donkey.)

So much love to my family: to my daughter, husband, parents, brother, and sister, who all deal with more than their share of book-induced lunacy. My sister, Brooke, has been my first reader and best critic on every single one of the books. As for my parents . . . there aren't enough words to say thank you for all the hand-holding, sustenance-bringing, whine-listening, and, more recently, babysitting. (Not to mention all those years of raising me and reading to me and singing endless rounds of "Do You Know the Muffin Man?" and all that sort of thing.) Thank you to my husband for takeout, reassurance, and toddler-wrangling (not necessarily in that order), and to my daughter for being so insanely adorable. Because, really, when a book isn't behaving, there's nothing like hearing a toddler's rendition of *"Frère Jacques"* to put life back into perspective. Thanks to Lutchmie for entertaining said toddler for extra hours during those crucial weeks when *"Frère Jacques"* became incompatible with deadline: this book wouldn't be here without you.

Over a decade and twelve books, there are so many people who have offered love, support, caffeine, gin, and laughs along the way. This is, necessarily, a very incomplete list, but hugs, hugs, hugs to, among others, Claudia Brittenham, Nancy Flynn, Liz Mellyn, Jenny Davis, Weatherly Ralph, Marie Gryphon, Emily Famutimi, Abby Vietor, Lila de Tantillo, Lara Lorenzana, Chris Ray, Stella Choi-Ray, Will Crawford, Francine Crawford, Justin Zaremby, and Vicki Parsons.

A special shout-out to my writing sisters: Tasha Alexander, Tracy Grant, Deanna Raybourn, Sarah MacLean, Cara Elliot, Alison Pace, Karen White, and Beatriz Williams, for book tour adventures, plot help, gossip, and always reminding me that the point is the stories we're telling. Thank you for keeping the writing joy alive—and just being such fun.

To all the baristas at my bat cave (i.e., Starbucks) on Fifty-seventh Street between Eighth and Ninth, a heartfelt thank-you for letting me spend months at a time hogging the seat next to the outlet, starting my drink before I'd even ordered it, not commenting on my haven't-done-laundry-in-days chic, asking after my book and my toddler, and, generally, being wonderful. Those cheerful good mornings—and caramel macchiatos—made such a difference.

Last but not least, a huge thank-you to my readers. When I wrote that first Pink book twelve years ago, the last thing I ever suspected was that it would lead me not just to an imaginary world, but to a very real community, filled with some of the most talented and generous-spirited people it has been my privilege to know. Together, we've built traditions, like the annual Pink Carnation Peep Diorama contest (aka Pinkorama), shared our weekly reads, engaged in adventures in baking (thank you, Christine Moon Angeles!), and so much more. Thank you to everyone who has been a part of my Web site, commented on my author Facebook page, popped by a reading, or taken the time to drop me a note via e-mail. When I was given the choice of dropping the Pink series or doubling my workload in order to see it through, you were the ones who gave me the courage and the energy to see it through. In oh so many ways, this book is for you.

Thank you all!

Historical Note

M ad monarchs provide excellent fodder for fiction.
Because I already used George III in a previous
book, it felt a bit greedy to seize on another afflicted monarch,
but Queen Maria I's condition made a perfect premise for a
novel set at the outbreak of the Peninsular War. Like her coun-
terpart, George III, Queen Maria descended into a form of
dementia that some speculate may have been caused by por-
phyria, although other theories have also been mooted. (One of
the details that surprised me most in my researches was the
amount of inbreeding in the Braganza family tree. Maria herself was married to her uncle; one of her sons was married to his
own aunt, Maria's sister.) Mental instability ran in the family.
Maria's grandfather King Philip V of Spain believed that he

was being consumed by fire in retribution for his sins; her uncle Ferdinand VI zigzagged between depression and mania, assaulting his servants and banging his head against the wall. Queen Maria went with the "all of the above" approach: by 1790, her behavior, in the words of her biographer, "swung between extreme lassitude ... and violent excitement." George III's own "mad doctor," Francis Willis, was called in, but was dismissed after he stipulated that Queen Maria would have to be taken to England for further treatment.

By 1807, Queen Maria lived confined to her pavilion in her palace at Queluz, where shrieks of "*Ai*, Jesus! *Ai*, Jesus!" could be heard echoing through the halls, along with the sound of crashing crockery. I have tried to keep the details of her condition—her violent rages, her fear of her servants—as close to the historical record as possible. You can find more about the life and times of Queen Maria in Jenifer Robert's biography, *The Madness of Queen Maria: The Remarkable Life of Maria I of Portugal*.

Meanwhile, as Queen Maria raved in her pavilion at Queluz, her son was dealing with pressure from both England and France. In July of 1807, Napoleon ordered the Portuguese Regent, Dom João, to close Portugal's ports to its old ally and trading partner, England. By August he had upped the ante, warning Dom João that unless he wanted to be deposed, he had better declare war on Great Britain, arrest all British subjects (of which there were many in Portugal, including one of the sons of George III, who had settled there), and hand over his fleet to the French. Caught between a rock and a hard place, aka Britain and France, Dom João dragged his feet, trying to pacify both sides. To the French he offered to arrest British subjects, declare war, and close the ports. To the British ambassador he promised that the war would be in name only, trade could continue with Brazil, the British could lease the isle of Madeira, and no British property in Portugal (of which there was a great deal) would be confiscated. Both sides responded with the diplomatic version of "You've got to be kidding." The British fleet moved to blockade the Portuguese ports. And as for Napoleon . . .

Poor Dom João. On the twentieth of October, Dom João decided that the French were scarier than the British and reluctantly kicked all Britons out of Portugal. It was too late. Even as he offered concessions to Bonaparte, the French army, headed by Jean-Andoche Junot, was already on the move. Napoleon invaded Portugal under the aegis of the Treaty of Fontainebleau (October 27, 1807), a deal with the King of Spain and his minister, Godoy, in which Portugal would be divided into three parts: one for France, one for Spain, and one an independent principality for Godoy. (This, as you can imagine, did not go well in the end for the King of Spain or Godoy. And by "in the end," I mean a few months later, when the troops supposedly marching through allied territory on their way to Portugal turned around and took Madrid instead.) On November 24, Admiral Sir Sidney Smith (who, as a side note, some claim was the model for Orczy's Pimpernel) presented

Dom João with a copy of *Le Moniteur*, the French newspaper, in which Napoleon had announced, "The House of Braganza has ceased to reign." The paper was dated October 13, 1807. The British "I told you so" was implied. The issue had been decided before Dom João had said a word.

In a panic, Dom João flung himself on the mercy of the British. Junot was all of five days' march from Lisbon. A rather straggling march, but Dom João, unlike historians, didn't know that. Hastily he gathered the court for departure. As the rain pounded down, paintings, objets d'art, furniture, government documents, gold ingots, anything that could be salvaged was piled onto wagons and pulled onto the docks as courtiers desperately tried to secure berths, and royal servants hung about, hoping to be taken along. Space was scant and the confusion was extreme. As the royal storekeeper described it, "Many people were left behind on the quay while their belongings were stowed on board; others embarked, only to find that their luggage could not be loaded." There was unrest and looting in the town. Dom João took a plain carriage to the docks to avoid being mobbed. The Queen was less subtle. As described in the novel, her cries could be heard all the way down to the docks. Some accounts have it that she shouted, "Not so fast! It will be thought we are running away." It was that line that gave me the idea of the Queen's staying behind— although, when I learned the extent of her illness, it became more realistic to render her a pawn than a principal.

It was a last-minute flight. As Junot's men marched into

Lisbon, they could see the sails of the fleet as they bore the Portuguese court away to Brazil. They also discovered a number of carriages and crates left abandoned on the quayside; according to one historian, these included "sixty thousand volumes from the Royal Library of Ajuda and fourteen carriages of church silver and other treasures." In confusion like that, who would miss one mad monarch?

Little did Dom João know, if he had stood and fought, Napoleonic triumph wasn't a done deal. As Jack informs Jane in the book, the invasion was a mess. Napoleon looked at a map, found the shortest distance between two points, and told Junot to go that way, rather than take the usual road, ignoring the fact that the usual road was the usual road for a reason (i.e., it was much more passable). The Emperor further gummed the works by ordering Junot "to ignore the temptation to gather supplies, as it would lead to unacceptable delays," insisting, "Twenty-thousand men . . . can live anywhere, even in a desert." As historian David Buttery dryly puts it, "Unfortunately for the French, [Napoleon] was about to be proved wrong." Short on supplies, Junot's starving and barefoot men found themselves wading through rivers in full spate, falling down gorges, and generally dying like flies. Junot entered Lisbon on November 30, 1807, with only four battalions of infantry. His artillery was still on the road, far behind him. One of his officers, Baron Thiébault, recounted, "As everyone knows, Junot took possession of Lisbon, of the army that was there, and of the entire kingdom, without having at hand a single trooper, a single gun, or a cartridge that would burn. . . ." Exaggeration, certainly, but not by much.

Hungry, ragged, and desperate, looting and pillaging along the way, the French troops did not make themselves popular. Nor, for that matter, did Junot, who was not generally known for his subtlety or tact. The riot in Rossio Square on the thirteenth of December on the occasion of the lowering of the royal standard did, indeed, occur as depicted. The impositions of curfews, decisions to quarter troops in monasteries and nunneries, and an enormous tax levied on the Portuguese people fanned the flames of rebellion.

In reality, it took some time for that rebellion to coalesce into organized resistance. I moved the time line up a bit, inventing a local loyalist group, headed by the Bishop of Porto, intent (in my fictional version) on using the Queen as a rallying point. In real life, the Queen did make it onto that ship to Brazil, and the Portuguese resistance movement, which coalesced under the Bishop of Porto, only really took off six months later, in June of 1808.

If you wish to learn more about the Peninsular War, and this first phase in particular, I recommend David Buttery's *Wellington Against Junot: The First Invasion of Portugal, 1807–1808*. For the Peninsular War generally, Michael Glover's *The Peninsular War, 1807–1814* condenses a great deal of information in a highly readable narrative inflected with dry humor.

Many, many English and French passed through Portugal in the eighteenth and nineteenth centuries, before, during, and after the Peninsular War. At times it seems like most of them wrote about it. Given the timing of this novel and the changes wrought by the conflict, I relied most heavily on those travel narratives written before the war, since the landscape through which Jack and Jane traveled was still largely untouched by the devastation that would occur a scant year later. That being said, I also consulted the memoirs of those who traveled in and through Portugal during the war (bearing in mind that some of what they saw might have changed). The story of the corpse at the inn came straight from the memoirs of Junot's wife, Laure. For the details of the march to Lisbon, I relied, among other sources, on the memoirs of Paul-Charles-François Thiébault, who did not mince words when describing the straits in which Junot's soldiers found themselves. Descriptions of contemporary Lisbon were taken, in part, from William Graham's memoir, *Travels through Portugal and Spain, During the Peninsular War.*

There are both benefits and drawbacks to travel narratives written by outsiders. On the upside, strangers are likely to notice and report on details that inhabitants take for granted. On the downside, they're also likely to misinterpret, misunderstand, or misreport many of those details, blowing certain elements out of proportion and ignoring others. It was necessary to read the reports of the French and English in Portugal with more than a grain of salt; the English tended to both exoticize and denigrate Portugal, seeing it on the one hand as foreign and romantic, and on the other as backward, priest-ridden, dangerous, and dirty. For an excellent unpacking of the attitude of the British towards Portugal in the early nineteenth century, I highly recommend Gavin Daly's *The British Soldier in the Peninsular War: Encounters with Spain and Portugal, 1808–1814*. Since both Jack and Jane are outsiders, albeit from rather different backgrounds, it was instructive to know not only what Portugal had been, but what the English perceived it to be, which were often two rather different beasts.

It was the 1790 memoirs of James Cavanah Murphy (the same Murphy's *Travels* Jane references as required reading for the English visitor to Portugal) that inspired the scenes set at Alcobaça Monastery, as well as my depiction of the snobbish abbot. I should like to offer apologies to the actual abbot—one gets the sense that Murphy's description may have been more than a little biased. Murphy clearly took quite a shine to the prior of Batalha Monastery and something less of a shine to the prior of Alcobaça. The comments about there being more pipes of wine in the cellar than books in the library are taken straight from Murphy, who seemed to be a little bit uneasy about the wealth and grandeur of Alcobaça. (For the record, Murphy—and Jack—were both entirely wrong about that. Alcobaça had an impressive library of medieval manuscripts. At least, that is, until the French came through in 1810. The remains of the collection can be found in the National Library in Lisbon.) But I do owe at least one major plot point to James Murphy. It was his comments about the rarity of strangers being admitted to the hall of novices as well as his description of the mysterious chalice that provided the inspiration for key bits of my story.

Although the monastery of Alcobaça is very much a real place, I took some liberties with its inhabitants and furnishings. Unfortunately, although there were those, like Murphy, who stayed at Alcobaça and wrote of it afterwards, I was unable to find any description of the guest chambers as they would have appeared in the eighteenth century. The reception rooms in the strangers' wing, yes. The actual bedchambers, no. I also adjusted the layout of the novice's wing just a bit. Eighteenth-century visitors report traversing a corridor from the chapel to the cells. But I needed Jack and Jane to be able to see the chapel from the inside of a cell, so, for plot reasons, I dispensed with the corridor and had the cells open directly off the chapel. I hope my readers and the shades of past novices will forgive me.

I would be remiss if I didn't mention another source to which I owe a great debt: a Web site called myneighborwellington.blogspot.com, which exhaustively and entertainingly chronicles the minutiae of the Peninsular War, largely from the Portuguese perspective. It was from My Neighbor Wellington that I learned of expressions like *saudade* and *amigos de Peniche*, period costume, local living conditions, contemporary recipes, and a thousand other details, most of which I sadly had no opportunity to use, such as folk-song lyrics (which I so very, very much wanted to use—but Jane wouldn't know them and Jack stubbornly refused to break into song). There isn't much that isn't covered on that Web site. To the proprietress, a heartfelt thank-you. The details of daily life on the site brought the early nineteenth century to life for me and, I hope, for the book.

Finally, I couldn't resist sneaking in a taste of Jane's and Jack's future adventures. (Of which there are, of course, many.) The Ottoman sultan Mustafa IV did indeed attempt to have his twenty-three-year-old brother, Mahmud, assassinated in 1808. Accounts vary, as they do, but one version of the story has it that as the assassins approached the harem, a Georgian slave girl named Cevri Kalfa held them off by throwing ashes in their faces. Mahmud then fled to safety, although no one seems to agree on where he hid. I went with the version that had him hiding in a furnace, although other accounts place him on a roof or elsewhere. The rebel leader Alemdar Mustafa Pasha did show up and announce to Mustafa that he was being deposed, although he was not, in fact, fetched by Jack Reid. The bits I left out? Mustafa did succeed in murdering his predecessor, the deposed Sultan Selim III (some of you will remember hearing about him in *The Passion of the Purple Plumeria*), and the story is that the sound of the hullaballoo surrounding Selim's noisy murder alerted Mahmud and his mother, Naksidil, to his danger.

Legend has it that Naksidil was Josephine Bonaparte's cousin, Aimée du Buc de Rivéry, who was captured at sea and sold to Barbary pirates at the age of eleven. As far as I can tell, the legend is purely a legend, despite a number of historical novels that treat the identification as fact. Unfortunately, the timing just doesn't seem to work. Aimée du Buc de Rivéry was kidnapped in 1788. Naksidil Sultan's son, Mahmud II, was born circa 1785. Proponents of the Aimée theory argue that Mahmud was actually born in 1789. It seems more likely, as some historians claim, that Naksidil was not French at all, but from the Caucacus region. Although the Aimée theory is certainly more dramatic. . . .

For the purpose of this novel, though, it seemed fun and fitting (given that the first Pink book takes place at Bonaparte's court) to hint at the story that Naksidil was Josephine's cousin.

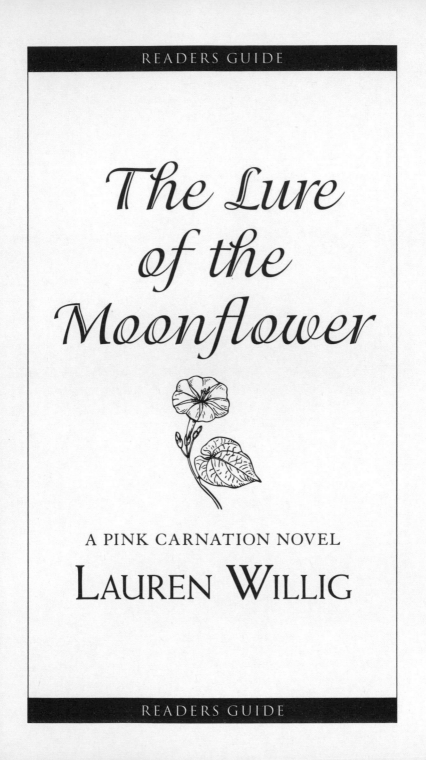

The Lure of the Moonflower

A PINK CARNATION NOVEL

LAUREN WILLIG

A CONVERSATION WITH THE COMTE DE BRILLAC, AKA THE CHEVALIER DE LA TOUR D'ARGENT, AKA THE GARDENER—BUT LET'S JUST CALL HIM NICOLAS, SHALL WE?

"Author? Author?"

I can hear myself being summoned. The character has a faint French accent and a roguish pair of hazel eyes.

"Oh, Monsieur le Comte! Hi. You do know the book is over, right?"

I look over my shoulder to make sure he's not being pursued by any other characters. Henrietta, after all, still holds a grudge. And you know what Henrietta is like when she holds a grudge. She's worse than Miles without a ginger biscuit.

The comte, aka Nicolas, seems less than pleased with me. "What, may I ask, happened to my Grand Revelation?"

"Your what?"

"My Big Secret? The one to which you have been building

for oh so many books?" He casts me a decidedly inimical look. "Don't make me take this to the guild."

I've had my run-ins with the Pink Carnation characters' guild before. Miss Gwen is fond of filing complaints. Too much purple, not enough purple, the poor quality of parasols . . .

"Ah," I say. "Right. Sorry about that. You see, I'd thought we were going to do this big showdown scene on Berlengas at the end of the book and you could do your reveal then, but . . . It just didn't work out. Sorry."

"What does it mean, this 'it just didn't work out'? First you cancel my novella, and now you take away my scene?"

"Well," I say apologetically, "I ran it by my little sister and my college roommate, and they both agreed that doing your Big Reveal would take too much attention away from Jack and Jane and their happily-ever-after. So I cut it."

Nicolas looks sulky. "I do not care about their happily-ever-after. Jane, she was supposed to be happily ever after with *me*."

"Actually, you're going to be very happily ever after with Jack's little sister Lizzy." Nicolas looks somewhat aghast. "I know, I know—family Christmases are going to be a little awkward for a while, what with the whole Jack-and-Jane thing, but trust me: it'll be worth it. You and Lizzy? You two are meant for each other. And does it make you feel better to know that you're going to do very, very well out of the Bourbon Restoration? Lizzy is going to adore being your countess. It'll be great. I promise."

Nicolas looks partially mollified. "That, it is good news. But you promised me the Big Reveal."

And since a promise is a promise . . . Pink Readers, brace yourselves.

Remember those hazel eyes of Nicolas's, which get mentioned with annoying frequency, starting in *The Temptation of the Night Jasmine*? (Yes, he was that Frenchman.) And the fact that Henrietta finds something really annoyingly familiar about him?

The Marquess of Uppington is Nicolas's father.

Which makes him . . . Richard and Henrietta's illegitimate half brother. (He's also their brother Charles's illegitimate half brother, but since Charles has managed to keep his head down and stay out of this whole flower-named exercise, I think we can pretty much ignore him for the moment.)

Originally, this news was meant to come out in a novella about Jane and Nicolas, "The Pink Carnation in Love," in which the whole topic—and what it meant for Nicolas's childhood—could be explored in rather more depth. But since I got rather behind schedule, that never happened. I had also intended, one of these days, to write a series about Lord and Lady Uppington in their youth, in which we would learn Lord Uppington's side of it. But . . . see "behind schedule," above.

So here's the short version: like the second Duke and Duchess of Richmond and Lennox, on whom I based Lord and Lady Uppington, the Uppingtons had an arranged marriage when Lady Uppington was scarcely out of the schoolroom. (She had just turned fourteen.) Lord Uppington, who was seven years older, very aware of his own consequence, and less than thrilled with his incredibly outspoken, juvenile, prank-pulling bride, went abroad, serving in a diplomatic capacity in France. While there, he had an affair with a sophisticated older woman, the Comtesse de Brillac. The Comtesse de Brillac was very unhappily married to the comte, who was a brute and a bully.

Edward, Marquess of Uppington, returned to England entirely unaware that the comtesse was carrying his child. Back in England, he proceeded to fall in love with his own wife, much to both their surprises. (And they solved many mysteries together—or will, if I ever get around to writing that series.) His affair with the comtesse was an unimportant blip in his past, part of the PH era (pre-Honoria).

So, there you go. The Chevalier, aka the Gardener, aka the Comte de Brillac, aka that mysterious Frenchman in *Night Jasmine*, aka Nicolas, is really Henrietta and Richard's half brother. And, given that he's going to marry Lizzy, this is something they're going to have to learn and to come to terms with.

But not within this book.

THE LURE OF THE MOONFLOWER: THE LOST EPILOGUE

Speaking of things that didn't happen within this book . . .

Originally I'd planned a final Jack-and-Jane chapter, a wedding scene to parallel the wedding of Colin and Eloise. In this planned epilogue (which I persisted in thinking of as an epilogue, even though it was slated to come before the final Colin and Eloise chapter), Jack was going to have staged a reconciliation between Jane and her parents. I wanted to tie up that last, lingering loose end so that Jane and Jack could sail happily off into the sunset together.

Also, Pink Carnation wedding. Enough said.

But epilogues and I have a checkered history, by which I mean I never seem to use them. So far I've written three epilogues: one for the first Pink book, *The Secret History of the Pink Carnation*, one for my second stand-alone novel, *That Summer*, and now one for the final Pink book, *The Lure of the Moonflower*. (There's some nice symmetry there, no?)

The Curse of the Epilogue continues. As soon as I started writing Jack and Jane's epilogue (aka chapter twenty-seven), I knew it just wasn't going to work. Too much cute, too much too much. So away it went. I replaced that lost epilogue, eventually, with a very different chapter twenty-seven. But I'm not calling that one an epilogue—because, clearly, if I did, I would then have to get rid of it.

Here, for your amusement, is a fragment of the lost epilogue of *The Lure of the Moonflower*:

Epilogue

*T*here were two dukes, a dowager duchess, a marquess, and a viscount in attendance at the wedding of Miss Jane Wooliston and Jack Reid. There was also a man in a carnation-embroidered waistcoat who appeared to go by the name of Turnip, a small child named Parsnip, a butler dressed as a pirate, and, much to Jack's annoyance, a French count who had once gone by the name of the Gardener and who now appeared to be flirting outrageously with Jack's sister Lizzy.

The Earl and Countess of Vaughn sent regrets and a silver tea service.

"What are we meant to do with this?" muttered Jack.

"Drink tea?" said Jane. She hefted the solid silver tray. "Or possibly beat off assailants."

Their trunks were already packed—new trunks, Jane's old one having been left behind somewhere on the road to Santarém. As for Jack, the last time he had traveled with a trunk had been when his father sent him off to school in Calcutta. Since then he had traveled light, his worldly goods fitting in a pack on his back.

There was something strangely satisfying about seeing his breeches folded in with Jane's gowns and false mustaches. Something solid and lasting. They had designed the trunks together, with the maximum number of false panels, mock keyholes, and other devices designed to frustrate and annoy.

As soon as the last of the lobster patties had been devoured, the happy couple was to depart for Constantinople, where they would infiltrate the court of the Sultan disguised as a ci-devant French aristocrat and her feckless soldier-of-fortune husband.

Jack had only one stipulation: there would be no plum velvet involved in the deception. Jane had, with some persuading, agreed.

What with all the persuasion, it hadn't occurred to Jack until later that he'd left himself open to bottle green, periwinkle, and other shades of velvet.

She was a tricky one, that Pink Carnation. Jack was rather proud of her for bamboozling him. Not that he had any intention of wearing a velvet frock coat, bottle-green or otherwise. And he was quite sure he could persuade his wife on that point.

Wife. Even with the vicar's blessing still echoing in his ears, Jack couldn't quite believe she was really his.

Along with a rather large extended circle of family and friends. The transition from his old life to this—well, it took some getting used to.

"I do wish you weren't leaving so soon," said Jane's cousin Amy wistfully. She grimaced and rubbed her stomach as a little Selwick-to-be kicked in agreement. Jack was having trouble

keeping track of all the various offspring running about as it was. There appeared to be a vast number of them, all underfoot. "We've only just— Percy! Give Plumeria back that basket!"

Amy's son looked at her with wide-eyed innocence. "But, Mummy—"

Percy's words turned into a startled oomph *as he was tackled by a small purple fury. Carnation petals scattered everywhere.*

Jack's newest sister might come up only to his knees, but she had a mean right hook.

Amy turned calmly back to Jane. "We've only just got you back."

"I shall return." Jane looped an arm through Jack's. They watched together as Jack's father separated the brawling children, carrying them off, one under each arm. "In a few years."

Amy turned to Jack. "I am sorry about that frog in your bed. Percy meant it as a wedding present."

"Hmm?" Jack had been looking at the door. "Think nothing of it. I'm just glad it wasn't a snake."

He hated snakes.

On that note, just in case you were wondering . . . any resemblance between Jack and various characters played by Harrison Ford is more than coincidental.

The epilogue went on a bit after the snakes line, but once

we started getting into lines from *Raiders of the Lost Ark*, I knew that the epilogue had passed the point of no return.

Just in case you were wondering, though, Jack does track down Jane's parents. They arrive late at the wedding, but they do make it. Because Jack is that kind of guy.

And they all live happily ever after.

A CONVERSATION WITH LAUREN WILLIG

Q. Was this how the first Pink book came to be? Did you write it because your advisor refused to accept your dissertation?

A. The answer is no, again no, and absolutely no. When I realized, a few books ago, that the series really needed to start wrapping up, it occurred to me that it might be fun to go all meta, bring everything full circle, and make Eloise the "author" of *The Secret History of the Pink Carnation*.

It also solved a very real problem for me (and for Eloise), which was how she and Colin could reconcile their careers in such a way that they could wind up in the same place with neither feeling like they had sacrificed too much or abandoned their principles. I couldn't—and wouldn't—have Eloise give up her career for a guy, but I also couldn't see Colin following Eloise around the United States from junior faculty job to junior faculty job.

Confession: over the course of this series, a happily-ever-after for Eloise and Colin was never a given. Until the end of

The Mark of the Midnight Manzanilla, I had no more idea than you all did what was going to happen with them. So it was a great relief to me when Eloise's career change shifted the dynamic and brought a relatively realistic happy ending in view for them.

As to how the first Pink book really came to be . . . Well, I've spoken at great length about that elsewhere, but the thumbnail version is that I started writing it as a means of dissertation avoidance right after I passed my general exams back in 2001. It was an advisor-sanctioned form of dissertation avoidance: my advisor had advised me to take the post-Generals summer off and take a rest. For "rest," I read "go write a novel." I continued to amuse myself with Amy and Richard's story through my research year in England (during which I found no private collections of family papers), and finished it up when I returned to the States in the spring of 2003. Unlike Eloise's fictional advisor, my advisor was nothing but supportive, urging me to keep going with the dissertation even after I'd made the decision to jump ship and move down the block to the law school.

The one particular in which our stories dovetail? Like Eloise, I had a friend who handed the manuscript to an agent, after which everything moved fairly rapidly. In real life, though, I got the call from that agent in late summer 2003, the manuscript was sold to Penguin in the fall of 2003, edited and revised over the course of that year, and, at long last, published in February of 2005.

Because I hadn't originally planned to sync Eloise's story line with mine, astute readers of the Pink series may have noticed that Eloise's draft of *The Secret History of the Pink Carnation* is first purchased by a publisher in June of 2005—four months *after* the publication of the actual book.

As they say, details, details . . .

Q. Is there anything you would have done differently?

A. Hindsight is always 20/20, right? When I wrote Pink I, I intended it as a one-off. I never planned it as a series, which means that the series as we know it is a rather ad hoc, trial-and-error affair. For me, that was part of the fun of it. I loved stumbling on new plotlines and getting to know characters who might or might not be important down the road. But it did also mean the occasional meander or missed opportunity.

As I mentioned above, Eloise's time line is out of sync with the real-life publication of *The Secret History of the Pink Carnation*. Had I known that she was going to "write" the book, I would have moved her story line a year earlier, starting in 2002 rather than in 2003.

The largest change I would have made? In retrospect, it would have made the most sense to have Pink XI be Tommy Fluellen and Kat Reid's book rather than Sally Fitzhugh's. Tommy Fluellen was a side character in Pink V, *The Temptation of the Night Jasmine*. Kat Reid is Colonel Reid's oldest daughter (Jack's big sister). Their story line would have followed very logically off Colonel Reid's book, *The Passion of the Purple Plumeria*, and led perfectly into Jack's. But that only occurred to me months after Pink XI, *The Mark of the Midnight Manzanilla*, was already in print—about a different pair of characters.

Q. Did you always know that the last book would be Jane's book?

A. Yes, but as with everything, there were some changes along the way. Originally I'd thought that if I were very, very lucky, the series might stretch to three books. I'd entertained thoughts of pairing Jane with Geoff for that highly hypothetical book three—but by the time I was two-thirds of the way through *The Secret History of the Pink Carnation*, it became clear that Geoff and Jane had all the sexual tension of cooked spaghetti. Without sauce.

By the time Pink I came out, back in February of 2005, I knew that Geoff was going to Ireland for his book, and I was very, very sure that Jane's book was going to be set in Portugal at the beginning of the Peninsular War—around, oh, book six or so, if I could keep the series going that long.

I had an image of an adventurer sitting in a rocky landscape, his slouch hat pulled down low, the remains of a campfire in front of him, tipping his hat back as a very put-together lady in a frilled gown approached. He would say something like "Who the hell are you?" And Jane would reply, "Your contact." All I knew about this man was that he was a soldier of fortune, he looked a bit like Harrison Ford as Han Solo, and his name was probably Lucien.

And that was where my image of Jane's book remained until summer 2008, when I was writing Pink VI, *The Betrayal of the Blood Lily*. Jack Reid slouched onto the scene—and I recognized him immediately. His name might not be Lucien, but I knew, just knew, that this was the man I'd seen across the campfire from Jane. They were going to drive each other crazy. (And his father, Colonel Reid, was destined for Miss Gwen. I'd figured that out somewhere after chapter two of *Blood Lily*, so it was already a given in my head.) It was perfect.

These things are always perfect—until you start writing them.

As you can see, while Jack and Jane are very much the people I knew they would be, that original campfire scene went the way of the dodo. As did pretty much everything else I had planned for them along the way.

There are two Pink XIIs. There's the book you're holding in your hand. And there's the book I meant to write. My original plan for Pink XII (and when I say "original," I mean the plan I concocted when I began writing this in 2014, not the thousand vaguely imagined plans I entertained over the past fourteen years) involved a foil for Jane, a Portuguese marquesa who would be ally, suspect, and rival. She would also be a way to get some Portuguese history in there and have a glimpse of the elegant, cultured world of the Portuguese aristocracy. The idea was for her to be one of Jack's contacts. When Jane approached Jack about tracking the Queen, he naturally would suggest they stop in and see the marquesa on the way to Porto. It would be at her house that they would encounter the Gardener, aka the Comte de Brillac.

But then Jane went and pulled that stunt at the tavern, posing as a French soldier, and the next thing I knew, Jack and Jane's book had taken a very different, much more rough-and-tumble path. Instead of traveling by the marquesa's carriage, they acquired a donkey.

Part of me wishes I could write that book, too, just to see how it would turn out. But I'm not sure Jack and Jane would let me. They had very strong feelings about the progress of their book—most of them entirely contrary to the wishes and plans of their author.

Q. Will you ever write another Pink book?

A. I never say never. Well, hardly ever. The truth is, I just don't know. Are there Pink books I want to write? Absolutely. Kat and Tommy's story is still waiting to be told, Lizzy and Nicolas are just taunting me with the prospect of their romance, and I never did get around to that mystery novel featuring Colin and Eloise, or that prequel series about the elder Uppingtons.

But the market changes and so do authors. I've been writing this series for a very long time now—through grad school, law school, practice at a firm, multiple moves, a marriage, a baby—and it was time to try something new. I tried to juggle the stand-alone novels and the Pinks, but it was tough, and proved to me that, for the time being, at least, I need to focus on either one or the other.

Q. What happens to all of the characters after the series ends?

A. I started to write pocket histories of all of them, which is when I realized, Wow, there have been an awful lot of Pink books and an awful lot of heroes and heroines.

Some of them, like Laure and Andre or Mary and Vaughn, have their future history recounted in the Eloise sections of their own books. So I've left those out and just concentrated on those characters whose futures haven't been explored. As far as I can remember. After twelve books, one does start to get a bit blurry. . . .

Richard and Amy continue to run that spy school, and, to everyone's surprise, make such a success of it that it becomes genuinely secret and shadowy and has to be moved from the grounds of Selwick Hall to an Undisclosed Location. The school continues within the family well into the reign of Victoria, although, given the whole secretive and shadowy thing—and they do become very good at secretive and shadowy—it's hard to tell just how long it lasts. Either way, the spy tradition continues strong in the family up through the present day. Even if Colin is not, in fact, a spy.

Miles never does succeed in getting that ginger biscuit recipe out of Cook. (Clearly this was a cunning ploy on the part of Lady Uppington to ensure that her daughter, son-in-law, and grandchildren could never stray too far from Uppington House.) Henrietta continues meddling happily in the lives of her friends, and, not to put too fine a point on it, eventually turns into her mother. Only slightly taller. Miles eventually succeeds to his father's title, and Viscount and Viscountess Loring are always in great demand on the social circuit.

Geoff and Letty are enormously prolific in every possible way. When not looking after their nine children, Geoff is busy with the House of Lords and a seat in the Duke of Wellington's cabinet. He also takes a great interest in the police force being formed by Sir Robert Peel. Letty, in the meantime, has written the *Practical Viscountess's Book of Household Advice*, a book that absolutely mortifies her older sister, Lady Vaughn, who feels that no member of the peerage should have anything to do with a) practicality, b) household advice, or c) books.

Robert, to everyone's surprise (but most especially that of the Dowager Duchess of Dovedale), warms to the idea of being duke and begins to experiment with ways to improve the lives of the tenantry. With Charlotte's assistance, he plots out a series of model farms—although Charlotte does secure his promise that she will not have to wear traditional shepherdess costume. At least, not in public.

Aside from a few brief visits to England, Penelope and Alex live out the rest of their lives in India, where Alex is commissioner of a small (and imaginary) district, Karnatabad. Although Penelope finds herself unable to carry a child to term, she adopts five children from a nearby village whose parents died of cholera, shocking the English community, especially the wife of Alex's assistant district commissioner. While shocking the English community was the main point, both Penelope and Alex become deeply attached to their wards and consider them their true sons and daughters.

Turnip remains Turnip and lives happily ever after with the Arabella, who loves him, their five children, and a large supply of raspberry jam.

Sally Fitzhugh adores being Duchess of Belliston. And the Duke of Belliston adores the Duchess of Belliston—although his feelings are slightly less warm, and rather more fuzzy, in regard to her pet stoat.

Agnes Wooliston shocks everyone by coming out of her shell with a vengeance as a very early supporter of women's suffrage, deeply influencing Jeremy Bentham's 1817 *Plan of Parliamentary Reform*. She strongly lobbies journalist (and later MP) Augustus Whittlesby for his support for votes for women. Augustus tries, but is deeply outnumbered during the debates over the Reform Act of 1832.

Parsnip Fitzhugh (née Jane) grows up best friends with Plumeria Reid and Emmeline Pinchingdale-Snipe. Don't even think of asking about the Season of 1825. Or, for that matter, the Season of 1826. You just don't want to know. . . .

Plumeria Reid, after causing the maximum amount of scandal and bother, eventually marries Percy Selwick, a match that surprises no one except, potentially, the two parties primarily involved.

But what can one expect of a son of Amy and a daughter of Miss Gwen?

Have I left out anyone or anything important? If so, just e-mail me through my Web site, www.laurenwillig.com, and I'll be happy to answer any questions you might have.

Q. What are you working on now?

A. Right now, Beatriz Williams, Karen White, and I are just polishing up the manuscript of *The Forgotten Room*, a novel set around a Gilded Age mansion in New York, the women who live there in 1892, 1920, and 1944, and the secret that connects them all. *The Forgotten Room* will appear in stores in January of 2016. We had a blast writing it, and we already have our heads together over another one.

Once the *Forgotten Room* revisions are done, I'll be hunkering down over my fourth stand-alone novel, a multigenerational family saga sweeping from Gilded Age New York to Belle Époque Paris, the Roaring Twenties, and World War II France.

For more on those and all the other books, just stop by my Web site, www.laurenwillig.com, or visit me on my Facebook author page, http://www.facebook.com/LaurenWillig.

QUESTIONS FOR DISCUSSION

1. Even before they had a chance to work together, Jack and Jane had already formed fairly solid judgments about each other's characters. What do you think this says about the power of reputations? Was there some truth to their assumptions? How are their assumptions about each other proven wrong by their actions?

2. Discuss the role that societal norms and class play in the book, and how the main characters are affected by their perceived status.

3. Jack and Jane are both very determined individuals who prefer being in control of a situation, rather than sharing the reins of power. Do you think that either of them had the upper hand at the beginning of the book? What moment (if there is one) brings about a shift in the power dynamic between them? How does this shift affect their relationship going forward?

How do you think things might have been different if they shared the decision making from the start?

4. Talk about Jane's resistance to conventions such as manners, marriage, and mores. How might her life have been different if she'd lived in a more modern era? Do you think she still would have become a spy? How would that have been different?

5. What characteristics do you think make Jack and Jane good spies? What about them makes them good partners—and lovers? Are the characteristics the same?

6. How do you think Jack's childhood—his mother's suicide, his strained relations with his father, his outside status as a half-caste—shaped his character and the way he views himself and the decisions he made?

7. Was it surprising to you that Colin's great-aunt was a spy? Do you think it is fitting that the descendants of the Selwicks would still carry on spying in the modern world?

8. What name do you think Jack and Jane should finally settle upon for their pet donkey?

9. Did you know much about Portugal during the Napoleonic era before reading *The Lure of the Moonflower*? Did you learn

anything new about this period in time? Do you prefer learning about history through fictional characters or through narrative nonfiction accounts?

10. If you were Jane, would you have chosen Jack or Nicolas? Discuss the merits and shortcomings of each of them.

11. Out of all the characters in the Pink Carnation books, which one would you choose to take out for a cup of tea? Who was your favorite couple? Discuss why.

"   *T*he city of your birth awaits your return. Please
• • •   send word of your travel arrangements by courier
at first opportunity. I remain, your devoted brother, Edouard."

"The city of your birth awaits your return." Amy whispered the words aloud.

At last! Fingers tightening around the paper in her hands,
she gazed rapturously at the sky. For an event of such magni-
tude, she expected bolts of lightning, or thunderclouds at the
very least. But the Shropshire sky gazed calmly back at her,
utterly unperturbed by the momentous events taking place
below.

Wasn't that just like Shropshire?

Sinking to the grass, Amy contemplated the place where

she had spent the majority of her life. Behind her, over the rolling fields, the redbrick manor house sat placidly on its rise. Uncle Bertrand was sure to be right there, three windows from the left, sitting in his cracked leather chair, poring over the latest findings of the Royal Agricultural Society, just as he did every day. Aunt Prudence would be sitting in the yellow-and-cream morning room, squinting over her embroidery threads, just as she did every day. All peaceful, and bucolic, and boring.

The prospect before her wasn't any more exciting, nothing but long swaths of green, enlivened only by woolly balls of sheep.

But now, at last, the long years of boredom were at an end. In her hand she grasped the opportunity to leave Wooliston Manor and its pampered flock behind her forever. She would no longer be plain Amy Balcourt, niece to the most ambitious sheep breeder in Shropshire, but Aimée, Mlle de Balcourt. Amy conveniently ignored the fact that revolutionary France had banished titles when they beheaded their nobility.

She had been six years old when revolution exiled her to rural England. In late May of 1789, she and Mama had sailed across the Channel for what was meant to be merely a two-month visit, time enough for Mama to see her sisters and show her daughter something of English ways. For all the years she had spent in France, Mama was still an Englishwoman at heart.

Uncle Bertrand, sporting a slightly askew periwig, had stridden out to meet them. Behind him stood Aunt Prudence, embroidery hoop clutched in her hand. Clustered in the doorway were three little girls in identical muslin dresses, Amy's cousins Sophia, Jane, and Agnes. "See, darling," whispered Mama. "You shall have other little girls to play with. Won't that be lovely?"

It wasn't lovely. Agnes, still in the lisping and stumbling stage, was too young to be a playmate. Sophia spent all of her time bent virtuously over her sampler. Jane, quiet and shy, Amy dismissed as a poor-spirited thing. Even the sheep soon lost their charm. Within a month, Amy was quite ready to return to France. She packed her little trunk, heaved and pushed it down the hall to her mother's room, and announced that she was prepared to go.

Mama had half-smiled, but her smile twisted into a sob. She plucked her daughter off the trunk and squeezed her very, very tightly.

"*Mais, maman, qu'est-ce que se passe?*" demanded Amy, who still thought in French in those days.

"We can't go back, darling. Not now. I don't know if we'll ever . . . Oh, your poor father! Poor us! And Edouard, what must they be doing to him?"

Amy didn't know who *they* were, but remembering the way Edouard had yanked at her curls and pinched her arm while supposedly hugging her good-bye, she couldn't help but think her brother deserved anything he got. She said as much to Mama.

Mama looked down at her miserably. "Oh no, darling, not this. Nobody deserves this." Very slowly, in between deep breaths, she had explained to Amy that mobs had taken over Paris, that the king and queen were prisoners, and that Papa and Edouard were very much in danger.

Over the next few months, Wooliston Manor became the unlikely center of an antirevolutionary movement. Everyone pored over the weekly papers, wincing at news of atrocities across the Channel. Mama ruined quill after quill penning desperate letters to connections in France, London, Austria. When the Scarlet Pimpernel appeared on the scene, snatching aristocrats from the sharp embrace of Madame Guillotine, Mama brimmed over with fresh hope. She peppered every news sheet within a hundred miles of London with advertisements begging the Scarlet Pimpernel to save her son and husband.

Amidst all this hubbub, Amy lay awake at night in the nursery, wishing she were old enough to go back to France herself and save Papa. She would go disguised, of course, since everyone knew a proper rescue had to be done in disguise. When no one was about, Amy would creep down to the servants' quarters to try on their clothes and practice speaking in the rough, peasant French of the countryside. If anyone happened upon her, Amy explained that she was preparing amateur theatricals. With so much to worry about, none of the grown-ups who absently said, "How nice, dear," and patted her on the head ever bothered to wonder why the promised performance never materialized.

Except Jane. When Jane came upon Amy clad in an assortment of old petticoats from the ragbag and a discarded periwig of Uncle Bertrand's, Amy huffily informed her that she was rehearsing for a one-woman production of *Two Gentlemen of Verona*.

Jane regarded her thoughtfully. Half apologetically, she said, "I don't think you're telling the truth."

Unable to think of a crushing response, Amy just glared. Jane clutched her rag doll tighter, but managed to ask, "Please, won't you tell me what you're really doing?"

"You won't tell Mama or any of the others?" Amy tried to look suitably fierce, but the effect was quite ruined by her periwig sliding askew and dangling from one ear.

Jane hastily nodded.

"I," declared Amy importantly, "am going to join the League of the Scarlet Pimpernel and rescue Papa."

Jane pondered this new information, doll dangling forgotten from one hand.

"May I help?" she asked.

Her cousin's unexpected aid proved a boon to Amy. It was Jane who figured out how to rub soot and gum on teeth to make them look like those of a desiccated old hag—and then how to rub it all off again before Nanny saw. It was Jane who plotted a route to France on the nursery globe and Jane who discovered a way to creep down the back stairs without making them creak.

They never had the chance to execute their plans. Little beknownst to the two small girls preparing themselves to enter his service, the Scarlet Pimpernel foolishly attempted the rescue of the Vicomte de Balcourt without them. From the papers, Amy learned that the Pimpernel had spirited Papa out of prison disguised as a cask of cheap red wine. The rescue might have gone without a hitch had a thirsty guard at the gates of the city not insisted on tapping the cask. When he encountered Papa instead of Beaujolais, the guard angrily sounded the alert. Papa, the papers claimed, had fought manfully, but he was no match for an entire troop of revolutionary soldiers. A week later, a small card had arrived for Mama. It said simply, "I'm sorry," and was signed with a scarlet flower.

The news sent Mama into a decline and Amy into a fury. With Jane as her witness, she vowed to avenge Papa and Mama as soon as she was old enough to return to France. She would need excellent French for that, and Amy could already feel her native tongue beginning to slip away under the onslaught of constant English conversation. At first, she tried conversing in French with their governesses, but those worthy ladies tended to have a vocabulary limited to shades of cloth and the newest types of millinery. So Amy took her Molière outside and read aloud to the sheep.

Latin and Greek would do her no good in her mission, but Amy read them anyway, in memory of Papa. Papa had told her nightly bedtime stories of capricious gods and vengeful goddesses; Amy tracked all his stories down among the books in the little-used library at Wooliston Manor. Uncle Bertrand's own taste ran more towards manuals on animal husbandry, but *someone* in the family must have read once, because the library possessed quite a creditable collection of classics. Amy read Ovid and Virgil and Aristophanes and Homer. She read dry histories and scandalous love poetry (her governesses, who had little Latin and less Greek, naïvely assumed that anything in a classical tongue must be respectable), but mostly she returned again and again to *The Odyssey*. Odysseus had fought to go home, and so would Amy.

When Amy was ten, the illustrated newsletters announced that the Scarlet Pimpernel had retired upon discovery of his identity—although the newsletters were rather unclear as to whether they or the French government had been the first to get the scoop. SCARLET PIMPERNEL UNMASKED! proclaimed the *Shropshire Intelligencer*. Meanwhile *The Cosmopolitan Lady's Book* carried a ten-page spread on "Fashions of the Scarlet Pimpernel: Costume Tips from the Man Who Brought You the French Aristocracy."

Amy was devastated. True, the Pimpernel had botched her father's rescue, but, on the whole, his tally of aristocrats saved was quite impressive, and who on earth was she to offer her French language skills to if the Pimpernel retired? Amy was all ready to start constructing her own band when a line in the article in the *Shropshire Intelligencer* caught her eye. "I have every faith that the Purple Gentian will take up where I was forced to leave off," they reported Sir Percy as saying.

Puzzled, Amy shoved the paper at Jane. "Who is the Purple Gentian?"

The same question was on everyone else's lips. Soon the Purple Gentian became a regular feature in the news sheets. One week, he spirited fifteen aristocrats out of Paris as a traveling circus. The Purple Gentian, it was whispered, had played the dancing bear. Why, some said Robespierre himself had patted the animal on the head, never knowing it was his greatest enemy! When France stopped killing its aristocrats and directed its attention to fighting England instead, the Purple Gentian became the War Office's most reliable spy.

"This victory would never have happened, but for the bravery of one man—one man represented by a small purple flower," Admiral Nelson announced after destroying the French fleet in Egypt.

English and French alike were united in their burning curiosity to learn the identity of the Purple Gentian. Speculation ran rife on both sides of the Channel. Some claimed the Purple Gentian was an English aristocrat, a darling of the London *ton* like Sir Percy Blakeney. Indeed, some said he *was* Sir Percy Blakeney, fooling the foolish French by returning under a different name. London gossip named everyone from Beau Brummel (on the grounds that no one could genuinely be *that* interested in fashion) to the Prince of Wales's dissolute brother, the Duke of York. Others declared that the Purple Gentian must be an exiled French noble, fighting for his homeland. Some said he was a soldier; others said he was a renegade priest. The French just said he was a damned nuisance. Or they would have, had they the good fortune to speak English. Instead, being French, they were forced to say it in their own language.

Amy said he was her hero.

She only said it to Jane, of course. All of the old plans were revived, only this time it was the League of the Purple Gentian to whom Amy planned to offer her services.

But the years went by, Amy remained in Shropshire, and the only masked man she saw was her small cousin Ned playing at being a highwayman. At times Amy considered running away to Paris, but how would she even get there? With war raging between England and France, normal travel across the Channel had been disrupted. Amy began to despair of ever reaching France, much less finding the Purple Gentian. She envisioned a dreary future of pastoral peace.

Until Edouard's letter.

"I thought I'd find you here."

"What?" Amy was jolted out of her blissful contemplation of Edouard's letter, as a blue flounce brushed against her arm.

A basket of wildflowers on Jane's arm testified to a walk along the grounds, but she bore no sign of outdoor exertion. No creases dared to settle in the folds of her muslin dress; her pale brown hair remained obediently coiled at the base of her neck; and even the loops of the bow holding her bonnet were remarkably even. Aside from a bit of windburn on her pale cheeks, she might have been sitting in the parlor all afternoon.

"Mama has been looking all over for you. She wants to know what you did with her skein of rose-pink embroidery silk."

"What makes her think I have it? Besides," Amy cut off what looked to be a highly logical response from Jane with a wave of Edouard's letter, "who can think of embroidery silks when *this* just arrived?"

"A letter? Not another love poem from Derek?"

"Ugh!" Amy shuddered dramatically. "Really, Jane! What a vile thought! No"—she leaned forward, lowering her voice dramatically—"it's a letter from Edouard."

"Edward?" Jane, being Jane, automatically gave the name its English pronunciation. "So he has finally deigned to remember your existence after all these years?"

"Oh, Jane, don't be harsh! He wants me to go live with him!"

Jane dropped her basket of flowers.

"You can't be serious, Amy!"

"But I am! Isn't it glorious!" Amy joined her cousin in gathering up scattered blooms, piling them willy-nilly back in the basket with more enthusiasm than grace.

"What *exactly* does Edward's letter say?"

"It's splendid, Jane! Now that we're no longer at war, he says it's finally safe for me to come back. He says he wants me to act as hostess for him."

"But are you sure it's safe?" Jane's gray eyes darkened with concern.

Amy laughed. "It's not all screaming mobs, Jane. After all, Bonaparte has been consul for—how long has it been? Three years now? Actually, that's exactly why Edouard wants me there. Bonaparte is desperately trying to make his jumped-up, murderous, usurping government look legitimate . . ."

"Not that you're at all biased," murmured Jane.

". . . so he's been courting the old nobility," Amy went on, pointedly ignoring her cousin's comment. "But the courting has mostly been going on through his wife Josephine—she has a *salon* for the ladies of the old regime—so Edouard needs me to be his *entrée.*"

"To that jumped-up, murderous, usurping government?" Jane's voice was politely quizzical.

Amy tossed a daisy at her in annoyance. "Make fun all you like, Jane! Don't you see? This is exactly the opportunity I needed!"

"To become the belle of Bonaparte's court?"

Amy forbore to waste another flower. "No." She clasped her hands, eyes gleaming. "To join the League of the Purple Gentian!"

Photo © Sigrid Estrada

The author of eleven previous Pink Carnation novels, **Lauren Willig** received a graduate degree in English history from Harvard University and a JD from Harvard Law School, though she now writes full-time. Willig lives in New York City.

CONNECT ONLINE

laurenwillig.com
facebook.com/laurenwillig